I0831816

The Unholy Servants

a novel

Andre Cole

Anna Wynn Press

For information address
Anna Wynn Press

Visit our Web site at
www.blackcloudfilms.com/annawynnpress

First Edition: July 2011

Cataloging considerations

Cole, Andre.
The unholy servants: a novel / by Andre Cole. --1st ed.
ISBN-13: 978-0-9836842-0-6
ISBN-10: 0-9836842-0-0

1. Mystery--Fiction 2. Corporate corruption—Fiction. 3. Mythology--Fiction. 4. Religious--Fiction 5. Female friendships--Fiction

Fiction I. Title

ISBN(ebook) - 978-0-9836842-1-3

Printed in the United States of America

For Grandma, Aunt Rucker and Jim-Jim – I know you will welcome me… or come get me if need be.

BOOK ONE

Prisoner's Psalm

CHAPTER ONE

THE TUBE

The liquid in the large cylindrical tube was a murky yellow tinged gel. Its purpose was simply to recreate the womb. It provided the skin with the electrolytes it needed to continue operating as the body's largest organ. The small fiber optic cables transferred electric pulses in rapid succession to the muscles of the body insuring complete muscle operation for lengthy times of sedate immobilization. The body in the tube was in need of it. He had been floating in this particular tube for close to eight months without a twitch and frankly Dr. Lisa Lucas was sick and tired of babysitting him. It got to a point where she stopped checking his vitals on the computer readouts every 15 minutes and maybe got to it every 45.

Now, she was just sitting reading one of the many Stephen King novels she'd brought with her to the facility.

To call it a facility is a slight misnomer. Sure it was built for medical study and had all the bells and whistles of a laboratory, but it also had all of the accouterments of an operating room and all of the security measures of a zoo.

The place was also kitted with every creature comfort of a mansion. There was the full kitchen with island and two modernly designed living rooms with plush micro fiber couches sitting in the middle of them. There was also an indoor heated pool and full gym. The gym's equipment was beyond state of the art. The track that surrounded the gym was built to Olympic specificity and was getting its full use every morning by the facilities inhabitants. All six bedroom suites were enormous. Each California king sized bed was fitted with five star hotel quality plush linens. To counter the lack of windows, the lighting was warm, inspiring and structured to radiate all the goodies the sun offers. This was the facility officially named CG-406J, but known as "The Country Cage" to all who wished to work there. Right now, Lisa didn't care about all of the other doctors who were standing in line to work at The Country Cage. She didn't give two shits about the "primo assignment" she'd received. Right now, she wanted to be on a beach somewhere with the scent of salt water in the air and her body feeling a warm breeze. Hell, she'd even go topless, maybe even nude, if she could get the hell out of The Country Cage.

"Girl, you're reading that book a-damn-gain?" Her roommate shouted.

"Well if someone didn't spill coffee all over the other two then I wouldn't have to...but this is a good part so be quiet for a second." Lisa said not moving her eyes from the page.

It's rare to find two women of such expertise in the same lab. It's even more rare for both to be Black and even further that they shared a similar past and goal.

Lisa's lab mate was the highly certified, seriously relaxed, Dr. Marjorie Houston. Everyone called her Jury as in "judge, jury and executioner". Jury's demeanor was laid back but her methods and work ethic were unmatched. How'd she get her "primo position"? She walked into the office of the head of the research project with one sheet of paper. On that sheet of paper was a list of all the other contenders for the position. Next to each name was a sentence. One sentence - just one horrible sentence of damaging evidence explaining why that name wasn't qualified for the job. Those sentences were so horrible; the head of research immediately shook her hand and welcomed her onto the project. Lisa's name was on that list. Her sentence read:

Dr. Lisa Anne Lucas – This bitch never knows when to stop working.

As she did at least three or four times a day, Jury walked up to the tube, extended her arm, placed her hands lovingly on it and stroked. If there were no glass, her hands would caress the arms and shoulders of the man inside it.

"How is my favorite pet today, huh?" She cooed with her best Marilyn Monroe voice.

"He's still floating in the tube, still in stasis and still keeping me here." Lisa said.

"What's wrong with you? Don't take your mood out on my pet." Jury said. Her playful taunts cracked a smile on Lisa's pretty face.

"Yeah your pet needs to wag his tail or something so I can get some action in my life."

"If he wags HIS tale I might jump on it. Two chicks alone locked in with one man...ONE MAN who's catatonic! That's just fucking with a bitch's emotions." Jury turned to her favorite pet and rubbed the glass in the area of his genitals. "Come on baby, wag that tail for mama."

"You know you're a sick person, right?" Lisa said as she joined her partner at the tube. She pulled Jury's hand away and looked into the tube. She tilted her head adjusting her view of the form fitting shorts covering his genitals. "I think the pet had his tail snipped."

"I'm sure he's a grower not a shower. Leave my pet alone."

"Well he needs to show something so we can write a progress report, do an interview and get on out of here. You ready for a run?"

"We have to do it now?"

"Yeah the call is at 10 so we'll have time to get showered, dressed and eat before the meeting."

"Ok, but you're cooking."

"Whatever."

"Goodbye, my handsome pet." Jury petted the tube lovingly again. Then as Lisa turned her back and walked towards the door, Jury kissed the tube right where his neck would be.

The two of them exited as the lab lights automatically turned to sleep mode. The tube's security lamps remained on, bathing the room in blue light.

Had they turned around just at that last moment, they would've seen his eyes slowly open. He watched their ample behinds magnified by the curvature of the glass and distorted by his weary pupils then they disappeared through the doorway.

Their thick strong legs trotted side by side thumping the man made track surface. They sweated profusely as their matching ponytails bounced in tandem. The daily run had begun as a means of exercise then became therapy. Now it was just another regimented part of their lives. There was the 7am wake up call. The 7:15 vitals check. The 7:15 to 8:15 alone time which usually meant more sleep for Jury and reading and/or writing for Lisa. The 8:20 run was followed by a shower and then breakfast. At 10 AM, there were the daily reports to be wired to the main facility and on Thursdays the weekly conference call. By noon they were watching television in the lab, only interrupted by the vitals check every 15...um...45 minutes.

The last three days had been nearly unbearable since the satellite went out. They knew not to watch movies in the screening room during the day since they only had a limited number of films left and those had slowly dwindled to the final three in the system. First run films at home, The Country Cage really did have its perks.

So the two friends and colleagues ran the track again, quietly pounding out their thoughts until the electronic beep signaled the end of the run.

"What's for breakfast?" Jury said as she wiped her face with a plush white towel.

"Fruit. Granola. Low Fat Yogurt?"

"Umm..Let's try waffles and sausages!"

"And eggs. Let's shower before these bastards call."

"Let's? You trying to shower with me? All these months in this place finally drove one of us to lesbo land, huh" Jury laughed as Lisa shook her head in disgust.

"You couldn't get this, if your kitty had diamonds falling out of it." Lisa said.

"Oh it does. And The Pet is gonna be the jeweler."

On occasion, the hot water was on the fritz in The Country Cage. It could spritz out like a child spitting water from its inflated cheeks then sprinkle to small drops then back to full power, the horrible cycle continued over and over again until the doctors gave up. Today it was all too perfect. The warm water massaged Lisa's skin, relaxing her tension. Her caramel skin appreciated every individual droplet that cascaded across her full breasts. She threw her head back and let it kiss her neck. Warm wet kisses ran down her neck and across her breasts. A slight chill hit her spine perking her nipples to attention. Mmmm this was nice.

Instinctually her left hand placed her weathered loofah on the soap dish as her right hand slid lower. It crossed her stomach; her fingers lingered around her belly button then dipped below. She felt down there was just as wet as the outside. Her right index finger knew where to touch and did so slowly in a circular motion. Before her knees went weak, she used her left hand to focus the stream of water higher then she stepped backward and took a seat on the shower bench. The stream's trajectory was perfect. The water massaged her hand as her hand massaged her spot.

Lisa threw her leg over the side of the shower bench exposing herself fully to the water and her fingers. She was using two fingers now and they were massaging faster. Her mind summoned imagery. Maybe it was the water or the talk of tails, but she imagined him, the man in the tube.

His hands were on her breasts, on her stomach and her thighs. Then a white-hot electricity shot through her body. Her muffled moans bounced off the bathroom tiles as she relaxed back in post-orgasmic sedation.

BWOMP! BWOMP! BWOMP! BWOMP!

The call alarm was sounding early, a sure sign of an emergency. Lisa hopped from the shower, her legs still slightly unsure and grabbed the plush robe hanging on the door.

Her robe was still flapped open and undone as she trotted barefoot through the carpeted hall. Jury came running down from the opposite hallway wrapped in a towel that barely covered her curves.

BWOMP! BWOMP! BWOMP! BWOMP!

"What's this shit?" Jury yelled as they met at the staircase and bounded down the steps together.

"Ridiculous!" Lisa said as they turned one corner then another. The two of them sprinted the final hall. Lisa reached the door first, placed her palm on the sensor and the door released. She struggled to close her robe with one hand as Jury held the flaps of her towel near her nearly exposed crotch. They hustled through the chemicals lab before reaching a conference phone in the specimen holding room. The motion lights shot on quickly.

"H-h-hello?" Lisa yelled as she pressed the on-call button. She shoved her face close to the camera filling the frame.

"Lisa? What's going on?"

Neither had to look up to the monitor to know it was Dustin Carver, head of research and the boss, for all intents and purposes. Just as she was getting closer to the camera, Jury's towel unraveled at the top, half exposing a breast. She spun backward turning herself toward the tube to fix it. Lisa checked the output monitor insuring she was the only face seen.

"I was in the shower." Lisa fumbled.

"WE!" Jury yelled off camera.

"*We* were taking showers...separately. You guys are calling early today."

"Everyone's not on. It's just me. Where's Marjorie?" Dustin looked confused on the video monitor and his voice sounded different.

Jury bent over the main console pushing her face into view right next to Lisa.

"I'm here, Dustin. You could've given us a heads up before calling." Jury adjusted her towel higher as she bent conspicuously further over the console. Her behind arched high in the air, her toes barely touching the tile floor. Her bare behind and more was on full display for the man in the tube.

"Yeah, I'm sorry about that."

"Or you could've just called on the main line. You know we still only have one video conference center." Lisa said. She had been hounding them for several conference units throughout the complex since before they had arrived.

"Listen..." Dustin said. He was tentative.

Lisa looked to Jury their eyes registering the same concern.

"I just found out and I wanted to tell you ladies before the call. I didn't want you to feel beset upon."

Lisa slid a chair over with her hand and kneeled on it while adjusting the camera to get more of Jury's face in the shot. Her robe fell open, but her breasts were only facing the man in the tube and he was catatonic so she could care less.

From inside the tube, her nipples looked like soft round half dollars. He could see her nipples were pert. It was a delicious view. Not as delicious as the other one. Her very round behind was arched well over the console. He could follow the brownish globe downward to the place below. The place below was speaking to him. He liked the female form. For the first time in a long time he could feel a slight electric rush.

That rush showed up on the vital stat monitors as a bump in the normal heart rate and an increase in blood flow. It would've been automatically obvious to the two doctors had they not been intrigued by Dustin's statement.

"Beset upon by...?" Lisa's voice cracked just slightly.

"They've assigned someone else to your lab." Dustin began. "No it does not mean you can leave." He finished quickly before Lisa could ask.

"Who are they sending?" Lisa was speaking in measured tones. She was sick and tired of disappointments. It had come so far that she couldn't even bask in the afterglow of a self-inflicted orgasm without some kind of disruption.

"They're sending a theologian."

"For what?" Jury said, slipped on her toes and almost knocked over the camera. Lisa's breasts were nearly revealed on camera in the ruckus.

She threw an angry glance at Jury.

"They're thinking maybe the theologian can decipher some of the wounds on him. It's just a theory, but well that's what they want." Dustin said.

"The wounds?" Jury probed.

"Yeah well not just the markings, but the wounds too." Dustin reiterated.

"You're sending someone here to look at wounds and markings?" Jury continued. It was easy for Jury to forget the wounds on her pet in the tube. She was so used to seeing him that they had almost become part of his outfit.

For a first time viewer, the man in the tube had the skin of a battered person with a severe history. The tattoos, if you could even call them that, were dark tribal like symbols running from the right side of his neck and down the side of his arm. In all, there were close to two hundred symbols viewable to the naked eye. They seemed to billow out from his neck and float down his arm on clouds...or perhaps burned into his skin with fire.

The wounds were even more curious. There were the two long scars on his back just behind the trapezium muscles of his shoulders. The skin on the palm of his right hand looked loose and floated slightly detached from the hand. There were several stab wounds. One each on his stomach, chest and right thigh. Lastly, there was a superficial wound to the left side of his lower lip as if something or someone had burned off a small piece of the corner of his mouth and it had healed slightly asymmetrical from the right side.

"And this is all "them"...?" Lisa said.

Her inference was clear. Was Dustin hiding behind the other people and playing a game of point the finger by calling early and pleading his case? Was this another one of his decisions that would cause more problems for them?

"Yes. I suggested you guys scan the body and send the images. You guys have a holographic camera, it's not like they won't get proper images for her."

"Her? You're sending another woman up here? We can't even get a man. Someone that can help us change some of these light bulbs or take out the trash?" Jury said.

For the first time, Dustin's face broke and he registered a smile. He hadn't smiled often lately and talking to these two was normally when he did. There were times late at night when he wanted to just pick up the phone and hear their voices. He liked their voices. Lisa's had a smoky timber to it, while Marjorie's was all sweet honey. Outside of their femininity they offered a true understanding of this project and had trusted him and his leadership. Unfortunately, his leadership meant almost nothing with the new regime at the top of the totem pole.

"So when does she arrive?" Lisa was business as usual.

"She'll be there tomorrow." Dustin's face sank.

"Tomorrow?" The two of them echoed. For the new theologian to be arriving the next day there had to have been at least a month worth of planning done, a month worth of planning behind their backs.

"Yes, she's coming with the next supply shipment. I do have some good news. Not that she's bad news."

"Oh please regale us with your good news Dusty." Jury said.

Lisa pinched Jury for her smart mouth.

"Ow!"

"In the supply shipment is a new converter for your satellite so you're television can be fixed."

"Good." Lisa mentally tossed aside that appreciated but minor creature comfort.

"We've also included some new load-ins for your home theater and we were able to get almost all of your requested sundries."

"What's missing?"

"Ummm..." They could see Dustin looking over a list. "The yogurt isn't low-fat and they just couldn't find the sunflower seeds." Dustin shrugged.

"Still?" Jury said adjusting her towel yet again. "Who do I have to flash to get some damn sunflower seeds?"

Lisa smirked. Jury had a way of making her do that.

"I have another surprise, but I'll keep that under wraps. You guys get ready for the meeting. I'll see you all again in a half hour. Miss you guys."

"Miss you too, Dustin." They echoed.

As the transmission ended, Lisa turned off the camera and sat her head in her hands. So many ideas were swirling in her head. The most prominent being disappointment. When Dustin first called ahead of the main conference call she hoped that he would announce the end of the project and she could finally get a vacation. This was unlikely, but she at least wished they could get a break. Of course for most working people, spending all your days in a high-tech complex with minimal work and no costs, was a vacation. For Lisa, tedium became the remains of her days. In that moment she decided she would go back to her shower and treat herself to one more orgasm before finishing her shower, eating and joining the conference call.

That thought left her quickly as she raised her head. Her eyes grew, wider her jaw slacked.

“So now we have to make room for some Bible thumper, huh. I hope she realizes as big as this place is there’s no room for…L what’s wrong?” Jury saw a change in Lisa’s face; there was something there… What was she looking at?

Still hoisted over the console with her behind in the air, Jury craned her neck over her shoulder. It took a moment for her eyes to adjust to take in what she saw.

Her favorite pet was standing in the tube, eyes open, with an obvious erection.

“You were right…definitely a grower.” Lisa said.

He could tell the two women were looking at him, but he couldn’t muster the energy to move. Why were they staring at him? Did they always stare this way? Where was he? Who were they talking to with such intensity and why were they seemingly talking to this person through a camera? The pretty one with the pretty lips and exposed breasts had started staring first. The cute one with the bare ass and the...pretty lips had looked to him. Almost immediately the first covered herself with her robe and pushed back away from the console. The other spun around adjusting her towel to cover herself. Did this have anything to do with the lust he felt? It had been so long since he felt something, but he knew that it was lust.

They were heading towards him watching. They were looking lower. It was the lust. Was his body revealing how lustful he could be? Would they take him from this wet, warm place now? Would they punish him for his lust? He was used to punishment and these two didn't look capable of inflicting the types of punishment he felt in the past. Although, he had been fooled before.

The first one ran back to the console and started pressing buttons and reading screens. The second one just stroked the outside of his confines. She was talking to him. He could not hear a word. He forced his ears to act but still all he could feel was a warm fluid on his body. When she waved her hands from side to side in front of his face, he tried to follow with his eyes, but they wouldn't budge.

He noticed how her breasts pushed against her towel as she spoke excitedly to the other woman. With her this close to the glass her features were now more pronounced. Her lips were full and were constantly repeating a word, a word he could not make out "bear"? "Bed"? "Pell"? "Pen"? She turned over her shoulder and said something to the other one. She was nodding and running to another console. The other one was typing something and then the closer one stepped back from the glass.

The first one spoke again. Her face was urgent. The closer one took another reluctant step backward. The first one pressed a button. White heat shook his body. He tried to hold on but all of his muscles burned. His heart thumped and then...He felt the world go dark again.

"All I want to know is if his dick got hard because he saw us half naked or because there was some kind of blood flow change." Lisa shoved a protein bar in her mouth furiously as she poured a glass of orange juice.

"Look at YOUR ego." Jury joked as she checked the date on her yogurt before opening it.

The two of them headed back to the lab with handfuls of portable breakfast food.

"The defib put him out again, so I don't know..."

Jury didn't have to say it. Lisa knew the rest of her sentence. Had she risked the entire project by trying to jump-start him into further consciousness? His heart rate was better than the previous eight months and had increased some just a few minutes before they saw him. With the defibrillation he was lingering right above his stasis. Would he get better? He had to get better!

BWOMP! BWOMP! BWOMP! BWOMP!

The call alarm sounded. Lisa pressed the button straight away then another that broadcasted the video in a hologram right in front of the tube. Six people sat at a conference table. Dustin sat at the head of the table, but didn't look to be in power. There were 3 other men and 2 women.

"Hey how are you guys?" A board member said.

They nodded.

"So, we have some news for you ladies." Dustin started...

"Actually, we have some news for you!" Jury shouted.

The conference call didn't go exactly as they hoped. While the panel seemed encouraged by their news, they weren't overwhelmed. Most of the discussion revolved around the impact of the development on the arrival of the theologian. By the time the call ended, the doctors were exhausted and embarrassed. It's no small fete to explain to a panel of government officials and military researchers that your nude body in a laboratory may have caused a hard dick on a specimen.

"This is some bullshit. He needs to open his eyes right now!" Lisa said. "I want him to open his eyes, get his dick hard and break through that fucking tube with it!" She marched toward the tube.

"What are you doing?" Jury shouted from the console.

"I'm waking his ass up!" Lisa banged on the tube with the side of her fist. "Hey you! Let's go! Open your eyes again! Please just do it! I'll show you a tit, just give me a sign!" Lisa cupped her breasts.

PLINK! PLINK! She banged.

"Hit him with a pulse." Lisa ordered.

"What?" Jury was sure Lisa had lost her mind.

"Hit him with a pulse. Not the full defib but 30% more than on the muscle charge." Lisa's voice didn't waver.

Jury typed in a few commands. Her finger lingered over the button.

"Ok. Safety line." Jury shouted as Lisa stepped back behind a small yellow circle that surrounded the tube. She pressed the activation and his body jerked slightly in the tube. The pulse caused air bubbles to form at his nostrils that quickly imploded back to gel. Nothing.

"FUCK!" Lisa stepped up to the tube and banged again "Wake the fuck up! You wanna see some ass? Maybe you're an ass man. She turned and placed her round expansive ass against the tube. Still nothing.

"Girl, you're crazy. You should at least show him some skin." Jury laughed.

"Yeah right." Lisa broke out into a giggle. Then taking the joke too far she untied her baby blue sweatpants, turned her behind to the tube and dropped her pants. Nothing. She bent over brushing the tube with her bare ass. "There's my ass for you! Just wake up!"

As if on cue, his eyes opened. Lisa jumped and pulled her pants up.

"HOLY SHIT! Maybe he is an ass man!" Jury said.

"Check the vitals." Lisa shouted as she whipped a small flashlight from her pocket and aimed the beam into the pupils of his eyes.

"The pulse increased his heart rate, he was steadily increasing since then. Sorry to bust your...um...bubble...

ass..." Jury typed in more commands and received more feedback.

"So, are you going to come out here and get me or what?" Lisa whispered to the tube as she searched his pupils with the flashlight.

And then, swiftly, he raised his hand to the glass blocking the light from his eye.

CHAPTER TWO

 DECISIONS DECISIONS 

The specimen was pushing against the inside of the tube. He wasn't trying to break out so much as pleading to be removed. Upon regaining consciousness, his attempts to take a big deep breath were met with a throat full of the yellow tinged gel. He sucked heavily on the air hose in his mouth, but the fluid had already filled his lungs. He could tell the two women outside the tube were worried about him. One was frantically speaking to the other while pressing buttons on the console. The other was rummaging through binders. Why was she looking through papers? Didn't they know how to get him out of the tube?

"No it's the green book!" Lisa was panicked as she searched through various menus on the console. None of the screens told her what was wrong.

Jury had properly initiated the removal sequence. Why wasn't the fluid draining? With every step there had been a new prompt for an authorization code. Finally, they had run out of codes and answers. The specimen had been running out of patience and presumably air. Flinging yet another manual from the shelf, Jury quickly found the index and flipped through to the specimen removal section.

"This shit says the exact same fucking thing. We need the "Master authorization code", but we went through every damn code." Jury was more pissed than confused.

"These bastards..." Lisa's face registered a slight smirk. She knew they were kept on a short leash, but had no idea of the size of the egos of those in control. "THEY have the master code. We can't remove him without them giving us authorization." She quickly pressed the on-call button then the code for Dustin's office.

Jury watched the tube. His eyes bulged; his body was pressed against the tube. A gigantic shroud of darkness had overtaken her. Her pet was dying in the tube, he was dying right before her eyes. The electronic beeps began. Dustin wasn't answering the call.

"Pick up! Pick up!" Lisa yelled.

"You've begun an extraction..." Dustin's voice was calm, but there was a small hint of excitement in it. "He hasn't died." It was odd now. Dustin was asking rhetorical questions. They knew that the vital stats data was accessible from the main headquarters. Yet he was playing cat and mouse.

"He's conscious, Dustin. We need the master authorization." Lisa's patience was worn nearly gone.

"His heart rate is up, blood flow is low. How conscious is he?" Dustin said obviously monitoring their specimen.

"Dustin! Cut the bullshit. He's fucking smothering in there! Drain the fucking tube!" Lisa shouted. She watched Jury's pet push back from the front of the tube and start to lower himself to one knee as he held the air hose in his mouth.

"Listen to me first, I'm going to drain the tube, but I'm not going to release him."

"Not GOING to release him?" Lisa didn't believe her ears. She and Jury had long said they were babysitters, but now Dustin was proving it. "What the fuck exactly is our purpose here then, Dustin?"

"You have to understand, there's a reason why we put in these safeguards. I told you, we consider him to be a very dangerous individual. Just because he's been quiet in that tube for months doesn't mean he won't step out and lay that entire complex to waste."

Suddenly, there was stillness in the air. Lisa could hear her heart pounding against her chest. Jury stopped flipping through errant manuals and watched the speaker console. She was waiting...as if Dustin was going to step through the console in physical form and type into the keyboard. His words had been echoing through Lisa's ears. She had been given warnings about Jury's little pet before, but there never was such intensity in Dustin's voice. He had mentored her. Even through some of the most demeaning power struggles in his career he had been such a pillar of strength. Suddenly, he sounded fearful. She could hear him quickly unlocking something. She was sure it was the safe that he kept beneath his desk. She had seen the safe once when dropping something off to his desk after hours. She wondered why a "suit" would have a safe under his desk, but never brought it up to him in conversation.

There was a click, then a loud metallic sound closer to the phone. He had placed something next to his speaker and returned to the safe. He was rustling through papers then he was back to the speaker again. He nervously cleared his throat.

"Ok here's the code." He said.

Jury glanced up to the tube. It was the most peculiar thing. She could've sworn she saw her pet peek up from his kneeling stance. It was a small peek to see if anyone was watching, like a kid cheating on a third grade spelling test. Or was it a look to see if they were even trying to help him? She stepped closer to the tube as she listened to Lisa typing into the keyboard. The specimen grabbed the air hose with both hands and opened his mouth. Jury banged on the tube.

"Wait! Don't! Not yet! Stop!" Jury yelled at the top of her lungs as if she were saving the life of one of her dearest friends. She saw him peek up again, but this time the look was smeared with sinister, evil eyes.

He was slowly dislodging the air tube from his esophagus; little by little he was pulling the tube from within him. She turned to Lisa to speak but no words left her mouth. She saw Lisa nodding as Dustin talked her through the process.

"The Final sequence is 7-L-1-B-G-8-Q-N-S." Dustin said.

"I got it. There's another box. What do I type in there?"

"Another box?" He sounded totally confused.

Jury's pet convulsed as he pulled harder on the tube. Finally the blood smeared final piece slid from his mouth and he exhaled causing big bubbles to erupt from his nose and mouth.

"He's taken the air hose out, L." Jury said. The effort took a lion's share of her energy.

Lisa looked up, shaken but not panicking...yet.

"OH! Just type in your normal pass code." Dustin sighed.

Lisa typed quickly and pressed return. Nothing happened. The specimen held the hose in his hand, the air erupting from it created waves in the fluid. He peacefully stared at Jury. There was intent here. He was leaving the entire situation to fate. No not fate. He wasn't giving up. It was a look of defiance. Jury pleaded with him through her eyes. Just take some air. He dropped the hose, took a step backward so his back touched the tube and exhaled. Bubbles erupted from his nose and mouth.

"What are you doing?" Jury screamed at the tube.

"I'm trying to get this thing to work" Lisa answered. She punched buttons on the console not understanding why the initiation hadn't started. She inadvertently hung up on Dustin as she jabbed the console with her slender fingers. The phone made an electronic clicking sound before rendering Lisa and Jury alone again.

"No not you. Him!"

Lisa looked up and caught his eyes. He stood motionless in the tube. The air hose created waves in the liquid giving him a ghostly appearance.

THUMP! THUMP! THUM-THUM-THUM THU-THOOOOOOM!

The suction pumps had started. The fluid was slowly emptying through small drains on the inside perimeter of the tube. He looked down watching the fluid flow quickly down and disappearing through the grates. Small air bubbles rose from the drains like carbon bubbles in soda pop.

Lisa and Jury watched him closely. By the time the fluid level reached about six inches above his head, his body had started to convulse from lack of oxygen. However, he didn't jump for air. He stood and accepted the pain in his body. And there was pain, the painful feeling of thousands of little needles pricking his lungs, his throat and head. Just as the fluid level was about to pass his shaven head, he doubled over falling deeper into the tube. Jury gasped, but when she made to approach the tube, Lisa held her back by her arm. Jury flinched, surprised at how quickly Lisa had arrived at her side.

"But..." Jury started.

"He'll be ok. There's nothing you can do. If he wants to live he'll stand. If he wants to die, it's too bad! That fluid will be out of that tube in a couple of minutes."

"Yeah but it's not like we can go in and resuscitate him."

The fluid was moving faster through the drains now. The more it drained the faster the pumps seemed to work. Slowly, the fluid drained from around his head, but he kept his head bowed. The yellow-tint of the fluid left his body and for the first time they were able to see the true soft brown color of his complexion. The fluid was swirling around his body quickly. It was a torrent of swirling yellow, like a man hunched over in the eye of a tornado. Lisa realized now that he was kneeling, almost in prayer, his head bowed. His arms were at his side, his hands rested on the wires protruding from his thighs, his feet were tucked under his bottom. The air hose lay next to him bobbing up and down emitting air bubbles. Occasionally the hose jumped into the air, swirled wildly then fell again at his side. Both of them stared in awe. It wouldn't register to them then, but the way the blue security lamps collided with the yellow liquid created an alternating green glow around his body, especially near his head. There was a shallow gurgling sound. The air in-take was now clear. The fluid had left the tube.

"Are you ok?" Lisa said beating Jury to the question.

He didn't move. He just sat quietly. He wasn't dead. They saw his stomach slowly rise and fall with large deep breaths.

Jury walked to the console, punched a few buttons then stretched a connected microphone up to her full lips.

"Can you hear me?" She said softly, but the sound seemed to startle him. His head jerked up. He stared at her.

"I guess that's a yes" Lisa said with a smile.

"Are you feeling ok?" Jury said softer.

He reacted similarly, this time his eyes winced. He covered his ears with his slick palms.

"Turn it down...It's too loud." Lisa said with a bit of excitement in her voice. Her excitement was lost on Jury who slowly turned it down while giving her a look that clearly read 'watch your tone, honey.'

"Is this better?" Jury cooed into the microphone stopping just short of calling him her favorite pet.

He nodded fluidly.

"Ask him how he's feeling..." Lisa stepped closer to the tube. His attention directed towards her.

"I think he can hear you too." Jury whispered after removing her finger from the talk button.

Staring in Lisa's eyes, he nodded fluidly. She felt the hairs on the back of her neck stand. Her arms prickled with goose bumps, but her face felt flush. His stare had touched her soul, handled it and left imprints with one look. Jury pressed the talk button.

"We need to know..."Jury started, but was interrupted by a thunderous grinding sound erupting from the speakers outside the tube.

The sound was her pet clearing his throat. He coughed a hacking cough then spat a mouthful of the fluid into one of the drain vents. Lisa jumped back at his sudden movement. He cracked a smile realizing how easily he had startled her.

"We need to know..." Jury started again looking at Lisa. Lisa already knew what the question would be. "Who you are."

He stared at Lisa, his expression turned serious. His head swiveled to Jury. The look caused her finger to slide off the talk button. His lips upturned in a slight smirk then parted and a soothing low rumble of a voice rattled the frame of the speakers.

"Apparently, I'm your pet."

Dustin's face wore the troubles of many bad experiences. His pale blue eyes were chilly. His features were that of an aging big man on campus. He still had the charm. The looks tried to fade, but with constant exercise and healthy eating he had kept all of the negatives of getting older at bay. Those pale blue eyes stared at his satellite phone.

Unlike his regular desk phone, which sat on his desk of course, his satellite phone sat on a small but beautiful mahogany table on the left side of his desk. He had the table placed there to further shield the safe that was installed under his desk shortly after his arrival. The table didn't match anything in his otherwise boring office décor. The walls were white, the desk was black finish, there was a black leather executive chair and the visitors' chair was hard and uncomfortable. The otherwise spacious corner office wasn't impressive, except for the table. Soon after it arrived, that beautiful table had a rather large phone sitting on top of it. It was a shame. That table was a gift from his assistant, Janice. She considered herself quite the weekend antique warrior and picked it up at a quaint little antique shop downtown.

The dark wood and intricate craftsmanship were perfect symbols to celebrate the anniversary of their two-year affair. It was dark, complex and had plenty of history. That affair was over now, but the sexual tension still bubbled to the surface now and again. Janice hated that her perfect gift was now being used as a phone holder. On occasion her eyes would drift to the small knick the phone had caused when it was placed there. That knick would make her bristle. Dustin was now thumping that knick with his fingertips, waiting for the phone to ring again. Why hadn't Lisa and Marjorie called him back immediately?

Dustin checked the open screen on his computer monitor. There were several computer "widgets" open on his screen. He never got used to widgets. They were little applications that served a singular purpose. What ever happened to programs that did everything? The widgets gave information about what was happening in the tube at The Country Cage. He could see the specimen's heart rate and vital statistics had improved. The widgets were on a fifteen minute delay, but as far as he knew, all was still well. His fingers drummed against his desk waiting for the phone to ring. The improvements in heart rate had spiked suddenly. He glanced down at the other three dark widgets at the bottom of the screen wishing they hadn't gone out. They ceased working at the same time as the television satellite at The Country Cage. Then he realized something even more pressing.

"Janice! Janice!" He yelled.

"What's wrong?" Janice's voice responded through his telephone. He'd often overlook the call button for yelling and she always responded in the correct manner instead of yelling back to him.

"Hold my calls. If anyone from tech calls or any of the research board...especially the board, tell them I'm in a meeting."

"What's the meeting about?" Janice said with a sly tone.

"I'm looking for a new assistant." He responded with a smile as he rummaged through the file folder on his desk.

"In that case, you're *very* available."

"Thanks, sweetie" Dustin hung up as he shifted through page after page in his file.

His eye caught his computer screen. The widgets were signaling an increased heartbeat, the specimen was doing miraculously well, incredibly quickly. What the hell was going on there? Had the specimen spoken to them? Was he fully lucid? Impossible. But if he had, Dustin was going to do what he thought was best. Reading from the file, he quickly typed in several codes into his monitoring system. Prompt after prompt asked him if he was sure. He stared at the final prompt blinking on his screen...

Are you sure you want to disable all monitoring of sector tube A818?

Dustin knew that pressing the yes button would create all sorts of questions. The first being, why the hell did he cut all monitoring of the specimen? This didn't just effect him, but also the board of directors, the other researchers and security operatives. His official answer would be that he mistakenly reset the system in an effort to save information and fix his own widgets. In actuality, he just wanted their hands off of his project. It was too personal a quest for him to stop now. So, he pressed yes and watched the widgets turn dark.

Dustin slowly gathered the papers and reorganized them back into the folder. He placed the folder back into the safe on top of the other files and closed the door. Just before it locked, he remembered he'd left something out. He picked up the heavy metal of the fifty caliber desert eagle that sat right behind his satellite phone. He didn't like handling guns, but it had often become a horrible necessity. With training he was good with guns, not great, but pretty skillful. Either way, he didn't like them. He eased the hand cannon into the safe with a thump, closed the door and gave the combination dial a whirring spin.

Dustin stared at his screen wishing those bottom three widgets were still operational. But for some reason the hidden cameras he had installed in The Country Cage weren't working anymore either.

"What's your name?" Jury blurted out. It was the first thing she could think of that would mask the flush overcoming her body. A warm heat of embarrassment had taken her as soon as the man in the tube said the word "pet."

"You're telling me, you have me locked in a little cage and you have yet to give me a name?" The man in the tube glared at her.

Lisa had tuned the volume down to a bearable level. She watched the monitors to get a sense of how the man in the tube was feeling. She was also keeping a close eye on Jury who had seemed a slight bit nervous and entranced by the man in the tube.

"We didn't name you, but right now your name is "specimen A818". Personally, I think it's a bit cold, but if you want to stick with that name it's fine with us." Lisa spoke into the microphone. Her words hadn't changed his staring at Jury, but his expression did alter from glaring to pensive.

"What is your name?" The man looked at Jury.

"I am Dr. Marjorie Houston, you can call me Jury. She is Dr. Lisa Lucas, you can call her..."

"Dr. Lucas." Lisa spoke loudly into the microphone.

"Lucas..." He repeated. "Lukas...Lucian...Lucio." He thought aloud shaking his head at the last thought and continued. "Luka...Loki..." He continued. "Luke..." His demeanor changed slightly "Luke." He smiled. His smile was bright and seemed to bring some manner of calm to Jury.

"Dr. Lucas." Lisa repeated sternly.

"Dr. Lucas." He repeated.

"And you are?" Jury nodded.

"Allard. Call me Allard." The man bowed. "Now that we have made each other comfortable can you release me from my cage?"

"Umm..."Jury began.

"Unfortunately Allard we can't do that right now, but we will try our best to make you comfortable." Lisa heard herself say it and wished she could've swallowed every last word back down her throat. These were the words of bed-side manner. Words she had no urge to ever repeat again.

"Well...what would make me comfortable right now is being released." Allard smiled to Lisa. She found herself smiling back to him.

BWOMP! BWOMP! BWOMP! BWOMP! BWOMP!

The sound of the phone startled Lisa and Jury. Allard stood watching them immobile. They sent mental messages to each other. Was it Dustin asking what was going on? Was it the board? Was this the end of their days in The Country Cage? Lisa clicked the on-call button.

"Dr. Lucas speaking." She attempted to sound unmoved.

"Answer yes or no." Dustin spoke. "Are you and Jury ok?

"Yes." Lisa responded.

"Can I be sure?"

" Yes."

"Is the specimen doing ok?"

"Uh...yes."

"Lucid?"

Jury looked up to Lisa. Her eyes told her not to tell the whole truth. The way Dustin was asking the questions seemed off kilter and very much out of personality. Coded language must've meant the phone lines were being monitored...no not monitored, recorded. Recorded? They were never told that the regular calls were recorded, only the conferences.

"No." Lisa shrugged.

"We seemed to have lost monitoring capability here so until we get it back please take care. If there are any emergencies do not be afraid to light the beacon. I just wanted to check in on you guys since the data stopped so abruptly. I'll call later with an update. Until then, find out everything you can. Keep the line clear." Dustin's connection was gone as quickly as it had come.

"Keep the line clear?" Lisa asked, but Jury was already headed for the console.

Jury made quick work of the faceplate on the phone and was soon reaching into the twisted wires. She disconnected a green wire, then a white one. She reconnected the faceplate back as it was.

"The line was recorded. That's what he meant. He wanted us to disconnect the monitoring on the phone." Jury explained. She felt a slight bit of nausea attack her in fear of what Dustin had to reveal once the line was clear. It was the onset of a flashback. A flashback of the moment Dustin had crushed her entire world. She had heard that order from Dustin once before. It was a late night call to her house. She cleared the line and then Dustin broke the news that a strike team of fifty had been killed and he needed the details of the massacre to be kept top secret. The details of that massacre made her lightheaded and she threw up in her toilet after hanging up the phone.

Why hadn't he told them that the line was under surveillance before? Like before he gave them the news about their upcoming visitor? Unless, he wanted the board to know he was giving them this information. He wanted them to know that he was still in charge of the program and these were his people. However, the new developments were something he didn't feel comfortable with sharing. Jury felt herself get lightheaded.

"Let's go take a walk." Lisa held her shoulder. She turned to the tube. "Allard, we'll be right back."

"I'll stay here." Allard smiled. Lisa noticed the humor then walked out of the lab with Jury plodding ahead of her.

Jury sat on a stool hunched over the kitchen island. Her hands slowly rubbed her temples. Lisa poured a glass of water and slid it across the counter to her. The glass shook as it stopped against her hand. The condensation and the coolness of the glass startled her slightly. She picked it up and took a healthy gulp. Lisa studied her face.

"You gonna be alright."

"Yeah." Jury shrugged.

"No, that was a statement not a question, chick. You can't go along fine all this time and then in the middle of a crisis you start to get haunted by thoughts of your dead boyfriend. It's just not gonna work right now. Sorry. Just not gonna work." Lisa's face was stern as a dean to a student.

"I KNOW!" Jury wiped a few stray tears from her lids. "It was just hearing Dustin sound like that reminded me so much of the night he called me to tell me Boyce was killed. It was just kinda eerie, ya know."

"Sorry. But we know it's not death we're dealing with. And if its death, it's the death of the research project as we know it because of the new board. But for us, for US, life goes on. They could come in here right now, pluck that guy out that glass cage, shut this place down and tell us to go home, but guess what, they can't take away our strength or who we are. Hell, they're scared to get rid of us anyway, we're the only ones that'll put up with this shit and the only ones qualified to do it."

"Damn right!"

"So..." Lisa reached in the fridge and pulled out a carton. "You want waffles?"

Jury smiled and flashed two fingers. Lisa flashed one...the middle one.

Allard stood still in the tube as the motion sensor lights immediately went out. The tube was filled with the scent of the fluid he had been semi-floating in for months. It was pungent. Like someone had pissed burning leaves. He held onto the wires that were crisscrossing his left arm and pulled slowly. The ends were piercing his skin just slightly, so as he removed them, he a the slight sting when the wires disengaged his muscles. He reached over and removed the wires from his arms, then his legs. The wire in his back hurt the most. He felt a searing pain shoot through the entire length of his body. His hand held onto it for a moment then dropped it too. The wires dangled from the top of the tube like wayward Christmas lights.

The IVs were easier to remove. When they were out, he flexed his hands open and closed. His veins snaked in his hands as he pumped the blood through them. Oh yeah, how could he forget that other issue. Holding his right palm up to his face, he surveyed the piece of skin that was hanging from his hand. It looked like a translucent glove made of his skin. He slowly, peeled it from his hand. It hurt most by the fingertips, small droplets of blood rose to the surface of his fingers like dew on blades of grass. His hand felt raw and burned, especially at the palm. He licked his hand, God's cleanser, and tasted the sourness of the fluid. When he inadvertently swallowed it, he gagged.

Allard didn't look forward to the last bit of disconnection he was to do. He sighed heavily and cleared his mind. His hand snaked into the waistband of his wet shorts. His flaccid manhood lay in his hand like a short thick garden hose. He glided his fingers to the tip of it and found a thinner hose protruding from it. After so much time being attached to the catheter, his urethra was virtually fused to the plastic tube inserted in it. He tugged lightly and the tube barely budged. It was obvious he would be forced to pull with way more effort and lots more pain. His teeth bit into his bottom lip, he gave himself a count of three and tugged. A deep groan vibrated in his throat. The hurting in his manhood was a virtual cavalcade of pain. His eyes saw starbursts. Slowly, he lowered himself to a knee clutching the clear plastic tube. Looking out of the glass he wanted nothing more than to get out. He already knew he would, he already knew when and it was very clear to him how.

CHAPTER THREE

FLUID

The technical name for the fluid was Scilymax-Amnio. It was initially devised to keep once living evidence preserved for lengthy amounts of time. Often that evidence was used for research. The "evidence" never led to an investigation in the legal terms, so a memo was sent to all who used Scilymax-Amnio. The memo instructed all users to cease using the "evidence" stickers on all jars, vats and barrels. From now on, "specimen" was the proper term. The company, Scilymax, even brought in a team of drones to re-label and re-tag all previous "evidence" tags to the proper "specimen" tags. Scilymax was many things, effective being the first.

In their third trial of Scilymax-Amnio 332, scientists and developers discovered that the solution could help to preserve live test subjects that were in forms of shock or coma. The fluid had kept the animals in a form of stasis. The animals' circulation, respiration and organs all functioned well, but at slower speeds. It was as if they were submerged into a barrel of liquid slow motion. In order for it to fully take effect a small amount was injected into the test animal along with a sedative and a morphine derivative. The sedative was to calm the animal before it was submerged, the morphine to calm the severe pain caused by the injection of Scilymax-Amnio.

Why there was such pain when the S-A was injected had never been fully proven or researched. After the injections, the animal was attached to a respiratory tube and then submerged. The stasis was nearly immediate. Researchers found that the fluid on the outside of the body interacted with the fluid inside of it. They attracted each other like a beacon to a rescue crew. Soon the fluid outside the body would be absorbed into the body through the skin, but only in increments allowed by the S-A itself. It maintained its own balance without researcher regulation.

The development arm of Scilymax had come up with many ideas for the mass production and sale of S-A. The most internally popular idea was a hair growth repressive. A small amount injected into a woman's chin, for example, then applied topically would halt hair growth for well longer than any other popular remedy. Unfortunately, because of the volatile nature of the S-A molecules, the pungent odor could not be masked. Of course, then there was an issue with the pain as well.

Another puzzling attribute of various versions of the Scyilymax-Amnio was a temporary reduction of motor skills. The most widely reported within the Scilymax research community was the effect it had on a lab rat known affectionately as Rocket Rodney. Rocket Rodney held the record for executing the most intricate maze in the facility in only 6.8 seconds. After his S-A experience, his time doubled. However, once his system had fully purged itself of the S-A, he broke his own record. The new record for that maze still holds at 3.7 seconds.

The latest version of S-A, S-A 333, was carefully infused with nutrients. These nutrients helped to keep human skin functioning as the body's largest organ. The nutrients could also travel through the skin via the miraculous attributes of the Amnio and provide the body with self regulated vitamins and minerals. The researchers that added the nutrients didn't know how it worked, it just did.

Scilymax-Amnio 333 was in effect a miracle fluid. Fluid was to be used as a loose term. Research was being conducted to see if it could actually be defined as an organism. Although, there were thousands of pages of research on S-A 333, none of them, not a single solitary one, could pinpoint how, when or who created the first batch, but the research would continue.

It had been nearly five hours since either of them had entered the lab that held the tube. Neither could muster the courage. In fact, they had gone about their day as if the tube hadn't existed. They watched a movie in silence both preoccupied with the upcoming responsibility of going back into the lab. Finally, the two flipped a coin, winner would cook dinner, loser would check on Allard. The coin landed on heads, Jury let out a sigh and went to the refrigerator to find the steaks she had marinated the night before. Lisa was in no rush. She checked her email then read two more chapters of her novel before nodding to Jury and walking towards the labs. There was a silence in the hall, the only sounds were of the light bulb hums and her sneakers squeaking against the tile floors.

She inched toward the final door. Her stomach was queasy and she was unsure. She was scared to see what would greet her when she crossed the threshold. Would he lay dead at the bottom of the tube, the victim of relapse? Would Allard be waiting for her, broken from the bounds of the tube? Would he take her from behind by surprise strangling the life from her thin long neck? His hands looked strong even though one was partially mangled. Lisa could handle herself well. She was an athlete-minded, well-built woman. She could put up a fight. It was doubtful she could stop him though. Even if he'd been locked in that tube for months, she was sure he could handle himself well. The wires inserted into his muscles had insured they hadn't gone through atrophy, but surely he wasn't one hundred percent. He was waiting for her on the other side of that door. He was surely pissed. All she could do was take several breaths, clinch her right fist and slowly push open the swinging door.

The lights went on immediately. The quiet hum of soft white fluorescents behind warm lighting fixtures filled the room. She watched the tube and saw him sitting. His legs were crossed "pretzel-legged", hands were held up, but outward from his face, his eyes were closed. He was praying. Lisa typed her pass code into the console as quietly as possible and looked at the screen. All of the vital statistics screens were registering no movement. Was he dead? Was he stiff as a board with rigor mortis? Did he die praying solemnly to his maker? Pushing her head forward, she looked closer at the tube then pressed the intercom button.

"Excuse me." She was speaking softly as you would to a baby. He didn't move. "Allard are you..."

Alive?

"...Awake?" She paused. His hands lowered slowly, his eyes flicked open. His lips spread to a gentle smile.

"I'm sorry I was trying to take conference." Allard's voice was peaceful.

"Conference?"

"Yes..uh...praying?" He tried to make her understand the concept. She knew it well.

"Why did you take off the wires? Did you remove your...oh great..you removed the I.V.s too." Lisa couldn't contain her frustration.

"I'm feeling better. Not one hundred percent, but definitely no need for wires and tubes. Especially not one in my penis."

"Well we need to make sure you're remaining healthy, Allard" Lisa was watching him carefully. The last thing she wanted was to put her guard down and then somehow he'd come barreling through the three-inch thick plate glass straight for her.

"We? Where is your friend?" He asked.

"My colleague Dr. Houston wasn't feeling well. Right now, she's attending to other business."

"Your colleague, not your friend?"

"She's my friend also."

"I could tell. When she was having her little panic attack, you held her like a sister." Allard was now rolling his neck from side to side stretching it out.

"She's fine and she's like a sister to me." Lisa bristled at his words. He sounded too judgmental to be a man in a tube wearing a pair of shorts.

"What was wrong? Perhaps I can help her."

"She's fine. She's attending to other business. Without those wires and without the I.V.s we could have a problem sustaining your condition."

"You can let me out and replace them." Allard extended his arms to her. "Or you can come in and join me."

"No, I'll let things stay the way they are for now."

"For now..." Allard perked up. "Well you're welcome in my cage anytime. I am your pet."

"Jury called you that, not me."

"Oh did she? Is that what she was saying? There was a word she used. I didn't understand. Pet...pet..." he mouthed the word several times to himself, finally agreeing that was it by nodding. "So what do you call me, Dr. Lucas?"

"Guy in the tube."

Allard let out a loud laugh that rattled the speakers and briefly unnerved Lisa. Allard slowly rose to his feet. He seemed a bit tentative with his balance.

"Listen, if you're better off sitting, I'd suggest you stay that way." Lisa was concerned for his and her own well-being.

"No, it was rude of me to sit as you entered. It'd be even more rude for me to beg you from a sitting position."

"Beg me?" Lisa felt her jaw tense.

"Yes. If you or your colleague friend could be so kind as to provide me with a meal, I will be overwhelmingly appreciative. I'm not sure how long you've held me here, but I assure you I.V. entrees are not filling." He rubbed his stomach.

"Actually, we're going to have to figure that part out." Lisa hadn't remembered there being an access point to put things in, without totally removing the specimen. So much for the efficiency of Scilymax.

"Well when you do, I don't ask for much. Maybe some water, some bread, some fruit maybe?" Allard had sounded close to pathetic. His humility embarrassed Lisa.

"We'll figure that part out."

BWOMP! BWOMP! BWOMP! BWOMP! BWOMP!

The phone rang. Lisa turned off the intercom and answered the phone. Dustin's face popped up on the monitor.

"Lisa, are we clear?" He sounded hurried.

"Yes. You're back on camera now. I assume everything is better there than it was earlier."

"Something like that. Listen, I had all remote monitoring turned off to the tube. How is he doing?"

Lisa glanced to the tube to see Allard standing there watching her. He couldn't hear her so he was giving her face a strong focus. No. It wasn't her face he watched. It was her lips. He did infer to reading Jury's lips didn't he? She covered her mouth with her hand and faked a cough, but left her hand in place shielding her lips.

"He's awake and talking. Removed all of the cables and I.V.s"

"TALKING?? What is he saying?" Dustin tried to quiet his excitement. His eyes were darting back and forth on his side of the screen.

"Well, he wants to get out and he wants food. What would you want?"

"Shit, ok. Listen...ummm...try not to put him on guard too much. The board of directors were really trying to get the monitoring reinstalled by IT by the end of the day here but the day's almost done so it'll probably be back up sometime tomorrow morning or later if I can get IT to drag their feet."

"What is going on with the board?" Lisa knew there were some power struggles before but not to the extent that Dustin Carver, of all people, would sabotage the project. That was more something Jury would do.

"This new board, they've got a little fire under their ass and are trying to bring him back here for some...let's just say re-focusing. We have different goals here and I want to make sure that we at least understand who we're dealing with before we decide what we're dealing with."

"Hold on." Lisa turned her back to the tube because it was annoying holding her hand over her mouth for so long. She felt like a football coach giving instructions on the final game winning play. "You told us this guy was a witness to an investigation, a military crime. We were supposed to help him through getting conscious, getting his memory right and then getting your bad guys in jail. What IS there to re-focus?"

"He didn't just witness the crime, he was part of it."

"I figured as much with all your 'be careful' talk. So is the board pushing to charge him too? What the hell do we care? We're medical researching this deal. He woke up. He's talking. He's got an appetite. Let's get our data. What they want to do with them is on them!"

"I wish it was that easy. It *was* that easy until I got some new info. I convinced them to allow us to send in this theologian to help develop some theory."

"Theory?" Lisa was dumbfounded.

"Yes and she was a perfect fit for what I'm working on. I know you have concerns..."

"I just didn't think you'd turn this into a sorority house. I'm honestly surprised she wanted to come!" Lisa shook her head.

"Well, I made her a very lucrative offer."

"And I'm sure you used us as bait as well." Lisa poked her finger at the phone wishing it was Dustin's forehead.

"...Maybe just a little. Keep and eye on her while she's there. She has to remain safe, I'd hate to have put her in harm's way."

"Oh and you just throw us two bitches to the wolves, huh."

"No, not at all. Wait, where is Marjorie?"

"Cooking dinner." Lisa whispered extra low as not to even entice Allard's ear.

"Why are you whispering?"

"Mixed company..."

"He can't hear me, can he!!??" Dustin was louder than he needed to be.

"Not at all. I even have my back to him so he can't read my lips. So, hold on, this theologian is coming here to do what exactly?"

"She'll check out the wounds and the marks...and now that he's awake, counsel him. Hopefully, we can get some of it on tape as a pseudo deposition."

"Do you think this guy is Jesus? I don't know why else you'd ask a religious person to come here. As far as I saw there were no holes in his hands or feet and no scars from a crown of thorns on his head. So..."

“Counsel, remember? She’s great at that. It comes from a different place than Marjorie’s psyche exams.” Dustin sounded testy.

“Right.” Lisa felt a twinge of guilt for questioning Dustin’s motives.

“I have to go. Just remember what I said and make sure your new house guest gets everything she needs to do what I sent her to do.”

“Speaking of needs...Food.”

“Supplies are coming tomorrow remember?” Dustin chided.

“No, Allard.”

“Who?”

“His name is Allard. He wants food. How do we feed him? That thing is like a jar without a lid.” Lisa said.

“Allard? His name is Allard??”

“Yes and he’s hungry.” Lisa sat waiting. There was a long silence on the other end of the phone. Dustin obviously hadn’t considered this problem.

“The fresh air vent. Now that the tube is empty, there’s a vent on the lower left side of the base. You can open it, take out the filter, move the hose and pass it up through there. It’s small so he won’t be able to get much, but he also won’t be able to get out.”

"Thanks. Sounds like changing my own oil."

"Be safe." Dustin's line closed. The Scilymax logo popped up on the monitor as a screensaver.

Lisa turned around to the tube. Allard was standing waiting patiently. Lisa pressed the intercom button, said she'd return and left the room. Allard was disappointed in the abrupt end to their conversation. But there'd be plenty of time to talk to Dr. Lucas in the future, this he knew already.

"So this is just gonna be a dorm room, huh." Jury laughed as she brought her fork to her mouth. Mmmmm she did it again with those marinated steaks.

"Yeah, I told him it was a sorority house now." Lisa poured light balsamic vinaigrette on her slightly wilted salad then started cutting her steak. Damn Jury did it again with the steaks!

"How's he doing?"

"He's ok. He's just concerned about the board's menta..."

"No, not him. Allard, how is he?" Jury's eyes probed Lisa's.

“Outside of removing all of the monitors like I told you. He seems pretty good. When I walked in he was praying. He called it conferencing or ‘trying to conference’. He said he was hungry so Dustin told me if we were going to try to feed him something we’d have to dismantle the fresh air vent and shove it through there.”

“More technical shit. I swear when I leave here I’m not lifting a finger for at least 6 months.” Jury shoved another bit of steak in her mouth.

There was a peace between them as they ate at the kitchen island. They gave up on eating in the dining room a long while ago when they realized that it was silly of them to set a formal table for two and sit in a cavernous room when the kitchen island was so much more comfortable. Jury broke the silence.

“So I’ll take him the food later. I need to talk to him.”

“Ok, what time should we go in there?”

“No, I’ll do it myself. I need to start building his trust and see if I can get him to open up. See if he has what Dustin needs to make a case.”

“Uh oh the head shrinking starts now, huh.” Lisa smiled. She could tell there was something else there, but didn’t want to pry. Jury was a great psychotherapist so

Lisa was sure any of her own personal reasons for talking to Allard would be handled the right way.

"It'll be a short session. I think I need to get in on the ground floor before the Jesus freak comes and scares him with her deciphering and whatnot." Jury got up and made a second smaller plate for herself. She could feel a bit of excitement in her heart and mind. There was some between her legs too, but she would never acknowledge that...not yet anyway.

Allard sat with his legs crisscrossed. The tube was starting to stifle his breathing. He was never a claustrophobe, but with the combination of the rising humidity and the pungent smell, he was starting to feel uncomfortable. So Allard sat, crossed his legs and prayed. He tried his best to "Take conference" with his Creator. He pleaded for answers to his condition, for help with the situation, but nothing came. In his frustration, he lashed out and demanded a response, but none came.

Allard slowly inhaled the remnants of the odor and rubbed his muscles all over. Although he hadn't been active, his muscles had a distinct soreness to them. They felt as if he had been doing non-stop calisthenics for months with nearly no break. He assumed correctly that it had something to do with the wires he'd removed from his muscles. While there were the obvious side effects of muscle soreness, he liked the way his muscles looked. He was more solid, his muscles felt longer, stronger and their definition was more pronounced than he remembered. He was embarrassed by his own vanity until he ran his hand across the top of his head. No hair.

They had cut his hair. All of it! His anger built inside him. How dare they take such freedoms? Was this a way of making a fool of him? Were they trying to demean him? Or was this just a misguided attempt to keep him "orderly" in appearance. His long dreadlocks were gone. Obviously, they had read the story of Samson. They felt by cutting his hair that they could perhaps strip him of his power. Hadn't they read the whole story? Didn't they know that by the end of that story Samson regains his hair, regains his power and overcomes more than he had ever before? He smirked as he rubbed the stubble on the top of his head, lucky for him his power didn't reside in his hair or rather the Nazerite oath Samson was bound to hold. Regardless, of the matter, he wanted his hair back and he wanted his freedom, the freedom to finish his journey. Just as he felt a sincere feeling of hope evading him, his Creator answered his call.

"I brought you some food." The sweet feminine voice echoed through the tube.

Allard raised his head to see Jury holding the intercom button as she balanced a small plate of food in her other hand. He bowed his head in humility.

It wasn't long before Jury was horribly frustrated with the fresh air vent and all of its screws, plastic gadgets and hickamadoos. After removing the outside cover, things got a little more technical and she lost all focus. Allard found it endearing to see her struggle with the vent. She was persistent and tough. He read her lips as she spewed foul words hoping one of them would release the filter and move the hose. Finally, he tapped hard against the glass. She looked up at him, big brown eyes batting in damsel in distress mode. He raised both hands displaying all ten fingers and one horribly shredded palm. He slowly counted down using his fingers from all ten to the final one. He let the final finger linger for a while then pointed to the vent.

Suddenly Jury had found her error. She quickly unscrewed and detached the filter then moved the hose. A distinct odor was released from inside the tube. She closed her eyes and winced, pursing her mouth as if she tasted something sour at the same time as smelling something strong. It was like someone had urinated on a pile of burning leaves, she thought. She tried her best to ignore it. She didn't want to make Allard feel more uncomfortable and embarrassed about his situation than he already was.

The hole in the bottom of the tube was much smaller than she thought it would be. There was no way the entire plate would fit.

"Hold on let me see if I can shove this in one by one." She said to herself.

"Ok." Allard replied immediately through the hole in the base of the tube. She jumped slightly at his response. It was the first time she'd heard his voice not broadcasted through speakers. It was comforting and sweet like a smooth cognac.

Allard had noticed a new scent wafting up into the tube. It was sweet like honeysuckle with an accent of a fruit, pear maybe apple scented. He stared at Jury's smooth skin as she repositioned the food on the plate. He started to smell this now too, steak, a hot biscuit and green beans. As hungry as he'd become after smelling the food, it was still her scent that he preferred now. She positioned her hand into the vent again, this time the biscuit was peeping up through the hole. He lifted it up, holding it while she twisted the plate to the next item. He picked up the steak and balanced it in the same hand then did the same with the green beans. Try as she might, she couldn't find a way to fit the plate through the hole. He was left to feed from his own hands.

"Can you please leave that open for a little while?" He pleaded. His mouth savored the warmth of the melted butter in the biscuit.

Jury paused closing the hole. She sat back on her rear next to the tube. Happily, the odor from the tube wasn't as prominent where she sat. She watched him eat slowly with his hands. She left him to eat for a while, keeping herself preoccupied with matching screws with their errant nuts.

"I'm sorry. You wanted to talk..." Allard smiled swallowing the last bit of steak.

"I didn't want to interrupt. I know it's been awhile since you've had solid food. Dr. Lucas asked that I keep it light on your stomach, but what fun is that?"

"I appreciate it. I really do. Are you ok?"

"I'm sorry?" Jury was puzzled then realized her pet Allard had witnessed her breakdown. "Oh...Yes I was just a little upset earlier. I was thinking about a loved one of mine that I'd lost. Have you ever lost a loved one, Allard?"

"Yes, but not from death. More from...abandonment." Allard's words hung for a moment. Jury waited. "I caused it and I tried...I *try* my best to repair the relationship."

"When was the last time you spoke to this person?"

"Not sure, how long have I been here?" Allard watched her as he placed the last of the green beans in his mouth.

Jury smiled. She had set herself up for that. She knew that revealing too much about his length of stay and his current whereabouts were considered security issues. Allard watched her wheels turning. He could feel her soothing nature. He liked the way she addressed him. Their conversation continued. Allard felt at home telling her the pain his abandonment had left in his heart, but he was sure to explain that it was his cross to bear. He spoke in generalities, but Jury could surmise that this person was someone Allard looked up to. Someone he was ashamed to have caused such hurt that forced him or her to abandon him. She didn't want to pressure him too much. She didn't want to go too fast this early so she turned the conversation to lighter subjects.

His favorite color was gold, "a jubilant color". His favorite hobby was "people watching". He liked to observe people in their own element. His best skill was fighting. He could only describe it as "freeing". Jury made sure to take mental note that she would need to know what he wanted freedom from most...not including the tube of course. Siblings? He had several brothers and one sister. His sister was the youngest and by far the most aggressive. She had to be tough with so many older brothers. His father was a fair and kind man, but also ruled their home with a strong hand. His stepfather was less kind, but more open. Jury could sense some reticence when his stepfather was brought up so she backed away slowly from the topic.

"You call me your pet...is that a term of endearment?" Allard interrupted.

"Well yes..." Jury blushed.

"Did you have many pets as a child?" He sat with his back against the tube; he peered over his shoulder to her.

"Just a dog. How about you?"

"No. My father didn't allow us to have pets. My stepfather did, but I didn't like the pets he kept. Do you want to pet me?" Allard looked away from her.

"I'm sorry?" Jury attempted to catch his eyes.

"I'm your pet. Would you like to pet me?"

"Depends on what you mean by that." Jury peered over his scarred shoulder, but his eyes looked away.

"I mean you petting me. With those pretty fingers, that sweet scent. Your soft skin against mine. Pets bring comfort. Would you like me to comfort you?" Allard's voice echoed in the tube and escaped through the hole in the vent riding on a wave of sultry sweetness.

"Are you good at comforting? Is this what you would like to do for those around you?" Jury probed easily.

"I would like to comfort you. I've seen you want it and need it. When Dr. Lucas helped you away there was something missing from her comforting. You wanted a masculine touch."

"And how do you suggest I get that? Let me guess, I open up the tube and let you out..."

"No." Allard reached over and slid four fingers as far as he could through the vent, which wasn't that far. "This will do for now."

"For now? I have a feeling you're the one that wants comforting." Jury slowly slid over, her fingers extended slowly towards his. Their fingertips barely touched. His fingers were cold, moist and soft. He moved them slowly across hers and she felt a warmth flow from her hand through her body. It caused a shiver up her spine. His scarred shoulders relaxed as if he'd let the troubles of the world off of them for just a moment, then he pulled his fingers away.

"Can you do me a favor, Jury?" He spoke warmly.

"Anything."

"Can you leave the vent open or allow for more air to enter the tube when you leave? It's quite stale in here and I am rather tired."

Jury tried her best to not sound disappointed when she responded in the positive. She quickly re-installed the fresh air vent and with a few commands punched into the console, the air had begun to circulate inside the tube.

"Have a goodnight's rest Allard." Jury spoke into the intercom button. She watched his scarred back.

"Stay comforted, Dr. Houston."

Jury smiled and made her way towards the door. She manually turned off the working lights, bathing him in the security blue. He gestured to her; she reluctantly pressed the intercom button

"Yes?"

"This person you lost was a man? A loved one? A partner?"

"Yes." Jury felt her voice quiver.

"Be comforted. He's in a better place and I'm here with you."

Jury could only nod and walk away.

The first thing she noticed when she entered the halls were that they were darkened. That meant it was after eleven and the energy savers were activated. As she walked swiftly through the halls the lights turned on and off around her motion. In the kitchen, the dinner dishes were cleaned and the pots were sitting in the drain. She found Lisa sleeping in the living room cuddled around a throw pillow with her Stephen King novel sitting beside her. The clock read 12:03 AM. Had she really been talking to him for nearly four hours? It didn't seem that long. Not long at all. Instead of waking Lisa, she draped a blanket over her and turned out the lights.

After a nice long hot shower, Jury rubbed her body with her scented body oil and wrapped her hair in a head-scarf. Crossing her room in her towel, she boosted the thermostat to 80 and climbed in her bed nude. She liked the feeling of the fresh clean soft cotton against her body. Her head barely collided with the pillow before she was sleeping. She found herself riding through a swirl of color then smelled something foul, the smell from inside the tube. She returned to the bathroom doorway where she saw steam escaping the shower. It was unbearably warm. Allard's body was silhouetted in the steam of the glass doors of the shower. As she approached it slowly, she was totally unaware of her own nudity. The shower stopped abruptly. Her feet paused on the chilly tile floor, frozen in fear.

Allard stepped out of the shower with the steam rising from his body. Without drying off, he exited, his eyes met hers briefly as he passed her, his arm brushed hers leaving the slightest amount of moisture on her brown skin. She turned and followed him. His skin glistened; she admired his tight rear end as he walked toward the bed. She couldn't help but to reach out and touch the scars on his shoulders. He grabbed her hand quickly, spun her around so her arm was pinned behind her. He held himself against her firm round behind, his mouth close to her ear. His firmness was evident to her as it pressed against the back of her thigh. She could feel the hotness of his breath against her skin. Not just her ear, but all over her body.

Her face was in the pillow. He was behind her. She tried as hard as she could to concentrate, to wrap around what was happening to her, but her body was shaking too hard. He was deep inside her, filling her with comfort. She muffled her moans in the pillow and when her body shook with orgasm her fingers contorted in wild spasms. She could feel her essence flowing from her. He lifted his weight from her sweaty brown skin. Slowly, she rolled over and opened her eyes. His skin had changed to the color of a bloody crimson. His eyes were black and lacking pupils. His hand gripped around her throat tightly. She could feel the air leaving her lungs. She flailed her strong athletic legs, but they bounced off of him like rubber bands.

Jury awoke coughing loudly. Her sweaty skin stuck to the sheets that were tangled around her body. There was a loud noise echoing. A fire alarm? No it was something else. She jumped from the bed, tripped over the tangled sheets and fell at the foot of the bed. The room was unbearably hot. She opened the door and was hit with a refreshing burst of cool air. Small red lights were blinking in the hall. Then they stopped and the sound was gone.

"Lisa, what the hell was that?" She yelled.

"Proximity alarm, sleepy head!"

"What?"

Lisa came walking up the hall fully dressed in her workout clothes. Her eyebrow cocked at Jury's sweaty naked state.

"You smuggle a man in during the night?" Lisa joked.

"Why'd the proximity alarm go off?" Jury covered her breasts with her arms leaving the rest of herself bare. "The security team didn't have the new code when they crossed the marker. They're bringing our new roomie. Get some clothes on. She'll be here in a minute."

CHAPTER FOUR

A NEW RESIDENT AT THE COUNTRY CAGE

Dustin sat waiting in a low -key coffee shop far enough from the Scilymax complex that had a co-worker come in and spotted him, it would have been a clear case of spying. He was uncomfortable and fidgety and it had nothing to do with the frappa-whatever-you-call-it he was drinking. He doodled an odd symbol he'd seen somewhere recently on a paper napkin. He drew it large, small, upside down, all kinds of ways. Doodling was therapeutic for him. Dustin needed to talk to someone about all of life's issues.

With the new board of directors in place, work had become more stressful. Now that Janice was no longer in his life, his sex life was the pits. His marriage to his wife of twenty-one years was seemingly on its last legs and he wanted to vent to someone he didn't know. His only confidant in life was Lisa and he could never tell her the full story of Janice or the other three mistresses. Their friendship had cultivated during many consulting hours at work. However, he felt funny telling her the ins and outs of his home life, especially considering Lisa had met his wife several times and the two had become friendly. Dustin asked Lisa if she knew a good therapist or even better, a person of the cloth he could speak with. Lisa suggested a friend of hers, Michelle Bonds, a theologian who wasn't quite a pastor, but was close to a church. Michelle was also fairly liberal, very understanding and had done marriage counseling before. Lisa wrote down her number for him, but sensed his hesitation when he accepted it.

Dustin shoved the piece of paper in his wallet. It was tucked away with the errant receipts and dry cleaner pick up slips for a long time. Then one day, he found himself masturbating in his office to thoughts of Janice in her form fitting skirt while smelling the file folder that still held her perfumed scent. He finally pulled out the dog-eared paper and gave a call. Michelle had a pleasant voice. It was soft and professional. Had he not been sitting behind his desk with his pecker out and his jizz sprayed across the back of an empty manila folder, he would've been able to get another rise from the faint sex in her voice. Instead he asked her for a meeting.

As soon as she entered the coffee shop, an exasperated breath of air shot from his mouth. He knew automatically she was the one and he wasn't happy. Didn't Lisa have one friend that wasn't attractive? Why couldn't the "pastor friend" be matronly, bookish and gangly? Why was Michelle a caramel skinned, curvy woman with pretty brown eyes? He could tell her skin was soft...Geez. He waved signaling her to his table. Their introduction was simple. The ice was easily broken. He saw how Michelle was good at counseling. Soon he found himself explaining some of the most intricate recent disasters in his life. She listened, commiserated and seemed to know exactly what he was talking about. Had she been on a job interview, she would've landed the position thirty minutes in. Here they were working into their second hour when she checked her watch.

"It's almost two. I'm going to have to make my way back to the office, but we can set up another talk if you'd like." Michelle smiled sipping the last of her third herbal tea.

"Sure. I think that'd be helpful." Dustin smiled noticing not for the first time that Michelle had a healthy bosom.

Dustin helped Michelle put on her coat and as she did she noticed the napkin he had doodled on. Her head tilted this way and that.

"You in the Erasmus Club?" She asked pointing at the symbol.

"What's that?"

"I think that's the symbol for one of the local Christian sailing clubs, right?" She said unsure.

"Is it? I didn't know that. It's something I saw at work..." Dustin stopped short and peered at the symbol. "You said Christian sailing?"

"Well really it's the symbol of the Patron Saint Erasmus, the patron saint of sailors. It's what they call a windlass. I only remember it because the story is pretty horrid and it reminds me of a horror film I watched the other day."

"What's the story?"

"Well the Cliff's Notes version is, Erasmus was preaching the gospel and when it came the time that people were killed for such things they had a hard time killing him. They beat him until his veins burst, threw him in a pit of snakes, boiled him in oils, threw him in a barrel with spikes and threw it down a hill. However, every time they tried, he'd get hurt, but he'd keep living. They put him in prison and starved him, but he even escaped that. So finally, they slit his stomach open and used a sailor's winch used to raise anchors to remove his intestines." Michelle's face scrunched in the middle at the disgusting thought. She pointed to the symbol "The sailors winch was called a windlass. That's the symbol the sailor's club uses. The symbol of Erasmus, patron saint of sailors."

"Do any of the other patron saints have symbols?"

"I think all of them." Michelle said turning to leave.

Dustin grabbed her arm, which startled her. She could tell he was having some sort of epiphany. He pulled out his pen and started to draw another symbol. When he finished, he held it up to her.

"What about this?" He said peering into her eyes for an answer. This symbol was a little more abstract than the windlass, but in it she could see something.

"Is that an axe?" She tried to make it out from his horrible drawing. She could tell he was excited, even more so than he had been during his counseling.

"I don't know, but if it were, would it coincide with a saint?"

"Hmmm..." Michelle thought a moment and remembered one name. "Maybe Saint Thomas Moore...he was beheaded."

Nearly as soon as she finished speaking, he jotted down another image. Dustin could feel his blood rushing through his body. He couldn't believe that with all of his Catholic school education he hadn't considered any of the saints. No one he asked had considered saints either.

"Would you mind coming to my office? I'd like you to see something."

"I really have to go." Michelle demurred. She was actually kind of scared at his sudden manic behavior.

"Ok, what if I send you some pictures to your email? Do you think you could just look at them and give me some feedback? I'd be happy to pay you."

"You don't have to. I'll do it."

Later that day, Michelle checked her email and received five large emails from Dustin Carver. Her eyes grew wide when she opened the attachments. Each email contained a picture of the same person's arm. There were close ups of the person's tattoos. Well, they looked like tattoos except they also looked like engravings or brands. She saw the windlass in the symbols as well as the axe there were others that didn't look as familiar. All of the tattoo engravings weren't documented in close-ups, but she could tell that the artwork was very intricate. After some perusing, Michelle responded via email that the symbols she could identify seemed to be similar to some of the symbols of patron saints. Dustin's response landed on her desk early the next morning.

"I'm not sure I understand what you want me to do." Michelle spoke into her phone slowly like you would to a child.

"I'd like you to accept that offer to join this project as a consultant. For your limited time involved you will be paid the amount on the letter."

"How long would I have to work?" Michelle was confused. She stared at the number three which was followed by two zeros, a comma, three more zeros, a decimal point and two more zeros.

"Well I'd like to you to research the symbols we actually have pictures of and then see the rest of them in person as well as the markings on the body." Dustin explained slowly.

"Body? This person is dead?"

"Catatonic. When the person is lucid, I'd like you to come back and then speak to him about how he got those markings and why. Basically the same thing you did with me yesterday, but just counseling a person that has some disturbing tattoos. Two sessions for that number on the letter."

"I'll need to think about it."

"I understand. Just understand that if you can help, you'd be really doing a big favor for every one here. You'd also be helping Lisa and Marjorie on getting relief from the project they're on. They may be able to come home earlier." Dustin knew Michelle missed her friend. He'd felt a slight tinge of guilt in manipulating the situation, but it had a greater cause.

Two weeks later, his answer arrived on his desk in a small UPS Letter Pak. In the pak were color print outs of the pictures. Each symbol that Michelle could identify was circled, there was an accompanying explanation of the symbol and it's meaning affixed to the photo with a paper-clip. Dustin completed his own round of research without permission from and unbeknownst to the board of directors. When he had his own theory formulated, he presented the board with Michelle's research and secured her trip to The Country Cage. He locked his own research away in his safe. He wouldn't give the board that information just yet, if at all.

Michelle waved through the safety hatch window with a "surprise!" smile across her face. Lisa and Jury were in shock. They didn't know if it was all a mirage or the person being sprayed by the automatic air hoses bore an uncanny resemblance to their friend. The hoses slowed to a light spray then the vacuums started. The entire process only took about three minutes real time but nearly a lifetime in anticipation for the three of them. After the pressurized air blew across Michelle, the vacuums would suck up any possible contaminants that may have become attached to her. It was far from fool proof, but considering the location, there weren't any bugs or plant life to really worry about. The "all clear" alarm buzzed and the outside safety door (which was fashioned like any other home front door) released. Michelle pushed through and into the waiting arms of her friends.

After the big hugs and chatter, they convened in the kitchen. Michelle sat at the kitchen island as Lisa and Jury lifted the inside locks on the pantry and storage closets. When the doors opened a brisk chill blew into the room.

"Don't you wish you had this at home? You seal the doors then big ol' buff men come in from the other side, restock the pantry, unload the supplies, clean up on the way out and lock the doors behind them." Lisa laughed.

"I would think you'd want to invite the big 'ol buff men in after they were done." Michelle said to Jury.

"Uh-uh we said buff, not cute! Now if they were cute and buff we may ask a few to stick around." Jury laughed as she opened a bag of sunflower seeds and started the process of crack, suck, spit, shooting the leftovers into a handy plastic cup. "Want some?"

"No. I'm good. I'm still kind of nauseous from the trip." Michelle rubbed her face as Lisa got the hint and poured her a glass of ginger ale.

The three caught up on life as Lisa and Jury looked over the supply inventory. It took all three of them to figure out exactly how to patch the new converter box and reestablish the satellite link for the television, but it finally worked when they were done. Jury loaded the new movies into the theater as Lisa organized the fresh seafood they would have for dinner that night. It felt more like a bachelorette pad than a sorority house.

"Um, where's the body I'm supposed to look at?" Michelle asked nonchalantly. The other two stiffened. "What's wrong?"

“Shit, I forgot you were here for work.” Lisa stared back towards the hall that led to the labs.

“Did you check on him at all today?” Jury made her way towards the labs with the other two in tow.

“Yeah, I got up at regular time remember? He was fine. He was still sleeping, but I’m sure he’s up by now.” Lisa’s voice wavered.

“What do you mean up? Isn’t he in like a coma or something?” Michelle was taken aback by how comfortable the labs were even though they were fitted with lots of high tech equipment and fixtures.

“They didn’t tell you...I guess you were already on your way here when it happened...” Lisa used her hand-print for the scanner and the door released.

“What happened?” Michelle was confused as she turned the corner and saw the tube. Inside was a man in a wet pair of shorts bent over on his knees with his back facing them.

“Girl, he woke up after he saw some tig ol bitties and kitties.” Jury joked.

“Is he ok?” Michelle asked taking a tentative step forward as Lisa pressed the intercom box.

“Allard...” Lisa started but was rebuffed with a loud groan.

Allard turned slightly towards them and splattered the glass of the tube with projectile vomit.

It only took about ten minutes for Allard to regain his composure. Jury had jammed a small plastic cup through the small vent cover opening. He sucked water from it through a straw. She had surprised herself just how quickly she could dismantle the thing now that she knew how to do it. Michelle watched from behind the console. At a loss for words, she stood silently and prayed for the man's well being.

"Allard, do you feel any more pain? Are you still nauseous?" Lisa spoke into the intercom.

"No, I'm much better now. I guess it was the food. Maybe I shouldn't have eaten quite so much solid food my first time out." Allard smiled sheepishly.

"Solid food?" Lisa glared at Marjorie who looked away as she retrieved the cup from Allard. "What solid food did you have?" If Lisa's words were heat, she would've burned a hole in the back of Marjorie's head.

"It was quite good actually. Thank you." Allard retrieved the small sponges from Jury and started to wipe down the sides of the tube as best he could. “Your friend was holding conference for me. I must thank you for that.” Allard looked to Michelle.

Michelle could feel her entire face get hot. The heat traveled down her neck and flushed across her entire body. Small beads of sweat began to form at her hairline. She nodded unsure if she should speak. Uncomfortable with his glare, she turned to Lisa and mouthed, “Can he hear me?”

“I can only *hear* you if you speak louder, although, I am pretty adept at reading lips. You held conference for me. Prayed to The Creator for my well being. Thank you. You did a very good job. Obviously, He heard you and answered your prayer. Mine haven’t been answered just yet so I appreciate your assistance.” Allard passed Jury the sponges one by one as she collected them into a bucket without touching them.

The stench was so strong Jury covered her nose with her forearm and hurried from the room to dispose of them. Lisa’s eyes followed Jury from the room. She wanted to follow behind Jury and confront her about the food debacle, but didn’t want to leave Michelle alone.

“Why do you think your prayers aren’t being answered? You know God answers all of us. You just may not be getting the answer you want.” Michelle spoke slowly moving closer to Lisa not just for the intercom, but also for comfort.

"No I'm pretty sure *God* isn't answering me." Allard said assuredly. Michelle didn't like the tone he gave when he said "God". She decided from this point on she'd use the term "He" or "Him" in reference to God.

"Why are you so sure that you're the only one He isn't listening to?" Michelle wrapped her arm around Lisa'-s and held.

" Dr. Lucas, you haven't formerly introduced me to this beautiful young woman..." Allard stared into Lisa's eyes, effectively changing the subject.

"Allard, this is Michelle Bonds. She's an old friend of ours." Lisa said with a smirk as Michelle tugged her arm.

"Just Michelle Bonds? No, M.D. attached to this name? No prefix or suffix?" Allard brushed his shorts straight hiding his slightly protruding manhood. Those thin nylon shorts were not the best outfit for one to present themselves in formal introductions.

"Well, actually..." Lisa started then felt a tug on her arm. "No. She's just Michelle Bonds."

Michelle nodded.

"Nice to meet you Allard." Michelle spoke. Her voice trailed a slight bit.

"If you two beautiful young women can excuse me, I need to relieve myself and doing so by aiming into the catheter tube isn't the prettiest thing to witness." Allard bowed.

"Of course. I'll be back in a few minutes to check your vitals." Lisa said pulling Michelle towards the door. Allard watched the two of them exit admiring their curves as they did so. Something bothered him about the new woman. He wasn't sure if the questions she asked were disturbing, but he was sure that the way she prayed was an issue. She seemed very familiar, very practiced with her conferences to The Creator. He would need to talk to her more. She could be of assistance in his effort.

CHAPTER FIVE

INFLAMED FLORA

The Sun's light was unbearably bright. The heat was stifling even though it was a "dry heat". Allard's feet were burned, blistered and swollen. The sand beneath them and in between his toes was course, hard and hot. He continued to stumble ahead. His prints were the only visible prints in an entire desert of wind blown sand. The sweat on his body was slick and collected grains of sand against it when the hot winds blew at him, as it often did. The thin nylon shorts protected him, but barely allowed air to cool his nether regions. He dared not remove them for fear of what the sun and sand would blister next. Allard crossed mountain after mountain and dune after dune.

His throat and mouth were as dry as the sand he walked in. His lips were chapped and crusted with a white film in the corners. The long locks on his head blew wildly collecting grains of sand. When his legs couldn't carry him any longer, he fell to his knees and crawled. The shadow he cast resembled a lithe lion prowling the land. As he reached another peak, he looked to the valley and saw a small blue pool of water about two feet in diameter, in it floated a single flower. Allard wiped his eyes, closed them and hoped this was not a mirage. He crawled blindly downward a few steps then peaked from one eye. The water and the flower were still there. He scrambled to the pool on his hands and knees. He bowed before the blessing. Before he dared breaking the stillness of the water, he closed his eyes, raised his hands, bowed his head and said "And now?"

"You will continue as you have." A voice echoed.

Allard opened his eyes. The pure blue of the water wavered slightly. The single white lotus flower sat as if a still life. Allard cracked a dry lipped smile.

"Interesting choice of imagery." Allard said.

"I've always liked the lotus." The voice echoed causing the water to vibrate, the flower now bobbed and moved with each ripple.

"Since it's just me and the lotus should I assume we are both here because you like us?" Allard responded still bowing, still on his knees, still thirsty.

"You over look the water. You've never been one to miss details." The voice continued.

"Then you know I didn't over look it. I assumed it was here for a reason, but was waiting for your word." Allard sat back on his legs relaxing.

"Drink and you may continue. Do not and you will burn." The voice spoke rippling the water again.

"If I drink I will burn, if I don't I will burn. It seems I'm damned if I do..."

"Damned if you don't" The voice finished.

He waited and watched the lotus flower bob and bounce in the small pool of water. His head rose watching the wind blow across the sands. The sun was bright and golden like a shining gold coin in the sky. There were no clouds on this day, just a blue sky that extended into infinity. Allard bowed to the sand, kissed its grains. With one partially injured finger, he poked the lotus so it floated to the opposite end of the water. His hands dipped together in the ice-cold water cupping a double handful. He brought the water to his mouth; the chill soothed his lips and his tongue. As it passed into his throat it burned. The burn was overwhelming. Allard let out an echoed roar that did not move the water or the lotus.

Allard stood to his feet newly affected and turned his back to the water and the flower. He raised an eyebrow and with it a question. He glanced over his shoulder and watched the lotus combust into flames, but not burn.

"How's that?" The voice responded.

On her third day at The Country Cage, Michelle felt comfortable enough to get down to business. Besides, there was a conference call coming in two days and she would have to report something, even if it was as minimal as her opinions on the tattoos with or without deciphering every symbol. That afternoon she assisted Lisa's conduction of Allard's vitals check. Allard placed two fingers on his throat and counted aloud as his pulse throbbed against his fingers. Lisa checked her watch and noted an increased heart rate. Then Lisa passed a syringe with a vial through the vent opening and talked him through collecting his own blood sample. Lisa noticed it took quite a bit of pressure for the needle to puncture his skin. She worried this was an after effect of the S-A 333 exposure. He handed her the vial with a smile. She noted everything on her clipboard. Michelle gave her a nod, "It's OK. I'll try to check things out now." The nod conveyed. Lisa waved to Allard who winked back at her as she left.

"You're staying to talk to me, today?" Allard quizzed.

"You act like I don't talk to you, Allard." Michelle felt immediately exposed.

"I'm sorry. I appreciate the company. It's just you've never stayed to talk alone."

She had to admit he was very observant. Michelle took a seat behind the console and pressed the two-way conversation button. Allard settled in, intrigued by the alone time.

"You did really well giving yourself that shot. Had that been me, I would've passed out, either from the blood, the pain or just the needle. I'm not a fan of needles." Michelle sipped her cup of piping hot Chamomile.

"The blood is nothing, I've been in way more pain and that needle is nothing compared to the things that have pierced my body." Allard reassured her as he sat back against the tube.

"Now that you mention it..." Michelle tried her best to sound matter-of-factly, but really sounded like a low rent Nancy Drew.

"Yes, I've noticed you staring at my wounds." Allard looked up at her. From her vantage point, his eyebrows created arched horns over deep eyes.

"I'm sorry I didn't mean to stare. I was just wondering what having those kinds of wounds inflicted on you has done to your spirits."

"Oh my spirits?" Allard let out a loud chuckle that vibrated the speakers. "You're worried about my spirits? Well, being inside this glass tube hasn't helped my *spirits*, but somehow, as you see, I continue on." He smiled letting the awkward moment linger until Michelle felt totally ashamed. "They are quite a sight aren't they? All of them are well earned."

"Earned?" Michelle sat up, her hand picked up a pen, poised to write down any pertinent info.

"Yes." Allard stood holding up his thigh for inspection. "This was when I turned my eye away from someone that couldn't be trusted. He stabbed me right through the thigh. Also here." He showed another thigh wound. "This one..." He pointed to a rather garish jagged scar on his chest near his breastbone. "Was just a simple love tap."

"A love tap? That looks like they tried to stab you in the..."

"Heart! Yes! How else would you destroy someone's love than by taking away their heart?" Allard spoke plainly.

"What about that one?" Michelle's finger extended pointing to the healed scar just on his left side of his rib cage. Allard looked to it then back at her. He rubbed it with his left thumb and thought. "If you don't want to talk about it I understand..."

"No, it's just some things you forget and others you just kind of wish you could.

"In that case, let's talk about the ones on your back." Michelle's Nancy Drew pressed on ahead.

"You like battle wounds, Ms. Bonds?" Allard cris-scrossed his arms over his chest and wrapped his arms over his shoulders to rub the scars on his trapezium.

"Battle wounds? What kind of battle?" She asked.

"You wouldn't want to hear about that. Boring, tedious nonsense for people like you."

"What kind of person do you believe I am?" She allowed herself to be lured in by his bait.

"The kind of person that wants to jump to the good parts of the story. The intricacies of my battle scars don't intrigue so much as the totality. These are battle wounds from a very large war. I fought in a war and was unfortunately or fortunately, depending on what side you're on, was on the losing side."

"So, how'd that affect you?" Michelle wrote, "war - losing side".

"I did what any smart soldier does, I switched sides for awhile."

"So are you on the winning side now?" Michelle asked confused.

"That depends on who you ask."

"I'm asking you."

"I always feel like I'm on the winning side and honestly, whatever side I'm on IS the winning side." Allard smiled a bit of vanity showing through.

"But you just said you started out on the losing side." Michelle wrote "confused about which side he's on".

"Ahhh yes, but when you're losing in one way, you could be winning in a totally different way, now can't you." Allard spoke as if he was a professor.

"Ok, the riddles are confusing me now." Michelle's frustration bubbled to the surface.

"You take conference...uh...pray very well. I assume you go to church every week and may have studied beyond the normal Sunday school plan. Are you a pastor?" Allard seemed to be looking for something.

"No. Not technically..."

"But you've studied The Creator in a temple of some sort." He seemed to be reading her mind.

"I'm a theologian, Allard. I'm not the pastor of my own church, but I am well versed in Christian Theology." Michelle came clean hoping it would force him to stop speaking in riddles.

"Christian Theology, perfect! You know the story of Samson." He began with a minimal pause continuing when she nodded her head. "Well, see I once had long flowing locks like Samson and the people who put me in this tube must've cut them off to reduce my power, but obviously they don't know the end of the story. Samson regains his hair and his power and destroys all that opposed him," Allard had walked to the tube so his nose was almost touching glass as he spoke.

"Well...that's not really how that story ended. It was more like..."

"Right! The Christian Theologian...of course the end of that story really depends on where you heard it. I tend to believe the person that told me that story." Allard said.

"Who told you the story?" Michelle continued her notes.

"You want to know where this scar came from, Michelle?" He pointed to the one on his side.

"Yes." Michelle spoke quickly and excitedly hoping finally for an answer to at least one question.

"It's in a similar placement as Jesus' isn't it...where he was stabbed with the spear as he hung on the cross" Allard began.

"Well yes I did notice that, but I don't think you're..." Michelle tried to explain.

"It's a coincidence."

"I didn't think you were him."

"Good because I am a solider and when I was attacked, they made the mistake of not tethering me or nailing me. The side I'm on doesn't stop responding to attacks. So, when you go back and tell them how my wounds are doing, you tell them that they struck me and I wiped their slate clean." Allard's anger built. "I am a solider and I will continue to strike. I am a prisoner of war, but this battle hasn't finished yet."

"Who are you at war with?" Michelle could feel a shiver running up her spine.

"The losers." Allard smiled.

Lisa and Jury's feet pounded the surface beneath them. The sweat spots in their workout tops and small fabric shorts spread as they quietly thumped next to each other. The intensity of today's run wasn't noticeable in the muscles that flexed or the hard breaths that were exhaled, but in the silence. Both of them were deep in thought and this run was therapy. Although they didn't share their thoughts, they were both contemplating the same thing. Lisa's pace slowed slightly and Jury responded in kind.

"She's gonna be ok. He's in a tube, girl." Jury huffed.

"Yeah I know." Lisa replied and inhaled deeply.

"You think she'll get some info from him that'll get us out of here?" Jury grunted as she pushed her way up the elevated end of the track and kept pace with Lisa.

"Hopefully." Lisa wiped her brow with her towel then tucked it back in the side of her shorts.

"I'll talk to him after breakfast. Maybe something in her session will loosen him up and he'll be ready to talk about that night." Jury slowed down more and Lisa joined her.

"What if it's something you don't want to hear?" Lisa worried.

"I'm not a raving lunatic..."

"You're not..." Lisa's words had a spattering of judgment in them.

"No. He's a witness and can help all of this come to an end." Jury's heart pounded hard against her chest.

"What if he's more than just a witness?" Lisa's eyebrow cocked.

"I'm prepared for that now. With Dustin's warnings about him, I know there's more to it than he's been saying." Jury stopped jogging and started walking as she stared off to the side of the track by the entrance. Lisa's eyes followed her to Michelle who leaned against the doorway.

"How'd it go?" Lisa's smile slowly dropped as they got closer and saw the look of worry in Michelle's face.

"Umm...he says he's a soldier. I don't know. He seems to think he was attacked by people and beat them. I think he might be some kind of zealot." Michelle looked scared.

"Were the wounds self inflicted? Like some kind of sacrifice or self therapy?" Jury wiped the sweat from her strong thick legs.

"No I really think he was the guy that the strike team was after and they may have inflicted some of them."

"He has puncture wounds, some of them are really old. The strike team has guns, he would've been blasted to bits if they attacked him." Lisa's eyes darted between Michelle and Jury. She didn't want to shake Jury too hard today. For some reason today didn't seem like the right day, she felt it during the run.

"No. I'm pretty sure. He thinks he was the guy they were after and he says he wiped their slate clean." Michelle rubbed her eyes trying to clear the mental images of what he'd said.

"I'm going down there. If he's remembering stuff, then it's time we stop the bullshit." Jury pushed open the door and stomped out with the other two right behind her.

Lisa and Michelle had to trot to catch up to Jury as she bounded through the weight room and across the adjoining pool area.

"I need to talk to him alone. You guys can't come." Jury said.

"Just hold on one damn minute. I know you're trying to get some closure here, but don't forget you're also a part of an investigation. If you go and fuck up his memory or put things in his head that aren't supposed to be there then we'll be spending even more time here while you work to deprogram his ass." Lisa's voice echoed forcing Jury to turn around.

"Don't worry I got this. You know me." Jury said hitting her left palm with her right fist.

"Yes I do, that's why I'm telling you to calm down."

Jury stormed into the laboratory looking all business, well except for the fact that she was wearing her little sweaty fabric workout shorts and what amounted to a sports bra. She clicked the two-way conversation button, flopped into the chair behind the console and cleared her throat loudly. Allard stood with his back to her. She cleared her throat again louder, expectantly. He didn't budge.

"You don't want to talk to me? You sat here and made all kinds of comments and threats to Michelle. You talked all tough and angry to the preacher lady why don't you go ahead and tell me what's on your mind, Allard? What's making you so angry?" Marjorie tried to hide her brewing anger.

"Well..." Allard began just peering over his shoulder. "Right now I'm not too happy about the level of privacy I have."

"Yeah I noticed you like privacy and keeping secrets." Marjorie shot back sounding more like her Jury persona.

"Secrets? Privacy?" Allard raised his eyebrow. "Well, if I must expose all..." Allard turned to reveal the catheter tube aimed precariously near his exposed penis as he relieved himself into it carefully and with deadeye aim precision. "I guess you've seen it all before so there's no need to be bashful."

Jury felt the natural urge to turn her head, but instead stared directly at him. His light yellow urine shot into the catheter, swirled downward spiraling in the hose and disappeared beneath the tube's platform to a slight gurgling sound. The urine tapered to small drops. Out of habit, Allard shook the tube in concert with his penis to get out those last few drops then held the tube high to allow them to slide down into the plumbing hidden beneath the tube. He slowly returned his manhood into his shorts. Their stare didn't break. Jury hadn't been staring in his eyes the whole time, her vantage point allowed her to get a free look as well as peer at him without breaking the stand-off.

"Now let's hope you're as good with revealing your thoughts as you are with showing off your stuff." Jury said.

"Am I good with revealing my "stuff", as you called it?" Allard flirted.

"What do you remember about the day you were put into this tube? The day you were saved..."

"Which one do you want to know about, me being put into this tube or the day I was saved? I've been saved on more than one occasion so you may have to be specific with that one." Responded Allard.

"What was the last thing you remember happening before you were put into this tube?" Instinctively, Jury pressed the record button on the console. The computer's tiny audio widget blinked red on the computer monitor.

"Pain. I remember pain."

"What kind of pain?"

"All different sorts. Mostly I remember the pain of large darts entering my body and then my body not feeling like my own. Then there was a pain. As if my own blood hurt as it coursed through my veins. The men that shot me with those darts were far away. Far enough away that I didn't see them." Allard said.

"So they shot you from a far distance with the darts. The darts that sedated you." Jury followed. "Why do you think they'd do that?"

"Because they were scared. I understand that, fear can force people to act out of cowardice. Although, it's more liable to cripple people." Allard pontificated.

"Why would they be afraid of you?"

"They had just seen several of their comrades at arms killed. I'd guess they didn't want to suffer any more casualties." said Allard.

"And how could you help them? What did you see? Why did they want you? Have you thought about any of that?" Jury felt goose bumps growing on her arms. Either her adrenaline had slowed or the lab was chilly and her absence of clothing wasn't helping her. Most likely it was a combination of the two.

"I thought about all of that. I know the answers to those questions. Would you like those answers? If I give you those answers whom would it help more? You to leave this place, me to get out of the tube or your bosses to know what happened that day?" asked Allard.

"I would think you would help yourself in relieving any guilt in your mind. Maybe you could sleep better at night knowing you helped others..." Jury's finger drummed against the console.

"I have no guilt. I didn't do anything wrong. I only did what was right."

"And what was that?" Jury stood, walked to the other side of the console and leaned against it shortening the distance between them in hopes it would help Allard to open up.

"I killed those men. Each and every one of them." Allard's words lingered there like a stale odor.

"You killed what men, Allard" Jury took a deep breath.

"The men that attacked me, the tens of men who approached me with guns and grenades and all the other means of war. I'm a soldier Dr. Houston, when it's time to go to war there is no one better suited to it than I am." Allard said.

"I think your ego is getting the better of you. You expect me to believe that you took out an entire armed outfit by yourself? You're covering for someone. I get the whole idea of not snitching on your friends, but really, Allard, to take responsibility for the deaths of fifty people..." Jury huffed crossing her arms.

"Oh no, I've killed more than that. But on the night you're asking about, it was twenty-three souls." Allard placed his hands against the tube glass. Jury didn't notice it, but his once injured right hand was back to normal.

"I lost a friend in that assault...in that massacre. I suggest you re-think your answer. Were you the only person involved?" Jury stared hard at him.

Allard held his hands against the tube staring back to her. They slowly slid downward making a squealing sound as they rubbed down the glass.

"I'm sorry you lost a friend, but I am not sorry I killed him or the others. They were crusaders for the opposition. Every war has its unfortunate casualties. Alas, had he not been in that position, I may not be here to meet you."

"Sonuvabitch!" Jury heard herself say before she could stop herself. She stood watching him. Her breathing increased so much that her chest heaved up and down heavily against her body.

In the adjacent lab, Lisa and Michelle stood by the door eavesdropping. Their backs were pressed hard against it as they listened to the conversation through the intercom.

"Should we go in and break this up?" Michelle's voice cracked as she whispered.

"No." Lisa shook her head. "This is a breakthrough for her. She's getting all the information. If we go in now we'll contaminate the setting."

Michelle could feel her stomach bubbling. Her palms had become sweaty. This just wasn't what she had signed up for. Lisa's thoughts drifted to something she had talked to Dustin about before she came to The Cage and she started to quickly remember the details.

Back in the laboratory that held the tube, Allard and Jury were at a stalemate. They stared at each other through the glass, both waiting for the other to say something. Jury walked from her position and returned to her seat behind the console. She stared down at the computer monitor and the red record light blinking. She knew there was lots more to be said, lots more that needed to be hashed out for the record. However, there were a few things she needed to get off her heavy, heaving, and ample chest. She pressed the spacebar on the keyboard and the red light disappeared.

"What kind of monster are you?" Jury said in a faint whisper.

"The only kind of monster that matters..." Allard started.

"The kind that lets his partners hide behind him while he takes the blame. The kind that took fifty brothers, sons, fathers, husbands and boyfriends away from their loved ones. You're a coward, Allard. A motherfucking coward. You're scared shitless that if you tell on the others that helped you kill those boys they're going to do to you what they did to my man and those other men. You're not a monster, you're a fucking bitch." Jury shouted, stood up from the console and marched out. As she stormed through the door, Lisa grabbed her forearm. Startled, Jury swung a hard punch that Lisa ducked with a fighter's instinct.

"Marjorie you can't..." Lisa began.

"Don't tell me what the hell I can't do." Jury pulled away with tears in her eyes and marched off through the labs.

Allard sat with his legs folded, his hands raised, his eyes closed, his lips were moving quickly but no sounds were coming out. Michelle entered first, looked to Allard and turned back to Lisa intimidated. Lisa walked in swiftly and pressed the intercom button.

"Allard, I need you to check your pulse for me." Lisa commanded. He did not move, he did not stop mumbling to himself. "Allard, I need a vitals check."

BEEP! BEEP! BEEP! BEEP!

Lisa looked back toward the other labs. One of her alarms was sounding loudly through the open lab door. She hopped up and walked swiftly into the lab. Her blood work machine had a row of LEDs across the top of it. All of them were illuminated green. This high-tech piece of million-dollar equipment was responsible for the blood tests she conducted. It had finished its last process on the vial she had submitted that morning. Lisa pulled the three multi-colored pages from the printer and looked them over quickly.

Once again Michelle was left alone with Allard, this time she was way more uncomfortable. She glanced back to the labs wishing Lisa would hurry and return.

"Do you know the war hasn't ended?" Allard's voice echoed through the speaker startling Michelle.

"Which war?" Michelle said after a brief moment's shock.

“The most important one. The war between good and evil.” Allard said as he stood.

“Well yes I did know that, but there’s only one side to be on.” Michelle said.

“And by that you mean...”

“The good side of course.” Michelle finished and took a slight step backward.

In the lab, Dr, Lisa Lucas was reading over the blood test results. Allard’s body was low on amino acids as well as other nutrients as expected since the paste he had been eating was only a partial supplement for normal nutrients. She’d also noticed that the SA-333 had finally passed through his system totally. He was finally back to normal. Perhaps, Lisa thought, without the SA in his body, he had become more regular and more aggressive.

“Do you think you’re on the good side?” Michelle asked Allard.

“I’m on the right side.”

“Right, according to you the other side is full of losers.” Michelle said.

“And losers are relative. Kind of like these engravings on my arm.” Allard pointed to his tattoos.

“What do you mean?” Michelle could feel a slight bit of perspiration developing above her upper lip.

"Martyred saints, holy men, righteous warriors all symbols of the war between good and evil." Allard pointed to different symbols

"And you wear them on your arm. Are you saying they're losers?" Michelle asked.

"No. They're notches on his belt." Lisa finished as she stepped next to her friend. Lisa could hear Michelle exhale heavily.

"I wouldn't call them notches." Allard was amused by Lisa's grand re-entrance.

"So why have the symbols of saints and holy men that have been killed on your body?" Michelle felt emboldened.

Allard stepped back and leaned his shoulders against the tube so his back arched slightly. He ran his hand over the top of his head feeling the bristle of stubble, which now also littered his face.

"I approached Saint Patrick's Cathedral alone around eleven o'clock in the morning looking for an old acquaintance." Allard closed his eyes as he spoke. "It was odd because normally at that hour the building is buzzing with people talking, tourists, prayers, others waiting for a noon time prayer. However, on this day it was eerily quiet and even odder, it was empty. I walked to the back of the house, opened a few doors I wasn't supposed to and I admit I took a cookie or two from a plate that sat right outside the rectory. The silence was deafening. Here I was in one of the busiest Catholic buildings in one of the busiest cities in the world and not a sound, not a word, nor a person. It just wasn't right. So I headed quickly for the exit when I saw him. There he was, my friend, lying without air, without life between two of the pews. Someone had stabbed him right in the chest. I know because he clutched his heart, the dried blood caked around his wrists as his hands held the red flow of his essence. His eyes were fearful. His mouth was open. This wasn't a surprise. He was hunted down like an animal. He died in terror. Unfortunately, in the world we live in, it's harder to discover a body than to leave one. When you discover a body, all sorts of people want to sit you down and talk about how, when, why and sometimes they even accuse you of committing the crime.

So, I closed his shocked eyes and I ran for the front door. It was the oddest thing. I knew as soon as the door cracked and let in the light that I was in for a trial. I hadn't made it to the top step before the red lights shined against my body and the men in the black fatigues approached from every corner. The first two were bold enough to tell me to "freeze" as they ran behind me and attempted to shackle my arms. I broke both of their necks. Then I heard shots. Before I knew it, I was jumping into a bush and fracturing skulls. I was using their bodies as cover and advancing on the others.

By the time I realized there were more descending from the rooftop, I had already unsheathed my spear and had begun eviscerating most of those that shot at me from across the street. I spiked those that charged me. If you saw the shock in their eyes when they realized exactly how high I could jump, how fast I could move, you would've felt pity as I did. Unfortunately, they challenged me at a church. Churches are supposed to be neutral ground. A safe haven for everyone and since they chose to break the treaty, our war is now no holds barred. So I sacrificed all twenty-three of those men to make a statement. I am Allard, the holder of the spear and I am a soldier."

Clack Clack

Lisa and Michelle didn't remember hearing that sound, but the next one shook them.

BOOM!

The glass in the tube fractured with a spider web of cracks spreading across the surface as it held its shape. Allard opened his eyes, peaking at the tube and grinned. Lisa and Michelle hit the ground covering their heads with their hands.

Clack Clack

A spent shotgun shell clattered against the floor next to Michelle. She could only see a pair of running sneakers advance one step passed her.

BOOM!

The fiery slug collided with the tube causing more cracks, but was unable to break more than the surface. Allard moved inside the tube to the opposite side of the tube just as the bullet hit it. He stared back into the face of Jury as she took one more step closer. She cocked the shotgun again.

Clack Clack

"Marjorie what the fuck are you doing!!? " Lisa screamed from the floor as she stared up at her friend who aimed with one eye closed.

Jury's finger massaged the trigger then pulled back igniting the various mechanisms inside the gun. The slug erupted from the shortened barrel and emitted sparks as it rocketed toward the tube. In the tube, Allard watched the bullet approach, then moved his torso slightly to the left as the bullet collided with the tube. The tube cracked more, the spider web of splinters spread to the back of its shell. Allard glanced at the point of impact and let out a sigh of relief.

"JURY STOP! NO!!" Michelle screamed.

Jury's bloodshot eyes welled with tears. She wiped them with her sweaty forearm then cocked the gun again.

Clack Clack

The shell smoked as it bounced against the tile.

"Marjorie Jean Houston, put down the gun!" Lisa shouted crouching on the floor.

BOOM!

The tube cracked again. Allard touched the glass. He could feel the heat from the impact. The tube's structure was being tested. It now had a small amount of give and crackled under the pressure exerted from his fingers. He looked at Jury and cracked a smile.

"You wanna fucking smile??" Jury shouted as she took another step toward him clearing the console.

Lisa rose with Michelle standing just after her, they slowly approached behind Marjorie looking at each other for clues as to what to do.

"Marjorie, put the gun down sweetie. You can't let his talk mess with your head. Boyce wouldn't want you to do this." Michelle pleaded.

"Boyce taught me how to shoot. This is exactly what he'd want me to do and when I'm done, I'll plead insanity." Jury glanced over her shoulder at Michelle. Lisa grabbed her arm from the other side as the gun went off.

BOOM!

The glass shattered. Half of the tube clinked against the floor in a rainfall of glistening sparkles. Before anyone could take a breath, Allard was in the air. He leapt clear across the room, grabbed the barrel of the gun and forced it from Jury's hand with one yank. His arm wrapped around her waist, pulled her close to him and kissed her lightly on her full lips. He pushed Jury to the floor, grabbed Lisa's wrists with one hand and pulled her to him. His lips reached the side of her cheek, just to the side of her mouth before her knee rose quickly and hit him hard in the stomach. Lisa spun quickly delivering a roundhouse kick that Allard blocked with his palm but the sheer force of her strong legs pushed him back a foot or two. Allard stumbled backward in shock, bumped into Michelle and knocked her to the floor.

"Maybe we'll have our goodbye later then." Allard said to Michelle as Lisa lunged forward to protect her friend. Instinctively, he hit Lisa with a forearm that leveled her with a thud. Before any of them could recoil, they heard Allard's feet patter against the floor as he ran through the labs and down the hall.

Lisa scrambled on her hands and knees to the adjacent wall, made it to her feet, broke the glass and pressed the button inside. A loud screeching sound wailed as red alarm lights flashed throughout the complex. Jury picked up the dropped shotgun and cocked it as she made it back to her feet.

"I need to know what the hell you think you're doing!" Lisa shouted at Jury.

"Lock the doors." Michelle pointed as Lisa ran over and secured the lab doors shut.

The three of them backed away from the door with Jury aiming the shotgun at their only exit.

"Great! Now we're fucking locked in!" Jury shouted.

Dustin's stomach had been bothering him all night. Too much cheap Mexican food had been a bad addition to his diet and now he was paying the price. He sat on the cold toilet bowl finishing his business when his cell phone chimed loudly. Mustering a slight bit of contortionist expertise, he fished it from his slacked pants pocket and checked the message.

Red alert sounded at location CG-406J, please advise.

Dustin couldn't wipe his ass quickly enough. His belt buckle clattered back and forth as he ran into his adjoining office without washing his hands. His fingers tapped against the keyboard. He waited as it logged on then sat impatiently as one after another of his hidden camera widgets illuminated on the screen. He had felt a slight twinge of guilt when the widgets began to work again after Michelle's arrival to The Country Cage. She has unknowingly delivered the fixes for the satellite, which had fixed his cameras as well. He watched the widgets as they came into focus. Jury's bedroom was empty, Lisa's bedroom was empty and the final widget came on...

The Tube was broken and glass littered the floor. Jury held the emergency shotgun and aimed it off camera while Lisa and Michelle stood beside her. They seemed to be yelling at each other as their body language and hand gestures signaled quite a heated discussion. Dustin picked up his conference phone, dialed the access code and the extension for The Country Cage. He saw them react to the phone and then press the call button.

Immediately, Dustin could hear the loud screeching from the alarm as Lisa and Michelle looked into the conference camera. Jury still faced the door, her back to him.

"What the hell is going on?? Are you ladies ok? I just got a message about a red alert." Dustin shouted trying not to sound as aware as he was.

"How fast can the security team get in here? Our eagle has flown the coop!" Lisa shouted over the alarm.

"Did he just break out of the tube? There's glass everywhere." Dustin typed frantically into his phone responding to the red alert message.

Lisa looked behind her. There was no glass in the shot. In fact, the tube was the opposite way.

"How do you know there's glass in here?" Lisa asked looking upward.

"What happened in there?" Dustin yelled.

Lisa looked higher as Michelle watched her eyes dart back and forth. Both of them came to stare at the same small circular object which reflected a slight glare from the rooms light - a lens fitted into a high back wall.

"If that thing has a rewind button, you should press it." Lisa pointed into the hidden camera.

CHAPTER SIX

CRISPUS ATTUCKS

Mohana was a charming individual. He was tall with dark black hair, a bronze complexion and a thousand watt smile. At first sight, most people b would think he was of Middle Eastern descent, but would always settle on Indian because of the sharp British lilt with which he spoke. His good looks weren't to blame for the way he got what he wanted, but the fact that he was a charmer. His power wasn't simply "magic". He couldn't make a coin appear from behind your ear. His power was influence through spoken or unspoken suggestion. Mohana's charm was the reason he was asked to call the meeting. He also had a history with his friendly enemy and he took pride in the relationship he had with Allard.

For Mohana, being on a first name friendly basis with Allard was an odd thing. It was like being friendly with a celebrated enemy, the most distasteful yet inspiring nemesis. His peers would look at him in awe when he told stories of his association. Some of them had even asked Mohana if they could meet Allard; the answer would always be no. Not only did Mohana not want to risk his relationship with Allard, he also didn't want to risk his own life.

The charm he was sought to conjure was one of the broadest and most intricate he had ever done. As he stood on the eastern corner of Fifth Avenue and Fiftieth Street in Manhattan with his hands raised, he felt his power leave him in a great rush. The charm had taken quite a bit of energy from him, he didn't know then, how much. Suddenly, all of the people that walked the streets in and around St. Patrick's Cathedral decided they didn't want to be there. The faithful decided against going to a mid-day prayer. The tourists decided to take pictures in Times Square instead. Vendors moved their positions to Madison Avenue. Storeowners took their employees out for a long lunch. The streets, the windows and the stores were virtually empty. Only a few lingered. Later, when those few were asked, they would not recall what happened there just moments before.

Mohana entered the Cathedral, his steps made loud echoes in the hollow empty building. His dark eyes surveyed the artistry of the edifice and he shrugged his shoulders with a smirk on his face.

"That is incredible." The Man said as he approached him from behind.

"It is very credible. I know because I did it." Mohana bragged.

"Are you sure he'll come?"

"Yes. He wouldn't give up a chance to get more intelligence." Mohana stood with his back to the man, amazed at the colors the sun created as it shone through the stained glass. "You should leave before he gets here. He prefers to take meetings alone."

"I need to know something first..." The Man started as he pivoted on his heels looking around. "How did you make it so the rest of us could come here, but the regular people on the streets stayed away?"

"That..."Mohana turned with a smile "is why I'm so special." Mohana boasted.

"How long does it last?" The Man asked even though Mohana had already answered this question before.

"I told you, maybe an hour."

There was a slight squeak behind them. It was a soft rubber sole on the wood floor. The man's face dropped. Mohana turned to see several men clad in all black with black masks approaching him with their weapons raised...no... pointing at him!

"What are they doing in here? I told you to keep your men in their positions. If he even smells..." Mohana shouted.

The Man raised his hands and shrugged his shoulders as if to say "I can't control these guys sometimes".

Mohana turned and walked furiously towards the soldiers. He pointed his soft index finger at them and whispered with anger, but they kept approaching, some of them disengaged the safeties on their weapons. It was then that he knew. He turned, trying to put more space between himself and the soldiers. He raced towards The Man who stood with his hands behind his back.

"This is a diplomatic conference in a neutral place!" He yelled to The Man, but he knew it would not help. Quickly, he went to raise one hand, his energy was diminished but it roared quickly in his heart. Then it stopped with a cold striking pain. His eyes stared into the cold blue eyes of The Man and saw fear, he saw sorrow, but most of all, he saw conviction. Then Mohana looked down and saw just the very end of the blade that stuck in his chest. The Man's hand shook nervously on the pearl handle as Mohana grabbed it. They struggled for it. Mohana tried hard to keep the blade inside him, but he was weak, way too weak.

The Man pulled the blade from his chest and Mohana could feel his power leaving him. It left him in long hot spurts across his hand and across his wrists. His vision clouded as he watched the men with guns approach him faster then stop abruptly at The Man's behest. If he could only get back outside, he could recall the charm. One step after another he stepped between two pews. Slowly one step after another, he could make it outside. He could get his hand outside and recall the charm; all would go back to normal. Allard, his celebrated enemy, would know something was wrong and not approach. The men disappeared behind a wooden pew. No, he was on the floor now. Mohana clutched his chest trying to hold his power inside. He fought for air in his lungs. His simple black loafers kicked against the wood floor as he tried to push himself along.

The Man slowly walked toward him with a grimace on his face, hope in his eyes and that pearl handled knife in his hand. Mohana sucked his last breath in from his mouth and exhaled words. He was unable to use his charm in this place, but he could plant a seed of a curse. A lingering name implanted in the wood. If his celebrated frenemy touched the wood with his bare flesh, he would hear the last words of Mohana The Charmer... "Dustin Carver."

The five-member security team entered The Country Cage via the food pantry's rear entry system. Their faces were covered by white thermal insulate masks and goggles. They moved slower with the extra layers and pierce proof protection, but they were instructed that any and all precautions should be taken. They moved with precision through the small room and paused at the doorway as the Team Leader removed a small red card from his breast pocket. Cracking the card in half, he removed a small slip of paper from within it. The card was only to be used in extreme emergency. The paper had the security access code for the doorway leading into the facility. He dialed the code carefully on the keypad. A loud whining beep accepted the code and then there was a rush of air as the door unlocked.

Two members rushed through the door with weapons at the ready and "cleared" the kitchen area. They slowly cleared room after room and hallway after hallway on their way to the laboratories. They weren't as cautious as they could have been. Their only "threat" was a man running around the facility wearing only a pair of shorts. The only weapons he would find would be the utensils in the kitchen, as they also knew the emergency shotgun was in the hands of one of the doctors.

They walked carefully down the hallway on their way to the final lab. The hum of the fluorescent lighting buzzed like millions of angry mosquitoes. Their weapons aimed, swinging and swaying covering each dark corner as they headed into the outer testing lab in a one, two, one, one formation. The tension grew, as they got closer to the final lab. It had come over all of them at the same time. Why had they been ordered to extreme caution for one man? The crevices seemed darker; the hiding spaces seemed more numerous as they approached the final door. From the side of his eye, Team Leader caught a glimmer through the grates of an air vent. He raised his fist and the team froze with precision. His index finger pointed to the vent and all five aimed their weapons to it. They too saw a glimmer in the vent; two round orbs glowed staring back at them from within the darkness.

"Come out slowly...with your hands visible." Team Leader spoke clearly and slowly.

There was no movement.

"Move slowly towards the exit and come out...RIGHT NOW!" Team Leader commanded.

Suddenly the door to the laboratory opened. The security force spun on their heels having been flanked and totally caught by surprise. Their weapons auto cocked, red beams shot from their scopes once the triggers felt pressure from their nervous fingers. All of them illuminated on their targets...

Lisa, Jury and Michelle all held their hands high.

"Hold!" Team Leader shouted as they all lowered their weapons. "What are you doing coming out?"

"You just told us to come out!" Lisa shouted pissed and scared.

"Sorry doctor, we weren't talking to you, but..."

"Sir!" Another team member shouted as the team aimed focus and weapons back to the vent. "I think he moved."

"Step out of the vent!" Team Leader shouted.

Lisa glanced over to the vent with her hands still raised high.

"That's not him."

"M'am?" Team Leader leaned his head towards her while still staring into the vent.

"Unless he has cat's eyes, that's not him...It's the meter inside the vent. It checks the quality of the air being pumped into the labs." Lisa said as she dropped her hands, which caused the two security members closest to her to recoil.

"Two for flinching." Jury smiled.

Team Leader nodded to another, who quietly flipped a switch on the side of his weapon. A light shot on blazing a clear view of the cavernous vent and the two small nodes connected to a tube inside it. A short sigh of relief came over the team as they regained their ease.

"Lift your cover." Team Leader ordered. The five men removed their masks and goggles revealing sweaty faces and ogling eyes.

Jury looked down at herself. With all of the excitement, she had forgotten that she and Lisa were only wearing their flimsy workout attire.

"I assume you guys haven't seen him." Michelle interrupted with a stern voice that knocked them all quickly back to attention.

Lisa, Jury and Michelle sat in the lab that once held Allard and waited for Dustin and The Board to call. One security member stood guard inside the doors, one stood outside them. The other three including Team Leader had set off into The Country Cage looking for Allard.

"Did you like the sunflower seeds?" One of the men asked Jury.

"Yes, I like sunflower seeds." She responded confused.

"No...I mean the s-s-sunflower seeds that were in the p-pantry." He stammered over his words slightly as a smirk spread on his partner's face.

"Yes..." Jury said tentatively shooting a glance at Michelle who was equally confused. Lisa just smiled.

"Oh good. I heard they couldn't get you...ladies any sunflower seeds so when we packed your supplies I made sure to include a bag from our rations. I remember when we brought you here, you and I were talking about them so I figured it was for you, Dr, Houston." He seemed relieved to get it all off his chest.

"What's your name?" Jury asked with a smile.

"Welk...Agent Welk." He nodded.

"Ok, thank you Agent Welk for the sunflower seeds, darling, but if you haven't noticed there's a nutcase running around this place and you two are supposed to be watching the door. I personally saw this guy jump about fifteen feet from that tube to right about where you are now. So maybe we should talk about the sunflower seeds later when it's not possible that he'd bust through those doors, pull those guns from your hands and beat you about the head...ok, sweetie?" Jury sounded as sweet as a lemon-laced cup of honey tea.

"Certainly m'am." Agent Welk turned embarrassed.

"Doctor." Jury corrected him.

"Doctor." Agent Welk stiffened.

"Agent Welk." Michelle began.

"Yes...Doctor?" He responded sheepishly.

"Just Michelle...For future reference, I like Chik-Fil-A." Michelle smiled bringing a grin to Welk's face.

Allard had pulled yet another window treatment from yet another fake window and had become exasperated. All of the doors he had encountered were bolted or welded shut. All of the curtains with bright sunshine glowing through them were curtains with lighting fixtures behind them. They were quite nice windows, but nothing but brick and mortar were behind the lights. Allard broke through two of them leaving shards of glass in his fists. He shook what glass he could from his hands leaving glittering blood stained sparkles on the carpet and the couch. When he finally decided to return to the lab and recruit a volunteer from one of the women to help him leave this place, he heard the clatter of boots.

From his experience he knew there were about five different individuals in heavy boots headed toward the labs. They most certainly were carrying weapons. He'd heard the heavy metal collide with a wall as they moved through a room. If there was any sound Allard was familiar with, it was the sound of troops moving. He doubled back quickly and quietly up the carpeted steps to the bedroom area. He lay flat against the floor listening as they marched below. Yes there were five, he could hear them even in their stealth movements. There was a time when he would have challenged them straight away, but today was a new day. He would wait and strike when it was most beneficial to his strategy.

His search through the first bedroom rendered no clothes that could fit him. He rummaged through the chest of drawers. Nothing would fit and allow him full range of motion. There were only sexy underwear, comfortable sweat suits, tight women's jeans and small t-shirts. On the desk were pictures of a much happier Jury with her lost boyfriend. He touched the man's forehead on the picture and closed his eyes. His prayer rose from his heart and he knew this man's soul was protected. Allard was pleased that this wasn't another of the many that he'd condemned.

There was movement in the halls. Heavy boots moved swiftly toward him. Allard pulled the comforter from the bed and wrapped himself in it like a robe. He covered his head and held it tightly around his body from inside the comforter. He took slow steps toward the door and paused at the nightstand to rip the lamp from the outlet. He tore the lampshade from it then with a quick flip of his wrist, shattered the bulb against the wall leaving the jagged remains still in the lamp. Without hesitation Allard ran into the hallway. The sudden movement shocked the first security officer who leveled his weapon. Allard spun like a top sending the comforter flying in the air blocking the entire view of the hallway.

The security officer sent one warning shot high towards the comforter, blowing it backward. His view now clear, all he could see was the jagged edge of the broken bulb and the lamp flying towards him like a spear. It ripped through his shoulder with so much speed it sent him airborne four feet before he collapsed to the ground. His screams echoed through the empty halls. Team Leader hit the deck aiming his weapon at a now empty hallway. With a quick succession of hand signals the third member of the team quickly doubled back and down the steps.

He sprinted the long hallway on the first floor, his boots squeaked as they made contact with the wooden steps on the other end of the hall. He took the steps two at a time ready to flank their target when he felt a sudden powerful blow to his head and collapsed. Allard caught him as he fell limply and laid him softly to the ground as you would a newborn.

A hot blast inflamed Allard's lower back sending him to his knees. Momentarily ignoring the pain, he swiveled his body into a corner and yanked the weapon from the man that lay next to him.

"Put the weapon down and come around the corner with your hands raised." Team Leader shouted.

Allard felt the hot throbbing sensation in his back. He reached back to feel the damage, but there was no blood. On the floor sat a rather hard neoprene ball. He picked it up and rolled it through his hand. It was filled with hard rubber pellets. Allard surveyed the ammo in the weapon he held. It too was filled with hard beanbags. What good would this do? He tossed the gun out into the hallway in full view of Team Leader.

"Good. Now come out slowly. We don't want anyone getting hurt here." Team Leader shouted. He tried to sound as confident as possible, but you didn't need to be an experienced soldier like Allard to hear the uncertainty in his voice. The uncertainty built on the unfortunate order that the security team bring no live rounds with them. The best they had were rubber bullets. The most effective were the beanbags. The shot Team Leader scored should've rendered Allard crippled, but he was obviously still mobile.

Allard stepped into the hallway, his body covered in sweat. Team Leader stood and peered at his target. The man was leaner than he expected. The tattoos on his neck and down his arm gave him a freakish sideshow appearance. If Allard were to make a move, Team Leader would pop him right in his head. The shot wasn't according to orders and would definitely concuss him or worse, but Team Leader wasn't in the mood for games.

"Target is on the second floor by the C staircase." Team Leader spoke aloud, his voice transmitting through his ear set to the rest of the team in the labs.

"You aren't here to kill me. You have non lethal ammunition." Allard spoke.

"Hold your arms above your head!"

"Why aren't you using lethal methods to undo me?"

"GET YOUR HANDS ABOVE YOUR HEAD!"

The security member Allard injured with the lamp walked over slowly clutching the wound in his shoulder. His gun lay on the floor where he had been hit.

"My name is Allard. I am the unholy servant. Who do you serve?"

"Raise your hands, sir." The injured security shouted as Team Leader took tentative steps toward him.

"Why are you trying to capture me? Whose side are you on?" Allard slowly raised his hands.

"We have the target surrendering. Notify HQ." Team Leader spoke into his ear piece.

The facility intercom cracked and a female voice creaked through.

"Is he hurt? Did you shoot him? Should I come up?" It was Lisa. Her voice wavered nervously. "Dustin doesn't want him filled with holes, ya know!" She sounded more assure.

Team Leader saw Allard's reaction to the name "Dustin". It was a startled angry grimace. It all happened too quickly. Team Leader was sure he got off at least six rounds. Two of them hit Allard directly, but he kept coming. He blocked two rounds with his forearms; one was caught and thrown back almost as hard as it had been shot. Team Leader had ducked the throw, but it leveled his injured comrade. Allard reached him with incredible speed. He tried to duck Allard's blows, he even hit him once or twice, but the last thing he remembered was a flurry of hard elbows and fists then a hand jammed hard into his crotch another on his shoulder. He saw the wall, the ceiling...Was he airborne? The wall again....The ceiling then the floor and all went dark.

Allard stood over the men, his breathing barely affected. He was feeling more like himself again. The haze that had affected his judgment, his reflexes and skills had nearly disappeared entirely. With his palms stretched out in front of him, he opened and closed his hands. His strength was returning exponentially. All of his gifts were making an appearance suddenly. He would need them to escape this place. His arms criss-crossed his chest. His fingers rubbed his shoulders then lower to the scars on his trapeziums. If only he had his wings again.

CHAPTER SEVEN

COLD HARD TRUTH

The news of the murder of Mohana the Charmer and capture of Allard caused ripples through the unseen world. Saint Peter stood pensively unsettled at the gates of Heaven, behind him stood an entire brigade of warrior angels. They watched quietly and tried not to disrupt Saint Peter's normal movements, but they knew he was painfully aware of their presence. They were on alert as was he. Thoughts grew even more ominous when Michael, the archangel himself, crossed the line of his arcing brigade and spoke to him.

"My apologies for the disruption, but I'm sure you have heard." Michael whispered.

"I have." Saint Peter continued his watch of souls approaching the gate. His eyes never looked to Michael.

"It's just a precaution." Michael explained.

"I understand. I've never needed one nor do I expect to." Saint Peter breathed. Michael bowed and with a nod of his head his brigade of warriors took seven steps back, but not one let their eyes leave the horizon.

At the fiery rivers of hell, Maalik stood with his back to the flaming, pop and bubble of the roaring rapids as he always had. The nineteen guardians that stood at the coastline to Hell did not move or waver. It was business as usual. Maalik gave stern looks to the growing number of lost souls that lumbered toward the line. On occasion, a fallen angel would swoop dangerously close to the danger line a mere 30 feet from Maalik, but none dared cross it. That day, it happened ten times the normal amount. They were testing his reserve. They were nervous. Maalik bit the inside of his cheek angered, but with unnatural resolve.

"You'll stay put. All will stay the same." Maalik said to no one in particular.

Dustin sat in the cold lifeless conference room his thoughts were in a whirlwind of what-ifs, most of all, what if he was wrong. What if he was totally, the Earth is flat, Bigfoot lives in the woods, size doesn't matter – wrong? The Board of Directors filed in one by one nodded, shook hands and greeted him. Some of them seemed way more cheerful than he'd expect considering they had an entire project in jeopardy and under siege by a raving lunatic.

"What do we know?" The Chairman huffed taking a large gulp of his exotic coffee.

"There's a strike force deployed inside the facility. There has been some contact with Allard."

"The captive." Corrected a board member.

"Allard The Captive." Dustin continued hating to be disrupted as much as he hated to be corrected. "We're not exactly sure how many of the strike force is still operable, but we're positive – "The Captive" has attacked them. Drs. Houston and Lucas are holding up in the laboratory with the Theologist Ms. Bonds and a strike force guard. We may need to consider the option of lighting the beacon and prepare for an extraction as soon as possible." Dustin stared around the table awaiting the reaction.

"You may be right." The Chairman sipped his coffee.

"Of course, we're not sure what, if anything caused Allard..uh...the captive's escape. It may also be an issue that we've just wasted an extraordinary amount of resources to study him and now we're just going to..."

"Has your theologian made any headway or received any new information?" One female board member spoke.

"We haven't spoken since all of this occurred. I understand that you want to at least be able to talk to him but we may have enough DNA to replicate a viable clone." Dustin said exactly what the stockholders would want to hear.

The silence was deafening. He could tell all of them had made up their minds and this was probably the scariest of all. The part where he learned he may be in the midst of true enemies.

"Instruct them to light the beacon."

"Light the beacon."

"It's the only option at this point."

"I concur."

"Me too."

"Dustin?" The Chairman sat awaiting his vote.

"Well I'm concerned that the extraction won't go as planned and we'll end up losing not only the data and the specimen, but two of our best doctors." Dustin watched each of them with his best poker face.

"We'll leave that up to the powers that be." The Chairman croaked.

With that, Dustin was positively sure that there was something wrong with his plan and it was too late.

"Try calling again!" Lisa shouted at Agent Welk whose "never let them see you sweat" moment had clearly passed.

Agent Welk pressed the call button and calmly uttered a few incoherent, indecipherable phrases as Jury and Michelle stared at the door in near panic. It'd been nearly ten minutes since Welk's communicator erupted in so much noise and clatter he pulled the earpiece from his ear in pain and tossed it to the ground. Now there was silence. With Allard roaming the halls of The Country Cage, they could only hope he wasn't coming back to do to them what he seemingly had done to the rest of the armed strike force.

"Let's try Dustin again." Lisa dialed on the conference phone.

"For what!? We already know he can see in here. He's not doing shit. He's left us to die." Jury waved the shotgun wildly at the once hidden camera.

"We're going to leave a message." Lisa glared patiently as Dustin's phone rang through the speakerphone.

"You've reached Dustin Carver, Head of Research and Development sector five of Scilymax Corporation..." Lisa impatiently pressed the number one key interrupting the rest of his incoming message.

BEEP!

"Dustin it's Lisa Lucas, Marjorie Houston, Michelle Bonds and Agent..." Lisa snapped her fingers at Agent Welk.

"Duane We..."

"Agent Duane Welk. We are trapped in the facility with the hostile captive named Allard whom we have been studying under your supervision. Allard has attacked part of the security force and we are in fear for our lives. At exactly 4 pm Eastern Standard time we will be forced to light the beacon." Lisa took a deep breath as Marjorie and Agent Welk turned to her. "Our extraction point will be noted on Agent Welk's GPS system." She nodded to Welk who immediately checked his wrist Global Positioning System to make sure it was still working. "Hopefully, you get this message before we light the beacon because frankly this shit sounds fucked up and we're not even properly equipped for a proper extraction, so call US BACK!!" Lisa took a deep breath. "I'm going to forward this message to the entire board and the CIA office of terrorist development as well...just in case Allard escapes. But, I'll give you until four before I do that."

Click!

"Great. You're going to threaten him with exposure after you ask for help. Think that'll work?" Agent Welk chided sarcastically.

"Baby...can you please shut up and watch the door?" Jury shoved Agent Welk from Lisa's face before things got really ugly.

Allard sat legs bent sitting on his heels. His hands outstretched in front of his face as he tried as hard as he could to make conference. All he could hear was the slow steady thump of his heart and a slight whistle of breathing from one of the strike force members lying unconscious on the floor near him. He'd dismantled the team much faster than he had expected. His original thought was to keep one of them conscious so he could find out how to get out of The Country Cage. But then that last one had to shoot him with those beanbags and well his temper got the best of him again. Now Allard needed an answer. Which way was he to go?

The answer came minutes later, not with a voice, but with the sound of breathing. A measured pattern that grew closer then there was the sensation of cold hard metal on the back of his head.

"Ok bitch, these aren't rubber bullets or bullshit bean bags. I have hot live rounds in here and if you make one move faster than the speed of a constipated turtle shitting, your brains will ponder why the fuck they're laying on the floor!" Team Leader spoke slowly with a slightly raspier voice. He was still woozy from his toe to toe with Allard, but still very alert.

Moments later the rest of the security team were up and tending to their wounds and aches. Allard sat quietly with his eyes shut not making a single motion. He looked like an eerily serene statue sitting amongst the armed modern day gladiators. Finally team leader spoke to him again,

"Slowly raise your hands directly above your head as far as they can go."

He did.

"Now raise up to a kneeling position."

He did.

"Now slowly. SLOWLY. Stand. Keep those arms high above your head." Team Leader said as Allard felt the rest of the team step backward cautiously.

Allard could sense their weapons. He could smell their fear.

The walk back to the laboratory was painstakingly slow. Allard could feel the burn of holding his arms up for so long as they baby stepped through The Country Cage. When they reached the laboratory floor, Allard shuffled his feet against the cold tile floor.

"Pick your feet up slightly higher. I don't want any mistaken slipping." Team Leader spoke.

"Sorry. I didn't reali..." Allard began but was shooshed.

The cocking of Agent Welk's gun shocked Lisa, Jury and Michelle, Welk quickly opened the lab door and propped his foot against it holding it open. A slightly relieved smirk brightened his face as he watched out the door.

"Do you see them?" Lisa took a step back.

"All of them." Welk smiled as he aimed his weapon closer. The other door opened quickly causing Michelle to jump. Another strike team member held it open with his back as Allard entered in his submissive position.

The women were stone faced. Jury's gun slacked to her side as she watched Allard in his half naked glory, sweat trickled from his head and fell to his tattooed arm, he slowly walked towards them with his eyes squeezed tight.

"Slightly left..." Team Leader instructed and Allard followed making his way carefully pass them.

"What are we supposed to do with him?" Lisa's anger was building. "If you haven't noticed the holding tube is shattered to shit."

"It'll have to do."

"Watch the glass!" Michelle spoke just as Allard's feet stepped on the sharpened edges of broken tube glass. He stepped across them slowly with an imperceptible acknowledgment of the sharpness of it. She felt her heart sink at the sight of him humbled.

"So you could take out fifty guys in New York, but not five at The Cage, huh. Someone must be losing their swagger." Jury chided as Allard reached the tube and stood just outside of it.

"Fifty? He told me twenty-three." Michelle watched the security team as they prepared shackles to bind him.

"No there were fifty people killed that day. He hunted them down one by one all day until they were all gone." Jury responded and raised her shotgun to the back of Allard's head. Lisa stepped beside her, placed two fingers on the side of the barrel and eased it downward.

"We've had enough of Annie Oakley today." Lisa said.

"There were twenty-three souls. I did not lie." Allard spoke.

"Shut your fucking hole, prisoner!" One of the security team yelled. His itchy index finger rubbed the trigger of his gun.

They had prepared a triple locking system from three separate pairs of shackles. When all was done Allard was to be hog-tied with shackles on each limb bound by three cuffs

"There were fifty..." Jury started.

"People. Bodies." Michelle finished as she took a step closer to Allard and the team.

"Raise your left foot at the knee and hold your balance. Don't try anything slick." Team Leader commanded as the shackles clanged to the floor ready to be locked onto their prisoner.

"What's the difference between a body and a soul?" Michelle asked without thinking.

Allard raised his left foot slowly. He turned his head just slightly towards Michelle's voice. She could swear she saw a smirk. A member of the security team slid low and locked three cuffs to his left ankle.

"Did you hear me? What's the difference?" Michelle spoke louder.

"Can you please wait until we're done with this?" Team Leader said with an icy tone. "Left foot down, then slowly raise your right foot." He continued to Allard who followed him as instructed.

"You are a soul." Allard responded.

"What makes me different from a body?" Michelle was tying together her loose thoughts.

"Michelle." Lisa looked at Michelle with a motherly 'don't start this now!' expression.

"Drop your right foot slowly. Then slowly lower your left arm and place it as straight behind you as possible." Team Leader spoke louder as if to drown out the thoughts of Michelle's question.

"You have a soul." Allard spoke following the instructions. The metal cuffs were locked one by one onto his wrist.

"What makes you soulless?" Jury spoke causing a wave of heads to turn towards her.

"You too?" Lisa said.

"I have a soul?" Allard smiled a devilish smile.

"Lock the others in." Team Leader instructed the other security member who promptly grabbed the chains from the left wrist cuffs and organized them to lock onto the chains near the right ankle cuff shackles.

"Do we all have souls, Allard?" Michelle stepped passed Agent Welk toward Allard. Welk reached out to grab her shoulder, but she shrugged him off slowly. He didn't protest.

"What's taking so long?" Team Leader spoke to his subordinate.

"I'm going to braid these to make them harder to break." He said as he slowly intertwined the three chains in a iron cuff braid.

"How many souls are in this room, Allard?" Jury asked.

"Eight." Lisa answered quickly feeling uncomfortable with the tone of the question.

"No." Allard said.

"What?" said Lisa.

"Six!" Allard snarled.

With lightening speed, he ripped the shackled chains on his wrists from the team member's hands, spun on his heels whipping the cuffs to and fro slashing the weapons from the security teams' grips. It all happened too fast. Team Leader saw it in an altered speed. Everything was happening and he could not move fast enough to stop it. He finally steadied his hand and felt his finger let off one, two, three bullets.

The slugs flew toward Allard with screaming explosions as the other team members were hit with cuffs and chains that sent them falling to the floor. The chains whipped back into the air like wild cobras blocking the bullets one, two, three and sending them ricocheting passed Lisa, Michelle and Jury. They found themselves ducking well after the bullets squealed by them with intent. Everyone lay on the floor in a clatter of weapons and bodies. Team Leader ducked for cover behind the console for safety. The only two standing were Allard and Welk.

"You must be a rookie scout." Allard spoke.

"How do you know?" Agent Welk returned.

"Because you haven't run yet!" Allard shot back whipping the chains wildly as he charged forward.

Welk recoiled getting hit in his forearm by one of the chains. He aimed his weapon wildly blasting a hole in the tube behind Allard as they clashed. Welk whipped a blade from his side and swung it quickly toward Allard. Sparks shot from the chains as they connected. Allard swung his chains with precision, each cuff operating independently attacking Welk, who did his best to block them with the blade.

Team Leader fired a shot that was ducked by Allard just as it whizzed by his nose. Allard spun, using the chains to knock the gun from his hand. Welk saw a moment to attack; his blade sliced the thinnest of cuts on Allard's ear before he was kicked through the doors of the laboratory and into the other room. Allard charged spinning and swinging the chains of the shackles quickly. Loose cut links of the chains clattered and clang to the floor as Welk's blade collided with the shackles. Allard moved slowly with a shuffle being careful not to get his feet tangled in the shackles locking his feet together.

"You will not win. You can not win." Allard groaned as he moved closer.

"I don't have to. I'm not meant to." Welk shot back as he sliced at the air with his blade.

In the laboratory, everyone had regained his or her footing. The security team rushed the doors weapons aloft.

BAM! BAM!

Allard ducked and dodged shots. He was covered by gunfire on both sides.

"Watch out for Welk!" Team Leader shouted as Allard somehow spun his opponent's back to the security team.

"All I need is to sound the cry." Welk groaned as he pushed forward slicing at the air.

BAM!

Allard felt the hot thump of an explosion on his swinging arm. He dropped it slightly then recoiled as Welk's blade came dangerously close to his throat. Allard knew the pain; luckily it was just a beanbag. However, the distraction was enough for Welk to get a head start on an escape through the labs and up the stairs. Allard pursued as shots from the warning rounds and Team Leader's bullets exploded in the doors, walls and fixtures around him.

"Shit!" Lisa shouted as she crawled for the console.

"Don't do it!" Jury screamed.

"No choice!" Lisa started pressing buttons on the console feverishly. "What was the bypass again?" Lisa banged on her head trying to remember

"Can we at least get our shit together first, bitch?" Jury shouted.

"What is she doing?" Michelle screamed.

"She's lighting the beacon!" Jury said as she ran out of the lab.

"Go with her!" Lisa pointed Michelle out the door to Jury. Michelle hesitated but sprinted as fast as she could behind her.

Jury ran through the corridors then up the steps two at a time. As she crossed the living room the wall exploded above her head with gunfire from the adjoining room. She waved Michelle down as the two ducked and ran up the steps.

Jury bust open her closet and pulled from it what looked to be a red leather flight suit. She quickly collected a black one from Lisa's closet as the sound of banging emerged from the kitchen.

"They're headed for the pantry." She said as they ran to a closet in the hallway.

"The entrance...Welk's going to show him how to get out." Michelle realized as Jury pushed the sliding door open revealing a closet full of similar suits. Jury grabbed one about Michelle's size in camouflage green and tossed it to her.

"Put that on. I'll be back, I gotta give Lisa hers." Jury instructed.

SKREEEEEEEEEEE! An alarm sounded.

"SHIT! She started already." Jury wailed as she ran down the steps two at a time.

Michelle tried squeezing the suit over her clothes, but it was way too tight. She pushed and prodded at the zippers then realized she'd have to strip naked to get it on correctly.

The chains whipped through the air like hot tattered lightning connected with a team member's chest, knocking him out cold. Allard charged backward fighting off the security team while attacking Welk. Welk jumped up slicing the metal poles that held the elevated potholder sending cast iron pans and pots tumbling on top of Allard. Allard used them to block high-powered rubber bullets from hitting him directly.

"Give it up, Allard!" Team Leader shouted as he and the remaining team took cover behind a wall.

Welk burst open the pantry and high stepped it to the rear access. When he realized he didn't know the code to open it, he sliced at it exploding the electronic panel in sparks. He pulled the panel off, disconnected wires one by one and waited for a response.

Allard stepped into the pantry and the entire room rumbled.

"What the hell?" Lisa whispered as she pulled her suit on over her thick brown calves then shimmied her thighs and hips into the skintight experimental material.

"They said the shit would hit the fan when you lit the beacon." Jury said curtly as she zipped her suit up all the way to her neck.

"If someone told me it would be diarrhea maybe I would've rethought it" Lisa chimed back. "How the hell did you get this thing on so fast?"

"I wear shit like this all the time." Jury said as she helped Lisa squeeze her arms into the suit.

"You're a loon...watch it! Watch it!" Lisa yelped as Jury zipped her suit up quickly over her bare breasts. "If we make it out, I need THOSE!"

Unable to bend her limbs very much in the suit, Michelle slid down half the steps. When on, "The Life Suit" looked like a cross between a wet suit and a dominatrix outfit. The security team hid for a cover in the hallway outside the kitchen. When they saw her, their eyes bugged out as they stared at her plentiful curves. She crawled toward them slowly.

"I have a few pounds to lose. You don't have to stare." Michelle whispered.

"Why do you have the suit on?" For the first time Team Leader looked panicked.

"Jury told me to put it on because..."

A loud rumble began beneath them. It sounded like a freight train was approaching underground.

"Oh no...Ok, we gotta get out. Pyramid form let's get in and put this guy's lights out before all hell breaks loose." Team Leader whispered to his team.

"You're strong for a rookie scout." Allard grunted as Welk's blade pushed closer to his chest. Allard held it back with one arm as Welk pushed forward.

"Not...just...a...rookie...scout. I'm...the little..angel... that could." Welk panted spitting and huffing as he pushed with both hands using the closed rear access door for leverage. The weight from his foot pushed the door open just slightly. A high whistle of wind erupted through the miniscule crack. "I will sound the cry...you will be damned." Welk sputtered using every ounce of energy he could to push the knife toward Allard, his feet slowly pushed the crack in the door wider.

"That's if you can make a sound." Allard warned then threw the chains around Welk's neck.

"Grab the goggles." Lisa shouted as she and Jury pulled soft helmets from a supply closet near the laboratories. They bounded up the steps looking like wild dominatrix, scuba divers. As they reached the main level they couldn't believe what they saw.

Michelle was walking slowly into the kitchen with the security team crouched behind her using her as cover.

Welk's eyes bulged as the chains tightened around his throat. For the first time, he saw the legend in Allard's eyes. There was the death, the madness and the serenity all in his pupils. Welk's feet kicked hard. He fought for dear life. His blade clattered against the floor as he resisted the idea of holding onto it while he attempted to separate the chains from his throat.

"Go ahead, sound the cry..." Allard huffed as he pushed harder and harder tightening the sliced and splintered chain links around Welk's throat.

Welk sputtered, sucked air between his teeth and then a small nearly inaudible squeal left his mouth. When he realized he wasn't going to win, Welk did what any rookie scout would do...he let go and felt Allard bring the darkness over him. His body dropped to the ground with a thud. Allard took a deep relieved breath then turned his attention to the door. He rubbed the wood patterned metal with his bare hand, found the edge and held it. One foot found leverage on a corner, the other on Welk's body.

"Don't do it Allard." A soft voice pled.

Allard turned to see Michelle with her hands extended motioning him towards her. Had this been another time and another place, her skintight outfit and sweet voice would've conjured feelings below, but now he had a mission to complete.

"I must." Allard replied then looked away.

"If you open that door, you will die. That will be it. All of these conversations of souls and servants will be done. I want to know more about you. I need to understand you." She said.

The security team waited right outside the pantry door with Lisa and Jury right behind them wearing their soft helmets and goggles. Lisa checked her wrist timer. It was hurtled towards the lighting of the beacon. The deep rumble grew louder beneath them; the "freight train" was getting closer.

"I'll give you one more question, Ms. Bonds." Allard held the door with his right hand.

"Can I get three?" She cracked to Allard's amusement. "Ok." She thought deeply. She stared at this figure that had moved so gracefully, yet horridly, this man with so many contradictory views, this man of riddles and knew what she wanted. "Why the tattoos?" She stepped forward into the pantry ignoring the instructions of Team Leader. She was now blocking a quick attack.

"They're symbols...of people, places, things from my life." Allard glanced at his arm.

"I KNOW that already." Michelle's voice became slightly urgent as the rumble below them grew.

"People, places, things..." Allard stared at the symbols. "I've killed."

"What?" Michelle felt her heart drop. She was confused and then she saw it, a dark brand formed on his arm. Allard's eye winced slightly as what looked like a brand burned into his arm from inside. When it was done, she saw a reddened black mark perfectly formed within his arm art. It looked like a seashell.

"But I don't understand how you could have..."

"Maybe next time." Allard smiled.

"DON'T!" Michelle screamed and then felt a blast of the coldest air she could ever imagine. She hit the floor with a thud.

The darkness was serene. Allard felt icy pins all over his exposed skin. The wind caused him to take a step back. His eyes adjusted to the darkness then he felt them ice over. His tears froze in space leaving sparkles in his lids. He heard thumps behind him, saw a beanbag fly errantly passed him into the darkness and then he jumped.

He fell into the cold. His feet collided with cold, hard, sharpness. This was a cold his body had not known. He collapsed to his knees as wind exploded around his body. Frozen, blinding needles exploded into his muscles. He did what he thought was best; he started to move forward. Each labored step was met with more cold against his feet and the clatter of the freezing shackles. He could barely keep his eyes open and his skin felt as if it were being torn from his body with a razor. Move. He had to move forward. He had to leave.

The pantry was an explosion of action. The team rushed through pulling their goggles and soft helmets over their heads. They stepped over Michelle's body and ran towards the door. Lisa and Jury quickly poked in and dragged Michelle into the kitchen. Jury listened for breath while Lisa checked her pulse. When they knew she was fine, Jury covered her eyes with goggles and her head with a soft helmet and the two of them lifted her arms over their shoulders. Michelle hung like limp between them. They pushed back into the pantry into the wind as they watched the security team jump out into the darkness.

As the rumbling underneath The Country Cage grew more ominous, they reluctantly lugged Michelle toward the door. When they passed Welk's body, Lisa glanced down and could've sworn she saw black space where his eyes had once been. Perhaps, the cold had sunken them in...

"OK." Jury's voice whined with the sound of the air filters and mechanical gadgets in her helmet. "On the count of three."

"What the fuck are we counting for?" Lisa shouted. "Just jump..Go!"

The two jumped holding Michelle's body between the two of them and landed hard against the ice. The pitch black of the place was eerie. The only sound they could hear was of their own breathing as they made their way behind the security team. The team stood next to the large Humvee sitting just feet from the door. Had it not been so dark, they would've noticed that instead of wheels, this armored vehicle was fitted with swiveling tank tracks. It was a streamlined version of the vehicles that brought them to The Cage and a smaller version of the vehicles that brought their supplies.

Team Leader helped hoist Michelle into the waiting arms of another security guard then helped Lisa and Jury climb in next to her. The remaining team sat inside strapping themselves with safety harnesses. With a flip of a switch, heat blasted into the cabin. Then with a chug and a rumble, the Humvee's engine turned on.

"OK, let's see where he landed." The Driver said as he flipped another switch. Large L.E.D. bulbs broke the darkness illuminating at least a quarter mile in front of them.

"I don't see him." Lisa screamed.

The Humvee lurched forward as the truck began to move sluggishly to the left. The lights focused to that side and there about thirty feet in front of them was Allard walking slowly and intently. His skin had turned gray from the ice and windburn. He pushed forward walking like a zombie. His feet were blackened against the ice. Step by hard step he moved in the bluish haze of the lights.

"Oh My God!" Jury's voice cracked with the sight.

"Please save him." Tears formed in Lisa's eyes.

Allard stumbled as he looked back towards them shielding his eyes with his darkened hand. He tried to see what was caused the light, decided it didn't matter, turned his back and walked with faster steps.

"It's gotta be at least negative sixty out there. How the hell isn't he dead?" The Driver said as the tracks caught traction and pulled the Humvee forward toward Allard.

The wind kicked up and the snow blew hard pushing Allard sideways and causing the lights on the truck to sway. Haunting shadows were cast against the ice. Allard kept walking and was picking up speed. He was gaining a rhythm now. He had forgotten about the pain of the ice and was now warmed with the thought of leaving.

Huff......huff....huff He walked.

"The tracks are slipping. This wind is brutal man." The Driver whined.

"Drive! Drive! Drive!" Lisa shouted as she pulled her helmet and goggles off. She couldn't stand the way the heat in the cabin had made the helmet sweaty and uncomfortable on her face when she spoke.

Allard pushed harder. He wasn't to be stopped. The wind was like punches in his face; punches from large bricks of ice. With each breath he took, his lungs contracted and stuck. He swallowed and had no saliva. Then he remembered the desert and the warmth.

Huff..Huff..huff..huff..huff he began to trot, as the lights got closer. Then he was trotting harder and the lights got further away. Then his legs found a rhythm and they were moving faster. The ice was hitting him but it was melting fast against his body. He was running now. He was running so fast his toes barely touched the ice and then there was no light and he was running toward more darkness.

“How in the hell?” Team Leader screamed as Allard’s sleek form ran swiftly through the wind and ice beyond the range of the lights and disappeared in the darkness. He could see the wind pushing outward far ahead of them, around the form of a man on the horizon and Allard was gone.

BOOM!!

The Humvee shook. Everyone looked back as a large explosion ripped through The Country Cage. The roof shot outwardly in halves as an intensely bright beam of light shot from within their home and soared high to the heavens. A sustained beam of burning light erupted from The Country Cage as it rocked with explosions.

BOOM!

About five hundred yards away another explosion shook them. A bright beam of light burst from another facility.

"There goes our headquarters..." One of the team members said watching the security team building explode and spark.

Michelle opened her eyes slowly and reflexively ripped the helmet and goggles off of her head.

"Where's Allard?" She asked.

"He...ran away." Jury shrugged.

"Excuse me?" Michelle turned toward Lisa. Her eyes winced from the light's intensity.

"He ran away." Lisa pushed her hands out like 'hey whatdayaknow'

Michelle turned to look at the beacons of light that shot high up through the whiteout conditions. Whiteout conditions weren't a new phenomenon on The Antarctic's Masson Island. The lights would catch the attention of several U.S. military satellites. Those satellites would send the message that there was something wrong on the laboratory island Scilymax was funding. Eventually, there would be questions and issues and talks of treaties broken and what exactly was Scilymax doing on that island anyway, but for now...

"Beautiful." Michelle watched the lights dance through the sky against the snow. "So, what now?" She said.

"We wait for someone to come get us." Jury shook her head in disgust.

"Allard will probably get home before *US*." Lisa laughed causing a contagious bit of laughter from everyone in the Humvee, which grew and grew.

Little did she know, Allard would be on his way to the next island and then the next, swimming hand over hand in freezing waters. He had one person on his mind, "Dustin Carver..." and one mission "My war has begun again..."

END OF BOOK ONE

BOOK TWO

Sewn With Dragon's Needle

CHAPTER ONE

The plane was the only thing rumbling harder than Mark Silverman's stomach. The walls shuddered and there was an audible gasp from the passengers as the plane dipped slightly under the invisible forces of turbulence. His stomach rumbled more. As an experienced business traveler, he was all too familiar with turbulence and wary passengers. He however was not used to sitting on the cold hard plastic seat in the airplane bathroom sweating out a dump. This particular dump wasn't hard pressed to retreat his bowels so much as he was scared to release it. That damn burrito was to blame. In a rush to grab a bite of substance, Mark had the taxi pull over to the first burrito stand he saw. He had a double chicken burrito and heaped on the sour cream and guacamole in the back seat to the protests of the taxi driver. That first bite was like heaven, rich, well-seasoned pieces of meat, moist rice and beans all wrapped in a wonderful tortilla.

Four hours later, he was now in a new kind of hell. Sitting on the toilet bowl, he hoped he could slowly eek out the remains of that rushed burrito lunch. The last thing he wanted was the overpowering ass explosion of diarrhea, which could signal food poisoning and frequent trips back to the cramped lavatory. So, he sat and he sweated. Normally, he wouldn't sit on a public bowl, but today he needed control and balance. With a sigh, Mark relaxed his gut and held his palms tightly against his sweaty face. There was a rush within him and then the extreme force of flatulence pushing large amounts of feces into the small bowl. It was liquid shit and it flowed like a river. He heard himself call for God's help as his sphincter fluttered with each spurt and then as if the evil had been exorcised, Mark felt better. He flushed once, then again, wiped, washed his hands and took a deep breath. The last thing he wanted now was to walk out and see...

The pretty twenty something year old was standing in the aisle. Her pert bra-less nipples poked straight out of her thin t-shirt, a testament to Hollywood plastic surgery.

She flung her bleach blond hair over her shoulder while her blue eyes stared an embarrassing hole through his face. He fumbled a smile.

“That Indian guy ahead of me must’ve had one too many curry. You better hold your breath.” He warned.

“Ughhhh.” She grunted as the smell wafted directly into her face igniting her nose hairs. The next two rows grunted in tandem.

Mark shook his head in mock derision and pinched his nose closed relinquishing all blame to the bomb he laid. The plane rocked slightly. Had his ass thrown off the air quality? The flight was perfectly serene before he went into the bathroom and now he was a passenger on Parkinson’s Flight Shake Me Up. He brushed his hands across the luggage compartments steadying his self until he reached his seat. Wait, no, that wasn’t his seat; a guy was sitting there. He looked up at the seat number.

9B

This was definitely his seat. He sized up the guy in his seat...short, slightly stocky and nebbish. The man held a burlap bag in his lap. The handle was made of an odd interwoven construction of braided wood. It was like poor man’s wicker.

“Excuse me sir, you’re in my seat.” Mark spoke firmly. The man looked up at him, confused. “This is 9B, it’s a business class seat.”

The man looked left and right accessing his position. Neither of the two sleeping business types next to him budged. He looked behind him and ahead, then shrugged his shoulders unawares to the issue.

“You sat in the wrong seat.” Mark said slowly as if he were speaking to a child. The man shook his head, wrapped his hands around his burlap sack and looked straight ahead. “What the shit?” Mark huffed and signaled the nearest flight attendant.

“Sir, you have to take your seat. We’ve come upon some turbulence.” The flight attendant spoke immediately as if she weren’t summoned.

“We have a seating conflict. This was my seat and this guy is confused or something.” Mark gestured as a few of the nearby passengers pretended to not be listening to every word.

“Can I see your boarding stubs?” The Flight Attendant requested with Mark immediately fishing his from the breast pocket on his button down shirt.

The man checked his shirt, pants and jacket softly, but presented nothing.

“I don’t have one. This is my seat. It was empty.” The man said softly.

“That’s not how it works, buddy...”

“Sir, I’ll handle this.” The Flight Attendant cut Mark off at the ass. “Sir, can you please come with me? I’ll help you find your seat.” She gestured with her bright red fingernails.

The man floated from the seat carefully and out into the aisle with a spacey look in his eyes. Mark grumbled as he brushed by him and retook his seat, immediately waking the passengers next to him. Glancing up and down the aisles, the Flight Attendant saw that every seat on the flight appeared to be filled except one.

“Ahh there you go.” She led him toward the seat mistakenly colliding with the pretty twenty year old leaving the bathroom. “Oh, sorry miss. Umm...what seat are you in?”

“Right there...?” The Blonde sighed as if “duh” then sauntered to her aisle seat plopping down with a sigh.

With a cocked eyebrow, the Flight Attendant led the man toward the back of the plane. He was obviously trying to get over. He must’ve been seated in that horrible last row that didn’t recline. She walked swiftly through the plane with the man in tow. He clutched his burlap sack by its wooden handles. As they got closer, she noticed the seats were all impossibly filled.

"What's up dear?" Another attendant smiled crookedly at the nebbish little man with the odd bag.

"I can't find his seat."

"Where were you sitting, sir?" The Second Attendant asked as if the first attendant didn't have the sense to ask him herself.

"I had a seat in front. She told me it wasn't mine, but it was empty."

"It belonged to someone else." The First Attendant explained to the Second.

"Well people don't just hop on flights in midair now do they?" The Second Attendant smiled with a sarcastic bitchy wit.

"Can you find me another seat? I must deliver this parcel immediately."

"Well it'd help if we knew where you were." The First Attendant said hoping not to offend the obviously slow man.

"I'll check the roster. What's your name, sir?" The Second attendant stepped passed them and eased toward the front of the plane.

"Herman." He said slowly.

"Ok, Mr. Herman. I'm sure I'll see it on the way up and if not, maybe someone plopped their kid down in your seat until you got back." She smiled a false toothy grin.

Soon there was a call tone, the First Attendant picked up the phone. She looked down the fuselage to the Second Attendant, whose hands were sprouting from her arms like wild tree limbs.

"There's no Mr. Herman on the roster. I just asked Jack if he checked all of the bathrooms before we boarded and he did. He's not a stowaway..."

"This parcel is for Allard. It must reach him." Herman said.

"You think he was hiding in...luggage and came up?" The First Attendant could see the Second Attendant speaking as she pressed the emergency call button to the pilot.

"Sir, how did you get on this plane?" The First Attendant turned to Herman who stared down the fuselage at the other attendant.

"Allard is out there. I must get this to him." Herman spoke in a forceful whisper.

"Sir?" The Flight Attendant felt a chill shoot up her spine.

A man quickly approached the two of them one hand holding a small pager, the other hand tucked under his suit jacket by his right hip.

"Sky Marshal, m'am. Sir, you must take your seat at this moment or you will be placed under arrest." He spoke firmly tucking the pager into his pocket and removing the handcuffs from his belt clip.

"What are you doing here?" Herman spoke angrily looking directly through the Sky Marshal.

"I am a U.S. Sky Marshal. You are disrupting this flight and not following the directions of flight pers..."

"Kronus, are you supposed to be here?" Herman spoke louder to no one in particular at the other end of the plane.

"Quiet down, sir. We're going to settle this nice and easy." The Sky Marshall raised his hands.

"Do you have BUSINESS here? Answer me?" Herman shouted as the passengers stirred, turning to the three of them. He quickly sidestepped the Sky Marshal and stood in the aisle facing the Second Attendant.

The Sky Marshal grabbed Herman's arm, forced it behind his back and fastened one of the cuffs on his wrist. With what seemed like the ease of breathing, Herman pulled his hand from the cuff and took two steps toward the front of the plane.

"If you have business, take care of it immediately or you will have business with me." Herman spoke strongly as a few fearful screams were shouted in the seats.

Suddenly, the plane dipped hard, rocked, trembled and tumbled hard downwardly sending the Sky Marshal and the Flight Attendants crashing against ceilings and walls. The death curdling screams of passengers competed with the groaning and wails of the aircraft. The engines sputtered and whined as gasps and screams were shouted.

Herman stood stiffly in the aisle staring into space. He held the burlap sack in one hand by it's braided handle then held it aloft and spoke to no one in particular.

"THIS belongs to Allard!" He threatened.

Immediately the plane leveled, the turbulence ceased and all trouble ended. Groans and moans, gasps and heavenly praises erupted from the passengers.

Herman stood holding the bag out. At the other end of the plane, standing behind The Second Flight Attendant was a tall, hooded figure. The Figure's face was unseen in the darkness of the hood, his robes tattered and filthy. His hands were mere bones with pale waxy skin stretched across them. A scythe was clenched in his fist. He hovered over the Second Attendant staring back at Herman, the only person that could see him.

"Now find me a seat..." Herman whispered.

With lightening quickness, the scythe howled through the air flying directly at Herman. The screams of millions of souls screeched as the dull iron blade with the solid oak handle shot through the plane. Herman had no time to react as it shot passed him and struck the rising Sky Marshal. Deafening squeals shattered Herman's ears as a blast of chill filled the aircraft. The Sky Marshal collapsed again. Herman turned toward him as The Flight Attendant screamed for a doctor. It was too late, his soul was ripped from his body, pulled, twisted and contorted into the blade of the sickle.

Herman picked up his sack, walked to the Sky Marshal's seat and sat. He placed the burlap bag on his lap and clutched it tightly as the attendants and a doctor tried to revive the Marshal, but it was too late. Herman carefully watched Kronus as he collected his scythe. Then with a nod, Kronus disappeared through the floor of the plane and was gone.

The architecture of the Scilymax Physical Experiments building was ornate and vintage. The cold white stone color matched many of the neighboring edifices there in the Flatiron District of Manhattan. The hustle of the streets below the twenty-floor structure was in deep contrast with the quiet halls within the building. While the climate control and tight security could have been to blame, the real answer was that it was Friday and all of the doctors, researchers, assistants and support staff had gone home for the weekend. All that was left were the roaming security guards...and one physician, Dr. Lisa Lucas.

The time had come for even Lisa to call it a day. She shut down her computer, rubbed her tired eyes and closed the various file folders of blueprints and lab tests. She stashed the folders in the file cabinet and locked it. Her Christian Louboutin heels clicked against the hard tile floor as she made her way across the expansive square footage of her new corner office.

“Goodnight, Asis.” Her smoke filled voice echoed as she made her way through the archway.

“Goodnight, Dr. Lucas.” A computerized voice responded in kind, shut off the lights, drew the blinds and sealed the frosted glass door behind her.

The halls, as comfortable as they were decorated (by an expensive interior decorator no doubt) felt cold and lifeless compared to The Country Cage. Of course that facility had been her home and work for months and she had been here for...wow had it been a year already? She checked the face on her Horsebit Collection Gucci watch, a gift from the Scilymax board of directors for her “exceptional service”. The expensive timepiece read Eight-Thirty, just like any other watch would. She was leaving work early for once.

She stepped into the elevator and pressed the ground floor. As the doors closed, she felt a slight tingle in the back of her ear and she quickly pressed the button for fifteen as the elevator descended.

The Fifteenth floor was way more personal than hers. The paintings had more whimsy, the carpet a richer color. She guessed the head shrinks wanted their specimens to feel more at home while they were mentally fucked. She was within seven feet of her intended destination when she saw the door was closed and no light shone from beneath it. Of course, there was no way Marjorie Houston would be caught dead at work late on a Friday. As Lisa turned she saw a large silhouetted figure approaching her in the hall. A hollow scream left her throat before her brain had time enough to register what she had seen.

"Sorry Dr. Lucas! Just making my rounds. Didn't mean to sneak up or anything." His face lit up embarrassed. His too tight security guard uniform stretched against his biceps as he held his hands up in surrender.

"It's...ok...Roscoe." Dr. Lucas huffed. Her eyes blinked a few times making sure it had actually seen Roscoe and not a scarred man dressed only in shorts.

"Dr. Houston left early. I think her security detail picked her up around quarter to four." Roscoe provided way too much information in an effort to comfort her. "Do you want me to call the agents and have them escort you home?"

"Nah." She shrugged at him with a grimace. "You know me, I don't like all that secret service type shit." She cussed to help him feel more comfortable. "Have a good weekend, Roscoe."

"You too Dr. Lucas." Roscoe nodded. As he passed her in the hall, he took a deep breath of her perfume then was sly about taking a look back at how her business slacks cupped her round behind.

Lisa knew he was looking, she was used to it, especially from the security guards and the fellas in the mailroom. As long as they were slick about it and not leering, she didn't mind. For her own amusement, she brushed her hand across the ass of her pants as if removing some invisible dust. She heard the air whistle between his teeth in exasperation as she stepped back onto the open elevator.

Lisa studied the many faces that passed her on Twenty Third Street as she approached the west side of Manhattan. Looking at faces had become a hobby...no... more like a preoccupation of hers; looking at faces. Once or twice she had seen a familiar face or two, but not the one she was looking for. There were so many faces, so many people and so many possibilities. The fear had worn off earlier than she'd thought. In fact, she was never really scared, more anxious that she would see Allard walking down the streets of New York. Maybe he was selling hot dogs with Osama Bin Laden down by Washington Square Park.

The fear was what led Scilymax Corporation to provide round the clock security detail and transportation for her and her friends Dr. Marjorie "Jury" Houston and Michelle Bonds. Lisa halted the security detail three months after they returned, after the classified congressional depositions and reports had ended. After being followed around with two very square secret service types attached to her ample hips had become more of a drag than a convenience. She still took advantage of the transportation every now and then, like when she needed a designated driver after a tipsy night on the town. Michelle addressed the fear by moving away from the attention and made her home in a quiet town in the south. Jury kept every bit of security she could. She watched over her pretty brown shoulders with every step and navigated through the city with the secrecy of a third world diplomat.

Lisa watched the faces as she passed them, looking, searching for him. She waved to the whistling encampment of homeless men who greeted her every morning and bid her goodbye every evening as she passed through Madison Square Park. Her spare three quarters clattered into the cup of the man sitting against the fence with his head down, his long tattered locs were wild against his head. Her fingers waved in the air at the rest of her homeless fans as she trotted across the street to make the light. The homeless man reached in his cup, pulled out one of the shiny silver quarters, held it up and watched her over the top of it.

Lisa was unwinding with a glass of Chardonnay in her kimono robe when the buzzer disturbed the hilarity of "Sixteen Candles" playing on her television. She turned the channel to the security monitor. Jury waved back at her in grainy black and white security cam view. Her high wattage smile had a few more kilowatts than usual. She was drunk. Lisa pressed the intercom button on her remote control.

"What do you want, drunk?" Lisa said.

"I wanna come up and talk!" Jury whined from the television. She waved a bottle in her hand. "I brought wine AND chicken!"

"Where's the chicken?" Lisa cocked her eyebrow.

Marjorie reached off camera and tugged a security agent into view; he held a big box of Popeye's chicken and a non-too-pleased expression on his face.

"Open up, baby!" Marjorie laughed.

Lisa and Marjorie were well through the box of chicken and biscuits and the wine had reached its final drops when Marjorie cleared her throat.

"Ahem...do you...have you...wondered if...he's ever going to come for us?" Marjorie laid her head against Lisa's thigh as she stretched out on her plush couch.

"Ehhh." Lisa brushed Marjorie's hair down trying to force concerns away with it. "He didn't make it sweetie. That place was just too cold."

"They found his tracks down by the water." Marjorie slurred with the wine coursing through her bloodstream.

"We've talked about this before. Even if those were his tracks and he made it to the Arctic Ocean...it's THE ARCTIC OCEAN!"

"They never found him..."

"It's sad. He really was a misunderstood person. I'm sure if he did make it, he'd be more concerned with other things besides us. Like maybe finding how to get the frostbite off his balls." Lisa laughed.

"You're not concerned, you didn't try to blow his head off with a fucking shotgun, Leez." Marjorie sat up and picked through the left over chicken strips.

Lisa sat quietly. She hated replaying those last moments in The Country Cage. Her life here in New York was so much more comfortable albeit lonely. She was in a city of millions of people and she felt just as alone here as babysitting the man in the tube on an Antarctic island. There was only one constant, Marjorie, the drunk broad that was stumbling her way to the bathroom eating a chicken strip. Maybe things weren't that bad after all. Lisa stood and looked down out of her window. Even from her high-rise apartment she could spot the security detail SUV parked in front of the building.

At the same time Lisa was looking down, one of the agents was peering upward to her apartment window as he let the cigarette smoke escape his lips and out of the window. All was the same here, nothing new to him. But had he not been so tired and lulled into boredom, he may have noticed the homeless man pushing the small laundry basket full of belongings towards him, flipping a shiny new quarter in his hand.

The electronic rumble of Michelle's phone jarred her from sleep. She bolted straight up in her bed searching every dark corner of her bedroom. Nothing. What was that sound? The phone rang again to her surprise. The phone? She checked the clock. At twelve fifteen in the morning. It must be an emergency. Lisa? Marjorie? She fumbled with the receiver and placed it close to her ear.

"Lisa?" She said.

"Uh no. Michelle Bonds, please?" The gruff voice spoke.

"Speaking." Her heart sank. He definitely sounded like the authorities. Her mind thought of every horrible possibility in the short moments it took for the man to speak again.

"Ms. Bonds." He emphasized the "Ms." a little too hard for her liking. "This is Douglas Kind, Director of Investigations, Department of Homeland Security. Are you expecting any out of town visitors?"

"No..." Michelle's mind wandered because either it was so late or she wasn't really awake yet or because hmmm was this the weekend Lisa was coming to visit her? Who else could be visiting her from out of town? Her heart dropped.

"Do you know a man named Herman?" She could hear him tapping the phone with his fingertip impatiently.

"No. Mr...ummm..."

"Director. Kind."

"Director Kind. It's kind of late for a call like this. Can you get to the point?"

"Sorry. I'm sure you've seen the news reports of the disturbance on the airliner today and the death of the sky marshal. Well, your name came up in the subsequent investigation. It took quite a bit of time before we could interrogate witnesses at the center of the investigation, a man named Herman, says he was coming to visit you."

"Me?? I don't know anyone named Herman. He gave you my first AND last name?" She hopped out of bed and walked across the hard wood floor to her bathroom.

"And your address. He says he was supposed to deliver a package to you." Director Kind waited a few beats to let the information sink in. Michelle could feel herself being placed in the middle of interrogation 101. "We'd like you to come down and take a look at him. Maybe he's using an alias. Maybe if you come down and he sees you, he'll cop to not knowing you. The quickest we can take you out of the variables, the better."

"I can see about getting the morning off and coming down tomorrow if it'll help. I really..." She projected her voice to hide the low hiss of her peeing. "I just don't know if all of this is necessary, I don't know anyone named Herman. You guys have all kinds of illegal access to my life and records. I'm sure you've already checked that." She stood, wiped and nearly flushed but decided to save herself that bit of embarrassment.

"If you can come down tonight, it'd be of great help to us and the investigation."

"It's late. I don't even know where the local Department of Homeland Security is." She huffed with biting sarcasm. "And you expect me to drive around at night wasting my gas?"

"Actually, Ms. Bonds." Emphasis on the "Ms." again. "We have two field agents at your house right now..." His tone was a direct warning.

Michelle rushed toward the front of the house. She peered through her curtains and saw a black SUV sitting on her quiet country street in front of her house. A man in a suit with no tie stood just outside her fence looking at the house. His focus seemed to drift in her direction. She pulled away from the window.

"What the hell?? Do you think I'm going to leave with a pair of strangers because you claim to be from the government?" Michelle said as she trotted through the living room. She pulled the longest butcher knife from the butcher-block holder and squeezed it tightly in her hand.

“You can call your local police department. They know we’re there. They actually should be sending a marked car to your address very soon. We’d just rather not have them cuff you; turn on the lights and sirens and all of that. That can embarrass you in front of the neighbors. You’re in the south now, Ms. Bonds, people talk.”

Michelle thought for a moment. Didn’t he say there were two agents? She slid quietly to her kitchen window and nearly squealed when she saw a dark figure standing in her backyard by her back door. What the hell was this Butch Cassidy & The Sundance Kid? They had the house surrounded.

“I’ll wait for the police to get here, but they don’t have to turn on the lights and things.” Michelle clutched the knife as she slid back into her dark bedroom and shimmied into a pair of jeans under her nightshirt.

“Great. I really do apologize and I appreciate your cooperation.”

Michelle hurried to put on her bra and some sneakers. By the time she peaked back outside, she could see two uniformed police men talking to the two field agents by the gate. One of the uniformed men walked up to the door and gave a light knock. Michelle flipped on the porch light and opened the door keeping the chain link locked.

"Good morning m'am." The officer displayed his badge in the crack. "You can come with us or ride with the field agents. Whichever makes you more comfortable."

Michelle thought she wanted to ride with the uniformed officers until she realized she'd have to sit in the back like an everyday perp. The field agent held the door for her as she slid into the cushy leather backseat of the SUV. It reminded her of the security detail she had when she first made it back to New York from The Country Cage.

"It's about a twenty-five minute drive from here, Ms. Bonds. You can nap or we can play the radio if you'd like." The Driver said.

"The radio is fine, thanks." Michelle turned to make sure the marked car followed them out of her street and down the avenue. The agent in the passenger seat turned on the radio, smooth jazz, then nuzzled into the seat getting comfortable for the drive. He looked much shorter than he had in her backyard. Actually he was quite different from his ominous silhouette.

The dark figure was still standing there in her backyard. When he knew everyone had driven away, he approached the back door and pushed it open with one firm shove, breaking the lock and the doorjamb without much effort. He walked through the kitchen quietly listening for other inhabitants. The phone rang suddenly breaking his reserve. It rang again loudly as he walked toward the phone and peered at the caller ID.

Lucas, Lisa

212-555-1110

His head cocked to one side, confused. Why wasn't she dead already? Then he went about his search of the property.

The squeaky wheels of the over packed laundry basket squealed all the way up to the front door of the black SUV. The homeless man waved at the two agents with his fingers. His smile was bright, clean, definitely not what you'd expect from a man with seemingly no future. The agent in the passenger seat noticed and sat up just in time to feel the sharp pain that exploded in his head. It felt like the worst migraine he could ever feel. As if every blood vessel in his brain was trying to escape through his forehead. His sudden screams shocked the driver into a quick sweat. He reached for his partner with one hand while drawing his weapon with the other. Pulling back his partners face, he saw blood gushing from his nose like a water fountain. His eyes were closed tightly. The driver looked every which way through the tinted windows of the truck.

"What happened? What's wrong? What the fuck?" The Agent screamed to his injured partner who had stopped screaming and began to convulse in his seat. The Agent started the truck immediately and peeled off from the curb nearly rear ending the car in front of them. The quiet of the street was broken by the rapid acceleration, near collision in the intersection, erupting horns and screech of tires as the agents barreled away looking for emergency medical attention.

The homeless man stood in silence with his small-overstuffed laundry basket and pushed it towards Lisa's apartment building.

CHAPTER TWO

It was nearly break time for Tómas Colon. All he had to do was finish unloading the rest of the meat from the refrigerated extended trailer into the freezing warehouse. Normally his graveyard shift down in the trendy meatpacking district of New York would be used to cut the sides of beef with band saws before that meat was shipped to the local super markets. During his breaks, he'd watch the scantily clad partygoers stumble up and down the cobblestone streets to and from the late night hot spots. Unfortunately, there was traffic on I-95 and one last truck eased into the loading dock late by several hours. Tómas knew he'd be the one chosen to unload the truck. He was always chosen for the heavy details. His thick arms and wide neck was a reminder of his younger days. In his native

Columbia, he was once known as "El Cuello", The Collar. The infamous Pablo Escobar had many sinister henchmen and assassins, but none more ruthless than "El Cuello".

"El Cuello" was credited with creating the Columbian necktie. The necktie was the heinous practice of slitting the throat of a snitch, government official, hated boyfriend to a younger sister or random victim, then pulling the victim's tongue through the jagged cut and leaving it to hang down the victim's neck. However, Tómas Colon didn't invent the Columbian necktie. He learned it from watching his father during his toddler years in Columbia in an era known as "La Violencia". As a toddler, Tómas witnessed his father use the bloody tactic on government officials and opposition party members as a scare tactic. He grew up with the Columbian necktie as his birthright. Soon, when CIA pressure became too much, "El Cuello" would have his own face cut. Those cuts would change his appearance and send him to New York as part of the witness protection program.

Today he was an aging scarred and stout dockworker pulling hanging sides of beef along a track then lowering them into large carts to be cut in the warehouse. With every hard strike of his hook, he'd pierce the top of the meat, haul it to the end of the track, unhook it and heave the heavy carcass into the bin. The more he finished, the further into the truck he had to go to retrieve the meat.

Sometimes those motorized tracks just wouldn't function after a cross-country trip in freezing temperatures. As he got further into the truck, he noticed a "parts hamper", a long rubber bag that resembled a body bag. These bags carried the unintentionally broken, ripped, shredded and dismembered portions of the animal that were used in meat processing.

Tómas swung his meat hook catching the hanging hook holding the "parts hamper" and dragged it slowly to the exit. It was heavy and unwieldy, his hook slipped from the icy hanging hook constantly.

"Ay Díos mio!" He shouted. He'd had enough of the hanging hook. He swung his hook repeatedly hitting against the bag trying to puncture it with the tip so he could pull the bag itself. The thudding impact against the meat was sickening. Finally, he made a hole and dragged the hamper slowly to the door. He watched the exit come slowly closer. Was this hamper full of cows' heads? Why was it so heavy? His hand shook under the weight as he hauled the bag behind him. As the exit got closer, his hand shook more. Turning on his heels, he looked up to see the bag shaking and moving. It was alive! Quick thinking and with his murderous spirit tapped, Tómas ripped his hook from the bag and swung hard striking the bag with heavy blows. The bag shifted to and fro as it hung. Tómas' hook ripped away at the bag until it became unstable and fell from its hook landing with a thud against the floor of the trailer.

With a rage befitting a former henchman, he pounded against the bag attempting to beat it into submission. Heavy-handed blows with a deathly rhythm echoed through the trailer and the loading dock. He swung hard and built a sweat as the bag shuffled, shifted and squirmed. With each rip and shred created by the hook, Tómas would start to see the resemblance of a body in the bag. It incensed him. There was no way a person could travel so many miles for so long in the refrigerated trailer. It must be a zombie, a devil, El Chupacabra. His rage and vengeance grew as he swung. It would not stop moving. It would not die. Was it Pablo Escobar returning for revenge for Tomas' betrayal? Suddenly, a hand shot from a tear in the hamper and clasped the hook. Using Tómas' bodyweight as leverage, the hand tugged, pulled itself upward and ripped itself from the hamper. "El Cuello" was notorious for being fearless. On this day, "El Cuello" stared into the eyes of his fear. His hand dropped from the hook, which stayed in the hand of the figure that ripped from the bag.

"Please, do not kill me. I am a God fearing man now."

"Now..." The rusty, low voice repeated for effect.

“I am. I really am.” Tómas “El Cuello” Colon dropped to his knees with tears in his eyes, his arms shook; spit shot from his mouth in deathly fear.

“El Cuello? YOU beg for mercy?” The voice grew stronger though still shook in the cold air.

“Sí. Por favor. I am with God.” Tómas prayed.

“Now...” The figure repeated again. “If you are with God then you won’t mind joining him.”

“No..No..Please. I have grandchildren. They wait for their abuelo.”

“As does God, if you are with him...”

The loud screams of drunken coeds and the pounding bass of car stereos echoed outside the trailer masking the sounds of the pleading in the truck.

“I guess being with God isn’t as good as being with your ninos.” The figure said placing his hand on the back of Tómas’ lowered head then walked passed him. Tómas could hear the figure jump from the back of the truck.

“Gracías. Thank you God for mercy.” Tómas moaned then turned to see the back of the man clad only in white overalls and construction boots. His long dreadlocks swung back and forth across his back. The man turned to him and nodded his head. “Goodbye Allard.” Tómas whispered.

Ron Popeil has an annoying voice. Lisa was sure she hated it three fold tonight as she pried her eyes open to see one of his infomercials playing too loudly on the gigantic television. Why the hell did she let the cute sales guy convince her to buy such a big television anyway? Oh right, he was cute and had a swagger about him that she was sure meant he knew what he was talking about. Of course now, Ron Popeil's head was enormous and his mouth looked nearly big enough to swallow her head. Head? Yeah, the thing that spun on her shoulders. Too much wine and Ron Popeil's voice, two things that never go together. She sat up on the couch placing both bare feet on the hardwood floor. She looked over the takeout bucket, napkins, wine glasses and bottles...oh there had been more than one bottle of wine? No sign of the remote. Her thick, once sturdy legs wobbled her to the television as she felt around and finally turned it off.

The silence was deafening, but welcome. She looked over to the love seat. Jury wasn't there. Lisa parted her small lips to call Jury, but just knew the sound would cause her head to throb. She shuffled down toward the hall with her kimono robe undone. Her cami set was not enough material to block her from feeling the crispness of the air. She held the wall and peered down the long hallway. The mahogany floors gave way to the ivory travertine floors of the bathroom and the mocha colored skin of Jury who lay crumpled against its coolness. Lisa chuckled as she made her way to her.

"You sick?" Lisa's groggy voice echoed in the cavernous bathroom.

"Not anymoooooore." Jury replied with a slow growling whine, her eyes still closed.

"So why are you still on the floor?" Lisa nudged Jury's butt with her foot.

"Cuz it's so cool down here. It's refreshing. Remind me to get the number for the guy that did your bathroom floors." Jury replied as she slowly pulled herself up into a sitting position. "Head. Still. Spinning, baby."

Lisa shook her head and made her way slowly to the kitchen.

"Why'd you leave me?" Jury moaned from the bathroom.

"I'm getting you some water."

"Just get it from the bathroom sink. I'm not picky right now."

"And then later you'll scream on me for letting you drink bathroom sink water. I know you!" Lisa shook her head as she poured a glass of spring water. She took a gulp of her own then refilled the glass.

Her hand clutched the marble countertop preserving her balance. As her fingers shifted, they collided with the handset of her cordless telephone. That was an odd place for the phone. She hadn't made a call at all tonight, had she? Her stomach dropped...

"Marjorie." Lisa used her friend's full name for motherly scolding effect.

"Yes..." Her friend's weak voice responded.

"Who'd you drunk dial?"

"Huh?"

"Who'd you call?"

"That was me." The low rumble echoed from the darkness of the adjacent dining room.

Lisa's heart sank. She grabbed a carving knife from the butcher block on the counter and aimed it at the darkness and backed towards the doorway.

"I called Michelle Bonds, but she didn't answer." His voice was coarse as if his vocal chords had been massaged with broken shards of glass. "I used your caller ID. It saved me from having to pry the number from you."

Lisa was at the threshold between the kitchen and the hallway. She hoped Marjorie would be looking up.

Hoped she would see her pointing the knife and would understand the circumstances without warning.

"Someone else must've gotten to her."

Lisa's hand shook. She needed to see his face. She needed to know he had come to do harm and that he was there to make her eyes go black like Agent Welk's did at The Country Cage. She heard a chair rumble as it shifted and heard him stand.

"Don't come any closer." She wanted to see his face. "I'll cut your fucking throat." She wanted to touch him.

"I need to know where he is."

She heard him take a step toward her.

"Dustin has security, a hell of a lot more than we do." Lisa stepped backward and gave a quick glance to the bathroom. Jury wasn't there. Where the hell had she crawled to?

"I'll find him another way." The voice was closer.

Lisa thought about the lock on the bathroom door. It could keep Allard out for at least five seconds. She could use the bathroom phone, dial 911, leave it off the hook, just long enough for...the operator to hear her being killed. The bedroom was closer. How fast could she leap over the bed and make it to the window? If it were locked...and she was sure it was, she'd waste precious seconds getting it open, but at least she could reach the fire escape in time for him to...throw her from the window.

She could scream and get attention. Maybe someone would see her body falling and thudding against the concrete. Maybe Jury's dumb ass security guards would hear her screams and come running too late to save her. Screaming was her best bet, but she still needed to know if Allard had come to kill her.

"What do you want from me, Allard?" She tried to sound as stern as she could.

"Allard..." The raspy voice began. "Is what I want from you." Stepping from the darkness into the kitchen was the dirty bedraggled homeless man. His face was expressionless.

Lisa's screams echoed in the hallway as her bare feet thudded across the wood floors. She heard his feet banging quickly behind her. She could feel his presence closer as the bedroom door got nearer on her right side. Instinctively, she ducked to avert his hand grabbing her and swiveled into the bedroom nearly colliding with Jury who held something in her hands.

Lisa ducked underneath Jury's arms. Just as he turned the corner, Jury swung down hard with all her might and the large picture frame glass shattered across his face, stunned him and knocked him backward into the hallway. Lisa closed and locked the door as Jury pushed the nearby armoire towards it. Lisa helped to push the heavy oak piece in front of the door when there was a bang. The armoire teetered just slightly as the door pushed against it. He'd made much quicker work of the lock than Lisa had expected.

Jury was already headed for the open window screaming for help at the top of her lungs. She yelled as she pulled herself through and started descending the steps two at a time. Lisa pulled the cordless phone handset from the night table cradle as she ran for the window. The knife dropped with a clang as she pulled herself out into the brisk air. Behind her were the constant heavy bangs of the door colliding with the armoire. As Lisa made it to the next floor below, she heard the loud boom of the armoire hitting the floor. If nothing else, they had succeeded in making a scene.

Jury could feel the cold air bashing her lungs. She knew she wasn't sober, but the adrenaline-pumped fear had given her focus if not coordination. Her bare feet slipped across the cold metal. She descended swiftly. Every now and again she banged on a window to wake the neighbors. Lisa's feet were clattering against the metal steps maybe two floors above her. Below, she saw a quiet empty street.

There wasn't one police respondent, not one curious neighbor.

"There's a homeless man trying to kill us. YES! We're running down the fire escape!" Lisa's voice echoed through the quiet night. She had finally gotten the sense to use the damn phone, Jury thought. Then there was a light squeal and the sound of tumbling. Jury stopped and looked up to see Lisa trying to break her fall as she tumbled down the flight of steps. The sounds of joints and bones smashing against the metal echoed in the quiet night air. The telephone exploded into pieces and rained diodes, plastic and buttons down over Jury's head.

Her eyes shot up studying the fire escape looking for the man. Lisa had obviously been running fast, but had she left him that far behind? No, he was standing just outside her bedroom window looking down at Jury as he played with a silver coin in his hand. He wasn't pursuing them... just waiting.

"Lisa get up! Let's go!" Jury shouted.

Lisa didn't need a cheerleader. She had scrambled to her feet and bounded down more steps. Her ankles were sore and her knees were scraped. She thought she felt blood trickling from her elbow, but she didn't care. She was getting the hell out of there.

Jury wanted to see if he would move, but he just stood and watched. Lisa was coming towards her quickly. She would wait for her, again. She would make sure her friend was on the same level playing field as she had done earlier. As she'd done when she heard what she thought was Allard's voice in the dining room. As she'd done when she dragged herself quietly into the bedroom, unlocked the window and stepped out, but came back looking for a weapon and decided Lisa was more than her friend, she was a sister. Jury knew this was her fault and now she would be fair. Lisa was just two flights above her now. That was close enough wasn't it? No. She'd watch the man to see what he was doing then they'd take the rest of the fire escape together. Lisa saw Jury motionless and staring above her.

"What are you doing? RUN BITCH!" Lisa screamed.

"I'm waiting for you!" Jury shouted back then she saw what she knew was a smile on The Man's face. Just as Lisa reached Jury's level The Man jumped over the side of the fire escape and dropped two floors down, grabbing the metal fire escape with his hands. He arched his back and braced himself with his feet like a monkey jumping in a tree.

"OH MY GOD!" Lisa shouted as she too had stopped to look up. "GO!" They ran the steps with deliberate rhythm.

The Man jumped with a CLANG two floors at a time down the side of the building. The two sped their pace as the noise grew closer and closer.

CLANG!

CLANG!

CLANG!

CLANG!

CLANG!

The floor they were on rattled and shook as he landed on it then leaped lower. They continued to run as the sound of his jumping moved further down the escape. Lisa realized they were running towards him, not away from him and grabbed Jury's shoulder heaving both of them back against the building.

CLANG!

CLANG!

CLANG!

THUD!

The two of them peered down to the ground dead into the eyes of the man flipping the coin. Lisa had finally recognized him as the man she'd given the coin to in the park. He was looking back up to them and motioned with his finger. COME HERE!

Michelle was fed up with waiting. Sitting on the once comfortable chair in the nondescript building near the airport had lost its luster about three minutes after she'd arrived. There were continual stops and starts, "We're ready...oh wait some one else needs to be here." Then "Wait, we can't have him here and not have this that and the third one" and then there were hushed whispers of "the bag" and something about "a body". She'd had two cups of the not so tasty coffee and one very tasty Krispy Kreme donut and now her attitude was peaking out and ready to play. They propped her up in what appeared to be the best office in the building and turned on the TV being sure to leave it on "Lifetime" because that's what all women watch when they're home alone. They hadn't asked many questions since the officers of Homeland Security picked her up at home. The next person that walked through that door was going to get a hardy helping of attitude.

“Ms. Bonds, I’m so sorry they kept you in here.” A Female Agent opened the door and made a beeline directly for Michelle with a hand outstretched.

“I want my lawyer.” Michelle fumed with her hands stiffly against her sides. She looked at the woman’s hand as if it were covered in feces.

“If I was called earlier, there was no way they would’ve roused you out ya bed at this time of night for this.” Her southern drawl peeked through. She kept her hand extended and Michelle just pursed her lips. The creamy complexion of her face became flushed and she dropped her hand. “If you could please just ask this man some questions for us. You won’t be alone at all and since you say you don’t know him, I’ll help corner him.”

“I SAY I don’t know him because I don’t.” Michelle was still fuming on the outside. On the inside, she felt a little shame she was giving the hardest time to the only woman involved in the whole fiasco.

“I’ll happily call your attorney. It’s just at this time of night…” She glanced at the clock. “Time of morning, it could keep you here even longer because then we’d have to call even more people in as well to deal with the legalities.”

Michelle let out a deep sigh. She just wanted it all to be over.

The halls twisted and turned. Michelle had the correct inclination that the building was designed to confuse prisoners so they couldn't easily escape. Wait, did that mean they were confusing her as well? Was she a prisoner?

The woman went over the issues again. The man's name was Herman. He had been found on-board a full flight on the way to New York City. He was carrying a bag made of burlap. It took five TSA agents to wrestle the bag from the man and they found it to be empty so they gave it back. The man said he was returning the bag to another man. He said he knew Michelle and would give the bag to her instead. Another man, a sky marshal, died during the fracas.

No matter who told her the story, they always left the death part for the end. They always brushed it away as the sky marshal's own heart issues. On the way to the building, one agent said something about TSA injuries, but was hushed by the other.

"Here we are." The Female Agent opened the door and waited for Michelle to enter. Michelle balked then relented. The room was surprisingly full. There were four or five agents dressed in suits; their ties were pulled loose. There were six uniformed TSA guards standing behind the schleb of a man who sat behind a metal table. He was shackled to the chair and the table and clutched a burlap bag that resembled a purse in his lap. His fingers flexed on the wood twig handle. The two agents that brought her there sat at the back of the room bleary eyed. Douglas Kind had greeted her when she arrived to the building and was now whispering to another man. He glanced toward her, gave a brief smile then returned stern and kept his low tone. The man he spoke to nodded as if making mental notes of everything he was told.

The schleb of a man didn't raise his eyes from the table. He looked like a "Herman". There was no other way to describe him. The Agent led Michelle to a chair towards the back of the room. The men parted and created a semi-circle behind her facing Herman with the TSA guards behind him. A small microphone was attached to her lapel.

"Give us a mic check." The Agent whispered.

"Uh...microphone checka one, two." Michelle had only heard rappers give mic checks. The Woman nodded asking for more. "Three, four, five, six..." Michelle noticed one of the TSA Agents had a fresh bruise on his right cheek; another was clutching a bandaged finger. The Agent looked through a mirror instead of into it, raised her hand then dropped it.

"Here, read from this." She said and pointed to a piece of paper with at least thirty single spaced typed questions on it.

"Herman, are you ready to talk now?" Kind's voice boomed.

"Only when Michelle Bonds is brought here." He sounded like a Herman.

Hearing the strange man say her name brought chills to Michelle's spine. Everyone glanced around the room. Either Herman hadn't noticed Michelle had entered or he didn't know what she looked like.

"She's here." Douglas said sternly.

"Have you found another decoy?" Herman spat with a little venom in his voice. His eyes never left the table. Michelle could see his fingers flexing on the bag in his lap.

"No more decoys Herman." Douglas breathed.

Herman raised his eyes and looked squarely into Michelle's eyes. A smirk spread on his lips.

"You haven't changed one bit." Herman smiled.

Michelle's heart began to thump. She had never seen this man in her life and now he was gazing at her like an old friend. The Female Agent sensed Michelle's uneasiness and tapped her fingernail against the paper in front of Michelle. Michelle looked down and read the first question to herself.

What is your full name?

She licked her lips, took a deep breath and raised her head.

"Michelle, where is Allard?" Herman stared dead in her eyes. As if on cue, everyone's head turned to Michelle.

"What is your full name?" Michelle ignored him. After Allard she was sure she could interrogate this homely non-assuming Herman.

He sat quietly. Well "sat" isn't really correct. Herman looked as if someone had poured him from a large pitcher into the chair.

"My name isn't important. Finding Allard is. I have this parcel for him. He must receive it. You know where he is. Tell me."

Michelle looked at the second question on the list.

What is your nationality?

"Where I'm from doesn't matter." Herman answered almost as soon as she'd read the question to herself.

Michelle looked at The Female Agent. She pointed her finger at the air as if pressing a button.

“If I knew where Allard was, why would I tell you? You don’t have any proof that you know him and I don’t know you. So, we’ll just sit here and wait until we get to know each other.” Michelle tried her hardest to sound unaffected.

“The longer we sit here, the more danger there is. You have friends...Marjorie Houston and Lisa Lucas. They also know Allard. Do they know where he is? I’m sure they are in just as much danger as you. While you sit here with me keeping me from bringing this to Allard, I’m sure they are being hunted.”

“Hunted by who? What are you talking about?”

Donald Kind cleared his throat loudly. The Female Agent pointed to the list of questions. Kind gave a nod to the invisible people behind the two-way mirror. It was a directive.

How did you get on the flight?

“You don’t really want to ask that question. You want to know about your friends, the ones that also know Allard.” Herman said calmly.

“Sir, you said you would cooperate if we brought her in. This is not cooperation.” The Female Agent barked.

"I said I would only talk when Michelle Bonds was here." Herman's eyes glared at her. His expression was icy and dismissive.

"You..." The Female Agent began.

"...Were on the flight. Can I ask..." Michelle interrupted and tried to stay with the interrogation.

"If I explained it, you wouldn't understand...or you wouldn't believe. Well, *they* wouldn't. Something tells me you would, Ms. Bonds."

"So tell me."

"What was the message he gave you?" Herman surveyed the room.

"A message? You mean Allard gave me a message? Well, he told me something, but I don't think it was meant for you."

"All messages are meant for me. I'm the courier. Every thing delivered comes from me." Herman shot back dutifully.

"He asked ME to deliver this message." Michelle felt she was finally gaining the upper hand.

"Did you?"

"Excuse me?"

"Allard told you to deliver a message. Did you indeed deliver it?"

"I've had it with the riddles!" Douglas yelled. "Lock him up in the holding cell. We'll put him in front of the judge first thing. I hope you've enjoyed playing your little game. Now it's my turn!"

The TSA guards reached for the chains and began to undo them. Several agents in the room covered their weapons with their hands.

"You didn't deliver the message because I am the intended recipient." The guards unshackled Herman from the table and the chair. "May I have my message?" The guards lifted him to his feet. His hands clutched the bag.

"He said..." Michelle thought. "He told me to tell them..."

"Them?" Herman listened as the room became chilly.

"The losers. He said to tell the losers, that they attacked him and he wiped their slate clean. He said he is a soldier and he will continue to fight." Michelle shouted over the sound of the chains being collected.

"Well...I have my answer and my message." Herman extended his hands with the bag in them. "Here you are."

Everyone in the room shifted their eyes toward Michelle. A guard reached to grab the bag and without warning, Herman's shackled hands smashed his nose clearly flat. Blood exploded across the wall as the other guards tackled Herman to the floor. Guns were drawn. A commotion ensued. Michelle felt a large hand grab her elbow and she was tugged through a back door into another room. There were screams, grunts, moans and the clicks of weapons being cocked filling her ears. The door closed behind her and soon the noise was broadcast through speakers. She was on the other side of the double mirror. There were cameras and recording devices with technicians and other observers. Through the glass she saw the guards having more than their fair share of trouble subduing Herman.

"That's not necessary. Why didn't you just let me talk to him?"

"This has been going on for hours." The Female Agent yelled over the noise.

The technicians were yelling and screaming at what they saw on the screens and through the mirror. Michelle tried her hardest to get closer to the glass when a uniformed guard pushed her back and covered her with his body. There was a loud explosive sound followed by a fierce bright light. Michelle heard the sound of glass shattering and heat on her body. Then she fell. There was weight pushing her towards the floor and all went black.

"If you think we're going down there, you're crazier than I think." Jury shouted down to The Homeless Man.

"Don't make me come back up to get you. I'll make it all very not nice if I do." He was stern and very believable.

Quickly, the quiet street was disturbed by a screeching sound, sirens and police lights filled the sky. In the wisp of moments, three police squad cars converged on the sidewalk. Officers jumped from cars with their guns drawn and pointed at The Homeless Man. There were commands of "raise your hands" and "freeze". The Homeless Man was soon the center point of a broken semicircle of police officers. More sirens could be heard rushing towards them. However, Lisa and Jury did not relax nor did they feel relieved. They had seen some strange things in recent memory and they learned never to count their chickens early. The Homeless Man did not follow the policemen's directives. In fact, he hadn't stopped staring up at Lisa and Jury. There were more shouts of "raise your hands" and threats of shooting, but none were obeyed by him.

"Stop shouting and shoot that sonuvabitch!" Jury screamed as neighbors had begun to peak through windows and blinds.

A taser arrow shot from an officer's gun and imbedded itself just below The Homeless Man's skin. They saw him jerk slightly with the pulse then he pulled the arrow from his arm, annoyed. He turned towards the officers and a rousing amount of commands were shouted. He raised his hands high above his head.

Lisa saw a large cube truck approaching the scene at a high rate of speed. Behind it were three black SUVs. On the door of each vehicle was the Scilymax logo.

"Here comes the cavalry." Lisa huffed sarcastically.

The Homeless Man slowly approached the police officers with his hands raised. The officers approached him with measured steps. His lips were moving rapidly, but Lisa couldn't make out one intelligible word. Her experience taught her it wasn't a good thing when crazy people mumbled to themselves.

The Scilymax Field Captain hopped out of one of the SUVs as his men followed and began gearing up at the back of the cube truck. The Field Captain introduced himself to the police captain and explained why they were there.

"Watch his hands! His hands!" Jury yelled.

There was steam rising from the man's hands. They looked withered and dead like those on a corpse. The police officers looked confused. The Police Captain took steps toward The Homeless Man and was held back by the Field Captain.

"Cover!" Yelled The Field Captain as all of his men stopped what they were doing and jumped behind the cube truck. The Field Captain pulled the Police Captain down behind a squad car just as The Homeless Man dropped his hands. A sandy mist exploded from them. It hit the police officers hard. Within seconds they had all fallen to the ground. Their bodies were emaciated. The Homeless Man's mouth hadn't stopped reciting his incantation. He watched the officers as they curled in pain.

Lisa felt a tug on her arm as she stared frozen with fear. Jury had pulled her up nearly an entire flight of stairs before she realized she was running. After three more flights, she looked down to see the strike team advancing from behind the cube truck fully geared in all black with large helmets fitted with gas masks. They looked like an alien force of sinister warriors.

The impact of concussion grenades nearly knocked Jury from the fire escape. Lisa caught her by her elbow and whisked her back to her feet. They saw The Homeless Man clutching himself amongst the smoke and being covered with a large tarp made of a shimmering metal.

By the time they had reached Lisa's window, the strike team had loaded their cargo into the back of the cube truck and was checking vitals on the police officers lying on the ground.

Jury couldn't stop her hands from shaking. Lisa was slipped into a cotton sweat suit. There were firm knocks at the door. Not a second later, the knocks were more forceful.

"I can't move. I can't move!" Jury mumbled.

"Grab your EEB and let's go." The Field Captain said in a huff when Lisa opened the door. Lisa pointed to a small black satchel sitting in the foyer. He reached down and picked it up. "Where's Dr. Houston?"

"She's sitting on the bed. She needs a minute." Lisa tried to block his way, but he pushed passed her. Moments later he returned with Jury slung over his shoulder like a wardrobe bag.

"Let's move." He said.

Lisa locked the door behind them as they marched to the elevator.

"Why is he carrying you?" Lisa asked Jury as her head bounced up and down with each of his labored steps.

"I told him the only way I was leaving was if he picked me up and carried me and his crazy ass did!"

"There's no time for games. The individual we picked up outside." The Field Captain began.

"Oh you picked him up too?" Jury said.

"He killed part of your security team, Dr. Houston. You're lucky we were able to get here when we did. We were mobilized for a call in North Carolina, but were sent here in emergency."

"North Carolina?" Lisa fumbled as she pressed the elevator down button.

"Was it for Michelle Bonds?" Jury's head popped up.

"Can you please get your big ass off his shoulder!?" Lisa shouted.

"No, he's carrying me all the way to the truck." Jury shouted stubbornly back to Lisa.

"I believe the name was Bonds." The Field Captain said. Jury leapt off his shoulder just as the elevator doors opened.

"What!?" Jury huffed.

"Is she ok?" Lisa asked.

"We were told the situation was past critical." He responded.

"What does that mean? Can you stop speaking GI Joe and TELL us something!?" Lisa held the door open refusing to get in with the others.

"I understand Ms. Bonds was taken off site to meet with a person of interest. At the offsite there was some kind of explosion. She's missing so we're sending a small remote team to her residence. Please, Dr. Lucas, you have to step onto the elevator." He tugged at Lisa's jacket leading her on to the elevator.

"I'll radio the teams down there to get an update as soon as we've lifted off."

"Where the hell are you taking us?"

"Only the pilot has that info, but I'm told it's safe and secure."

As the elevator descended, Lisa had the strange sensation things weren't going to get better.

Michelle didn't have to open her eyes to know where she was. The scent was unmistakable. It smelled like disinfectant soap. The temperature was just under comfortable with a slight chill in the air. The blanket over her body was thin. Her back and her ass were touching twenty-five thread count sheets. She opened her eyes to see institutional colored walls, an IV on a stand and a heart monitor.

"I'm sick and tired of waking up after the action happens." She mumbled to herself.

“At least you’re awake.” A soft voice startled her. ”The rest of the people in that room weren’t as lucky.” She saw The Nurse making note of the readouts on the monitors.

“Are they dead?” Michelle spoke slowly as she mentally tried to categorize her injuries, but found none.

“A lot of concussions, a couple of comas, some are going into surgery to remove glass, internal bleeding, broken bones and then there’s you...” The Nurse nodded sarcastically.

“What about me?” Michelle sat up in the bed. The Nurse helped her by adjusting the bed with the controls.

“Usually, I let the doctor tell you the specific diagnosis, but you came in pretty much, just sleeping. I think the guard landing on you may have just knocked the wind out of you. He definitely took the brunt of the glass. It’s none of my business, but I think you may have a nice little law suit against the company that made that boiler. That thing exploded right under y’all feet. Hell, you can sue the government too.”

“I just thank God that I’m alive.” Michelle said trying her best to digest the cover up story in contrast with the real one. If a boiler had exploded, it was sitting in the middle of that interrogation room.

"That's one way to look at it. The other way is someone needs to pay you for your lost personal items, risk of internal injuries and couple hours of inconvenience."

"Couple hours?"

"Yeah, you've only been here about two hours. I thought you'd sleep until at least seven, but you're resting... Your stuff is over here on the chair." The Nurse pointed to a pile of things on the chair against the far wall. "They cut your clothes off, but they're here and your purse and your shoes are OK and this other bag. I'd have thought this would've burned up, but I guess it's sturdier than it looks." The Nurse held up the burlap bag with the twine twig handle. "Your brother is coming to check on you. We asked him to bring you some clothes over for when you get released."

"You talked to my brother?" Michelle stared at the burlap bag.

"Yeah, he sounded worried and asked where he could come get you. He should be here any minute."

"From New York?" Michelle turned to The Nurse confused.

"No, at your house. We called there and he said he'd come right over. He sounded sick with worry. Maybe that bump on your head was a little worse than the docs thought." The Nurse said turning to leave. "You just get some rest. I'll get someone in to see you. Maybe we can let you go in a couple hours." The Nurse closed the door behind her.

Before the latch could fully click, Michelle had grabbed the phone and started dialing. All she heard was the recording telling her that service had not yet been connected for the room. She jumped out of the bed ripped off the heart monitor wires and dragged the IV stand over to her things. She rummaged through the plastic bag containing her purse and found her cell phone. She let out a sigh of relief when it turned on with no problems. She scrolled through the address book looking for one number.

He was rummaging through Michelle's clothes attempting to pack a bag of things that would look convincingly like something a brother brings to his sister. To the layman, the bag contents looked exactly like what it was, a hodgepodge of clothing. He closed the irregularly large bag and limped from the bedroom down the steps. His frail limbs barely held themselves together especially with the added weight of the bag. As he reached the bottom floor, he spotted two men approaching the front door holding machine guns ahead of them.

Stumbling backward, he limped quickly toward the back door where he had entered the house. A bright light gleamed into his face from beyond the windows.

"There's a subject inside!" He heard a voice warn. He turned and headed back toward the stairs. There was a banging at the front door.

"Open up, step out with your hands raised high!" The voice commanded.

He limped up the steps ditching the bag halfway. The bag rumbled as it hit the steps on its tumble downward. He wheezed as he stumbled through the house trying to maintain a mellow head. Bad things happened when he wasn't mellow.

The doors broke on their hinges as the mini Scilymax strike team stormed into the house. Even with their small numbers, the team was incredibly efficient. They cleared the bottom floor of the house and were stepping over the luggage and headed up the stairs in seconds. Their gun lights lit criss-cross patterns on the wallpaper as they swayed to and fro in search of the man. The team could only hear the sound of their mechanically enhanced gas masks as they cleared the rooms one by one. The silence was broken by a loud clatter and crash of glass followed by a thud. The team focused on the room at the end of the hallway.

They approached slowly and once they were all carefully in position, they broke the door down with one thrust and held their weapons at the ready. The room was dark and quiet except for a wheezing sound. The Man lay on the floor, his chest heaved up and down heavily. They rushed over to him. His skin was an ashen grey. His jaundiced eyes rolled to the back of his head. His mouth gaped revealing a mouth full of rotten teeth and a blackened tongue. They checked his vitals and thought it best to put him on a stretcher and get him medical attention. As they loaded him into the back of their truck they asked him who he was. He called himself Dezi, said he was Michelle's brother and was sick, very sick. The rest was inaudible, but because he seemed so ill the team left their masks on as they drove him to the hospital.

The madeira red painted Rolls Royce Phantom sped across the tarmac slowing easily as it arrived in the private hanger. The driver, a tall European with a long nose and dark brown hair, stepped out quickly and opened the back door. A high-heeled shoe with red bottoms, Christian Louboutin's, gracefully eased to the ground, followed by the other foot. The Driver extended his hand helping the occupant from the car. She wore a black form fitting high-waist skirt which helped show off her small waist and curvy hips. Wolford tights covered her legs, but her legs were so soft and smooth, she could go without them. Her button down shirt was a crisp bright white and just enough buttons were open to reveal the top of her black La Perla bra. Her skin was a copper hue. Her lips were plump. Her long black hair flowed easily with the breeze. Her eyes were accentuated by a smoky eye shadow, which gave the white of her eyes an even brighter glow. She was pretty and on first look had no discernible nationality, but was closer to Hispanic or East Indian with a dash of African-American and a taste of Asian.

The Driver popped the trunk and loaded two sizable Gucci trunks onto the baggage handler's handcart. There was a man waiting by the private jet with an annoyed look. He had been waiting much longer than he expected. When she turned to him she flashed a smile. As she quickly approached, her scent caught the breeze and filled his nostrils. Her smile erased any attitude he held onto.

"Sono così spiacente per rendergli l'aspettare me." She said in perfect Italian. *I am so sorry for making you wait for me.*

"Nessun problema." He said with an American accent. *No problem.*

"An American?" She nodded. "I apologize for keeping you. I really appreciate your sharing your flight with me. My pilot got sick, he says the flu, I think he had too many sips of the vino and is praying to the porcelain god."

"Let me take that." He offered his hand to her large Gucci handbag.

"No. That's fine. This is just my personal stuff." She extended her hand. "My name is Alala."

He bent and kissed it.

"A gentleman. I'll be sure to thank Jake for putting me on a flight with such a mannered man. He was the only person I could think of who may have had a flight ready to go at such short notice. I didn't know you were waiting until we got caught in that traffic. Mr..."

"I'm sorry." He was mesmerized both by how beautiful she was and by how she name-dropped the Scilymax CEO's name. He had only called the CEO by his full first name "Jacob" or the more formal "Mr. Mora". "I'm Dustin Carver." He held her hand as she boarded the Scilymax designed and manufactured Sci-Jet 9.

The two were comfortably sitting in leather captain's chairs with their choice of wine when the plane had begun its taxi.

"No matter how many times I do this, private or commercial, this is the one part that I can never get used to." He said as the plane picked up speed and began to rumble down the runway.

"Don't worry." She put her hand on top of his. "I won't let anything happen to you." She sensed his pulse quicken. Tapping the top of his hand, she changed the subject. "How do you know Jake anyway?"

"He's my boss. I'm an executive for Scilymax Corporation." Dustin replied holding his breath as the plane began to lift from the runway.

"Oh, so should I call him something more formal to you? I don't want to get him in any trouble. You guys practically own a piece of every industry, don't you?"

"We haven't gone into comic books just yet, but if you have any ideas..." Dustin turned on the charm.

"I'm surprised. There's the obvious medical research stuff, the government engineering projects, cosmetics, manufacturing, you guys own a portion of a media conglomerate, right?" He nodded uncomfortably yet she continued. "Foods."

"Food processing." He corrected her with a bit of sarcasm.

"And you have all of those Scilymax soldiers fighting terrorists in secret wars all over the globe. Did I miss anything?"

"I don't think so. The way you listed all of that stuff it seems impossible not to work for us. Yet, you don't. What do you do?"

"Actually, you guys are one of my biggest clients. I'm a weapons engineer. I designed three or four of your military products."

"Really?" He thought it sexy that such a beautiful woman was smart and knew her guns. "Which ones?"

"I don't think I'm at liberty to say, but if it looks and works like something out of Star Wars, then I may have designed it."

"You a Star Wars fan?"

"Nothing can overcome the power of the dark side." She imitated Darth Vadar's voice.

"Sounds ominous." He laughed.

"Which division do you work in?" She crossed her legs and tipped her wine glass back draining it of its contents.

"Research and development. The medical division."

"So you're the one I'll blame when I'm sitting in a restaurant and my clone walks in looking thinner and sexier than me and can go all day on a small side salad and a glass of water." She pushed his arm playfully.

He felt warm where she touched him.

"I'm not sure there could be a better version of you." His words trailed off embarrassed at how the wine had relaxed him.

"You're sweet. If you guys really are making clones over there, I'll have plenty of space age guns for them to shoot."

"If there are clones, I'm not saying there are, but if there were, I work in medical research so we'd want a clone to help make cures, repair illnesses...Parkinson's, Lou Gehrig's, that kind of thing. I'm not into building super soldiers."

"Shame." Alala took a sip from her glass. "I think a super solider could be interesting."

"And lucrative for you." Dustin took a deep breath as the plane hit some turbulence.

"Maybe, but everything I design I try to keep simple. You know what my favorite weapon of all time is?"

"I don't like to judge people's weapons of choice." Dustin said.

"The slingshot." She said. "Simple, effective design, range is good and it's easy to reload and unload."

"Anything good enough for David is good enough for me."

"You religious?" She said kicking off her shoes and stretching her legs out.

“I’m a believer.” He said.

“So am I...” She raised her glass and the attendant immediately approached to refill it. “I believe you’re going to be on my side by the time we finish this six hour flight.”

“You’re that convincing?”

“I am.”

“Then I think I’ll have some more wine as well.” He said as the attendant refilled his glass.

Lisa sat in the back of the SUV feeling like a head of state. There were the accompanying two trucks, one led them and the other followed them. The armored and armed security sat in the seats in front and behind her and loud sirens cleared the pedestrians as they fled the scene. She realized, the discomfort she felt on her leg was her cell phone jamming against the bruise caused by her staircase fall. She quietly slipped the phone from her pocket and pressed the power button. The power-on sound was muffled against her leg. Looking at the screen, she scrolled through the numbers in her phonebook. The Field Captain’s earpiece began to crackle.

“Yes...what?...you sure?” He craned his neck behind him to look at the passengers. “Who just turned on a mobile phone?" He said as serious as cancer. Everyone looked around at each other. Lisa shoved her phone under her thigh concealing the lit display. "Dr. Lucas? Dr. Houston? We're tracking cell phone network activity in the area. We don't want our position compromised. Which one of you has a cell phone on?"

"We don't have our cell phones on." Jury said. "Why don't you stop being paranoid? We're the ones that are supposed to be scared and you're sitting there..."

Ring

Ring

Ring

There was a muffled sound coming from Lisa's thigh. A security agent reached under her leg, grabbed the phone and tossed it to The Field Captain.

"Don't you ever put your hands on me, again" Lisa pointed her finger in the agent's face. The Field Captain looked at Lisa with a disappointed expression. Lisa looked back at him with fire in her eyes. "Can you at least answer it? I was trying to call Michelle. That could be her!"

The Field Captain quickly ripped the battery from the cell phone, cracked the door on the SUV and dropped both of them out.

"What the fuck are you crazy!!?? If Michelle is out there, she's going to call us first. That was our best way to get in touch with her!" Lisa screamed at the top of her lungs.

"If her phone has been compromised then that's the easiest way for someone to find you two. You've already had one smoldering freak of the week try to attack you. Your friend in North Carolina may have had a second. I cannot risk you or my team. There's an assault team down there. IF she's found, then they'll tell us directly. Dr. Houston hand over your cell phone." The Field Captain ordered.

Jury gave him a sideways glance then rummaged through her purse, retrieved it and tossed the phone at The Field Captain's face. He caught it just before it hit his forehead.

"Thank you." He removed its battery and disposed of it through the open truck door.

The team arrived at JFK airport clearing security through a side guard post. The trucks drove swiftly to a group of military hangars at the far end. Lisa and Jury were daunted by the commercial jetliners landing and lifting off nearby as their SUV convoy raced across the tarmac. The SUV drove into a large military hanger bearing the Scilymax logo. Jury craned her neck to see the humongous cargo plane that occupied it. The SUVs parked alongside it, like ants next to an eagle. They hopped out of the trucks and rushed toward the airliner. A brawny man with cut off sleeves carried Lisa's bag. His arms looked too big to be contained by normal clothes. The Field Captain led them to the back of the plane.

"Dr. Houston your emergency evacuation bag has already been secured from your apartment and loaded onboard. I'm happy you followed instructions and kept it exactly where we suggested." He said as he made hand signals to several members of the team.

"So you guys just ran up in my place, huh. I hope you wiped your feet, the carpet is expensive." Jury said. She had started to lose patience with them even though they were the ones that saved her and Lisa's life.

Lisa, Jury, The Field Captain and three others from the security team boarded the plane. The once hollow cargo area contained several large crates. Lisa recognized them as supply crates. There were also some shipping containers and one fairly large container labeled "fragile: live specimen." Her stomach dropped. She stopped in her tracks.

"Where are we going?" Lisa turned to The Field Captain.

"I told you, I don't know that. Only the pilot does." The Field Captain checked his watch. He was obviously under time constraints.

"Ask him." Jury looked over Lisa's shoulder.

"Have a seat on the second level. I'll go up to the pilot." The Field Captain huffed.

The second level of the plane was impressively luxurious. It had none of the hollow bare attributes military planes were usually known to have. Lisa brushed her hand across the leather captain's chairs and eyed the large LCD screen that broadcasted a security camera of the cargo being loaded onto the plane. The onboard entertainment system was impressive.

"They're sending us to another facility." Lisa sat down. Her stomach bubbled. She couldn't imagine months more in the Antarctic somewhere.

Jury rummaged through a kitchen area, pulled a bottle of whiskey from the cabinets and fetched two glasses from the counter holder. She dropped them on the table in front of Lisa and poured both of them a full glass. She sat the bottle between the two glasses. They sat staring at the liquor. On the screen, the cargo door began to close. They could feel the plane's mechanical wizardry rumbling. They felt the plane shake as the door closed. The lights in the cargo area turned on. Everything on the screen was bathed in red light. Jury picked up her glass. She sniffed the contents. It was strong.

"A toast?" Jury raised her glass.

“To being safe and yet another adventure.” Lisa said staring at the brown liquid. They clinked their glasses and took mouth-numbing sips. Lisa sat her glass down and bowed her head. “And to Michelle, God willing she’s safe.” The two of them silently prayed together.

The Field Captain stepped into the threshold holding a piece of paper. He stood quietly in the doorway watching them pray. It would be in poor taste to interrupt them with a question during such a private moment. He turned and walked down to the lower level. The co-pilot would only provide the information written on the piece of paper. It was a code The Field Captain hadn’t seen before.

TF-619R

Michelle sat on the hospital floor staring at her cell phone. Lisa didn’t answer. It had rung then gone straight to voicemail. Now she was along again. She hated to be alone. Her room door burst open. The Nurse scanned the room, saw her on the floor and ran to her.

“Ms. Bonds, what are you doing?” The Nurse chided.

“I needed to make a call.” Michelle stood gripping the back of her hospital gown to conceal herself.

"You NEED to rest. I told you we have your brother coming to see you." The Nurse said helping Michelle back to the bed then resetting the heart monitor. She reattached Michelle's finger and chest sensors.

"About that...can you give me a warning before you let him in? Just let him wait out in the waiting room or something while I get my head together." Michelle began to plan her escape even as she lied to The Nurse.

"Definitely."

The emergency room doors slid open quickly and in ran four men wearing all black with masks on. They pushed another man on a stretcher. The Team Leader tore off his mask and shouted for help. He described the man's health needs to the head nurse as a resident and an intern ran in to help. The hospital staff began working on the sick man inside a small curtained area with the security team watching closely. The doctors preferred to have more space, but they knew that the logo on the teams' uniforms gave them carte blanche in many places. They especially observed open permissions in a hospital built with money provided by people that sent paperwork bearing the same logo.

The man, they called Dezi was definitely sick. His heart rate was extremely low. His skin was thick and it had taken an intern several tries before a syringe could be inserted into his arm. Immediately, Dezi began to shake. He was losing his cool. He didn't like the pain of the syringe; the excitement was too much for him. As the blood tube was inserted into the syringe, the intern backed away quickly.

"DOCTOR!" She squealed and pointed.

"What?" The Doctor was sick and tired of squeamish interns. He turned to the tube and saw it slowly filling with a jet-black liquid. He squinted his eyes trying to readjust their weariness to what he was seeing.

Dezi began to cough loudly trying to clear his throat. The anesthesiologist braced his mouth open attempting to intubate him with a breathing tube when a thick black liquid shot out over the medical staff. The Scilymax team jumped backwards on guard and watched as the medical staff writhed on the floor in seizures. The Team Leader quickly covered his face with his mask.

"Subdue him and lock down this area. No one gets out." He shouted as Dezi rose to a sitting position and glared at him.

CHAPTER THREE

THE REZ NOTIFICATION

Michelle hadn't realized she was sleeping until a large bang woke her. She lunged forward in the hospital bed and screamed at the top of her lungs. A man dressed in black army fatigues, body armor and a horribly technical mask was standing at the foot of the bed. His machine gun dangled on his side but was held close by his right hand. He shook her foot with his left hand.

"Ms. Bonds? Are you Michelle Bonds?" His voice projected a muffled metallic hollowness as it escaped the mask.

"NO!" She screamed in fright. He looked confused. She backed away towards the head of the bed as he pulled her chart from the foot of it. His eyes darted toward the door. He too was scared. He was the one holding an automatic machine gun. What was he scared of?

"Ms. Bonds, you have to come with me now!" He yelled tossing the chart over his shoulder

Her eyes glanced to her belongings sitting on the chair. Her purse, the odd burlap bag and...where were her clothes?

"They gave you a sedative. I know you don't feel like yourself, but it's time to go...NOW!"

Michelle recognized the symbol on the patch on his chest. It was the letter "S", very ornate. A logo. She was wearing her cut and torn clothes. How did they get on? The door to her room burst open. He spun on his heels to angle his weapon, but lowered it immediately when The Nurse came in yelling. Michelle had seen The Nurse yell before recently. It all was coming back to her now. Michelle had put on her clothes as best she could and was calling a cab when The Nurse had come in telling her she couldn't be discharged just yet. The two of them had a few words and The Nurse seemed to acquiesce. As she walked out, she'd pressed the button on Michelle's I.V. several times in quick succession. Sonuvabitch she'd sedated her!

CRACK!

The sound was muffled, but audible. The Nurse collapsed to the floor with a thud, her nose oozed blood. The soldier stood above her, his gun butt angled towards its victim. There were voices crackling like a robotic fire. They were coming the open walkie-talkie line was on his waist.

"Let's go! Move on it now!"

"Third floor is still clear. Staircase B. Repeat staircase B. I fired staircases A and C."

"Second floor is comped. I'm coming up!" Another voice screamed

"Where's the package? Get the fucking package. This whole wing is a wash."

The Soldier turned to Michelle, raised his mask and spoke quickly. "Ms. Bonds, we are taking you out of here, but I can not carry you. If I carry you, it only leaves me one hand and I need both to protect us." He lifted his gun. "So, grab your shit now or get laid out like Nurse Nightingale cuz I'm not hear to fucking die."

Michelle jumped to her feet and nearly sank to her knees. Her legs felt numb. She looked up and saw a surgical mask hurtling towards her, she bobbled it with her rubber band fingers and squeezed it for dear life..

"Put that on...I have the package. We're coming out." The Soldier spoke into his wrist as he replaced his mask. .

She put it on as instructed but felt silly as she tied big pretty bows in the back of her head with the ties. It was the only way she knew how to tie.

The door exploded open eliciting screams from Michelle and a raised weapon from The Soldier. Another soldier barreled into the room, his weapon held high.

"We're coming out." The First Soldier shouted to him.

"No, we're coming in. He's headed towards us."

"Who? What?" Michelle's head cleared quickly.

She'd seen these types of soldiers panic before. She'd seen these types of soldiers before on Masson Island at The Country Cage. Only one person could cause this. Allard had arrived here and he was raising hell.

"Clear." The Second Soldier shouted into his wrist. There was gunfire in the hallway. The First Soldier ran to the chair with Michelle's things and tossed them to the floor. Her mind in a haze, she ran to collect them. She hadn't noticed that he was lifting the heavy chair above his head. As she reached the floor and collected the two bags, she heard a loud bang and the chair came crashing to the floor next to her. The window had a large spider web of cracks spreading the length of it.

"CLEAR!" She heard as yet another soldier entered the room.

Thud! Crack!

The Soldier had smashed the chair against the window again. This time, he held it aloft and swung again without dropping it.

SMASH!

There was a tinkling sound of small glass fragments that had fallen to the floor, but the window still held together albeit weakened in the middle.

"What are you doing?" Another voice shouted.

She looked around to another soldier in the room, The Team Leader. His mask was smeared with a black liquid that had seemingly been wiped off haphazardly.

"Move." He shouted. The Soldier dropped the chair and blocked Michelle. A trio of shots rang out exploding the window and letting in the chilly late night air.

In seconds, Team Leader and the first soldier were tying ropes to spikes while the other two watched the door. The spikes went into the wall, the ropes thrown out of the window.

"Recon!" Team Leader commanded The First Soldier who fastened a hook to the rope, jumped into the windowsill with his back to the world and jumped. Before she could scream she heard the rope whiz, it tightened and the pressure from the rope on the spike pulled some of the plaster off of the wall.

"You don't expect me too..." Michelle's voice quaked.

"Stop! Don't move!" She heard someone scream.

An ashen colored man was looking through the glass on the door. It was Dezi. He looked horribly ill, but stared with intent at them.

"This won't be comfortable, but it won't last long." Team Leader had said to her before throwing a wide belt around her hips. He pulled her close and dragged her to the window. "Step up!" He shouted as he hoisted her into the windowsill. She gripped the sides, her hands held for dear endangered life. "We're going down together. Do not let go of me. Hold me under the armpits like a bear hug and lock your fingers. You understand?"

He didn't hear her unsure response because the sounds of gunfire erupted. Dezi stood just inside the room. He was pushed back against the door. Bullet holes exposed a slick black liquid leaking from his body.

"I need to speak with you." Dezi spoke to Michelle who stood there dumbfounded.

"Raise your hands above your head." One of the soldiers shouted.

Team Leader hopped in the windowsill with the rope in one hand. Michelle felt crowded, but happy she had company up there. Pulling the belt tight around her hips, he smashed their genitals together and clipped the belt to the rope. They were squeezed tight as if sharing one pair of pants. His size was more obvious to her now. She was nearly face to face with his armpits. How was she to bear hug him all the way up there?

BOOM! BOOM! BOOM!

Shots echoed. Team Leader blocked her view, but she could tell there was commotion happening in the room. She felt a push and found herself quickly spun around with her back to the soldiers and the sickly man.

"Clear!" The Soldier's voice vibrated from Team Leader's earpiece so loudly she could hear him perfectly.

"Hold on!" He shouted.

She felt a tug and they were falling from the window. She heard his heavy breathing, as he seemed to be timing something then she felt his arms tighten and the two of them jerked to a stop.

"Arghhhhhhh!" He screamed in her ear and she had started to feel guilty about how much she weighed. "Hold!" He screamed through clinched teeth, she squeezed and they began to fall downward again repelling down the side of the building. They stopped hard. This time he muzzled a loud grunt.

"Don't let him stand there too long. Pin him with fire and get out." Team Leader shouted into his wrist. "Do not let that black shit get on you. Do not!"

Michelle looked up realizing the last instructions were for her. She had been holding her face against his chest and only inches above her, near his collar, was the black liquid. She pushed her head away from him and felt the wind rush across her face as they plummeted again. Gunfire erupted from above them.

The ground moved closer to them, faster and faster without a stop. Her eyes glanced up to his face. His eyes were intent; looking at the window they'd jumped from. They jerked for a brief stop and plummeted again before the force could tear his shoulder from the socket. She could tell they were closer to the ground. Then they stopped about eight feet from impact.

"Got you Cap'n."

The First Soldier held Team Leader by the legs and lowered the two of them to the ground slowly.

"Clear!" They both yelled, as Michelle was un-buckled from the belt. There was more gunfire from above.

"You will not stop this. I need to speak with her." Dezi's voice was broadcasting over the walkie-talkie. They could hear a tussle and more gunfire.

"Get back Joe. I have the shot." A voice yelled.

"No you don't!"

"I have it!"

"Go!"

Michelle looked around for help, but the grounds looked deathly quiet. She couldn't fathom such mayhem and not one police car. Not one officer. She peered into the emergency room window and saw them. There were bodies...bodies laying everywhere. Bodies that had fallen in their tracks like they had been robots turned off. Some of them had pools of black liquid around their faces and on the floors.

The sound of the zip line brought her attention back above them. A soldier was repelling quickly. He was yelling into the walkie.

"Joe, concussion grenade! Grenade! Grenade!"

"No tell him to jump!" The First Soldier shouted.

It was then that Michelle realized that she heard him through the walkie. He was now thirty yards away in the middle of a clearing, looking into the sky.

"Noooooooo!" The screams erupted from the walkie just as they saw the soldier fly through the window and hit another soldier as he fell. The two of them plummeted to the ground with a hard thud.

"Go with him." Team Leader pointed Michelle in the direction of the clearing as he ran to check his men.

Michelle paused for the slightest of moments until she saw Dezi in the window above her.

"Where is Allard?" He shouted. His voice wavered and cracked.

Team leader exploded the side of the building with rapid fire forcing Dezi to cover his face from the flying bullets, brick and dust. Michelle had no sooner made it to the clearing than the other soldier ran passed her. He helped Team Leader drag his comrades toward the clearing. There was an echo of thunder rushing towards them. A bright light erupted and soon a Scilymax HBR Hummingbird helicopter descended on the clearing. Michelle crouched as flat as she could, holding her hands on her head like they do in the movies. The soldiers stood upright, comrades at their feet, weapons pointing at the building. A solider hopped from the helicopter and dragged one of the injured into it.

She watched Team Leader keep guard as they loaded the other injured man into the aircraft. Over the low thunder, Michelle heard gunfire. Dezi was falling from the window feet first...or had he jumped? She got her answer when he landed in a crumpled heap then rose slowly to his feet and limped toward them. His cold dark stare iced her spine. He stared at her trying to see what she looked like, but the mask prevented it. She felt a hand on her shoulder and jumped in fear. The solider from the helicopter pulled her toward the aircraft. She turned to face Dezi one last time. He limped as he shielded his face from the gunfire. He glimpsed the burlap bag in her hand and stopped in his tracks. The little color left in his face evaporated.

Team Leader stopped firing, looked over his shoulder at what caught Dezi's gaze and cocked and eyebrow.

"Get your ass in the copter!" He yelled as he backed toward her. His comrade fired two rounds that seemed to be swallowed by Dezi's body.

Michelle had heard the term "stuck like a deer in headlights" before, but this was the first time she felt she really understood it. Dezi was staring at her...not her...the bag, as if he had seen a ghost. She felt a silence wash over her. She was moving in slow motion. She ripped the mask from her face and tossed it at the ground beneath her, glared at him and boarded The Hummingbird. Finally, the soldier and Team Leader jumped on board and closed the door leaving Dezi alone in the clearing. The Hummingbird

Captain raised a fist to insure everyone was buckled securely.

Suddenly with a speed and agility not seemingly possible for his sickened frame, Dezi leapt forward and rammed the copter with his body. His face pressed against the glass. He said something. Michelle could only make out one word "Allard". The pilot dropped his hand and The Hummingbird shot up into the sky with tremendous speed. The G-force pressed Michelle hard against the seat. Through the window, she could see sirens, trucks and a very large tractor-trailer speeding towards the hospital. The copter shot straight into the air like an elevator then stopped abruptly, coasted downward a few feet and shot forward. They were gone.

The cleaning crew gathered their stuff together in the special hangar at New Jersey's Teterboro airport waiting for their next job. All of them had the work worn hands and expressions of "third world" workers except one. He was new to the group. The shift manager gave in to his pleading for a chance at a job after he'd offered to do one job for free. With the economy in the pisser, his eagerness was understandable, but his work had better been as energetic or he'd be sent with his dreadlocks packing.

Allard had the skill to convince souls, he was earnest and well meaning even when he wasn't honestly well meaning...especially when he wasn't honestly well meaning. However, his ability to know where souls were, the ones he was looking for in particular, was a God given gift.

Allard arranged the cleaning supplies in size order on the cart he was given. It was something to do with his hands before he truly had to use them. He watched the faces of the two other men on the clean up crew. They were illegal aliens here in America. He wouldn't have to worry too much about their eyewitness accounts. They would say just enough to seem as if they were cooperating, but not too much that they would be called to court to testify or to have their phony immigration papers scrutinized. They were well versed in reprisals and knew that snitches often found themselves on the business end of death dealing. They weren't the focus. The focus was landing on the runway.

The small jet eased into the hangar. Allard had been briefed in etiquette. Stay out of eyesight. Easy. Don't let the travelers see you looking at them. Perfect. Get on the plane quietly, clean thoroughly and leave immediately. Allard was sure he wouldn't clean anything, though he may have to get on the plane quietly and leave immediately after he was done. He stood huddled with his crew as he heard the door open and lock into place. There was only one car waiting, a red Rolls Royce and a driver that waited outside of it. There would be one passenger/victim and one driver to render unconscious. He found it odd that there were no security cameras inside the hangar, but knowing the secrecy by which the Scilymax executives flew; this was a blessing for them and him.

Allard joined the short convoy leading towards the plane. He pushed his small clean-up cart with one hand while the other adjusted his large hair net. The rough fabric of his grey jumpsuit swished and swashed as he walked. He dropped his head in a mellow meditation and conference. He always knew when the deed was done and this deed was as complete as could be. His hands flexed against the cart in preparation of the work that lay ahead of him. The convoy stopped just on the other side of the plane. He waited as the baggage handlers laid a set of trunks and one suitcase into the trunk of the car and disappeared. Finally someone descended the stairs. He peered just under the fuselage to see a pair of causal men's shoes and slacks. Slowly, he slid around the fuselage.

Dustin Carver's face was just as he had envisioned. His visions never failed him. Dustin was speaking to someone on the stairs. Was it the flight attendant? This crew was slated to fly back out immediately. Surely, she wouldn't be leaving the plane. Dustin raised his hand to the person. Was the flight attendant descending to handle business in the hangar? No. He couldn't understand this. This one didn't have the same aura as these souls. The woman's curvy legs descended the steps on tall heels. Her hips swayed and the wind caught her hair as she threw it over her shoulder with a whip of her head. It took less than a second. Allard ducked backward and hid behind the plane again. The other members of the cleaning convoy motioned for him to join them at their position, but he stood still hidden by the plane. It couldn't be. He peeked around the jet as Dustin and the woman chatted briefly outside the car. She put her hand on his shoulder and smiled. She laughed. Her flirtatious gaze melted Dustin with each second. It was indeed Alala.

Her presence had changed every nuance of the moment, of the day and of the entire situation. She stepped into the car followed by Dustin and The Driver closed the door. The cleaning crew walked, the leader doubled back, tapped Allard and woke him from his thoughts. Allard grabbed his cart, pushed it to the other side of the plane not once raising his head or revealing his face to Dustin or

Alala. Allard watched over his shoulder as the car pulled away.

If Alala was there and talking to Dustin Carver then it was pretty likely the others were here as well. Who were they talking to? Why the sudden movement? Was it even sudden? Had the game been played while he was in the tundra of the Antarctic? Definitely not. He would've received word in the desert. But with Alala there, he needed his things and added assistance. Luckily enough, he wasn't far from where he had to be to get it.

Lisa and Jury watched the small yacht speed back towards the cargo plane. The heat was overbearing and they had already shed their jackets on the ride across the water. Lisa stood on the pier searching across the blue water. It was hard to imagine a more perfect time for a vacation. If it hadn't been for the cargo plane rocking slowly off the coast, this island would have been the perfect island getaway. The cargo hold on the plane closed slowly as the security team loaded the last crate onto the boat. It was a grand fete of engineering. A water landing and unloading onto what could only be described as a speed ferry. The first trip on the boat held Lisa, Jury, the four-man security team and the supplies. The Leader of the security team, Lieutenant Wellspring and another soldier went back for the large container with all of the large red "Live Specimen" warnings on it.

Right now Lisa didn't care what was in the crate speeding back toward them. She was standing on a pier in the sun on a beautiful island somewhere off the coast of South America. The pier had the look of a makeshift island pier with rustic looking beams and worn boards, but like a Disney World attraction, beneath it all were large metal beams, titanium cables, joists and all of the engineering wizardry expected from Scilymax. Mirages and make believe were something Scilymax had become impressively adept at creating.

Lisa preferred to live in the moment. With the combination of The Sun, the water, the heat and the beautiful white sand beach she'd seen as they landed, she knew they were in paradise.

"Now..." Jury sighed. "Why do they say The Country Cage is the best facility? Cuz babyyyyy..."

"You know White people like to snowboard and ski and shit. This is where I want to be."

"Hell yeah." Jury watched as two security members loaded the supplies onto a skinny flatbed vehicle. They strapped in, pushed and stepped on bins and crates making sure there'd be space remaining for the large container headed their way.

"Hey, you're not putting my bag on that truck kicking it like you're doing that other stuff." Lisa shouted.

"No m'am." The agent responded. "You can take your bags with you in the other vehicle. This is only for the supplies and us."

Lisa drove the topless Jeep Wrangler with Jury sitting shotgun. They followed the small windy road around the island. They passed by beautiful lush palm trees, fantastic ocean views and small beach inlets as they sped to their destination. The only sign of other life were the flying fish that leapt from the water landing with a splash and the birds that hovered over the Jeep in anticipation of a morsel to eat from human's waste.

"I hope she's OK." Lisa broke the quiet.

"She is. Think positively. You see how these guys picked us up and swooooop shipped us off to sun and fun? I'm sure she's probably on her way here." Jury nodded.

"You're probably sure...?"

"I am sure. We're both sure." Jury reasserted herself then whispered, "What did he want? The guy in the apartment... How'd he find..? I think this Allard thing is a lot more complicated than Scilymax thought."

"I'm definitely sure of that." Lisa's eyes caught the pretty pink flowers along the water's edge and zoned out.

"The Hut" was modest in size compared to The Country Cage. The four-bedroom house was carved in the middle of lush vegetation with a beach bordering the back of it. Inside didn't have any of the extra amenities of The Country Cage. There was a comfortable living room with wicker furniture, a full kitchen with dining area and a den with a very expensive entertainment center.

Out back was a covered area with patio furniture surrounding a fire pit. The volleyball net and barbecue grill were unused. Lisa brushed her fingers across the wind chimes made from wood, twine and coconut husks. The sound emitted was a hollow peaceful clatter. She dropped her bag on the bed in one of the four master suites and eyed the jets on the Jacuzzi tub. From her window, she watched the soldiers descend a small ramp in the sand leading beneath the house. They rolled, carried and pushed crate after crate until the last one, the "live specimen" was unloaded.

"Lisa!" Jury's voice echoed up the stairs. "Lisa!" She didn't sound rushed, just in need of company.

Jury stood in the hallway holding the brown closet door open. Her face none too pleased.

"What's wrong?" Lisa glided down the steps huffing as she reached her friend.

"Look at this..." Jury pointed.

Lisa's eyebrow cocked as she slid to the door and looked in. It was an elevator. Lisa looked back at Jury.

"I knew this shit was too cool to be true." Jury fumed.

The two of them stepped in. There were only two buttons, "main" and "LL". Jury measured the distance between the two buttons with her fingers. "Main" was a good seven inches above "LL". Lisa let out a sigh and pressed the LL button. The doors closed slowly and the elevator descended swiftly. The ride took longer than both thought it would, long enough for the two of them to give each other a furtive glance.

"Ohhhh shit." Lisa whispered when the elevator slowed to a stop then dipped another three feet.

The doors opened slowly revealing a near doppelganger of their labs at The Country Cage. The two stepped out and walked slowly down the hallway toward the lab doors.

"Did we just take an elevator to the Antarctic?" Jury shook her head bewildered.

“More like The Twilight Zone.” Lisa grumbled.

There was a commotion just beyond the lab doors. Before Lisa could push them open, Jury held her back with her forearm.

“If we push open this door and they have Allard in a tube on the other side promise me you’ll turn right around and demand they get us the hell up outta here.” Jury said.

Lisa shrugged her shoulders. “You just promise you won’t blast him out of the tube with a shotgun again.”

“True...”

The lab was a near exact duplicate of The Country Cage with the exception of large metal closets on the left side of the expanded area of the room. There were computer consoles on each closet. One of the soldiers filled the supplies into the closets like a vending machine while the other three connected wires, hoses and metal bars to what looked like a stainless steel deep freezer. The deep freeze was in too prominent position for Lisa’s intuition. It was almost as prominent as Allard’s tube. The size was much bigger.

“Doctors.” The agent unloading the supplies called to them. Once he had their full attention he began showing them the system. “It’s just like a vending machine. If you’re out of something upstairs, you key it in on the console like this. The unit sends the item to the dumbwaiter; it shoots up the little shaft and is available in the cabinet. It's really cool..."

"That's very nice darling, but hold up..." Jury turned to the other soldiers. "What is in there? It says live specimen, but I know it's not human because it's not in the monitor tube. I don't know what kind degrees you think we have, but we're not super-educated cat sitters."

"It's the guy from the apartment." Lisa said matter-of-factly.

"No they didn't. They didn't just bring us to a deserted island with the guy that just tried to kill us. Y'all might as well hand Allard a gun and sit me on his lap!" Jury shouted.

"Doctors! This unit is like a coffin, but way less comfortable. As far as we know he's in a monitored coma and..." Lieutenant Wellspring began, but stopped when Lisa raised her hand.

"Here's where we get confused. Why do you have him HERE WITH US! There's no place you can store this "coffin" in your barracks?" She snapped.

"To hell with that. We should've dumped him off in the ocean on the way out here." Jury growled.

Everyone stared at each other. The soldiers had no answers, the doctors too many. The tension was a thick musty rotting mess. Lieutenant Wellspring bent down engaging the valve on a hose. Immediately noises came from the pipes. There was a light humming noise.

“Consider this place a tomb.” He began. “He’s secure in this coffin in an induced coma and some kind of medical freeze ‘em up and bag ‘em way that you two probably know way more about than me. I didn’t want this sick freak on the flight, but we were under orders. It was safer for your neighbors and everyone else if we removed him immediately.” The other soldiers wrapped up their affairs and cleaned up behind themselves. “You saw him. He demolished those officers. I’ve seen some pretty sick things since I’ve been with Scilymax, but this one here takes the cake.”

Jury huffed and walked towards the door. “Don’t you forget that he was after you. There’s no reason to involve anyone else.” Wellspring said.

“So, we get sent to Gilligan’s island...”

“It’s a tomb. Consider it a tomb. You don’t have a reason to come down here. Seal it off. We’ll lock the freight elevator on the ground level. You don’t have to come down here for anything.”

“We won’t. They better hope I don’t figure out which one of those switches is for the oxygen. I’ll flip that bitch quick.” Lisa pointed at the large metal box.

“Yes m’am.”

Alone in the house, Lisa and Jury sat in the living room watching the news coverage of a hospital fire in North Carolina. It was a tragic story of oxygen tanks exploding in succession after what was believed to be a forgetful hospital worker lighting a cigarette in a restricted area. Scores were killed by fire or smoke inhalation, which rendered an entire wing of the building closed.

"Another explosion in North Carolina..." Jury stared at the screen.

"That's gotta be connected. I just wish the damn phone systems worked here." Lisa was frustrated beyond compare. With every quiet moment, she worried about her friend.

They heard a car pulling in front of the house, but didn't flinch. Their worries overrode any curiosity of visitors. Chances were it was just another Scilymax security soldier checking on something.

"Helllllllooooooo??" The cheery voice echoed in front of the house. Then she was inside and standing in the doorway. It all happened so quickly, Lisa and Jury both jumped up to standing position. "Hope I didn't scare you ladies." Her smile was bright white. It took a moment just to get passed it. Then they noticed her sun tanned skin. She looked to be Brazilian and her flawless body showed it. All she wore were cut off jean short shorts and a neon green bikini top. Her high heeled sandals were the only sign she didn't just jump up from the beach. The top of her bikini bottom peeked over the low-rise of her shorts. She was carrying a bag of groceries inside a large pot.

"This is private property." Lisa was confused.

"Boy is it!" This time her South American accent was audible. "My name is Iara. I'm the chef." She extended her hand to Lisa and gave her a firm job interview handshake.

"The what?" Jury winced at the strong handshake she received.

"The chef!" Iara smiled brightly. "I'm so sorry I'm late." She carried her stuff to the kitchen. "They always bring those old freeze dried things and I figured you guys would want some fresh local vegetables with dinner tonight." She went about putting away her groceries then paused realizing the uncomfortable silence. "No one told you, The Hut came with a chef...Of course, I expect as much from Scilymax. Well, I'm her. I know that was a long flight, can I make you something to snack on? Tapas?"

"Sure!" Jury smiled then cocked her eyebrow at Lisa.

“Great! Shouldn’t be long. Do you need anything else?” Iara said brightly as she threw her apron over her head and adjusted the straps.

“You got a phone that works out here?” Lisa huffed jokingly.

“Certainly.” Reaching in her small purse, she tossed Lisa her cell phone. Lisa caught it bobbling it in her hands and started to dial.

“You just dropped out of heaven!” Jury stared at her in amazement.

“Well...” Iara blushed. “I’m sorry, I know you’re doctors, but I don’t know your names.”

“Marjorie.” Jury pointed to herself. “Lisa” She pointed to Lisa then shushed herself when she heard Lisa speaking on the phone.

“Michelle, it’s Lisa. Jury and I are safe and worried about you. Please give me a call...umm...we’ll call you or...I don’t know what the hell. Just get word to Scilymax to contact us and tell us that you’re ok.” Lisa hung up quickly.

“Thank you, Iara.” She walked to the kitchen and placed the phone on the counter next to her as Iara was furiously dicing scallions.

“You’re welcome. Where is the other doctor?” Iara smiled as she hustled through the kitchen.

“It’s just us.” Lisa huffed. She was trying to be nice, but really all of the patience needed in meeting a new person wasn’t with her right now.

“Oh! I was told there would be three doctors.”

“Really? Well I hope it’s someone sent here to do some work because we’re officially on vacay.” Jury took a deep inhale of the fresh veggies and seasonings that were being mixed together.

The small antiques shop in New York’s Soho district had only been open for fifteen minutes that morning, but Allard was feeling anxious. He watched from across the street ensconced in a doorway near a dumpster as the young clerk raised the blinds and dusted off some of the stuff in the window. Allard looked for a sign, but there was none and Allard needed to move faster. He galloped across the cobblestone street and pulled the hair net from his hair letting his long locks fall down his shoulders. He gave them a quick tussle as he pushed open the door. The clerk reacted immediately to the door chimes.

“Good morning, sir. May I help you find something or are you just looking?” The Clerk was sure he was just looking, but tried not to offend. Many of the items in the store were extremely high-priced. Looking at the man, The Clerk wasn't so sure he could afford much in there.

"I'm here to see Shalako. Is he here?" Allard looked around at the high standing shelves of knick-knacks, large tables on the show room floor and hanging fixtures.

"Yes. He's in back. May I tell him who's here to see him?" The Clerk asked.

"Tell him Allard is here for his package." Allard tried to be as polite as possible, but he was in a rush and needed information as soon as possible.

The Clerk walked to the back of the store, his feet thudding across the hardwood floors. Allard surveyed the shelves again noticing things here and there. Shalako had done well for himself and had interestingly enough placed quite a few priceless items right next to worthless baubles on the showroom floor. It didn't matter. The souls wouldn't be able to tell the difference anyway.

"Allard!" Shalako was a stocky guy, shorter than him with a half smile. His oval rimless glasses gave him the appearance of a stately librarian of sorts. Allard was bemused by what he could only think of as Shalako's disguise. They gave each other a hearty back thumping hug to the surprise of The Clerk.

"It's been some time, Shalako. I hate to be rude, but I need my bag."

"Here's the thing..." Shalako took a deep breath, which did not sit well with Allard. He led Allard to another side of the store away from the Clerk's listening ears. "Your package wasn't delivered here. It's very unlike Hermes to not deliver something, but there's a reason. He dropped it at the alternate drop off position for you after he ran into some opposition on a flight."

"Opposition?" Allard took on air and folded his arms as he pushed out his chest.

"I'm told Kronus may have been there." Shalako began, but when seeing Allard's eyebrows furrow, quickly added... "But I'm told he was helpful all in all. So, the package is with your second option. I'm assuming you know when and where you can find this person...."

Allard thought, concentrated and felt his mind vibrate. "I do. Kronus was there? Are you sure?"

"I'm told he was. I'm told he was helpful to Hermes." Shalako was careful with his words and Allard knew it.

"Who told you this?"

"I'm not at liberty to say..." Shalako tapped Allard on his shoulder to comfort him, but Allard kept his arms folded. "Are you mad at me? What's wrong? What's going on here?"

"No. You're right. It's ok. You've been helpful." Allard began to walk and look at the antiques in the shop perusing the items intently.

"Ummm...are you on official business today?" Shalako walked carefully behind Allard.

"What do you mean?" Allard was preoccupied by some of the items he saw.

"Are you working? Are you...back?"

Allard picked up a pair of thick frame glasses with blue tinted lenses and held them up to the light.

"These are Soul Eyes. You're selling Soul Eyes? Has anyone bought these?" Allard said looking at the craftsmanship of the glasses.

"A few...um...actually a soul bought a pair. He said he needed them." Shalako chuckled.

"A soul needed to see how the rest of them see? Meaning...he could see how we can see..." Allard put the glasses down and looked on.

"Not sure he could see how WE see. Definitely not how you..."

"I'm going to need one more favor from you. You failed me on delivering my package and..."

"I didn't fail you. Hermes didn't deliver. I always deliver. He failed you if there's anyone to be called a failure."

Shalako was stern, but then realized he was speaking to Allard. "No disrespect to him, but I am doing my best here."

"I know you are." Allard put his hand on Shalako's shoulder and squeezed it. "That's why you're going to help me deliver something so I can get my package."

"Anything for you." Shalako nodded.

Lisa was laid back on the beach in a comfortable beach chair. She kept her eyes closed and focused on the waves of the ocean and the smell of the saltwater. The breeze was just right. The sun warmed her face and she could tell she was already getting a golden tan as she lay there. She meditated and tried not to think about the real world. She was alone now. No one was within view or within earshot of her. She told herself over and over again that she could relax. She tried not to focus on the obvious. She was nude. She was lying out in the sun, on a chair, on a beach, on an island in the nude. Her brown nipples were perked with the first breeze and stayed firm as she lay there.

She was sweating and the sweat had begun to pool in her belly button. The sweat was at first caused by embarrassment then the hot sun. Now she was relaxed. The sounds of fish, possibly dolphin, maybe whales were splashing in the water. She had finally relaxed and was dozing off when she heard feet approaching her in the sand. Security?? She covered her breasts with one hand, reached quickly for her clothes by the chair and covered her privates with her shirt.

"Sorry to scare you. I just wanted to bring you a fresh mojito." Iara smiled as she sat the cool drink on the table by Lisa. She placed a glass of ice water next to it. "You know we all go nude where I'm from. You shouldn't be ashamed you're a very pretty doctor."

"Thanks." Lisa tried her best to feel comfortable in front of this cheerful stranger. "Next time they send me to an island, I just wish they give me some notice so I can bring a bathing suit." She sipped the mojito. It was perfect.

"Dinner is marinating. Do you mind if I join you for a moment?" Before Lisa could respond, Iara had shed her bikini top and shorts and was pulling the string on her thong bottom. With her bottoms shed, Iara left no question as to her being Brazilian. Lisa's eyes shied away as Iara pulled up a chair close enough to her and laid back. "Thank you. This really is nice. These chairs are like none I've found on a beach."

"Mmmhmm." Lisa sighed and laid back down leaving her shirt draped across her nether region. Lisa felt a little silly. Iara was just a little too perfect and pretty and graceful in high heels and comfortable with her body and a ton of other ands...but all in all she was a nice person and made a perfect mojito and incredible tapas. Lisa decided to give her a chance.

The warm air coaxed Lisa back to relaxation. She listened to the splash of the ocean and the breeze caressing the trees on the grounds. Iara barely made a sound. She was indeed in paradise.

“Lisaaaaaaaaaaaaaaa!” Jury screamed in a high-pitched squeal.

Iara and Lisa jumped up. Lisa fumbled with her clothes as Iara ran to The Hut nude. Her long legs stretched in bounds across the back patio. Lisa was moments behind her, her pants on, but hanging open as she clutched her shirt over her breasts.

“Are you ok, Dr. Marjorie?” Iara stood just inside the sliding glass doors of the den.

“Yes. Girl, why are you butt naked?” Jury smiled clutching the phone. “The phone finally works and guess who calls... Michelle!”

Lisa stormed into the house, grabbed the phone from Jury and put it to her ear.

“Michelle? What’s going on? Are you alright?” Lisa clutched her heart.

"I'll step out and let you have your privacy." Iara nodded and pranced out quickly.

"I thought I was interrupting yours." Jury watched as Iara left.

Michelle clutched a rather large global phone to her ear. She shielded the other ear from the ambient sounds on the pier.

"I'm fine. We landed and they got word from Scilymax that you needed to speak to me so one of these security soldier guys lent me a global phone, but said I have to hurry. I'm safe. There's been lots of drama. I have to give this guy back his phone because he's leaving."

"Where do they have you?" Lisa shouted into the phone as if it were a tin can on a string.

"I'm on a pier and it's hot as hell out here. They told me someone is coming to pick me up."

"What? They're leaving you?" Lisa screamed.

"Apparently. I'm fine, but I have got to tell you about what happened. It may have to wait. I shouldn't say this on the phone."

"Wait...you said you're on a pier?" Lisa paused.

"She's here!" Jury shouted. "Ask her if it looks like a Disney ride."

"Michelle, we think you're on the same island as us. We'll call the security team and tell them to bring us to meet you."

"Cool. I'll just be sitting here on the pier I guess. See you when you get here."

The security team had already been activated. Lisa and Jury excitedly hopped into the Jeep and peeled out to meet them at the end of the grounds.

Iara kept her eyes closed and let the sun caress her. She listened to the water's ebbs and flows. She could feel the movement of the tides and the fish beneath it. They splashed and swam playfully giving the water a wild sound in places. Iara had been here long enough to sense the smallest things about her favorite beach. So when there was a loud wooshing sound in the air and a bigger splash, she sat up quickly and peered out to the horizon. It could've been a whale, but it sounded different. She wasn't positive, but she thought she saw the water flowing differently in one spot and the waves creating the letter V around it. Then it disappeared.

Iara sat her feet on either side of her chair, placed her elbows on her knees and watched the peaceful ocean quietly. The golden sunlight glimmered across the light blue water and reflected on the dark blue further out. Then she saw it again. There was something in the water heading towards the beach. It was moving too slowly to be a dolphin. Was she about to see a whale beach itself right here? She hoped not. She hated to lose the beautiful creatures of the ocean. The water rippled around the form as it gained more shape and drifted through the clear blue waters.

Iara arched her back and sat upright as she watched it nonplussed. Her pupils dilated. Her breathing quickened as goose bumps rose all over her nude body. Her head angled back as she took notice of what was heading towards her. It rose slowly from the water. The still water near the surface spread away from it easily. The figure eased out of the water and approached her directly. Water dropped and peppered the white sands. Large footprints spread from the water straight up to Iara.

"Hello handsome." She smiled flirtatiously as she looked up at him. "That was some entrance. Can I help you with something?" She ran her fingers through her hair.

"Yes. I need to speak with the ladies of the house." He said.

"They've run out for a moment. Who shall I say is calling?" She looked him up and down. His wet clothes clung to his body.

"My name is Allard." He nodded and extended his hand. She took it and shook it daintily.

“Really?” Her smile dropped partially. She sensed her change and immediately recovered. He did say he wasn’t here to see her. “You’re cuter than I expected.”

CHAPTER FOUR

The Rolls Royce Phantom eased up to the curb outside the biker bar in Williamsburg Brooklyn like a mouse to a mousetrap. The driver's caution was evident. The car idled just behind a long line of choppers. These were real choppers, motorcycles put together by parts from other bikes, like Frankenstein's monsters of the freeway. They were crafted with love then repainted to become new beasts. The precise beauty and engineering of the Phantom contrasted with the battle scarred love of the two wheelers. Inside the car, Alala crossed her legs and stared out to the sign on the bar.

TART'S

She smiled. Yes, this definitely was a tart on the eyes and she didn't mean the cake with the fruit topping. It was to eye candy what a punch in the mouth is to dentistry, a crude haphazardly designed option.

"Want me to come in with you?" The Driver raised his eyebrow hoping she would deny him.

"Sure. If you want." Alala called his bluff.

"Hmmm..." He pondered. "Maybe it's best if I stay outside with the car. We may need a fast getaway." He surmised.

Alala huffed. "You're see-through. Don't even get out to get my door. I don't want you to get scared of the mice on the street." She sassed, opened the door, grabbed her purse and closed the door behind her as she left.

The light broke the darkness inside Tart's. Several of the patrons shielded their faces from the light and from being seen. Alala high-stepped into the place letting the door slam hard behind her. She strutted with a switch of her hips, the clatter of her high heels against the grimy hardwood floors echoed over the grinding sounds of AC/DC. She made her way to the bar, but didn't touch it. The bartender was a slender dark haired version of Iggy Pop.

"I already gave the health commissioner his cut. Are you here to invite me to the Christmas party?" He cracked. "Or maybe you're my Thanksgiving turkey?"

"Where's Dragon?"

"Dragon ain't here."

"Yes he is. Did you notice I didn't ask if he was here? No, I asked where is he? That means I know he's here." Alala looked across the room. It was well occupied with the post-community service crowd.

"Who wants to see him?" The Bartender picked a semi-clean tumbler from behind the bar and began pouring a double whiskey shot.

"I want to see him. That's why I asked, dummy." Alala's sass had bubbled to the surface like acid reflux.

He chuckled at her and slid the glass to her.

"I don't want a drink. I came for Dragon."

"That drink is for Dragon. You'd be better off bringing him a gift than just sauntering your ass over there. He likes sweet pieces of ass, but he doesn't like mouth...unless it's the kind of mouth he likes."

Alala lifted the glass and peered through the brown liquid.

"This is some cheap shit. At least, I know things haven't changed. Where is he?"

She followed The Bartender's pointing finger to the booth in the left corner.

Dragon sat hidden partially by the high backs of the booth and the low swinging light. He was stocky with a goatee and a kind smile, which he flashed as soon as she approached. All thirty-two of his teeth gleamed. He wore a black t-shirt that was too tight for him and exposed considerable tattoos. They covered his arms in sleeves, peeked out from beneath his collar and were exposed on his neck. There were three on both of his hands, which were partially concealed by thick silver rings. The wrinkles in his forehead were more prevalent now that he was losing his hair. A shorter, thinner man sat across from him. She recognized him, but couldn't remember his name.

Alala dropped the glass on the table spilling drops of its contents. "Hello Dragon."

"These waitresses here are getting prettier as the years go on. I know this one. Old friend." He spoke to his friend ignoring her. "Actually not a friend, just an old fuck."

"You wish! Don't try to show off in front of company, Dragon. We both know your tiny tool couldn't please a fly."

"She has a lot of mouth too...I know because my cock played hockey with her tonsils a couple dozen times." Dragon didn't raise his eyes to her.

Alala lifted the glass and drained it of its contents.

"See? Swallows it whole!" Dragon laughed amusing his friend.

In a flash, she spat the liquor on the tabletop, took his friend's cigarette and dropped it in the alcohol. Flames shot in the air nearly burning Dragon's arms. The two of them reeled backward.

"Hey! Hey! Hey! What the fuck?" The Bartender shouted.

"It's ok...It's ok. We're just having a little fun." Dragon laughed.

"How much fun will it be when Allard walks in here?" Alala snorted.

Dragon's eyes dropped to his friend.

"Give us a minute. We need to talk."

His friend slid from the booth and took in the entire view of Alala. He walked away licking his lips.

"Have a seat, Alala." Dragon looked her in her eyes for the first time.

"No thanks. I'll stand." She stared down her nose at him.

"Allard is with me on this."

"Says who? Did he say it? Did you hear him say it?" Alala gritted through her teeth.

"That's none of your business. You just know that when the time comes, when the lines are drawn, he's with me.” Dragon’s temper flared. He didn’t like this pretty young thing questioning him.

She tossed her hair and raised her leg up resting it on the seat of the booth. Her skirt rose high nearly exposing the tops of her fishnet hose. Her heels dented the seat. “I see you have some new artwork.” She pointed to his tattoos. “Does it still hurt when you get those or do you get used to the needle?”

“I don’t think anyone ever gets used to a needle. Not even a seamstress. That’s why she wears a thimble. The constant pain...who can stand the constant pain?” Dragon smiled.

“I don’t think Allard’s ever had a hard time with it. In fact, a little birdie told me he has some new art of his own.” She watched him bristle. His forehead wrinkles spread back against his receding hairline. “I guess he’s a little stronger than you are then, huh.” She smiled putting her foot down to the floor. “You’re not winning this one. You can go ahead and bow out of this.”

“I WILL NOT!” Dragon’s voice bellowed. “You can talk all you want. Allard is my man. I know your ways and I know what you want. You can’t have it. He looked you in your face and told you no.” He shrugged. “So what does that mean? It means you can go ahead and do whatever you like. But at the end of the day, you're a mere suggestion, in a world of decision makers."

"He's requested The Needle." Alala stared at him watching the words soak in. "Ahhh, I see that working its way around in your fragile head. With The Needle, he's about as powerful as anything out there. So if he's with you as you say, you don't care. But if I speak to him, I'll ask him myself." She turned to walk away.

"Alala." He commanded with a stern tone. She turned to him. "Whose side are you on?"

"Mine as usual." She smiled and winked.

Dustin's normally long strides had shortened and he was creeping along in the hallway. Each step he took was a measured intentionally placed movement. He had been hurrying to the conference room when he read the first sentence of the security briefing. The words had knocked the wind out of him and now he read slowly and walked slower. He had to make sure he understood every bit of it. The details of the last twenty-four hours were attacking his senses. How had all of this transpired within his department without him being notified immediately? Perhaps, he really was on his way out. He couldn't let that happen. He wouldn't let it happen. His plans had been thrown too many twists and turns. He promised himself that he would succeed before they had thrown him out on his ass.

"Dustin!" The booming voice echoed in the hallway.

He took a second to finish reading the last line in the briefing before he turned around and gave a fake smile. "Mr. Mora. Thank you for allowing me to use your private aircraft."

"Don't be silly. That's as much every board member's aircraft as my own. Well, that's what we tell the government anyway." He laughed a big corny laugh his hand clutched a large mug of his exotic coffee. Dustin noticed The Chairman of the Scilymax board was a lot more pleasant since the destruction of The Country Cage. Dustin liked to think it was because none of his people were hurt and the government had turned a blind eye towards the Scilymax experiments in the Antarctic. However, he felt there was something else there. "How was your trip to Italy? Did you find what you were looking for? Was there a flower or a plant that will cure all of our ills just waiting to be plucked from the lawns of a palazzo?"

"No nothing that fortuitous." Dustin shrugged. "But I was able to clear up the production issues with the

Scilymax Amnio-333 adjustment so we may be able to get it stateside in cosmetics sooner."

"That. Is. A-ma-zing." Jacob Mora enunciated every syllable of every word as if he'd just seen the face of God himself. He was many things, but most of all he was charming and complimentary. "Fine work you're doing in research." He switched gears quickly. "Have you read the security briefing?"

"Yes I just finished it and..."

"Save your thoughts. I need everyone to hear you on this one." Mora smiled as he led Dustin into the conference room. The other Board Members were already seated and looked as if their patience had already worn thin waiting for the last two attendees. "Sorry we're late. Carver was just telling me about his HUGE inroads in Italy. Production issues cleared, we'll be making America's women much more beautiful and feeling younger in no time. Not that either of you need that." He winked at the two female Board members.

Mora stood at the head of the table. He pressed a button on his remote and a hologram sprung up in the middle of the table. The hologram was split in several boxes; each broadcasted different views from surveillance cameras. There were multiple views of the standoff outside Lisa's apartment building. The TSA building explosion could be scene in several different angles in some squares while in others were various angles of the hospital standoff and escape.

"Here it is. This is what it all looked like last night. A grand old ass fucking for the PR department and a hell of a time for our security forces." He nodded to Dustin. "Not to mention the endangering of some of Carver's...OUR...loyal employees...again. Do we understand and is it agreed that the cloning project has created it's own legs and is trying to walk away...NO..." He corrected himself. "RUN! Away from us.?" He bellowed as he pointed to a screen that featured Dezi evading several Scilymax security trucks and running off into the forest near the hospital.

"Do you think this is all connected?" One of the Board Members bristled.

"I think so. How could it not be? Are you kidding me? We happen to be working on cloning people with all of these added extra abilities and what do you know, we have escapees jumping into the Antarctic turning themselves into specimen pops, others popping up and hopping around buildings like Spiderman and hurting police officers, a sickly old man spreads his sickness across a wing of a hospital then jumps seven stories chasing after our security? Let's see..." Mora put on a fake thoughtful expression.

"Well there could be..." A Board member started.

"Nope!" He cut him off. "I'm still thinking about it." Mora stood with his finger tapping his temple for a very tense silent few moments. "Yes! I think they're connected!! And we haven't been able to tie this down. I NEED this to work better. Why *have* the most esteemed minds on this board if we can't figure this thing out?"

"Perhaps we should allow Mr. Carver to give his opinion and then he can leave and we can discuss this further." One of the women said. She was the one Dustin liked the least. She was the bitch that always wanted to dismiss him when the decisions were made. Mora nodded his head as he watched the constant loop on the screens.

"Dustin." Mora sighed as he sat down. "Are any of these ours?" He pointed to the men on the screens.

"I've never seen any of them." Dustin started and heard a roomful of disappointed huffs of air. "But remember my department just builds the structure. We're test tube jockeys. We create better immune systems and vision and we're still working on the agility thing. That was one of the reasons why Masson Island was so important."

"You were here when we voted on Masson Island. You were concerned about the data and the doctors. The captive was low on the priority list. It would've been nice to keep him, but he'd proven to be just as rogue as the others." That bitch said.

"It would've been nice to understand his mentality." Dustin shrugged.

"I think we found that out when he killed fifty of our men in midtown." The rat faced board member chortled.

"So..." Mora squeezed his temples then drained his cup of coffee. "None of these are ours as far as you know."

"No."

"Can we make them ours?"

"I'm sorry." Dustin was confused.

"Like the one at The Country Cage. Can we make any of these ours?"

"I suppose we can try, but you'd have to find one, capture him and then investigate. It's just like before." Dustin paused. Of course, he hadn't thought of it. "You have one? Which one?"

The Board members got still. All of a sudden they found the looping screens more interesting.

"That one." Mora pointed to one of the scenes showing the outside of Lisa's apartment building.

"Jacob!" That Bitch squealed. Her face was flush as if Jacob Mora had proclaimed he was going to fuck her in the eye socket right there in the meeting.

"The Hut." Jacob Mora gestured to the security briefing. Dustin saw some of the Board members squirming in their seats.

"But you sent the doctors there. Lisa and Marjorie are at The Hut." Dustin was confused.

"You're sure none of these are ours?" Mora sat up and stared deep into Dustin's eyes. Dustin felt the hairs on the back of his neck stand up.

"I've never seen them..." Dustin heard his own voice barely eek out.

"Thank you. If you can excuse us now." Mora smiled gesturing to the door.

Janice was standing in the hallway outside the conference room when Dustin stepped out.

"You had fun in Italy, huh." She said with a cocked-eyebrow.

"What?" Dustin wasn't in the mood for the ex-lover games. He bounded down the hall towards his office.

"You didn't only do work, but you had fun." Janice was trying to make it seem as if she wasn't prying and was doing a horrible job of it.

"I had a couple of good meals...alone." He emphasized the last word with a huff. He never saw Janice as the jealous type especially since she was the one that had broken off their affair.

"And you had a private flight back with company..." Janice sang.

“Yeah, one of Mora’s friends...or whatever.”

“You guys had fun on the plane with six hours all to yourself?”

“We talked.” Dustin couldn’t wait to get back to his office so he could ask Janice in private confines, hidden behind the big wooden door, if she was out of her mind.

“Must’ve been one hell of a conversation if she chased you back up here...” Janice searched his face for a reaction.

“Chased me back where?”

“Here. She’s waiting in the lobby. Alala...no last name. I went and checked to see what she looked like. She’s hot. I can see why you’re trying to keep her a secret from me.”

“I’m not. She’s here...why is she here?” Dustin stopped at Janice’s desk outside his office.

“She said it was private.” Janice’s mouth did a twist.

“Can you have her brought back?” Dustin forced nonchalance into his voice.

“I’ll go get her myself.” Janice pranced away.

As soon as Dustin opened the door he smelled the pleasant scent and was transported to a better more relaxed place. He stepped into the office to see Alala sitting on his desk facing him. She swung her curvy legs back and forth. Her legs weren't covered with hose this time. He took in the fullness of her caramel skin and the thick athletic curves of her calves. Her short stiletto boots rocked with her legs. Again she wore a skirt, but this one was more New York winter appropriate, grey wool, which complimented a black cowl neck sweater. Her large "Jackie-O" sunglasses blocked her eyes. She licked her bright red lipstick.

"Are you sleeping with your secretary, Mr. Carver?" She tilted her head.

"Excuse me?" Dustin's shocked tone was a clear giveaway, a hint at what used to be.

"She was way too concerned about who I was and how I know you. It was more than the normal secretary gatekeeper stuff. Kind of like a jealous lover."

"Janice can be very protective." Dustin nodded as he walked towards her.

"Mmmmhmm." She smirked.

Dustin pulled his uncomfortable guest chair out to face her.

"Please have a comfortable seat."

"No. I'm fine here, thanks. Sorry I let myself in, but the games with the secretary weren't fun. I have a meeting with Jake...umm...Mr. Mora in a bit and since I was here I decided to drop in and talk. I hope you don't mind." Her legs glistened as they swayed back and forth.

"Not at all." Dustin sat in the guest chair staring up at her. "What'd you have in mind?" He watched her toss her long hair over the right shoulder of her cashmere sweater. He'd barely had time to freshen up between the flight and his meeting and here she was shower fresh, new outfit and with what looked like a new hairstyle.

"I have to be very frank with you right now, Mr. Carver." She began, but stopped when she heard the door click.

"She left, she must've..." Janice barged in and stopped abruptly. She glowered at Alala then at Dustin sitting in the guest chair in his own office. The little bitch was holding court with Dustin in his office!

"It's OK Janice. She found her way back. She's meeting with Mr. Mora soon." Dustin stood quickly in attempt to alleviate any visibility of impropriety.

"Would you like me to show her to his office?" Janice's lips pursed.

"No thank you. I've been here before. I have carte blanche on the executive floors." Alala said matter-of-factly.

Janice thought to reply "and the desks, couches and wherever else, I'm sure" But she bit her tongue, literally.

Dustin walked behind his desk hoping Janice would leave, but he knew she'd force him to dismiss her.

"We'll only be a minute. Thanks Janice."

"You're welcome, Mr. Carver." Janice's tone could've chilled all the water in the Hudson River. She closed the door behind her.

"Mmmhmmm." Alala grunted and pushed her sunglasses up on top of her head. She kept her back to him knowing that he was admiring how her small waist gave way to her round behind. "Like I was saying before I was interrupted by your mistress."

"She's not..." He began.

"Former mistress. Anyway, I want to be genuine with you. I have a meeting with Jake and I intend to tell him what I'm about to tell you. But I think you may want to get your defense ready."

"My defense?" Dustin felt a slight tightening in his chest. She knew something. Would he be forced to use the gun in his safe? Janice was upset with him would she help cover up the mess?

"Damn your mind goes straight to violence and self preservation, huh." Alala's sassy attitude erupted. "I like that." Had she just read his mind? "What we spoke about on the plane. The clones and the soldiers."

"I told you I work in medical research looking for ways to cure the ills..."

"The ills of man. Whatever." She oozed sarcasm. Her back was still to him. She could sense him shifting on his feet. "Scilymax has a program for cloning or adjusting soldiers creating better stronger soldiers." She let him ingest the truths she already knew. "Your program was built on attributes created in your lab, but by trying to harness the extraordinary abilities of people you've found. One of these test subjects is extremely gifted and extremely dangerous." She looked over her shoulder at him. As she expected, he was white as a sheet. "Scilymax captured him and held him. He escaped. They let this very very dangerous man escape. He is alive. He's alive and I believe he has or is trying to obtain a weapon I created. The most dangerous weapon I've ever designed. I need to find him. Not only for my sake, but for yours. Scilymax can have its super army, but I want to know whose side he is on. Yours? Someone else? His own? If Scilymax can't control or contain him, I need my weapon back. It needs to come back home. His name is Allard. I need to know if you know him."

Dustin stared in her honest pleading brown eyes. He was scared. He feared for his life and by the look on her face, he knew he was correct in feeling that fear. He spun the dial on his safe slowly, placed his hand inside and gripped cold metal. He lifted it quickly with a sigh. Alala stared in his face looking for the answer. It dropped on the desk. It was a metal file folder. Her slender manicured fingers flipped open the file. A brightly colored photo stared back at her. It was an arm with tattoos. This one was a close up of one tattoo in particular, but there were others. There were lots of pictures of lots of branded art. She grinned.

"Whose side are you on Alala?" Dustin read her face. His mind was on the other cold metal object in his safe.

"You're on mine." Alala said.

Jury had just let out a loud whooping laugh at one of Michelle's hilarious observations about their predicament when she looked ahead and saw Iara standing at the front door. There was something in her stance that poured cold water over her sunshine. She, Lisa and Michelle had caught up on the ride back to The Hut and just begun to talk about fun things. Lisa turned the corner into the main drive up to The Hut just beyond the security gate and Jury's laugh stopped abruptly. In fact, Michelle was still making fun of their enormous luck in getting paid trips to far off exotic places when Jury interrupted.

“Why is she outside?” Jury quizzed.

“You trying to keep her locked up in the kitchen? With that attitude, you’ll never be able to keep hired help.” Michelle cracked.

“Something is wrong.” Jury huffed. “She doesn’t look right.”

“You’ve known her for hours.” Michelle sat back.

“She doesn’t look all sunny.”

“What?”

“She’s right.” Lisa added as she pulled the Jeep to the front door. “This one is always happy. She doesn’t look right.”

“What’s wrong?” Jury stepped out of the SUV swiftly.

Iara’s arms were folded across her torso. She shook her head reassuringly.

“I thought I should meet you outside. Dr. Bonds nice to meet you.” Iara sprung a shiny smile and gripped Michelle’s hand.

“Not a doctor. Just mizz.” Michelle smiled then winced with the pressure of the handshake.

Iara noticed Michelle clung tightly to her over-stuffed purse. Iara reached to relieve her of it.

“I have it, thanks.” Michelle demurred.

“You OK?” Lisa walked up behind Michelle. “Did you burn something?”

“Like the entire kitchen.” Michelle smiled, making light.

“No. We have a guest for dinner and I thought I should be proper and tell you ahead of time.”

“Who? Your boo? That’s fine! We won’t tell.” Jury shrugged it off happily and motioned passed Iara.

“He’s a friend of yours, but...”

Jury had already opened the door and stepped inside with Michelle steps behind her. Lisa slowed noticing Iara’s facial expression turned sour quickly.

“Dustin?” Lisa whispered.

The loud shriek from in The Hut sent goose bumps down Lisa’s smile and made Iara jump. Lisa swung the door open and barreled into the house. Only four paces in, she had to side step Jury and Michelle. Jury’s hand shot out and grabbed Lisa’s just as her eyes focused on the dreadlocked man standing in the living room. He was nice looking with a shy uncomfortable smile. He was wearing soaking wet cleaning crew overalls. His face was familiar. Lisa felt Jury’s nails dig into her skin. She looked back to his face, under the slight mustache and five o’clock shadow was Allard. Her stomach dropped. The other two seemed to be frozen with fear.

"And like a boomerang we're all back where we originally started." Allard said with his arms forming a circle.

"What are you doing here?" Michelle stepped forward, with Jury quickly grabbing her free hand. She felt less fear. It could've been her strong belief in God or what she remembered of their last conversation.

"I'm here to protect you." Allard took a step backward with hope they would step forward, but there was no such luck.

"The killer is here to protect us." Jury's temper had begun to bubble to the surface.

"The last time we were face to face you were the one shooting bullets at mine." Allard shrugged. "But I understand."

"Dinner is ready. Let's all get freshened up and have a seat." Iara walked into the house beyond the trio and smiled at Allard who returned her smile.

"Iara!" Lisa warned.

"He's fine." Iara shot back. "We've been talking while you were picking up Ms. Bonds."

"We're fine, aren't we Allard?" Iara shouted from the kitchen.

"Very. I understand your hesitation."

"Do you?" Lisa shouted pulling her arm from Jury's grip. "Do you understand that men have been chasing us asking us about you?" Do you get that we're a little concerned that you just may be here to cause more pain?"

"What men?" Allard turned serious.

"Enough!" Iara returned from the kitchen with a sternness they hadn't imagined. She was no longer her cheerful self. "We will eat dinner. Ms. Bonds your room is on this floor. You ladies get freshened up for dinner. Allard have a seat."

Allard motioned to sit.

"Over there. On the seat without a cushion. We don't need you getting the sofa wet." Iara scolded.

Allard sat immediately and shrugged his shoulders. Michelle pulled Jury and Lisa through the living room passed him. Allard watched them pleasantly. As they disappeared around the corner, he noticed a small piece of burlap sticking from Michelle's bag. He sat back and let out a heavy sigh.

Lisa, Marjorie and Michelle stood in their respective bedrooms alone but their minds covered the same steps. Should I call the soldiers? Will he kill me? Why is he here? The soldiers were as obvious an answer as any of the others. They absolutely could not call the soldiers. The last time, Allard had made quick work of them and seemed to be holding back. If he were the one that could kill fifty in a clip, then it would be certain obliteration here. If he wanted to kill them, he would've done so already. They would've come back to find him wearing Iara's dead body like a shawl. Only Michelle had a true feeling for the answer to the last question. She hid that answer between her mattress and the bedspring carefully flattening it away without a sign.

Michelle was the last person to return to the table. She was shocked to realize she was the only one that had showered and put on the only outfit she had packed that resembled warm weather attire. Of course, she had to apologize to her neighbors for the helicopter landing on their street so late at night and the yelling by the soldiers for everyone to stand back. And the guns, damn she forgot they had pointed guns. Never no mind. Her white blouse billowed in the warm breeze that blew through the open windows. She took her seat amongst the pensive faces at the table. Lisa sat at the head of the table on one end directly across from Allard at the other. Marjorie sat abnormally close to Lisa. Another chair sat pushed closer to Lisa's end. Michelle presumed this was to be her seat. The other two chairs sat pushed back from the table. Lisa and

Marjorie had formed a barrier of two empty chairs between them and Allard.

"Smells good." Michelle sighed as she sat and excused herself for taking so long. "What'd I miss?"

Silence.

Allard cleared his throat.

"That's about what you've missed." He said.

Iara entered balancing several hot serving dishes on her arms.

"OK. Now let's get you all some good food and some good feeling in your bodies."

Lisa watched Iara place the steaming hot dishes on the table without care. She was truly a chef. There was no way a regular person could take such heat and weight. The food did smell good, glorious even. Lisa felt her mouth watering when the scents hit her nostrils.

Iara presented the food then explained the multiple dishes and how they were prepared. Her accent gave the entire exercise a quaint quality that everyone couldn't help but to enjoy. Michelle led the prayer. The three women clinched hands in a tight circle leaving Allard to bow his head and hold his own hands together. Michelle felt extreme guilt about this. It poked at her conscious the entire time the four sat and ate quietly. There was barely a request to pass anything, especially if it required asking Allard. When Iara came to check on them, they all answered in unison that they were indeed fine. It was uncomfortable though the food was really incredible. Marjorie drained the remainder of the wine from the bottle and glared at Allard.

“You kill anyone today, Allard.” She spat.

“Marjorie.” Michelle gasped.

“Let’s not. Let’s just not.” Lisa whispered.

Allard slowly swallowed what remained in his mouth, sat his knife and fork on either side of his plate and sat up straight.

“I haven’t. I’m sorry my presence is so distasteful that even Iara’s wonderful cooking can’t mask my flavor, but I really am not here for trouble.”

“You’re all here to be illuminated by my wonderful food.” Iara entered as if on cue. She refilled everyone’s water glasses to the brim. When she approached Allard’s, he covered his glass with his hand.

“I’m fine thanks.” He said.

“You sure? It’s fresh, brisk, clean.” She smiled.

Allard tossed her a side look that only Michelle witnessed. It was a warning of sorts.

“Yeah I guess you’ve had enough of the water for one day.” She shrugged. Allard nodded knowing Michelle was watching.

Michelle tipped her glass to her mouth and downed nearly half of it. She licked her lips in Allard’s direction to his amusement. Iara refilled the glass again.

“Are you going to eat?” Michelle asked as Iara took away empty serving platters.

“Yes. I will eat in the kitchen.” She responded.

“Don’t do that. You can eat in here with us.” Lisa objected.

“Yes, please.” Michelle concurred.

The two of them looked to Jury to make it unanimous. She pursed her lips.

“If you don’t mind sitting next to him.” Jury laughed.

“Mr. Allard? Mr. Allard wouldn’t hurt a fly.” Iara walked back to the kitchen with the dishes.

“No, but he’d choke the shit out of a soldier.” Jury quipped before having a chance to secure the filter on her mouth.

“That’s not necessary. If we’re all going to be here then we need to clear this up.” Lisa cut her fish as if attempting to break the tension with her knife. “And no more wine for you.” She pointed her fork at Jury.

Jury drank a gulp of her water in deference to her friend.

“I’m going to ignore the obvious questions of how you got off Masson Island. I’m even going to forego how the hell you knew we were here and go straight to what you want from us.” Lisa said.

“I want to make sure all of you are OK.” He began. “And I need to retrieve something.” He saw Michelle’s head dip. She was going to avoid it. He wouldn’t press. “But most of all I wanted to make sure you were OK.”

“So, if we give you what you came to retrieve will you leave us alone? I don’t know what it is, but I’d help you find it if you get on your way after you got it.” Jury growled.

“Your heart is so hard and scared.” Allard said to her. He spoke so fluidly it was as if he’d read it in a book. His tone caught Jury off guard. “Who were these men? The ones that came to you.”

“He didn’t stop to give me a name. Between chasing us out of the apartment and playing leap frog down the side of the building, we weren’t trying to ask after he decimated a bunch of cops.”

“Decimated like made them sick or eroded them? Made them like skin and bones?”

"The man that chased me made people sick. That's what they told me."

"Dezi." Allard said. "Did he take anything from you?" Michelle knew exactly what he meant and he knew she did.

"No. Who was he?" Michelle tapped her water glass against the table.

"He didn't touch anything?" Allard stared in her eyes.

"No."

"And the one that came after you, what did he do? Did you see him do anything?"

"No, but if you want to see him, he's downstairs." Jury said.

"WHAT!?" Allard jumped from the table with a terrified shock. The look alarmed everyone.

Iara entered with her plate and sat at the table. She took a bite of her food as if unaware of Allard's frightened expression.

"He's in a holding tank in induced coma. The area is sealed off."

"Did he decimate people?"

"If that's what you wanna call it. Let me find out he's the bully of the bunch." Jury sipped her water.

Allard sat down and started mumbling.

“Should we be more worried than we already are?” Lisa asked with her voice wavering.

Allard shook his head and took a large gulp of water. “That is good water.” He smiled at Iara.

“Told you.” She smiled back.

“Are we safe?” Michelle was more concerned.

“You’re the theologist. I think you know these answers better than I do.” Allard deferred.

“What did you come to retrieve, Allard?” Lisa remained guarded

“Your friendship and trust.” He responded.

“See, Mr. Allard isn’t hurting a soul.” Iara smiled. “So, everyone eat up. More wine, more drink. Let’s enjoy ourselves.”

Dinner ended more relaxed. With a healthy dose of wine in everyone the cobwebs came off. When it was time to retire, Allard offered to sleep outside on the hammock with everyone else locked inside. It was a small, but welcome olive branch. Michelle peaked out of her window watching as Allard fluffed the pillow Iara had given him then balanced on the hammock as he removed his boots. Her eyes twinkled when he unzipped and removed his cleaning crew uniform revealing a bulkier build than he’d had in The Country Cage. He stood stretching in only his boxer shorts and a tank top.

She felt tingles as the full moon laid blue light over his body. The hard waves of the ocean lapped against the beach behind him. She'd sworn she had more water tonight than wine. Yet, she still felt intoxicated. Her tolerance was obviously lowered from more years than she could remember of not imbibing large amounts of alcohol as she'd done in college. Her only real alcohol consumption came with the weekly communion, which wasn't much to enjoy. With intoxication came a certain lust. A lust she hadn't tapped in so long. The lust hit her painfully with tingles as she watched him pull his tank top off. She'd found herself hoping he'd do the same with his boxers. A schoolgirl gasp left her lips when he turned toward the beach and pulled the boxers down to his feet.

Michelle watched as the firm globes of his backside flexed as he walked across the sand towards the water. She waited to see if he'd turn to her so she could see more, but he didn't. After a short delay to test the water with his toes, he waltzed into the ocean up to his chest and waded. She no longer ignored her tingles. She welcomed them. She looked down to find one of her hands cupping her breast. An erect nipple pressed hard against her palm.

Michelle turned and changed into her sleeping shirt then went to the bathroom with a tipsy swagger.

Allard had always loved the ocean. It was one of God's most powerful, yet silent creations. This particular inlet was so warm it was like being in a large bath with waves. He rubbed the water against his tired muscles and stared out to the horizon where whales were moving in earnestly large splashes. He was intoxicated with each wave that crashed against his body,

"You need a towel." Her voice was more of a groan than a whisper, though she tried to be quiet.

Allard felt a tingle of his own down his spine and lower. He turned around to face Michelle. She stood on the very edge of the water line. The water lapped against her toes.

"You can leave that there." He commanded.

Michelle dropped the towel behind her and felt the water lapping against her ankles. The sand was much softer now. The warm water felt comforting against her calves, but when it met her thighs, it was delectable. Her sleeping shirt was tight against her stomach then her brown nipples were exposed as the water kissed her breasts through it.

Her lips quivered as he led her by the very tips of her fingertips closer to him. His mouth was as warm and comforting as the ocean so she waded there longer and longer. His hands held her thighs as she pushed closer to him and then they held her behind when her thighs gripped against his torso. Her ankles locked just below his buttocks and pressed against his thighs. The water was warm and beautiful with the fabric of her nightshirt floating in the waves around them. She watched the moon on the horizon. The whales splashed in the water.

The pressure of him was uncomfortable at first then incredibly soothing. She heard a loud whale moan leave her mouth. She spoke to nature as Allard spoke to her. He swam deeply and she clutched his back, her nails scratched his muscles. Her hands pawed at the tattoos on his arm as he filled her. They rocked in the water with the waves. Her tingles grew with each stroke. She quivered with each ebb and flow. He grunted small words in her ear as if hypnotizing her. Her reluctance and guilt were chased away with each syllable.

Michelle nearly lost consciousness and thought when he dove deeply into her. Her unpracticed sex was unaccustomed to his large lust, yet she pressed on. She pressed with easy movements. They were just right movements that turned her tingles to fire and soon her fire into an inferno. Her mind was lost in an explosion. Her body rocked with wave after wave and then she felt herself standing on uneasy intoxicated legs.

"Please don't tell..." Her lips shook.

"Why would I?" He answered. "Are you OK?"

"Sore, but good. Very good." She blushed.

"I need the bag." He stared in her dazed eyes.

She nodded. Michelle turned slowly in the water and shivered as she walked back to the beach. It didn't bother her that there were grains of sand rubbing roughly against her as she dried with the towel. Michelle felt comforted as she opened one half of the wide French doors to her room and turned to see Allard still in the water watching her. The room was spinning. She dropped the towel on the chair then peeled the shirt from her body and welcomed the soft mattress and cool pillow. She fell asleep immediately and floated away.

Allard's face stayed concerned. He looked to the house hoping for an answer, but there was none. The water moved against his body. He heard a splash from the whales then another one much closer. He turned to face the noise. The ripples of the water rocketed towards him. The sand was uneasy beneath his feet. Allard pushed his tired muscles toward the high bank of sharp rocks, but the predator gained on him swiftly. With his back to the rocks, he peered out towards the water. His hands flexed open and closed in anticipation. He timed the attack. Any underwater predator would attack him either high or low. He knew by the ripples it was gaining speed and altitude. His hands flexed again as the surface of the water broke. He saw the figure hurtle towards him rapidly and grabbed it by the neck. He forced it back down with rapid recoil submerging it then lifting it again and pulled it close to his face.

"You'd do yourself a service being more careful. I am not the one to sneak attack." He gritted.

"Just playing." Iara gasped through her constricted throat. They stared at each other with only the sounds of waves and whale splashes amongst them. He released her throat slowly. "So my water worked well." She smiled. Her wet hair plastered against her forehead.

"In this case." Allard grimaced.

"Great. So now you can..."

"I can what?" Allard dared her.

"I was just thinking you could consider this favor." She touched his chest and moved closer. "Why don't you come take a swim with me?"

"A favor. You like favors. Well, I have a question for you Iara..."

She drifted closer to him, her hands beneath the water.

"I have only the answers to which I am concerned." Her hands began to cleanse him. She washed him beneath the water with sturdy strokes. She used her easy hands to cleanse. She stroked him until he began to react to her supple fingers and strong hands. "That feels like an answer not a question."

Allard led her hand to all the right places beneath the water then he pulled her hand away and pulled her closer to him. His tattooed arm was inches from her face. The symbol she saw most visibly caused her eyes to go wide.

"Welk." He said with menace in his breath. "That's one of yours isn't it?"

Iara tried to pull away, but his hand was painfully clenched to her bicep.

"I said that's one of yours isn't it? The shell. He was one of yours. I had many questions that needed to be answered after I strangled him to death and saw the blackness of the darkest regions erupt in his eyes." His eyes bore a hole in her face. "My question was, why would one of hers be a scout? Why would one of hers attack me?

Doesn't she know, I'm sure she knows, I would come for her if he failed his mission."

"Things aren't good. I can't control everyone. There are some who act against my order."

"So, you've lost control?" His nostrils flared.

Iara began to panic. She felt a searing pain as his fingers dug into her skin. The whales splashed louder. Allard felt activity in the water. There was movement deep in the distance.

"Have you lost control?"

"We made a deal." She pleaded. "I don't know what Welk was doing. He disappeared long ago. I hoped he wouldn't cause trouble. I had no idea,"

"No idea?" Allard pulled her closer as he felt the movements under the water become more orderly. The whales stopped splashing.

"We made a deal. I want the same. The same as h-h-her." Iara stammered.

"You'll get it, but not the same as her." He huffed.

Allard pushed her by her arm against the rocks. Her face felt the cool slippery surface. She tried to climb up, but he held one leg elevated and pushed her forward. She was bent and exposed beneath the water. Iara craned her neck backward and kissed him with a mouthful of salty water. Allard spat the water into the ocean while his hands forced her forward again.

Without warning or sensitivity he entered her hard. She grunted as he pushed further. Her hands slipped as she tried to brace herself to no avail. His hands pawed at her hips while he pulled himself deeper inside of her. His size filled her frame and extended further. He was rough, wild and ravenous. She pushed back toward him with vigor and screamed when he pounded back. The ocean splashed against the rocks erupting against her pert nipples.

"Are you mad?" She asked him. "If you're mad I can't tell." She taunted. He pounded harder inside of her. "Oh!" She squealed. "I think you're a little upset." She groaned. To her moaning agreement, he pounded harder. His manhood filled her with glee. She had plenty of physical pleasures, but not like this. Not with Allard's type. Not that there were others like Allard. So, in fact, this was truly a once in a lifetime experience.

She felt her legs getting weak. She pushed forward to rest against the rocks, but he wouldn't allow it. His hands pulled her back stumbling against him. Her eyes went wide with shock as he consumed her. Her moans echoed in the air. The whales had begun to splash again. The pleasurable pain had begun to tear her apart.

Allard pushed forward acutely aware of the fish that swam around his legs and feet. They began to brush him closely. Some nibbled at his legs. He pushed forward enjoying the squeeze and noise Iara provided. The nibbles of the fish became bites as Iara began to squeal louder. He covered her mouth with his hand muffling her moans then lowered his hand to her throat and squeezed. She bucked backward as her body spasmed against his member. Her body quaked in the water and with each shake the fish pinches became more numerous but less perceived by Allard. His hands held tighter to her throat, clinched as he shook and stared at the bright moon. There was a loud splash off in the distance shielding the moan that erupted from his throat. Iara collapsed against the slippery rock as Allard took a half step backward.

Allard's eyes focused on the muscles in her back then lower to the rising globes of her buttocks as she bobbed in the water. The fish dissipated and swam away. Remnants of his excitement now washed to the sand with the foam of the tide.

"Fight hard, love hard." Iara laughed as she turned to him. Her smile stopped with a yelp as he grabbed the back of her head and brought it to him.

"We had a deal." He said.

"What more do you want?" She choked trying to hold herself steady otherwise be pulled down backward into the water. Her back stretched with pain.

"I need the others."

"What others?" Her eyes shifted side to side.

"The other two."

"How?" She panicked realizing she indeed did not have the upper hand in their deal.

"That's not my problem. We had a deal!" He grunted and walked from the water.

CHAPTER FIVE

COOPETITION

Dezi swung open the door to the rundown dive bar. The effort it took to open the heavy large oak door caused a strain in his shoulder. He was used to straining. Even though he had incredible abilities, there were still simple things that made him dig in and commit full effort to complete; like opening that door. The rank stench of cigarette smoke and cheap liquor filled his sensitive nostrils. He almost emptied what little he had on his weak stomach in the doorway, but managed to swallow it back and continue inside. Dezi dragged himself to the bar and held it to control his balance. He saw The Bartender look at him with a judgmental expression before he slowly approached him. Just as The Bartender was within three feet of him, Dezi found himself in one of his coughing fits. The Bartender reeled back on the tattered heels of his combats boots and covered his face,

“Geez, man. You sure you need to be in here?” The Bartender’s hand muffled his words.

Dezi’s first attempt at speaking was thwarted by more coughing so he nodded his head vigorously then took a couple of deep breaths trying to maintain some control. The Bartender dropped a napkin on the bar in front of Dezi, took a full step back and waited.

“Dragon?” Dezi growled.

“We don’t serve that here, pal. Maybe you should go over to Soho for that.”

Dezi looked up to The Bartender with angry blood-shot eyes. He wiped his mouth with the napkin and sat it back down on the bar. There was a slight smudge of the viscous black liquid on it.

“Shit man! You come here to die?” The Bartender covered his face.

“I need to speak to Dragon.” Dezi sounded better without the black phlegm in his throat. The Bartender pointed to the hallway at the end of the bar. Dezi nodded and dragged towards it.

"You gonna take this with you?" The napkin seemed to be holding The Bartender as a hostage. Dezi craned his thin neck over his shoulder.

"That's your tip."

The hallway was a longer walk for Dezi than most people. By the end of it, he was sliding against the wall using it as support. As he pushed himself forward, he brushed some of the pictures that hung and left one side of the wall hangings slightly askew. His ashen gray fingers found the space in the maroon drapes, pushed them open and stepped into the back area.

Dragon sat there as wide and as big as ever. He was shirtless and sitting under the light, his rolls of body fat exposed. His heavily tattooed body glistened with sweat with his eyes tightly clenched in pain. He was sitting behind a small round table draped with a dingy red tablecloth. The table held a dirty ashtray and a bottle of whiskey. The cause of his pain sat in a very high stool beside him. She was pretty with bright purple hair. Her pale face was a contrast to her dark purple lipstick. Her healthy bosom tried to escape her too tight black bustier. She sat with her legs spread wide, the absence of length in her dark skirt, exposed her see through panties. She tapped one foot of her thigh high leather boots against the stool, the other pressed the pedal for the tattoo gun. The needle from the tattoo gun she held dug into Dragon's forearm whilst the buzzing sound ricocheted off the walls. Dragon grunted with every line she drew and sometimes when she didn't.

"Hello Dragon." Dezi announced himself. Dragon's eyes popped open and rolled from the back of his skull to focus.

"What the fuck are you doing in here? You know how I feel about being sick."

"You'll be fine."

"Don't fucking tell me what I'll be. I KNOW you and your sickness. The number one thing I hate about being like this is getting sick. OW! SHIT!" He groaned and gave the tattoo artist a pissed look. She smirked not even bothering to look up. "Actually being sick is number two. Pain...pain is number one. I can't stand it. It's just not a feeling I appreciate."

"So why put yourself through it?" Dezi moved closer and leaned against a wall. He had a better view of the tattooist's creamy thighs and exposed crotch there.

"Don't ask questions you already know the answer to."

"You asked me what I was doing here..." Dezi returned with sarcasm.

"That's right I did! Don't you disrespect me. NOT ME! I gave you a new life and new way to follow. You were a sickly little boy when I took you under my wing and now look at you." He chuckled to himself. "You're a sickly little man."

The tattoo artist let out huff of air in a half laugh. Dezi didn't like that bitch laughing at him, he had half a mind to infect her.

"I put you all together and made you a cohesive unit. I created this. This is my invention. Your strength meant nothing without me tying you all together and now you're all running around like you don't owe me anything. The nerve." Dragon's eyes fluttered, he drifted off in another place momentarily. The buzz of the gun brought him back. "Alone you're like swatches of fabric, but together you're a quilt. I am the reason you even make sense. That bitch Alala came to see me...sassy and speaking out of turn as usual. Don't you do the same, Dezi. You were always the smart one. What you lack in strength, you make up for in your head." Dragon drifted off again. This time he mumbled under his breath. He banged against the table with his large fist then it stuck there in mid-air and shook. His head fell backward, his eyes opened and unrolled from the back of his head.

"So, I came to tell you..." Dezi began, but stopped when the table rocked.

The tablecloth shifted and out from beneath the table crawled a woman. Her bright blue fingernails slid up Dragon's sweaty torso, her fingernails matched her hair. Her skin was a dark mahogany that glowed with unnatural sheen. She turned to face Dezi and seemed shocked that someone else was in the room. She wiped her wet mouth, grabbed the bottle of whiskey and took a light chug. It wasn't until she removed the bottle from her lips that Dezi realized that she was the exact twin of the tattooist except with brown skin.

"This is what I like about being like this. The pleasures. Oh the pleasures are wonderful!" Dragon smiled.

The other woman stood. She wore a white tank top so thin you could see her areola through it. She wore some of the shortest white shorts Dezi had ever seen and a pair of bright white sneakers. She took hold of the tattoo gun as the tattooist exchanged places with her and slid underneath the table. As the tattooist disappeared under the tablecloth, she winked at Dezi and waved with all of her fingers. Dragon flinched when the tattoo began again.

"Pain. Definitely do not like the pain." Dragon winced.

"Allard may have The Needle. That's what I came to tell you. I saw a woman with a parcel. I'm sure it held it." He stared at Dragon who seemed more preoccupied with what was happening underneath the table than what he was saying. "He has the..."

"I know he does. I'm preparing for it as we speak." Dragon motioned to his tattoo. "I've heard from all of you except Sundiata. Where is he?"

"I don't know."

"I'm sure Alala is looking for him." Dragon winced as his tattoo continued.

"You've heard from all of us?" Dezi's eyebrow cocked.

"Yes...except Kronus. You know how he is. He's a little too glib for his own good."

Dezi nodded in agreement. Kronus had always been the outsider on the inside, but because of his distinct abilities and his way with words, they allowed it.

"Sundiata took a trip, I need to know what he found. You go follow up on it; you're better at getting information anyway. I'll handle Alala and Kronus then we'll see what all of this Jacob Mora, Scilymax business is."

"What about Allard?" Dezi huffed.

"He's sending me a gift. I need to prepare for it."

"I'd rather go find Sundiata myself than going to retrace his steps."

"Alala won't have a hard time finding him. He has such a hard time hiding. But if she does try some shit and decides her and Sundiata are going their separate ways together, I need to make sure my interests are protected as well."

Dragon summoned a waitress and asked her to prepare his table for a guest. She quickly retrieved a crisp white tablecloth. When she cleared Dragon's table, she squealed in surprise at the woman beneath it favoring him. She tried as hard as she could to ignore the woman and act as if she'd seen nothing, but hurried to complete her task. Dragon ordered a fine bottle of Shiraz and two crystal stems. Dezi huffed. Good luck with finding either of those in this hole in a wall.

"You still here?" Dragon grunted as his eyes fluttered back into his head.

Dezi nodded and reluctantly began to walk away, but not before sneaking a glance at Dragon's new tattoo.

L

Jacob Mora sat alone in a private dining area of New York's exquisite Le Bernadien restaurant alone. He slowly savored his Kobe beef in silence. The only sound was the clink of his knife and fork. Occasionally he would slurp his exotic coffee from the cup. He spared his manners since he was the only one in the room. His security detail waited outside the closed doors on both entrances. One checked the food and wait staff entering from the kitchen, the other made sure no one entered from the main restaurant. Mora flipped open an old worn journal and read over the pages again. There were two pages in particular that he focused on. They were the pages his father wrote during his excursion through Northern Africa while serving in the war. The pages served as the impetus for much of Jacob's work and he was making sure, once again, that the puzzle pieces fit.

The security guard found himself taking a deep breath as Alala approached him. Not only was she beautiful, she seemed to be ready to walk straight through him. He raised his hand just as she reached him. She was so close his hand nearly touched her breasts. They were covered in a red corset, which contrasted with her long slacks. Her hair was tied in a tight bun. She wore glasses again, but this time with clear lenses and thick plastic frames, which made her look bookish. She cocked her eyebrow at his hand.

“I’m sorry miss, there’s a private party in this room.” He said staring down passed her eyes to her corset-enhanced cleavage.

“A party of one.” She deadpanned. “Tell Jake I’m outside please.”

“Sorry m’am. It’s a private party.”

“M’am? I was Miss a second ago. You trying to say I’m old now?”

“No Miss.” The security guard took a deep breath as he watched her pull her mobile phone from her pants pocket and start to type.

Jacob’s phone chirped startling his glass of wine from his lips. He stared down at his phone. There weren’t many that had this number. None of them would be calling him at this time of night. He checked the screen.

OPEN UP!

- A

“Let her in Franco!” Jacob bellowed, placed his glass on the table, stood and buttoned his jacket. As the door opened, he tucked his tie in and adjusted it.

"You getting all sexy for me, Jake? Don't bother." She said as she high stepped into the room with the security guard following her.

"It's ok, Franco." Mora waved the guard off ordering him to leave the room. He pulled a chair out and pushed it in after Alala had taken her seat. "Would you like something to eat?" Mora took his seat and sipped his wine. "Some wine?"

"No thank you." She frowned at his choice of cabernet in the wine bucket. "I need to go to your little island."

"Which one?"

"The one that you took my friend to. If you want my help and my services, there has to be some cooperation on your part."

"I'll cooperate fine, but I can't allow your freakish friends to run around rampant messing up my plan and casting suspicion. How do I know you can keep him under control?"

"Because I just told you. Why are you asking me so many questions? Would you like me to leave you alone?" She motioned to leave.

"NO!" Mora nearly yelped. "It's fine, I just..." He stared down at the journal. His eyes lingered there too long. He was sure of it when he looked up and Alala was smiling at him. "If I sign off on another private cargo plane, the Brazilian government will start asking questions again. Those public works 'donations' are getting expensive. I'll get you a private plane to Sao Paolo and you can take a ferry over."

"Ferry?" She scrunched up her nose. "Do you even own a yacht?" She laughed.

"It's in the Maldives with my ex-wife." He spat back.

"Oh, just one." She rested her hand on her chin bored with his solutions.

"The other..." He pushed his plate to the center of the table. "Is in Ibiza with my daughter and her friends on vacation. Are you sure this is all you need?"

"No. I told you what I need. I need Allard, but barring his popping up, I can't locate him."

"What else?" He tapped his fingers on the journal.

"Are you rushing me, Mora?" Her voice raised an octave.

"I just want to make sure we're prepared. This can go very wrong, very quickly."

"I have more experience at this than you. I think if there's anyone that knows what they're talking about in this room, it's me."

Her attitude had started to really get on his nerves. He appreciated her ass more than her sass.

"Dustin Carver is coming with me." She said nonchalantly as if announcing the weather was cold in November.

He stopped still, he nervously stared her in the face. Had she just revealed his innermost secrets, his lifetime goals, his personal mission statement and the entire reason how and why Scilymax was created to Dustin Carver? Dustin Carver the creepy research head with one too many questions and one less mistress. His hand instinctually clutched the old journal and pulled it closer to him.

"What does he know?" Mora breathed.

"He knows how to help the situation. He doesn't know the situation, but he knows how to help it. So as long as he stays useful, he stays close to me."

"He doesn't listen. He doesn't know the details of this..."

"He killed Mohana The Charmer. Most of you couldn't even get within one hundred kilometers of Mohana and Dustin stabbed him in the chest with a pearl handle knife and watched him bleed out. He captured Allard. He developed the Scilymax Seraphium Serum and had the intelligence and kindness of heart to be sweet to me. Sounds like he's done more for you." She pointed to his journal. "And your goals, than you have." She probed the inside of her cheek with her tongue. Pushing away from the table, she pranced toward the door. "Don't worry about the travel. We'll find another way." She huffed as she pranced from the room with her head held high.

Lisa's soft brown eyes fluttered open and stared out of the window. The sky was a deep purple with the faint signs of the beginning of sunrise. She closed her eyes again with the intention of drifting soundly back to sleep, but her mind had begun to travel. Soon her body shifted restlessly, her legs scissored underneath the covers, then her feet flexed up and down again and again. She tossed the covers off and dangled her feet off the side of the bed. Lisa had spent so much of her time as the protector of her friends, family and colleagues that it was hard to ignore the spark of instinct. She climbed out of the bed with an urge to quell her restless energy. Her emergency bag was still packed so she had to rummage through hoping she had packed something to wear while exercising. All that was there were a pair of basketball shorts and a tank top. She pulled them on quickly along with the sports bra that was smooshed at the bottom of the bag. Her ponytail swayed back and forth as she tied her sneakers. Even though she knew the chances of the temperature being below eighty-five degrees outside were very slim, she tied her jacket around her waist in case she needed it.

The Hut was silent and dark so Lisa snuck down the hallway on her tiptoes as if on a reconnaissance mission. She tapped on Jury's door lightly then pushed it open quietly. Jury slept tucked tightly in a fetal position, her hands covered her head protecting herself from all outside assailants.

"Marjorie." Lisa whispered. She repeated herself a little louder when there was no answer.

Marjorie slid one hand off of her head and perked her head up slightly as if to say 'I'm listening'. Lisa couldn't help but smile at the adorable child-like response Marjorie had to her mothering figure.

"I'm going for a run. You wanna come?"

Marjorie's face contorted in a frown. She covered her head with the pillow and huffed.

Lisa eased down the steps. The last thing she wanted was to wake Iara. She was sure Iara would want to run with her. With her energy, she was probably doing jumping jacks in her bedroom already. Lisa moved extra slowly as she slid down the hall passed Iara's room towards

Michelle's. She didn't bother to create more noise by knocking. She pushed the doorknob, but it was locked. Lisa grunted and huffed. Logically it made sense, if Lisa was in the room not too far from Iara's, she too would have kept her door locked. Her knuckles touched against the wooden door three individual times. She took a deep breath and stared down the hall for movement at Iara's room. There was no answer. She tried again. One knock... two knocks...

The lock clicked and the door slowly opened. Michelle peered out looking quite the worse for wear. She squinted at Lisa clearly expecting Iara to be standing in the doorway.

"What's wrong?" Michelle's voice was groggy and horse as if it had been strained.

"Nothing I'm going for a run. I wanted to see if you wanna come." Lisa shrugged. She was obviously the only one up with any type of energy.

Michelle answered by leaving the door open and dragging her feet back to the bed. Lisa stepped in and nearly recoiled when she realized Michelle was naked. Michelle bent over near the foot of the bed. Had it been daylight, she would've exposed way more of herself than Lisa would've cared to see. Still, Lisa averted her eyes towards the windows of the French doors. Brighter blue light now mixed with purple. The Sun was rising slowly.

“Here.” Michelle extended her hand.

Lisa reached her hand out and grabbed what she was handed without looking in an effort to preserve Michelle’s privacy, which Michelle obviously did not miss. The material was rough against her fingers. She looked down at the burlap bag.

“What’s this for?”

“Put that outside for Allard. He needs it.” Michelle yawned and climbed back into the bed.

A bag? Lisa was confused. When exactly had he said this? She wasn’t privy to this need. No one cleared borrowing bags with her. As she made her way to the door, she saw a crumpled wet towel sitting on a nearby chair. She turned to ask all of her questions, but decided against it when she heard Michelle let out a grumbling snore.

Again, she found herself moving on tiptoes. Allard laid nearly corpse stiff in the hammock. She wanted to place the bag close enough to him that he knew it was for him, but didn’t want to wake him or alert him to her presence. Granules of sand crunched beneath her toes as she eased closer to him. She placed the bag on the ground, pushed it with her foot in his direction and turned to walk away. Not good enough. She turned back and nudged the bag with her foot a few more inches. She watched him. He slept peacefully. It was the first time in a long time that she had seen the innocence in his face. She had first known the peaceful innocence when he was suspended in the tube, but now all of that had seemed to wash away.

Lisa bent down, picked up the bag, walked quietly over to him and sat it on the ground next to the hammock. She stood over him and watched his chest slowly rise and fall. His eyes darted back and forth beneath his eyelids. His lips quivered. She thought of his lips and how soft they looked. His hands were strong and rough. His shirt was tight against his chest. His shorts gave an insight into the bulge she had seen at full mass. He was an enigma and she knew that every day he slept there, every day he lived on that island with them, there would be more protecting to be done. He was her burden.

Allard's hands twitched then balled into a fist. His eyes flicked open quickly as he gasped himself awake. He reeled backward against the hammock in shock. Taken aback, Lisa jumped slightly.

"You snuck up on me." Allard laughed quietly.

"I didn't mean to..." Lisa began to apologize.

"No, it's ok. I haven't had someone be able to do that in a long time. You are very skilled if you can do that." Allard placed his feet on the ground and looked up at Lisa's smooth brown face. He admired her soft features and small mouth.

"You have to go." She whispered. "I can't have you here any longer. However you got here, wherever you came from, you need to do it again and go back there. Marjorie is getting less and less fun to be around, Michelle is...I don't know what to call it. You have to go." Lisa glared at him eye to eye.

"I'm leaving today." Allard said and then to make sure she believed she had intimidated him into leaving... "I'm sorry I caused you stress. That wasn't my intention."

Lisa didn't want to believe it was that easy, but she didn't care. He was leaving and maybe then the world would right itself.

"You really have no urge to hear my story?" Allard looked down studying the sand grains beneath his feet.

"Some things just have to remain a mystery. I'll deal with it and when the time comes, I'll know everything I need to know." Lisa backed up slowly. She felt a tinge of guilt in hurting his feelings.

"I sensed that in you." Allard looked to her and smiled.

The smile was too familiar to her. She felt as if she had been saying things he had already heard.

"Sensed?" Lisa began stretching her legs slowly in preparation for her run.

"Yes. You're stronger than the average soul. You're a strong willed person. Strong with spirit." He nodded. He was silent as he watched her stretch. She let him watch, but didn't look to see what he was watching. Like most men, she was sure he was looking at how her ass curved or how her thighs flexed. He watched her hands and wrists.

"As for the mystery." She finished stretching. "I'll think about that on my run." She smiled, waved and began to walk away.

"Want some company? It's still kind of dark out there. Jungle... trees...animals. Not really a place for you to be by yourself." Allard warned.

"I'll be fine. Strong, remember?" Lisa trotted away.

She ran onto the beach with sand kicking high behind her. Her pace had started out faster than she wanted, but it was all for the best considering Allard was back there and she wanted to show him just how fast she could be in a chase. Her feet pushed against the soft sand then headed toward the harder surface by the water. She looked out to the sunrise then a few hundred yards ahead to the trees. It was a dark desolate jungle. A small footpath led right through the center of it, splitting it like a dark axe through a black skull. As she got closer, she slowed. It was not the safest place to be alone. She trotted in place. Her breath inhaled then exhaled easy. Allard was many things and one of them was a formidable opponent for the unknown. Lisa craned her head over her shoulder and saw Allard standing at the edge of the beach watching over her. She waved him toward her. He trotted quickly without hesitation with the burlap bag swaying in his hand. The two of them ran off towards the jungle side-by-side breathing in tandem without saying a word to each other.

When Jury opened her bedroom door, the smell of French toast and omelets was unmistakable. She floated down the stairs by her nose like a cartoon character. She stopped and watched in awe as Iara moved swiftly about the kitchen preparing the fluffiest omelets she'd ever seen in her life. Jury had become used to Iara's cooking attire, but even today was different for Iara. She stood in one of the smallest bikinis created. Small patches of material covered with seashells hid her breasts and her bottom wasn't covered at all. The G-string bikini hid between the cheeks of her bottom. If it hadn't been for the long green apron, Iara would've been near naked. To top things off, she was completely bare foot. Jury shook her head.

"Babyyyyyyy, you are something else." She startled Iara. "I don't know about this half naked cooking you're doing, but I'm sure you'll make some man happy somewhere, so I'm going to have to take some pointers from you." Jury laughed.

Iara smiled, taken aback by Jury's relaxed tone. Jury hadn't cracked jokes with her often, if at all.

"I'll give you all the pointers you'd like Dr. Houston." Iara smiled as she shook powdered sugar onto a plate of walnut banana French toast.

"Right now, just point me to a plate. I'm starving."

Iara handed her a ready-made plate with a southwestern style omelet and French toast with fresh strawberries.

"Be careful. The plate is hot." Iara smiled being sure to hand it to Jury with a potholder. Jury walked the plate to the table, said her prayer, lifted her fork and stopped inches from tasty goodness.

"Wait...Lisa put you up to this didn't she. She's trying to test me on a diet or soften me up for something." Jury's eyebrow cocked.

"Not at all, Dr. Houston." Iara continued by squeezing fresh orange juice. "She's not here. I haven't spoken to her this morning. I guess she hasn't returned from her run. I saw footprints down by the beach, but none returning."

Jury made a guttural moan, as she tasted the eggs. They were beyond divine. The food had touched her in a place food had never touched before. She was in the midst of a full-fledged foodgasm.

"Where did you learn to cook like this?" Jury spoke with her mouth full.

"Wow! What is that smell?" Michelle entered the kitchen with a bright glowing smile on her face.

"It's breakfast, Pastor Bonds." Iara smiled handing Michelle her plate.

"Not Pastor. Please don't call me that." Michelle took the plate with a thank you and sat across from Jury. "Where's Lisa?"

"I believe still on her run." Iara looked up studying Michelle's reaction.

"Still? She's been out since sunrise? That's four or five hours." Michelle tasted her French toast and joined the foodgasm express.

“I’m sure she’s safe. Allard wouldn’t let anything happen to her.” Iara watched Michelle’s response again, but was startled by...

“Allard is with her?” Jury looked up with confusion in her eyes.

“I believe so. I saw two pair of footprints that lead off down the path. I assumed he went with her.” Iara placed two glasses of fresh squeezed orange juice on the table. No pulp for Jury. Some pulp for Michelle.

“I don’t think Lisa would go on a run with Allard.” Michelle tried to force any resemblance of jealousy from her voice.

“If she’s not back when we finish eating, we’re going out to look for her.” Jury ate quicker.

“What about Allard?” Michelle asked concerned.

“Well if they’re together then we’ll find them both, but I’m just concerned about my friend.” Jury huffed.

Michelle didn’t like Jury’s tone or inference of Lisa being only her friend, but she shrugged it off and ate. She needed the extra energy after her eventful night.

The three women stood looking down the beach at the two sets of footprints leading into the jungle thick vegetation. It didn’t take a gumshoe to surmise the two of them both headed into the jungle. Whether it was together or one chasing the other was unsure until they reached the point that the prints were side by side for the rest of the way.

“I can run it, but I don’t know if you two want to. Let’s get the jeep and follow the path in.” Jury said.

“We can’t do that. There won’t be enough space once we pass the tree line. There are no roads or cart paths here.” Iara shook her head vigorously.

“We drove here so there are obviously other roads we can take.” Michelle pointed out towards the front of The Hut.

“Those are the only ones....”

“Excuse me?” Jury looked over to Iara blocking the sun from her eyes to get a clearer view of her face.

“The only roads on this entire island are the ones that lead from the Scilymax pier to this facility and the security house. The rest of the island is foot traffic only.” Explained Iara.

“So how the hell did you get here?” Jury’s patience was wearing thin.

“I took my small boat around the island to the pier and security picked me up there. You’ll have to go on foot through the jungle until you make it to the water and get a boat. If they've been gone this long, then they're probably in town."

"This makes no sense." Jury shook her head. "Why would she go to that guy for protection?"

"She asked me if I'd go, but I was too tired." Michelle said guiltily.

"Yeah, she asked me too. SHIT! Ok, let's go." Jury was antsy now.

"Maybe I should stay here. I'll wait for them if they come back." Iara seemed just as fearful of the dark trees as they were.

"You have to come. What happens if we make it into town? I don't speak Portuguese and neither does Michelle. You're FROM here. You have to come." Jury rationalized. She didn't care why Iara didn't want to walk through the jungle. The only thing she wanted was a quick start.

"I think I should stay. What if they come back and then leave looking for us." Iara's bottom lip quivered.

"Wait." Michelle picked up a stick and wrote big letters in the sand.

We'll Be Right Back!

Michelle shrugged. "Should we tell the security guys to look out for them or contact someone in town or something?"

Jury shook her head and thought. The easiest way to begin the drama again was to tell them Allard was on the island.

Iara quickly changed into some clothes and the three trotted towards the dense ecological wonderland. Suddenly, the big breakfast didn't seem to be such a good idea.

The Clerk could tell how high maintenance a customer would be by how high they held their head when they walked in and how careful they were not to touch the old items in the shop. He surmised that the woman that had just walked in with the extremely long coat and high boots would be the worst challenge of the day. The man who lingered behind her, however, was a push over.

"Welcome to Heavenly Little Things. Did you come looking for anything in particular this morning?" The Clerk gave his best toothy smile.

"Is Shalako in yet?" Alala smiled as she whipped her hair over her shoulder.

"He's in a meeting. Is there something I can help you with?" He knew it was often Shalako's way of giving his name to the rich and telling them to ask for him personally. More often than not, Shalako didn't know these people. He'd meet them at a dinner party and was just being his normally talkative self. Although, The Clerk was sure Shalako would remember this one.

"Do you know when the meeting will be over? I'd like to talk to him at his earliest." Her lips twisted in concert with her eyebrow as she glared down at some of the antiques on display.

"I'll check for you. While you're waiting, please have a look around at some of our pieces." The Clerk excused himself quickly then stopped in his tracks. "I'm sorry, what's your name miss?" He doubted it much mattered with Shalako's memory, but he wanted to know for himself as well.

"You think he would remember it, if you told him?" She was all sarcasm.

Touche´.

"My name is Alala."

He excused himself again and closed a back door behind him. Alala turned to Dustin, who was looking over the wares. He studied many of them closely like the experienced antique buyer he was. He had never seen some of this stuff before. Many of it seemed to be art, others rather odd takes on normal products. He stopped and looked over a heavy marble carving. The base was solid which led to small oval shapes leading higher. Held atop it all was an animal tusk like object. He rubbed the top and let his hand slide down the smooth stone. He considered buying it for Janice as a make up gift for the Alala confusion. It looked slightly phallic, although the topped portion was crooked into a crescent shape. Then again, that could've made it even more phallic.

"The war horn." Alala stared at it alongside Dustin.

"War horn? I thought it was more of a fertility object." Dustin shrugged it off.

"Sorry, did I mess it up? Was it supposed to be a gift for your mistress...I mean Miss Assistant." She exposed him faster than a heavy gusting wind up a toile skirt.

"Looked familiar. Wasn't sure where I'd seen it before." He ignored her as he stepped away.

"Popular amongst East Africans..." She explained as she stared up at a large circular object above the counter. It was a polished metal that seemed to be molded by thousands of small fingers. The fingerprints were still embedded in the surface.

Dustin turned back momentarily and looked at the war horn. It did look like a symbol he'd seen in the pictures of Allard's tattoos. He turned back and admired the vast array of trunks and chests. Each one was intricately designed. The woodwork designs looked to be hand carved. He held a small trunk in the palm of his hand and pushed the top to open, but it wouldn't budge. He looked around the small box for a locking mechanism, but the sides and bottom were all smooth. The bottom was engraved with a small symbol.

"Leave that alone." Alala warned.

"I was thinking about buying it, but it won't..."

"You don't want that. Neither does your...assistant." Alala smiled as she held her tongue, for once.

"Am I supposed to be giving you something, Alala?" Shalako's voice echoed from above.

The two of them looked up to see Shalako looking down on them from a small catwalk that hovered above the main level. The catwalk connected two separate balconies. Each balcony was crammed with large bookshelves filled with dusty leather-bound books. Beyond one balcony, Alala saw the open door from which Shalako had emerged. He bent over with his forearms pressed against the handrails of the catwalk.

"Well hello to you too!" Alala smiled. "It's been a long time, Shalako. Way too long."

"It really has. When Jessup told me you were here, I was sure this was some kind of joke."

"You know, I am no laughing matter, honey." Alala winked.

Dustin couldn't help, but to feel the pangs of jealousy at their friendly flirtatious banter. He involuntarily cleared his throat bringing attention to himself. Shalako's head pivoted towards him slowly.

"Hello sir, welcome to Heavenly Little Things. My name is Shalako, the purveyor. Jessup can help you with any of your needs."

"He's actually with me, Shalako." Alala began. "This is Dustin Carver. A colleague of mine."

Shalako rose from his leaning posture, stood tall and crossed his arms. He pivoted his head slowly towards Alala and looked down at her none too pleased.

"Oh wipe that look off your face. He's helping me with something and I need these arrangements immediately." Alala conned. She watched him stroke his cropped goatee with his hand. "I wouldn't bring him here if he couldn't be trusted." She turned serious.

Dustin looked away and began to peruse some of the goods to avert his attention from the uncomfortable silence.

"I'm in a meeting right now." Shalako spoke extremely slowly. "If you can come back later, perhaps around noon. I'll be able to meet with you...in private."

"Be sure you're ready for me. I said immediately and I mean immediately." Alala gritted her teeth.

"And I mean privately. No offense, Mister Carver."

Dustin glared up at Shalako as he tossed the small trunk back and forth between his hands. Shalako peered back down at Dustin and batted the name around in his head trying to remember where he'd heard it before.

He waved as Alala and Carver exited the store then waited watching through the large glass window as they climbed into the back of Alala's car and eased away along the cobblestone streets.

"I'll put the 'be back soon' sign up, Mr. Shalako." Jessup's voice rang from the first floor as he walked to the door.

"Thank you. I'll be done momentarily." Shalako's leather soles clunked against the metal catwalk as he walked to the open door.

He closed it behind him. He dropped his glasses to the small wooden desk with a clatter and rubbed the sides of his nose with his fingers.

"So..." He rubbed his hands together. "Now that your friend has gone, where is it you need to be?" He stared at Dezi with an ominous expression.

It began with a run, turned into a jog, led to a hike and ended with a walk. Throughout the darkest portions of the dense cluttered foliage of the jungle areas, Lisa felt comforted by Allard's presence. They had passed through a clearing and had been walking much longer than she had expected, but civilization was clearly a destination the two of them had craved. The first sign of it lay just at the bottom of a hill. During the run, there was barely a word spoken between the two. The same was true for the jog except they occasionally warned each other of low swinging branches and the occasional pile of animal dung. The hike was more strenuous. Allard encouraged Lisa to dig deep and even took her hand and pulled her up several sharp overhangs. They joked and bonded during the walk.

Lisa was more relaxed now that her only concern was herself. She had given up being afraid of Allard long ago, but now she had formed a comfort in her heart while being near him. The comfort wasn't enough to allow him back around her friends. He seemed to bring out a difference in them that she could not explain. There was one in her as well, but she could explain that one. They rounded a small thicket of brush and touched their feet onto a wide path that led straight through a grassy field.

"Follow the yellow brick road." She laughed.

"This is an endless journey. I've only had a couple this long in all my life." He shook his head in disbelief.

"No one told you to jump into the icy waters of the Antarctic in a pair of drawers!" She elbowed his side.

"Yes, thankfully it's not as cold. That has an effect on a man."

"Shrinkage is not cute." She huffed as she pushed ahead wiping sweat from her brow.

"There's a building right there." He pointed ahead, changing the subject.

They rounded the building and found themselves on a long walkway littered with small shops and a few restaurants. Natives and tourists alike mingled along the paths which were just not big enough and not quite paved enough to be called streets. The two instinctively followed the path to a small restaurant. Lisa headed straight for the bathroom to freshen up as Allard found himself led by the hostess to a table by an open window. He wistfully stared out at the people and the light bustle of the market place. He preferred small areas like this with little pain and lots of character.

"You ok?" Lisa stood at the table looking down at his face. Her concern was evident in her slight smile. The dirt and grime were gone. Her hair was pulled taut and in place now.

"Yes." He stood, pulled her chair out and pushed it back in as she sat. "I was just thinking about some business I need to attend to."

"You have a job?"

"I have my own business."

"That's good. I couldn't imagine a place allowing you to take off so much time." She joked.

The waitress approached. She immediately began to speak quickly in English covered in an accent. It was barely intelligible to Lisa.

"Ummm...I'll have what he's having." She shrugged leaving the pressure to Allard.

"Very well then." Allard looked at the menu, perused momentarily, looked up to the waitress and began to speak fluent Portuguese.

The waitress smiled pleasantly surprised she didn't have to figure out the Americans' order from their finger points and body language. She nodded and swiftly walked away.

"Portuguese. I think you left that out when we talked before." Lisa cocked her head to the side.

"I speak several tongues. I'm good with my mouth."

"Oh are you?" She felt a slight tingle.

"With language and that sort of thing." He was careful not to offend.

"It's ok. I wasn't offended. I'm not that stiff. Work is work. This is..."

"Play?" He smiled flirtatiously.

"Not work." She corrected then smiled.

CHAPTER DCX

It was afternoon on Ilha Grande, Brazil, but it looked near night in the densest areas of the jungle. Jury, Michelle and Iara trotted slowly through the damp turf. Exotic flowers of every imaginable color bordered their path. These were the flowers of legend. They held cures for tragic unexplained illnesses and simple treatments for re-curring ailments. Uninterrupted, they were just beautiful exotic flowers avoiding the heavy stomp of three women headed toward the water.

"Break!" Michelle called. They slowed to a halt as she rested her hands on her sore knees.

“We should keep moving.” Iara peered through the trees for the unseen.

“I just need a minute.” Michelle huffed.

“Figures Lisa would pick somewhere like this to run. Always the daredevil that one.” Jury held the moist wood of a thick nearby tree and stretched her legs.

A strong wind gust blew the tops of the trees making them sway hard back and forth.

“OK, let’s keep moving.” Iara started to walk.

“Slow up. We all go together.” Jury shouted as Iara got further away. “At least she changed her clothes.” She whispered to Michelle. “Imagine if she came out here in that stripper-kini.”

Michelle stared down at the odd insects that seemed entranced by her colorful sneakers. When they got too close for comfort, she moved them side to side alarming the bugs. They backed away cautiously, stopped and looked at the large colorful objects again.

“I hope this isn’t too far, I ate too much to be running like this.” Jury rubbed her belly.

“We might as well walk. It’s not like we’re really going to rundown Lisa and Allard. They’re just too fast.” Michelle massaged her thighs.

“Tell that to stripper-kini, she’s been rushing ever since we got in the jungle.”

"I thought it was just me. What's she doing?" Michelle looked up to see Iara slowly and cautiously moving backwards.

"Are you ok? What's wrong?' Jury shouted, but knew she was asking way too late. Something was wrong. She could sense it.

Iara exploded into a sprint down an adjacent path screaming at the top of her lungs. Jury and Michelle ran after her unsure of what the danger was, but understanding the need for urgency. Dirt flew from their feet as they pushed hard to catch up to Iara. Jury, being the more trained runner, gained on her quickly.

"What's back there?" Jury panted between breaths.

"Go! Go! They're coming! Don't stop running!" Iara huffed as her long legs stretched in lengthy strides.

Michelle took up the rear still pained from not enough of a break. She pushed hard trying to gain on the 20 yards that separated her from the others. She was curious to look back, she wasn't convinced Iara was all there in the head and this was the final straw. However, there was something about her fear, her urgency. Sharp pains shot up Michelle's thighs as her quads began to burn. The thumps of her feet against the ground began to wear on her. Her pace slowed. She saw Jury and Iara had pulled further and further away and nearly felt a sense of desperation until she noticed they too had slowed.

"What are we running from?" She panted, as her quick strides became plodding thuds against the hard dirt.

There was a low sound. It was a gurgling hollow rumble behind her. Michelle looked over her shoulder and squinted. She couldn't see much beyond a hundred yards behind her. The jungle was just too dense and it was quiet except for the low sound. Was it a sound or was she listening to her own breathing? There was something about the darkness that was odd. The way the sun disappeared against it, not into it. Was it the darkness that scared Iara? She took deep breaths resigned to catch up to her friends.

"Come! Now!" Jury yelled.

"Ok...I'm coming." Michelle shot back.

The sound gurgled again. It was deeper now. It sounded like a snore. Michelle looked up to the darkness and squinted. She couldn't make out anything. Lifting her head, she turned to Jury and Iara and they weren't there. No one was there. Her legs began to move. She walked fast towards the spot she had last seen them.

"Jury!? Marjorie!?" Michelle shouted as she trotted ahead. The gurgling was louder. She turned behind her to the darkness. Nothing.

She heard steps and screams from further away. It was Jury yelling something. Michelle began to jog a little faster. Jury's voice was crashing into her eardrums yet she couldn't understand a word. The jungle was too loud. There were too many animal noises...wait...that was the problem. There were NO animal noises. The jungle had silenced. Michelle trotted faster through the jungle. Her legs brushed by wet plants. She smelled the musk of wild flowers and fungus. She looked back, but nothing was there. Jury's voice echoed and bellowed.

"Marjorie! Where are you?"

"HERE!" Jury's voice erupted in Michelle's ears like a siren rattling her eardrums as if a stereo was turned on way too loudly.

Michelle turned toward the path and was face to face with a sweaty faced Jury whose eyes exploded wildly from the sockets in shock. Her strong hand grabbed Michelle's thick arm too tightly. Michelle winced in pain as she was tugged stumbling forward. Jury pulled her as they ran.

"GO! GO! They're right there! GO! OH MY GOD! RUN MICHELLE!" Jury squealed so loudly her voice cracked.

Michelle heard everything in a hollow tube. It was as if she had water trapped in her ears and the loud sounds only vibrated the drum sometimes. Her arm was sore from being pulled, but she pushed forward with Jury's hand guiding her. Why were they running? She felt the silence, but what was the silence. Where was the snoring sound now? Where were the animals? They were behind her. It was all behind her now. She moved to look behind her, but was scared Jury would tug her over a tree root, she'd miss her footing and the two of them would tumble to the ground. She saw the muscles in Jury's arms flex as she tugged. Jury turned to Michelle; her eyes looked over her left shoulder and bulged again. She tugged Michelle harder.

"Come on!" She heard her clearer.

She looked passed Jury and saw the break of a clearing about a football stadium length ahead. Michelle pushed forward, but her lungs began to burn. Had she inhaled fiery needles on the run? Jury's thighs were moving at double speed; Michelle could see the strain of her leg muscles. Suddenly, Jury swiveled her body, pushed Michelle to the left as she pulled. Jury's fist flew over Michelle's left shoulder with speed and returned scratched. Jury pulled Michelle along. Without warning, she pushed Michelle aside again and threw another punch. This time her fist returned scratched and bloodied. Michelle turned to look back, but Jury pulled her forward.

"We're just passing through! She said we're just passing through!" Jury screamed without turning back again.

Michelle's body felt numb. She didn't want to run anymore. She wanted to face off with the darkness. Jury wouldn't let her. Jury pulled her. Jury punched at the darkness until they stumbled out into the clearing where things felt unbearably bright. Jury's legs stumbled forward and finally she lost her balance. Michelle felt her legs intertwining with others. Their forward momentum pushed them head first to the ground and they tumbled down a hill. Up and down. Sky and ground. Michelle had seen darkness on one side and Iara off in the distance on the other. Her limbs felt scrapes and hard bangs as the two rolled together, separately and on top of each other. Finally they stopped. Jury's hand dragged Michelle by her ankle a few more feet before she stopped and looked back toward the jungle.

Jury stared out toward the jungle shaking. Michelle lay collapsed staring up at her. She turned back and all she saw were trees and beautiful flowers. A serene view if any. Michelle took Jury's hand and held it. It was ice cold and bloody. Jury's body shook so hard it looked as if she were convulsing. Michelle grabbed Jury and hugged her sweaty cold body to hers. All she could think to do was to hold her, to rub her back and tell her it was OK. Jury slowly released the tension and collapsed in Michelle's arms. Her heaving breaths pushed against Michelle's body until Michelle's own fatigue set in. Michelle sat on her heels and looked up to the teary bloodshot eyes of her friend and knew she had missed something.

Jury shot up and ran towards Iara. It was the first Michelle had noticed Iara was sitting in a small fishing boat with an outboard motor. Jury put her index finger within an inch of Iara's face.

"You happy now? Are you happy now, bitch? We could've died! WE could've died!" Jury yelled at Iara with ferocity.

"Why are you...?" Michelle staggered over to Jury. She cooed easily trying to relax her.

"She's banned Michelle! She's banned from the jungle. You heard them!"

"Heard what?" Michelle was confused.

Iara just shook her head embarrassed and worried.

"They were telling her we were all going to hell. They were telling her she wasn't allowed...that WE weren't allowed because we were with her. You didn't HEAR that!?" Jury shouted keeping her finger in Iara's face.

Jury looked to Michelle who looked confused on top of being exhausted. “You didn’t hear that?”

“She’s not like you. She didn’t hear any of it. I was surprised when YOU heard it. What are you, Marjorie?” Iara glared.

“What is she?” Michelle shook her head trying to shake off the exhaustion. “What do you mean *what*?”

“She means am I like Allard?” Jury asked lowering her finger.

The two of them stood watching Iara. Iara realized she had said too much.

“Which means you are...” Michelle said putting pieces together faster and faster.

Allard and Lisa walked through the tight aisles of the market and trading place looking at small knick-knacks and souvenirs. They moved with the slow lumbering pace of well-fed and fatigued bodies. Occasionally Lisa leaned against Allard to brace herself. She was impressed that she could be so relaxed around him. He felt a mellow remorsefulness at how their relationship began. She was a very sweet person indeed. Regardless of her assisting in his capture and scientific study. She perused the hand made jewelry looking to find just the right things to bring back for Jury and Michelle. Turquoise beads and recycled metal were in vast abundance.

"You sure you have enough to cover this?" Lisa grimaced as she collected a few small hand carved idols.

"Yes. Don't worry about it. Get whatever you like." Allard held a bracelet against her smooth brown skin. "What do you think of this? I think this is really nice with your complexion." It was really quite simple. It was a cord bracelet with a few small metal carvings and one small symbol in the middle.

"Is that a dragon?" Lisa stared at the intricately designed piece. It was so small yet impossibly perfect in design.

"I believe so. In Chinese culture dragons are considered a very malevolent creature." Allard began.

"That's how you see me?" Lisa arched her head over her shoulder looking Allard in his eyes.

"But." He continued. "Some believe dragons are just protecting their young, their family, their place in life from the people, the man that comes to destroy the Earth. I think that's how the Japanese came up with Godzilla." They laughed together. "I'm buying this for you. I'd like you to wear it." He tied the bracelet to her right wrist without further discussion.

Lisa stared at the bracelet on and off the entire time they walked around the marketplace. It was pretty, yet foreboding, just like her. Allard collected the items she purchased in his burlap bag. They even found a little something for Iara. Allard picked out a small pen depicting a dolphin jumping over the moon.

The sun was slowly lowering across the sky as they sat on the steps of a bed and breakfast and ate fresh mango. They were the juiciest mangoes Lisa had ever tasted. The juice slid down her chin and she wiped it with the back of her hand. Allard peeled his easily and sucked from the seed slowly making sure to take every bit of fruit and sustenance.

"So if we take the ferry to the other side of the island." Lisa picked small fibers from the seed out of her teeth. "We'll just have to walk through the jungle to get back to The Hut?"

"Yes. It's not as far as a run as we did. You can cut the jungle off and get through it in maybe an hour walking."

"What do you mean "you"?" Lisa pulled more fruit into her mouth and sucked the juices.

"I thought it'd be best that since you'd like me to go... I wouldn't return." He saw Lisa's shoulders visibly slump. A small, embarrassed smile caught the corner of her lips.

"Right. You're right. I guess that's best." She thought it over. "That jungle was just pretty dark when we ran it. I'm sure it'll be pitch black by the time I get there..." She worked the mango for more fruit using just her lips this time.

"Well if you give me a head start, I'm sure you can call a security team and they can pick you up at the piers and take you back to The Hut by boat." In a very comfortable gesture, he wiped mango juice from her chin with his index finger.

Lisa blushed at his touch. Her skin felt warm where he had touched. She looked down at her wrist. The bracelet had a dull shine to it. Her arm was warm there too. Allard tasted the mango juice from his finger and bit his bottom lip in response to just how sweet it was.

"I guess I can go in here and make the call." She gestured behind her, stood and stretched her legs.

"And that is my cue." Allard smiled as he stood alongside her. "I'll just come in with you to make sure everything is ok. You may need a translator." He held the door for her and walked into the modest yet very well decorated bed and breakfast.

Immediately, a short older man began speaking horribly accented English at a rapid pace. Lisa knew this was the sales pitch. His hands gestured wildly to sections of the room showing off features of the space. Lisa's eyes were bright with shock and humor and glanced to Allard. He was gob smacked as to when he could interrupt the man. Finally, Allard held his hands aloft and spoke to him slowly in Portuguese. He punctuated each sentence by lowering his hands as if to say "slow down". Reeling back on his heels, the man shrugged his shoulders. He had an opposing deal. Allard nodded and smiled.

"Of course." Allard smiled.

"He doesn't want us to use the phone." Lisa bristled.

"No, it's just that his phone can't make long distance calls. Only the rooms have access. In order for you to make a call out to The Hut, we have to do it from a room. If we go into the room..."

"We have to rent it." Lisa shook her head.

"Right. Even though we're just passing through. But he'll give us a reduced rate and won't charge extra for the call." Allard shrugged as he reached in his pocket and peeled off several U.S. twenty dollar bills.

"I feel bad. I'm sorry. I'll just walk." Lisa tugged at Allard's arm.

"It's fine. I think I need a good shower anyway. It'll be a great relaxing way to shuffle off unto parts unknown." Allard rubbed her back.

The bed and breakfast was painted in deep ivory textures. Even with its diminutive size, there was a grand old-world feel to the place. The furniture was ripped straight from turn of the century Portugal. The extra large portraits on the walls stared down at the inhabitants silently judging them. The wood floors were laid from what looked to be whole logs. They were barely stained, but without a splinter. Lisa and Allard climbed the creaky staircase to the uppermost floor and walked down the hallway to the end. The number seven was carved into the door itself and inlayed with broken pieces of glass and seashells. Allard tried peering through the number into the room and only saw contorted images as if looking through the opposite end of a peephole.

He inserted the large antique key with no response. He twisted the other way harder waiting for a click. He felt Lisa's breathing intensify and then her body leaned against his. Her warm breasts poked at him mid back as she pressed forward. The door gave way to a small room with a rather large bed. The furniture wasn't as beautiful or styled as the rest of the place. The bed linens looked to be at least a decade old, but the fixtures and the wooden windows gave the place style. A small painting hung above the low laying bed. The picture was painted in cool blues and mint greens depicting a boat filled with men staring out to a woman wading in the water. The woman looked to be enticing them to come out further and her beautiful features seemed to be winning the battle of wills.

"A rotary phone?" Lisa's eyes went wide. "I haven't seen one of these since my Aunt Chauncey's house circa 1983. Yes I have an Aunt Chauncey, long story." She laughed.

"I'll hop in the shower so I can be out of here as soon as possible." Allard nodded. He opened the small door to the small bathroom and closed it behind him.

Lisa sat on the firm mattress with her back against the headboard lost in thought. The proper thing to do was to do as she said she would. She'd let Allard take his shower, she'd call the security force and just as Allard bid adieu to parts unknown she'd be picked up at the pier. However, what she was supposed to do according to Scilymax and especially Dustin was to call the security team and alert them to Allard's presence. They could have the entire town locked down within an hour's time. The security team with back up would slowly close the perimeter on the hotel until they surrounded it. Allard would be taken into custody again and Dustin's work, her livelihood, would continue to prosper. Even more importantly, her friends would be safe again. The phone seemed to ask her "The proper thing or the right thing?"

The sound of the shower erupted. Lisa looked down to her bracelet and the warm spot it occupied on her wrist. She could practically feel the warm water hitting Allard's body. He was in another world of relaxation. The phone was bright white with intentions. Where can I connect you? What will be your call? She lifted the receiver with a sigh, slid her index finger into the rotary and began to dial. After her call, Lisa crossed the small room and pulled the sheers and the curtains closed. The room remained bright but long shadows were cast against the bed. She fingered the bracelet with the dragon and that abnormally warm spot on her arm. Lisa slid from her clothes and stood naked at the foot of the bed. Her breath rose and fell deeply and her body with it. Standing on her toes, she walked to the bathroom door, turned the knob, stepped in and closed the door behind her.

The small motorboat sputtered across the waves. On occasion it sounded as if it would shoot sparks, smoke and die right in the ocean. Iara used her arm and wrists adeptly steering the boat by the tiller. They were in a rush and the urgency seemed to increase three fold since they had begun their water journey, but it had become obvious the boat just couldn't handle the high speeds for too long so Iara slowed it down.

Michelle sat at the bow staring ahead in silence. She barely flinched as the spray dampened her clothes. Jury sat with her back pressed to the side in deeper thought. She watched as other boats passed. She waved in a friendly gesture to them as sailors do. No waves were returned. None of he nods were acknowledged. This went on for another ten minutes before she noticed that reaction was split. More often the women just stared. On occasion one or two would nod. The men would not look. Some had even covered their eyes as the boat passed them.

"I have never been in a place where all of the men ignore me." Jury shook her head as the boat slowed over another rough area of the ocean.

"A lot of men think women are bad luck in the water. You think it's sexism?" Michelle finally spoke, but had not turned or motioned away from her focal point out in the distance.

"No. I think it's her." Jury motioned toward Iara. "So, did you take all of those people to the jungle too, boo?"

"I have a reputation of being somewhat of a man eater." Iara smiled. "Some of them just believe what they hear. It really is all gossip. So the women give me cold stares and the men peek through their fingers. At least they do out here. Let me go into Carnivale or even just sit and have dinner in town and everyone wants to be my friend. They all want to get close and touch me."

"They know about your abilities." Jury was intrigued that for once Iara seemed melancholy.

"No one knows. No one really. They just hear whispers from one or another. Gossip, like I said." Iara raised her voice slightly over the growl of the boat motor.

More boats, more people not looking. To amuse herself Jury made funny faces at a couple of the passerby. She caught one older woman giggling to herself.

"Gotcha, mama!" Jury patted herself on the back.

"Does Allard know you're like him?" Michelle turned looking back at Iara.

“Allard and I aren’t alike. Call it low self-esteem, but he is so much more special than I am.” Iara laughed.

A party boat playing loud Merengue music approached slowly. The partygoers swayed and danced as the ship coasted toward the small vessel with the three women. As they approached, Michelle waved with a smile at some handsome men on the deck that were taking pictures.

“Hey beautiful, can we get a ride?” One of the men shouted.

“Sorry.” Michelle’s face spread a big grin.

“You sure? I see some space right there.” Another young stud pointed next to Jury.

“Toss me a couple of those beers and I’ll think about it.” Jury shot back to the laughter of nearly half the boat. Their boats were closer now and were easing by each other so as not to cause any waves that would overcome Iara’s smaller vessel.

“Your captain is much sexier than ours!” The frat boy with the dirty white university cap pointed to Iara. Iara winked and perked up. She arched her back pointing her full breasts to the sky.

The party boat captain looked over the side of the boat and waved to Michelle, then Jury. Upon seeing Iara, his face went pale white.

"Olá! Capitão!" Iara smiled a devilish grin.

The Captain ducked his eyes underneath his cartoonish captain's hat and turned away with a gruff bristle.

"Maybe you boys should teach him how to greet a lady." Iara shouted as the boats passed each other. She blew a kiss to her suitors.

"Hey man! That wasn't cool. How you treat her so bad? She didn't do anything to you!" They heard one of the men shout. A small group of men turned on the captain and began shouting at him. Iara pressed down on the throttle and sped away kicking a spray unto some of the women that sat on the rear of the party ship.

"Was that your ability? Did you make that happen?" Jury perked up looking back at what seemed to be a mutiny erupting on the party boat.

Iara shrugged.

"Someone could get hurt. Like when you took us into the jungle. Why don't they want you in the jungle? What was that in the jungle? Did you have sex with Mother Nature's husband or something?" Michelle fumed never turning to face her.

"I told you by the pier, you're not ready for those answers. I don't even know how to explain it to you without destroying you. Dr. Houston may be a little easier to speak with." Iara slowed the boat.

"Why because she heard some voices in the jungle?" Michelle shot back.

"No, because she doesn't think she already knows the answers." Iara defended angrily.

"What they said was..." Jury began trying to clear the cold silence.

"You really shouldn't..." Iara warned.

"They said she was a traitor." Jury finished ignoring Iara. "They said she was banished to the water and that's where she'd stay. They called her a traitor and said she would die for crossing into their land. She would die and so would her friends." By the end, Jury looked spent. She stared off towards the island. Michelle reached over and rubbed her injured hand.

"What did they look like? What did this to your hands?" Michelle brushed Jury's scratched hands softly.

Jury sat quietly thinking about the flowers. The beautiful exotic flowers that swirled and rushed with tornado like speed. The precision was impeccable. The thorns from stems swayed and lashed like whips. She thought about how they exploded from the ground collecting together in the darkness creating more darkness and barreled toward Michelle to smother her. She thought of how she punched at them and they ripped at her knuckles and would not stop moving forward. The smell of the pollen they omitted created a cloud of dark green dust that seared passed the trees and had overcome Michelle's senses. The flowers floated as if possessed and followed the power of a wind that pushed them forward. She knew she would never look at flowers the same again. Jury looked at Michelle with a solemn expression.

"She's right. You're not ready to hear this."

Allard's hands roamed Lisa's body slowly as the washcloth spread soap around her torso. The hot water bounced off of her face as she stood with her eyes closed feeling the warm sensation of his hands and the steam that fogged the room. He was doing a great job of washing her body. There wasn't one area he hadn't covered with lengthy detail and circular motion. She placed her hands against the cool tiles and braced herself as his fingers slid up her thighs, this time without the washcloth. He eased up her smooth inner thighs and found the origin of her lust. His fingers coaxed her slowly. A warm tingle trickled up her spine giving her a shiver. Lisa's hand grabbed the shower head hard and hung from it as she dangled slowly rocking to the motions of his fingers. He eased her round and round. He soothed her forward and backward. His lips kissed her neck and swam lower between her shoulder blades. One of his hands pulled her waist backward arching her back more. Her rear poked back toward him as his fingers continued to work. She loved the sensation of the hot water as it splashed across her face and dribbled down her chest. She found her waist gyrating involuntarily with his fingers finding just the right spot and her legs became uneasy. His hand reached and turned off the water.

She backed into the bedroom without drying off. There was no need; she would only continue to get wetter anyway. She tasted his mouth slowly, his tongue protruded often, slipping along hers. She was impressed how he guided her hips with his hands back toward the bed without once steering her wrong. She relaxed and pushed closer to him allowing his manhood to press against her warm inner thigh. He was warm too. He was a near inferno in the length and girth of the area he touched there. She wanted to devour every piece of him like a ravenous hyena, but she took her time. Her hands, raised above her head then trailed down his chest as she kissed his stomach and lower. She looked up to witness his enjoyment as her mouth pleased him. His head fell backward and a groan escaped his lips. Her rhythm didn't waver as her mouth adjusted to the contours of his thickness while her hands helped with his length. She enjoyed pleasing him here and she grew more excited as his moans and murmurs increased.

His hands reached low and lifted her by her armpits. She eased her plentiful backside against the bed and smiled. She adjusted her position on the bed and used her finger to call him closer. He crawled across the bed toward her like the predator he was. The length of his body extended beyond hers as he met her face to face by the headboard. She pulled his lips with hers and then let her own head fall back as his mouth sucked at one nipple then the other. The sensation was enough to make her shiver, but she held herself together. His mouth was vigorous on her full-engorged breasts. Tiny sharp nibbles marked her hard nipples. The sensation was just enough to cause the floodgates to open again.

Lisa grabbed his hips and pulled him forward. She wanted him right now. There would be no mistaking her intention as she pulled him nearer. She reached between them and allowed her hand to wrap around the warmth of his weapon. She aimed it touching just the surface of her target and wound her hips against him. She opened slowly for him allowing him to feel her warmth and lust in stages. Unprepared for the power of his weapon, she recoiled slightly when he entered her slowly. She trembled at the stroke. Her hands reached from the bed to his back and back to the bed to clutch the sheets. She held herself in place so as not to miss a moment of him inside of her. His weapon hit her right on the bullseye. She grunted her approval then worked her hips towards him. She could handle more. She wanted more. He obliged with swift yet easy motions exploding her mental capacity for pleasure.

Her legs arched upward and locked the ankles around his lower back. A tightened vice from her strong thighs pulled him deeper within her.

"Harder." She groaned and he obliged with might.

His strokes increased and with it her energy. She wanted more. She wanted it all. Her legs pulled him deeper as he thrust harder.

"Yes. Don't stop." She spoke.

They were moving fluidly. Suddenly, she reached out to the bed and braced her hand against the cheap side table. She pulled him deeper and pushed against the table pivoting her hips and him within her. Her shoulders and elbows twisted in concert and she drove herself sideways. He pulled her by her behind upward then around and she was now on top of him. She panted with success as she immediately rode him hard. Her eyes glared down at him as she bore down against him. Her breasts bounced precariously above him. He lifted and met them with kisses then harder sucks. She groaned under the feeling. Not yet, she thought.

Her hand clenched his throat and pushed his head back against the pillow. Lisa held him there in place as her hips swiveled and bounced. She took as much of him as she could stand then took more. She moaned loudly with each new deeper thrust. Rocking backward she found an explosion within her core and thrust against him. Her button pressed against him while his weapon massaged more than one spot within her as it filled her. Her slender hand tightened against his neck as she felt a billion tiny explosions erupt within her loins and the dam broke with ease.

Lisa sat with erect nipples shivering above him quietly still. She was afraid to move, fearful that a movement would end it all or begin it all again. He reached and grabbed her wrist. Before she could protest, it was pushed behind her back, she squealed as he shifted his body. His member rocked within her. He twisted and contorted her body quickly until he was behind her. A lightning strike erupted within her as he filled her again with more thrusts and pounding punishment. Lisa held her breath trying her best not to lose the power, but it had already left in small trickles that slid down her thighs. Bone jarring teeth clicking thrusts pounded within her.

"Oh Yes!" She moaned and begged for more punishment and he obliged. She squeezed him within her and met his thrusts.

"Yes." He moaned as she gripped him tightly around his weapon. He pulled from her quickly. She moaned in disappointment until she felt the product of their lust explode across her backside in torrents. Allard's guttural moans subsided as he eased back and sat on his heels.

Lisa looked over her shoulder at the sweaty, muscle-tense man of amazement and smiled.

"I guess that's one helluva goodbye gift." She smirked and flashed her bracelet. "Ok." She looked at the clock on the wall. "I need to get cleaned up and go before..." She stared at Allard's soft smile. "The security team gets to the pier and decides to come looking for me."

Allard watched her leap from the edge of the bed, her smooth brown rear bounced and jiggled as she escaped into the bathroom. He took a deep breath as he climbed over to the floor and found the burlap bag. The contents scattered across the small desk. He pancaked his hand against the bag feeling the material. He worked it slowly inch by inch searching intently. He finally stopped just at the side seam. His fingers pinched into the seam and slowly removed a gold needle. Its glint was beyond brilliant. He stared at it wistfully in his palm then sighed deeply. He took the gold needle and pinched it from each side using his thumb and index finger on each hand. Slowly, he pulled the needle outward and it stretched and elongated as pliable as chewing gum.

Holding the now eight-inch needle in his hand, he waved it quickly to the right with one hand. With each wave, the needle gained width until it was as thick as a pencil. He peered at the point and it’s microscopically sharp end. Allard swept the contents of the bag back inside it with the back of his left hand and propped the bag against the wall.

Lisa washed her face and private area with a warm soapy cloth. She washed the remnants of Allard’s excitement from her backside and dressed quickly.

“Are you going to take the ferry? The hostess at the restaurant said the last one is at dusk. You may want to catch it.” She shouted.

“Yes. I’m thinking of doing that. But I don’t want to run into your Scilymax soldiers.” He returned.

“Right.” She hustled her clothes on knowing that she didn’t have much time before she had to make it to that pier. “You need your clothes, they’re hanging on the door.”

"Bring them to me, please." Allard sounded preoccupied and worrisome.

Lisa fixed her hair, grabbed his clothes from the hook on the bathroom door and stepped out.

"Are you ok?" She asked.

It wasn't a pain so much as it felt like she had swallowed a piece of ice, a piece of ice that touched her heart. Her hands gave way and dropped the clothes. Her eyes went blurry momentarily then returned to focus quickly. She glanced up and saw Allard looking at her with sad eyes. She looked down and saw a long golden needle sticking out of her chest. She felt no pain, just weakness. Her legs crumbled, but Allard caught her and lifted her high. She floated down onto the bed. Allard tucked the pillow underneath her head. Her mouth tried to form words, but she found she couldn't muster the energy. It was cold in there. So very, very cold. Her eyes got heavy. She needed to know what this was in her chest and why Allard put it there.

"Don't fight. Just relax. I have to take it out." Allard whispered to her. "When I do..." He tapered off. She could see a shiny glint in his eyes. The sparkle of the needle was reflecting off of water in the corner of his eyes.

Her body began to shudder and shiver. She could not control it. She felt a jarring in her head as if her brain was trying to dislodge itself from her skull. She needed to tell him something. She had to tell him one last thing before she left him there and now she could not speak.

"Just take off the bracelet." Allard whispered quietly in her ear.

She tried to do as he said, but she couldn't move her arms. She felt his soft lips kiss her forehead.

"No. Listen." He stared in her face as her mouth contorted.

She felt control leaving her. She could barely see anything anymore. She could only barely hear him.

"I'm sorry. You'll understand." He petted her head softly. His fingers wrapped around the needle and pulled it swiftly from her chest.

Lisa was gone.

Allard got dressed and walked down the steps swiftly. He stopped by the front desk and said a few kind words to the old man behind it. He explained that the young lady he was with wasn't feeling well and would be staying the night to sleep it off. The man was all too helpful in offering to bring her up some tea and a mix of his grand-mother's home remedy. Allard assured him it wouldn't be necessary. He paid the outstanding balance for the rest of the night in cash.

The old man lent an envelope and stationary paper to Allard and watched him as he wrote a short note. He sealed it in the envelope and signed the back of the flap along the seam to insure that if the envelope were pried opened, the intended would know someone had opened it before them. What struck the man the oddest was that Allard did not leave a name on the front of the envelope. He just asked him to hold it and instructed to give it to whoever asked for it.

Allard walked out of the hotel and headed swiftly down the main street. He turned toward the pier and looked to the water. There was no sign of the security team just yet. He looked above and saw a small plane swoop overhead. He watched it. It was lower than most planes, though smaller. The design was sleek. He watched it shoot back towards the other end of town and tilt. The way it moved and pivoted seemed robotic and erratic. The pilot was uncertain. He stared in the air as it swooped back across the town again. He caught a glimpse of the top as it corkscrewed a maneuver. The top had a small black dome over it. It was a robotic drone. A plane operated by remote control. There was no doubt the remote control was operated by Scilymax.

Allard quickly walked back down the main street. He looked in alleys and archways, through windows and at faces to see if he spotted Scilymax security agents. Without warning he was caught in a rush of wind. It pushed him forward as if someone was pressing against his shoulder blades. He could barely keep his feet beneath him. He stumbled and looked around, but no one seemed to notice him beyond the wind. His chest grew tight. He knew what this was and was confused as to why it was happening now. His feet flopped beneath him as he tripped and flailed. His feet burst from the ground with a loud bang that shook the entire area. Pedestrian screams were muffled in the wind that lifted him high into the air.

Allard was caught in one of Shalako's courier waves. This was the precursor to transport. It was like being trapped in your own private tornado. Shalako had begun moving him without permission. Allard took deep breaths trying to right himself. Dust particles showered across his face slapping him hard with bits of ice and rock.

With an arch in his back, Allard held his arms behind himself and shot high into the air. He faced upward and controlled his breathing, as he waited for the concussion. Something was wrong. There was something coming towards him at an even faster rate of speed. A black smoldering cloud of dust arched downward directly toward him. If he didn't move, there would be a collision. He would smack dead into this firing smolder.

Allard tucked his elbows to his side while raising his fists. He pushed the dust around him outward. His trajectory changed and pushed him sideways in an arc. The black smolder whipped in the opposite direction so that they created a bow in the air. He looked across and smiled. He raised his hand to his face.

Alala looked across the sky at the brown mist of dust mere arms lengths away. It was as if Allard ascended in an elevator while Alala descended sharply away from him. Her face dropped as he passed her and blew a kiss with his hand. There was a crackle in the sky followed by a loud thunderclap. Allard disappeared into the mist headed to a destination that he did not know and with a heavy heart for what he'd left behind.

EN[OF GOOK TI O

BOOK THREE

The Dark Ensemble

CHAPTER ONE

A NIGHT IN TONULLA

Boyce Linden didn't appreciate the treatment he received on the mission. As a Senior Team Captain, he was the second highest ranked and most battle experienced Scilymax soldier on the field. He'd served two tours in Afghanistan, led troops in three peacekeeping missions in Darfur and personally supervised the creation of the new member enlistees' training manual. All of this happened AFTER; he graduated from Exeter cum laude and served his country as an officer in the Marines. He was a gifted solider.

When he was given the assignment of monitoring the last platoon in a flanking position, he knew exactly what to call it...babysitting. He was a babysitter for not only this platoon, but for pedestrians. It was an action-less assignment. His platoon consisted of twelve men. They were all recruits in a Scilymax operation titled "Seraphim". In Boyce's briefing, he was told they were men with exceptional abilities with uncertain skills. If the time had come, he would lead them forward and monitor them, not engage, during battle. He was babysitting. The platoon was also required to keep pedestrians from entering the engagement perimeter. They were babysitting.

When the shit hit the wind turbine, it came as a surprise to him that he was ordered to move his platoon in as quickly as possible and capture the target immediately. He'd heard over the radio that the other teams were taking heavy losses quickly, but the command screamed to him seemed a desperate plea. A command not just for him, but for his platoon especially.

They had been standing right outside of The Ed Sullivan Theater where David Letterman tapes his nightly talk show. He led them quickly heading east from their position at Broadway and Fifty-Third Street toward the marker on his wrist-bound GPS. They weaved through the eerily empty streets running with their weapons shouldered. Boyce found himself in awe as they crossed an empty sixth avenue. The other teams had done a magical job of clearing everywhere, absolutely everywhere. He was also surprised by how closely his troops followed him. What had begun as a V formation became nearly a straight line. They were restraining themselves from crossing his leadership position. They were overly energetic and their strides consisted of long-legged leaps as if they were jumping over puddles. Boyce didn't like it. Excitement in battle usually got people killed.

"He's up high! Up high!" A voice spoke to him in his earpiece.

Up high? Boyce was confused "up high" wasn't a direction they used as soldiers. His eyes looked north toward Central Park, but all he saw was a clear street. He stared through the trees trying to catch a glimpse of action, but there was none.

"Jesus Kangaroo Christ!" He heard another Team Leader shout. "Fire! Fire! Fire!" The voice registered panic.

Boyce raised his fist high, a signal to stop. He was surprised when they did. They not only stopped, but they stopped on a dime. His index finger pushed at the air in a spiral motion, telling them to spread wide forming a circle. The Seraphim Soldiers were fast if nothing else. They quickly adjusted into a large oval formation and moved slowly towards Fifth Avenue. Boyce was the lead point.

"Up high again! Blue he's right on top of you!"

Blue was Boyce's position. On top of him, was within his radius. There was no one to be found. In a stroke of inspired curiosity, Boyce looked up the towering skyscrapers. There he was, their target was falling down towards them. His arms were stretched wide, his legs tucked tightly to his body. He was definitely up high. Before Boyce raised his weapon he knew it was too late. In mid-air, the man swung a long metallic object from nowhere. Shots fired wildly upward all missing the man as he landed on top of a soldier flattening him cold. He swung a staff like spear and swiftly demolished another soldier.

Tranquilizer darts whizzed by the target. His spear blocked others. He was fast. He was way too fast. Boyce could barely see him much less aim at him. His team had begun to fall out of formation. Boyce thought it was panic until he saw a few of them drop their weapons.

“What are you doing?” Boyce screamed.

Faster than he could imagine, two soldiers tackled The Target from behind pushing him steps forward. The Target flung himself to the left and threw one soldier off. His spear swung with a metallic schwinging sound and knocked off the other. He ducked a flying dart, jumped over another low shot dart, swung his spear high above his head and finished off another soldier all with quick cat like reflexes.

Boyce trained his aim and got off three rapid dart shots. The target evaded each dart swiftly. He’d ducked his head and torso around them like one would a slow moving bug. His eyes focused on Boyce with angry intentions, his long dreadlocks flung wide as he pivoted his head. He charged Boyce with those same puddle jump strides and screamed with a war growl. The sound sent a shiver up

Boyce's spine. His index finger held down the trigger and blasted darts from the muzzle. Boyce stumbled backward as the target covered fifty yards in seconds evading darts along the way. He grabbed Boyce's weapon and flung it and Boyce attached to it across the street slamming hard into a wall.

The thud was excruciatingly painful. Boyce tried his hardest to breath, but his diaphragm just wasn't in the mood to cooperate. He closed his eyes and forced himself to count quietly to himself.

"10...9...8..."

Boyce heard sounds of more darts flying and feet running to and fro.

"7...6...5..."

He heard the sound of a window exploding.

"4...3...2"

He heard screams of agony.

"1"

He could inhale. The pains stretched from his chest to his back across the left side. He knew there were at least three broken ribs in his body. When he opened his eyes, they took a moment to focus through the agony. He didn't believe them when they did. The Target was sword fighting with a member of his platoon. The Target's silvery spear swung quickly whistling as it sparked against the black sword the soldier swung. There were no Scilymax issued swords so Boyce knew he was mistaken. Was it a pipe in the soldier's hand? A broken rifle barrel? An extra thick windshield wiper blade? The Target was more skilled than the soldier. He looked to be playing with his food before he ate it. He spun, stepped back and two-stepped sideways with ease as the soldier charged hard flailing his...sword. It really was a sword. Boyce saw the handle; the blade was wide and sharpened to a point.

Boyce made it to his feet. His weapon was gone. A soldier laid half inside and half outside the broken window of a small jewelry shop. He hobbled to him and gingerly turned him over on his back. Large shards of glass stuck from his torso like stalagmites. Boyce didn't feel a pulse on his jugular. He pushed up the soldier's eyelids to check for dilation, but there was nothing. No dilation, no pupils, just black orbs in the sockets. Boyce recoiled with a scream and stumbled backward. His gloved hands pushed the bits of glass across the sidewalk as he retreated from the body.

"How dare you." He heard someone shout. It was the soldier. He had resorted to double handed swings like a lumberjack chopping logs. "You can't win." The soldier huffed.

"You won't win." The Target deadpanned and stepped back. With one quick swing of the silver spear, the soldier's head went flying over The Target's left shoulder and bounced to the street.

The Target looked around. No one else was there except Boyce. His eyebrow arched and a smile twisted his left cheek. Boyce shuffled on his hands and knees towards his fallen comrade's body. His only hope for survival was that soldier's weapon. Thudding footsteps moved quickly behind him. The glass wouldn't move fast enough. There were wooden shelves and metal brackets in his way. The footsteps slowed, stalking him as he climbed over the body. He peered into the store. Glass, glass and more glass. The steps were close behind Boyce now. Boyce would have just one chance. Finally, he saw the weapon wedged at the bottom of the display case. He lunged, grabbed it, rolled on his back, flipped the safety, looked up and fired.

The darts exploded from the barrel and wedged in the neck of a soldier. The soldier grabbed them in shock. His eyes grew as big as saucers as he clutched the darts to pull them out. He shivered and fell shaking and ceasing against the floor. There were four more soldiers behind him.

"Don't shoot!" Another soldier shouted. His weapon was trained on Boyce just in case. "Where'd The Target go?"

"He was behind me." Boyce leaned back on his elbows.

It happened too quickly. By the time the soldier in the tail position turned to look behind him, his eyes were watching his body fall in the opposite direction, and then all went black just like his eyeballs.

Boyce lay on the floor hidden behind a jewelry case. His shots were missing The Target by mere millimeters. The other soldiers were losing the battle horribly. Hand to hand, The Target could not be beat. There was a constant snap of bones impacted into the brain. Another soldier pulled out one of those black swords. He put up a great fight slicing and swinging at The Target. When his blade landed flat against The Target's forearm, Boyce tried to stop the carnage with two more shots aimed directly for The Target's head. Instinctually, The Target pulled the soldier by his arm directly into the path of the darts, his black eyes exploded on impact.

"Nice shot." The Target said. "Stay out of the way." He glared at Boyce and leapt through the broken store window out into the street.

A barrage of dart fire hit the sidewalk and concrete façade around him as he charged the direction they had come from. Boyce made it to his feet. He hobbled over the broken bodies toward the window. Though he checked each and every one of them, he knew what to expect. Each of the fallen had blackened eyes.

By the time Boyce staggered out of the store, he found himself following a trail of injured soldiers through the desolate and damaged streets of midtown Manhattan. He moved slowly with his weapon leveled. The pain of breathing with broken ribs was beyond the asthma attacks he had as a kid. He wanted to sit down and call a timeout. However, there was duty involved and Boyce Linden was very much about duty.

Sometime during the fighting he'd lost his earpiece and without verbal direction, he followed the directional compass of weapon fire. The fire led him back to ground zero, St. Patrick's Cathedral. The Target stood in the middle of an empty Fifth Avenue and defended himself against the onslaught of three soldiers and their swords. Again, he battled with swift moves. The Target avoided each matte black blade with spins and flourishes. His silver spear sung a song of terror as it sliced through the air occasionally clashing against the black swords. With each clash bright blue sparks scattered through the air the air.

Boyce approached slowly one foot after the other quietly stalking his prey. He watched The Target through the concave view of his scope trying to get a clear shot. His sweaty left index finger flipped the safety switch to auxiliary ammunition. He heard a slight hum and the rattle of darts collecting in the chamber. His heart dropped when The Target leapt high and with a lightning fast spin, stabbed one of the soldiers in the neck. The soldier crumbled to the ground. It was the first time Boyce noticed that when the sword-baring soldiers were killed, there was no thick red mess of blood left behind. Not one drop of blood to witness. He stalked slowly hiding in the doorway of a store. There was to be a shot. There had to be.

The Target went on the offensive. His spear swung hard clattering against a soldier's sword. The soldier's knees seemed to buckle with each concussion. He was done in with a solid blow that broke the sword and nearly chopped him in half. The last remaining soldier jumped quickly landing a slice across The Target's back. He let out a growling scream then spun to protect himself. Boyce moved swiftly, his shot was near. The Target swung wildly at the soldier who buckled and retreated step by step as The Target attacked with angry ferocity. Boyce aimed his weapon at the slash left across The Target's back.

"Take it now! Fire!" A voice shouted.

Boyce, startled by the voice, pulled the trigger and saw his three darts erupt from the barrel and swish across the avenue. The Target lunged forward grabbed the solider and used him as cover.

Thud! Thud! Thud!

The darts hit the solider and he spun on his heels like a top. The spear flew from The Target's hand hidden behind the soldier. Boyce didn't see it, he wouldn't have had a chance even if he had. His eyes glanced up to the Cathedral to see the owner of the voice that told him to fire. Dustin Carver's eyes looked back at him. They registered shock and sadness. Boyce didn't understand why it had become so unbearably cold. It was nearly April and he was freezing. His legs were weak so he let himself fall backward. It was harder to breathe now. He looked up to the beautiful blue sky, the cumulous clouds looked like large puffs of cotton candy. Lower in his gaze was the silver spear sticking out of his chest.

"I told you to stay out of the way." The Target huffed as his face came into view. Boyce could feel The Target holding his hand. It was warm. As odd as he felt about the action, Boyce didn't want it to stop. The Target's face looked blurry then cleared, then blurry again. His spare hand reached to Boyce's face and wiped the tears from his eyes so he could see clearly again. "Hold my hand. Relax. Don't fight, good soul. It will come swiftly. Just go with it."

Boyce nodded, he knew "it" was death and true to form, it came quickly for those it wanted.

"What's your name?" The Target asked.

"Boyce." He whispered.

"Boyce, I am Allard. Remember that name...Allard. It is important for you."

It was an odd name, but Boyce knew he wouldn't forget it. A name attached to the man that had just mortally wounded him. As for importance, the idea of importance had drastically changed for Boyce as he lay there. There were so many names that went through his fading memory as he tried to hold on to his life. There were so many memories that seemed to pass by him noisily like racecars on a track. He only had one name he wanted to say.

"Jury." He whispered. "Love." He nodded.

"You love a jury?" Allard's brow furrowed.

Boyce shook his head slowly. That's not what he meant. He took a slow breath to repeat himself clearly. He flinched when Allard screamed. Allard's hand clamped down on Boyce's, crushing the bones in his fingers. "Why are you punishing me now?" Boyce thought. Allard reached behind himself and pulled a dart from his back. The tip dripped blood. Boyce's heart would've begun to race if it could. It was the worst timing possible. His last words were uttered to a man that was now on his way into an induced coma.

Allard released Boyce's hand and staggered as he turned to face his assailant. Boyce saw the glimmer of the two remaining darts in Allard's back. Allard's body began to convulse as the Scilymax Amnio began to course rapidly through his veins.

Allard fell to his knees trying to maintain his equilibrium, but his body did not cooperate. His left hand clutched his spear but it struggled for a grip. He couldn't find the energy to swing it. The muscle relaxers had taken effect. His muscles were shutting off one by one as if someone was switching off lights at the end of the night. His eyes focused on Dustin's grey hair and pale blue eyes. Dustin kept his distance from Allard. He slowly stepped around an invisible ten-foot perimeter staring at Allard and waited for a reaction.

Boyce needed help, but Dustin was preoccupied with the catch. Dustin ignored the man he had known for so many years. He ignored the man who had eaten dinner at his house and lived with one of his best workers. Boyce felt more tears forming as his last breaths escaped his body. The last thing he saw was Allard collapse at the feet of Dustin. Boyce felt a welling of pleasure. His duty was done. He had contributed to the completion of the mission in a large way. Then everything went black.

Allard bolted straight up into a fighting stance. It was as if he had relived his capture all over again, but this time he awoke not in a tube of stinking yellow fluid, but in a rainbow of silk fabric. The fabric snaked around his body and head swaying and moving as Allard punched at the air. When he stopped, the fabric stopped and fell to the ground amongst reams of other fabric creating a thick quilt of color. Broken wooden boards creaked beneath his feet. He had fallen from a great height into a fabric cart. The vinyl tarp that once covered the silken wares had done little to protect the fabric, which was now getting wet from the torrential downpour.

The owner of the now destroyed cart had only momentarily stopped yelling when Allard jumped up swinging at invisible combatants. The owner had begun to scream again now that Allard had stopped and was looking around himself confused. He couldn't understand the words. It was another language, but a familiar one. If only the salesman would slow down enough so he could remember.

The salesman yelled and gestured to what was left of the cart. The rain poured down on both of their heads. The salesman grabbed his own in exasperation. Allard grabbed his head recognizing a throbbing. He looked at the blood-tinged rain in his hands. He must've had some fall. He looked around and for the first time noticed he was standing in an open market. Other vendors watched in amazement. Some were pointing towards the sky. Allard looked up to the darkened cumulonimbus clouds shedding their tears upon them. It really had been quite a fall.

Allard tried speaking several languages apologizing for the mishap. None of them seemed to match. He looked around at the faces, the garb and the architecture.

"I'm sorry. I will pay." He spoke slowly in the salesman's fluent Tunisian.

"How will you pay? This is my life you have taken."

"I will pay you by not taking what little of your life you have left." Allard stared with anger. The look alone struck fear in the salesman.

Allard reached in his pocket and threw all of his remaining Brazilian Reais to the salesman. He picked up a black strip of fabric, wrapped it around his head and face then stomped off through the market. Allard barely glanced at the confused and angry faces around him.

Shalako dropped him in the middle of Tunisia without word or reasoning. The dark grey skies of the rainy season were a stark contrast to the warmth and sun he had left in Brazil. Of course that wasn't all he had left. His stomach turned at the thought of Lisa's lifeless body lying on the bed. It churned when he thought of Alala descending as he rose. She would find the dead Dr. Lisa Lucas. Alala would use that dead woman in her favor. Hopefully Jury wouldn't get involved.

Allard's feet waded through the muddy ground pushing through the crowds of tourists who, even on a day like that one, were in search of bargains. They knew that the rain wouldn't let up anytime soon. Like them, he needed direction, but in a different way. Street names meant nothing to him there. There was no visible sun. He climbed a small fence, stepped across the top of a windowsill then climbed to the top of the three-story building. He looked across the span of closely built three and four story dwellings, open markets and tight alleyways. The larger buildings were new and meant nothing to his purpose. Allard strained his eyes looking at worn brick surfaces and symbols on signs. He saw what he was looking for carved into the overhang on the top floor of an older brick building.

Some things never change. Others don't because they have no choice. Allard ignored the shock of the passerby when he leapt from the top floor and sprinted into a run before his feet touched the dirt street. He ran through the puddles, evaded the slow moving residents and the animals drinking from the dirty puddles. He was headed south, which made sense to him. He thought to himself again, 'some things never change because they have no choice.'

Instead of kicking the door in, Allard banged against the heavy wooden door with the side of his fist. The sound of thunder erupted from his pounds. He wondered if the inhabitants assumed it was just another storm rolling in. The rain streamed down his face and added a matted glisten to his hair. He was soaked head to toe, but it didn't bother him. He raised his wet fist to unleash another wood-creaking knock when the small metal peak slot opened. It was set just at his chest level and he felt compelled to bend down to look inside. A pair of beautiful green eyes stared back at him. Her eye make-up richly adorned her very pretty eyes.

"What is the word?" She said in heavily accented Tunisian. She sounded like a native from a smaller area, perhaps a farmer's daughter.

Manesh sat his stout body on the floor of the large great room amongst satin and silk pillows sipping whiskey. His jokes were stale like his breath, but his drunken audience laughed loudly and often. Everything is funnier with cheap liquor in your system and beautiful whores on your lap. The women were covered, though barely, in see-through sari. Their ankles were adorned with anklets whose bell charms made clangy sounds when they gracefully walked here and there. They did not drink. They massaged their men.

When the men decided it was time, they would pay Manesh a rather large sum to accompany the women to their rooms. The rooms were decorated with plush reds and purples. There were beaded curtains and pillows filled with pheasant feathers. There were so many pillows there was no need for beds. Upon entering the room, the women would wash their customers head to toe from a large basin filled with warm water. The bath alone would often illicit orgasms from the men. For those who held on to their climax, many clutching just barely to the explosion, they would be treated to mind-blowing magical sex.

Manesh entertained another group of similar clients on that day. They were businessman, tycoons and one very low-key American politician. The green-eyed woman poked her veiled head through the curtain slowly and immediately all attention turned to her. Her eyes were all she gave and from the response, all she needed to give. Manesh shook his head slowly. “Not yet” his gesture said. She batted her eyes, bowed then raised her head again. Manesh awkwardly pushed his rotund body to its feet and wobbled to the curtain scratching his beard.

She whispered to him about the stranger at the entrance that did not know the password. He gave another odd word instead. It was a name. The smile washed from Manesh’s face like sand leaving with the outgoing tide. He turned to the two guards posed in opposite corners of the room. They were large, hulking men, the two largest men in Tunisia. They were athletic men with muscles and veins that popped from them. They walked swiftly out of the room following the green-eyed enchantress as Manesh rejoined his gathering. He was less jovial after his discussion with the woman. He was pensive and worrisome. His face tightened around his jaw. Sensing the change in his demeanor, one of his employees immediately began to massage his legs as she knelt between them. Soon he relaxed and rationalized his concerns away. The women really were great at their jobs.

Moments later the green-eyed woman's head popped back through the curtain. She shot a glance of terror to Manesh, but he missed it. Ever the Tunisian whoremongering version of P.T. Barnum, he ambled to his feet and waved her into the room. She didn't open the curtains so much as they parted for her. They caressed the ample curves of her body, which couldn't be hidden even by her burnt orange colored burka. She was curvy where it mattered and obviously very well toned. Her burka was the only one that could not be seen through. The sandals on her feet were adorned with shiny stones and beads. Her glorious green eyes flashed as she looked around the room.

"Gentlemen." Manesh spoke in accented English. "You saw Riesha when you entered. She is our most prized possession here. I guarantee when you remove her burka, you will find a body carved from the fullest and firmest of what your God has to offer. Her face is so gorgeous we prefer to keep it covered so as not to cause stampedes of suitors at my door. Inside her you will find a virgin fit. Man has never touched her. You can be the first. However, that price is only for the serious minded. This is too precious a treasure to hand over cheaply. If you would like to purchase this glorious beauty..."

On cue, Riesha stepped into the middle of the room. She raised one leg slowly allowing her burka to float upward revealing more and more of her soft tanned legs until her foot was above her head. She stood stone still. Only her leg was exposed. The customers attempted to look beneath her dress to no avail.

“The bidding will start at two-hundred fifty thousand Euro.”

Riesha swiftly lowered her leg causing a gust of air to billow her flowing outfit in waves. Seeing the desire, but hesitation amongst his guests, Manesh continued.

“Alas, you can purchase the companionship of the delectable beauties about you for considerably less, but I’m certain her...”

He stopped short when she raised her hand interrupting another long-winded sales pitch. She knew in the current slumping economy this would be yet another demeaning moment. These men were lucky to afford the twenty grand a pop for the regular women. Riesha had more important information to share.

As she parted her lips to speak, Allard’s head poked through the curtain. Manesh involuntarily stepped back in a motion of self preservation. Allard pushed through the curtains dragging the two guards, one in each hand, behind him on the floor. He dumped their unconscious bodies at his feet. The customers stood in shock. A couple of them made motions to confront Allard.

"NO! It's fine." Manesh assured them. "Everyone sit. Sit. Please sit. Allard is an old friend of mine."

The men reluctantly sat down. The women cut each other unsure glances.

"So, you know my name now. When Riesha here returned with these two meat hooks I thought you had forgotten me. Did you forget who I am Manesh?"

"A-A-A-Absolutely not." Manesh stammered. Manesh changed languages so he didn't scare his clients. "Please do not kill me. I wasn't sure if you were the real you or some kind of trick." He spoke in Tunisian.

The women's eyes bugged out in shock. They had never seen Manesh so fearful.

"If someone is using my name to play tricks, I'm certain you know that wouldn't last as long as it took for their damned tongues to speak it." Allard said with a smile feigning kindness to the rest of the room.

"Let's catch up in another room. We are distracting the fun." Manesh smiled as he spoke English to assuage the clients.

The two men left with Riesha in tow. The two guards had just begun to stir and groan their way back to consciousness, but everyone ignored them as they had already proven themselves worthless when it really mattered.

Manesh led Allard to a covered balcony, which sat under the symbol Allard had searched and found. The rain rolled down the sides of the building and splashed nearby. Riesha stood just in the archway watching quietly.

"You can have anything. Anything if you do not kill me." Manesh spoke immediately.

"I'll take that deal." Allard reached over, grabbed Manesha's hand tightly and shook on the deal.

"It's true. You killed my brother and now you've come for me." Manesha's eyes bounced around in their sockets aimlessly.

"Has it been that long? Do you think a deal can save you from my hand? You really think I would kill Mohana and spare his despicably disgusting older brother? Mohana and I shared and unlikely friendship. I never liked you. I doubt there will be a time that I will. Shalako sent me here. I didn't expect to receive such a reception. Was it a sign of a guilty conscious maybe? You're the only Being I know of in Tunisia."

"There are others."

"I see that." Allard glanced at Riesha.

"So, why are you here if not to kill?"

"Mohana was killed. Before he died, he left the name of his assassin embedded in the pews of a church."

"Why would he have entered a church?" Manesh gasped.

"He was being helpful using his many talents to get his brother out of trouble." Allard frowned.

"What trouble? I am in no trouble."

"That's what he told me when he asked to arrange the meeting with me. Your trouble became my trouble when I arrived and found him dead and myself ambushed. He told me in his letter that you had opened your mouth and spoke too much to a soul. That soul held some very secret information because of you, vital information."

"That's madness!" Manesh guffawed.

His next words were muffled by Allard's hand tightly wrapped around his throat. His feet dangled inches from the ground.

"We made a deal. Anyth-thing if you d-d-don't k-ki-kill me." He spat attempting to breathe through Allard's tightening fingers.

"I never said I wouldn't cripple you or crush this priceless voice of yours." Allard sneered. He always knew how to find a loophole.

"P-p-p-please. No." His voice grew strained.

There was a sudden calmness that eased Allard's anger. He felt a soft warm caress on his temper as if a gentle hand massaged his brain. Allard turned his glare behind him to see who was touching him, but no one was there. Riesha stood several feet away watching him with soft eyes. He lowered Manesh to his feet gently and his arms dropped to his sides.

"She's very good. A gifted young one." Allard smirked. "Makes me want to rescind the deal we made."

Manesh protested with only heavy gasping.

"What do you know about a company called Scilymax?"

"They made my toilet bowl...and I think the name is on my soft drinks." Manesh pressed his hand to his neck feeling the welts that were left by Allard's hand.

"You ever have a customer named Carver?"

"Once, about five hundred years ago. He called himself an explorer, but every place he talked about discovering was already on this Earth."

"What about a man named Mora?"

Manesh began to speak, but quickly closed his mouth and looked up at the rain pouring from the heavens. His mouth twisted and contorted.

"Hmm..." He thought.

"You remember every customer you've ever had, but now you're not sure? Riesha won't be able to charm me out of giving you a swift kick off of this balcony." Allard looked to her. "She's not that fast yet."

Even with her mouth covered by the veil, he could tell she was smiling.

"There was a Mora here. He was fighting in a war and came with several of his comrades. They had survived heavy losses and escaped away here for comfort."

"Which war was this?"

"There have been so many." He sighed. "I believe the secondary war here."

"World War II? That's not him. The Mora I'm talking about wouldn't have been born until after that. Mora, I said. Jacob Mora."

"Yes. Yes, that is the one. Jacob Mora. He was here with a Lexington, Caffey, Rumeo and Wichtenstein. The Americans and The Brits were losing horribly over at the Kasserine Pass. I just talked to them over drinks as usual before they received their comfort. Then a Being by the name of Welk came in and joined the conversation. I told him to stop, but he was a new scout and he just couldn't handle his liquor."

"Welk was here talking to Mora during World War II?" Allard was confused.

"You know him? He seems a bit young and next generation to..."

Allard raised his shirtsleeve revealing the multitude of engraved tattoos on his arm. He pointed at one. It was the symbol of a small seashell.

"This Welk?" Allard glared.

Manesh was taken aback. His eyes bulged.

"Oh...I didn't know...I...I...didn't know. I swear to you Allard."

Allard angled toward Manesh angrily waiting for more answers. There was a warm sensation spreading over his head like a head massage.

"Cut it out!" Allard shouted at Riesha and the sensation abruptly ended.

"Welk told them about the army and your war. He told them ways they could possibly win their war with help from other troops, your troops. Of course, the only way to secure a victory would be to get you. We all knew that was impossible so he left it like a riddle, a drunken riddle amongst soldiers. He told Mora he could help him fight his war with your troops for a price and a promise that he would make it his life's work to help Welk find you. It was drunken boasting and tom foolery."

"Jacob Mora Senior. It was the father of the founder of Scilymax that made a deal. A deal with Welk that his son is trying to fulfill."

"It wasn't a deal." Manesh tried to convince him that there was no concern. "When he came back asking if there was a way to get you involved, I told him definitely not."

"Came back?" Allard knew Manesh was hiding something.

"Yes. Welk helped him. He helped all of them. They won Tunisia then they went on to beat The Nazis.

"Welk and the troops fought a war here?" Allard was growing angry.

"Yes. Your troops."

"Stop calling them that. I don't stake claim on any of them. Welk couldn't have done that by himself with some troops. He would've needed a large number and I've seen many of them. They wouldn't be involved."

"Well Mohana got involved. He believed in the cause. He said it was a righteous war."

"Got involved meaning you sold him away. Or..." He stared at Manesh. "He was trying to keep you from trouble. You helped arrange the meeting with Welk and the

Senior Mora. You told him of the troops and the war. The secret was out and Welk was involved. Mohana had to come along and charm the American generals. He had to tell them how to win, stifle the enemy's resolve and change the tide here in Tunisia. He did it so you wouldn't be punished when things went wrong. He protected you then and then again when he had Hermes bring me the letter telling me you were in trouble."

"I didn't ask him to. Mora came to me and asked if Mohana could do the same to you. If he could help bring you out of hiding."

"Welk's dead." Allard tapped his arm.

"Does the Junior Mora know?" Riesha spoke abruptly out of turn.

"It wouldn't matter now would it? He inherited the knowledge of my existence. About the existence of an army that is powerful enough that if he could rebuild it..." Allard stared out into the dark gray skies. "Or use his science to recreate it, he'd be very powerful. So, he builds his foundation; his world dominating company while trying to rebuild the army. He finally finds a way to get Mohana to meet me and then..."

"He killed him." Riesha sighed.

"Why would you kill the one that you still may need?" Manesh spat angrily.

"That's a question for Carver. The man who killed him."

"I'll give you anything if you find this Carver and..."

"And what?" Allard roared grabbing Manesh by his collar. "Are you ordering me to do something? Am I your slave? You already owe me one anything. You must have a lot of anythings to offer, Manesh. You are a vile parasite that gains strength from the desires of others. Your only gift is latching on to those that have them. Your callous ways created this mess."

"He's just one man. He's one soul. How can this be so terrible?" Riesha spoke out of turn again.

Allard stared at Manesh eye to eye and dropped the bomb he held the entire time in anticipation of its impact.

"Because when I found Carver with intentions of avenging Mohana's death and getting to the bottom of it all, he had a companion." He waited a beat to clear the skies for the explosion. "Alala was with him..."

The sound of the pounding rains couldn't mask Manesh's gasp. His eyes grew big while his bottom lip quivered.

"W-w-what of the others?" Manesh stammered.

"They are also here."

Manesh wanted to ask the final question, but he was certain it wasn't his place. He was certain Allard would cripple him for being so forward.

"Dragon?" Manesh let the name hang in the air like a tethered helium balloon.

Allard stared at Manesh with a smirk.

"This "anything" you owe me." Allard changed topics. "I'll take her." He pointed to Riesha.

"What?" Manesh bellowed.

"Is there a problem?" Allard growled. "You offered me anything. I am taking your crown jewel."

"Allard please, I'll give you three of the others."

"You said anything. You offer her innocence and overwhelming gifts to strangers with the highest bid. Are you saying I'm not deserving of owning her innocence?"

"No. That's not it..."

"Do you covet the dollars you could get for selling it?"

"I...I...I"

"Yeah, it is all about you. So was it a trick? A bait and switch? You get your customers hot and bothered by her then when they can't afford her they spend more on the others? Are you that type of disgusting untrustworthy dealmaker? "

"No! It's real. She's too precious, too special, to give for free."

"I guess I should be happy that you're not so vile as to sell a woman's virginity for a low low price!" Allard shouted. "I will take her. It's decided."

"Why are you doing this to me?" Manesh was beyond distraught. "Fine. It is done. You can have her tonight. But please do not make it known to the others. I can still make the claim if no one knows she was with a man."

"Tonight? No Manesh, I'm taking her forever." Allard clarified.

"ABSOLUTELY NOT!" Manesh stiffened his back and stood up just within Allard's personal space.

"Then I'll kill you now." Allard smiled. "You weren't the only one Mohana was worried about. You were secondary on his list of concerns. His first was his half-breed daughter who was given extraordinary beauty and incredible gifts that rivaled even his. Of course if something were to happen to him, she would be left with her disgusting uncle. Who knows if he'd sell her like the whores he kept. Mohana had already had a rough time leaving her in his dirty brother's care while he was off in New York." Allard pointed a finger in Manesh's face. "I got here sooner than I expected, but apparently right on time. I'm many things and have been every evil known, but you are way too egotistical to believe saving your ass would be enough to meet with your brother in a church. You say I can't have her as my anything, that's fine. I'll kill you and then I'll take her. Makes no difference to me."

Manesh felt the shame and remorse Allard had intended for him. He glanced to Riesha, who again, Allard could sense a smile under her veil. There was a warm caress of his chest. Maybe it had gone lower, but he wasn't sure.

"If Alala is involved then none of this much matters anyway now does it?" Manesh rationalized.

It was late. Allard had given up waiting for Shalako to transport him home. His calls were not answered so he assumed Shalako had other pressing business that he would attend to and would pull Allard from Tunisia at his will much like he did in Brazil. He knocked on the old wooden door to Riesha's bedroom. The door opened slightly after a small click of the lock. She poked her eye through the small slit. Her eye looked up and down at him, then she left the door open and retreated further inside the room.

Allard slowly entered the plush boudoir. Unlike the other rooms, which were dark in décor, Riesha's room was brightly adorned with orange plush pillows, billowing curtains and lightly colored fabrics.

"Please lock the door behind you." Her voice traveled in from the adjoining bathroom. Allard did as requested. He stood by the door feeling too soiled and still too wet to sit on the pristine bed of pillows or to touch the soft fabrics.

"You can have a seat. I'll be right out."

Allard slowly surveyed the perimeter of the room. His curiosity led him to a small table and the family photos on top of it. He saw infant pictures of Riesha. She smiled widely in the arms of Mohana and her mother, a beautiful Tunisian woman. The pictures looked to be from the 1950s at the earliest.

"I'm sorry." Riesha startled him. Her hands reached passed him and collected as many pictures as she could. "The women told me that I should remove these before a man enters, but I forgot." Allard waved his hand as if to brush away her apology.

When he turned to her, she quickly removed her veil revealing a beautiful slim face. Her eyes sparkled from within her soft skin.

"I've planned that moment for a long time. I always thought I'd do it slowly, but it just makes sense to get it over with. Men are way more interested in seeing the rest of me." She said in accented English.

"When were these pictures taken?" Allard pointed at the oldest of the bunch trying to sound unaffected by her beauty.

Riesha just smiled and extended her hands.

"Please come. I will remove your clothes for you." She gestured.

"My clothes? You don't have to do that. I'll stay in these wet things. I need to rest. Do you have a pillow I can use?" The answer was obvious. He was standing amongst a hundred of them.

"Here." Riesha motioned to the pillow, which sat just to the left of a large porcelain water basin filled with steaming water. She quickly and carefully stacked the armful of pictures in the corner of the room.

"The nineteen-fifties?" Allard cocked his head at one of the photos.

"Forties."

"So that would make you..."

"A lot older than I look." She nodded. "I understand your concern, but I also know what is at stake. I have been waiting for a long time to get married, to find love. I've waited a longer time to feel the weight of a man. If this is the way I am chosen to transcend then I couldn't feel more honor." She stepped towards him lithe as a gazelle.

"That talk was for Manesh. I'm not going to have sex with you."

"Why not?"

"You'll be a virgin on your wedding day."

"If it ever comes. Then what happens? I have children; my husband dies leaving me brokenhearted then my children die and their children after them. All the while they are wondering why I have barely aged over time. I went through it with my parents. My father couldn't handle it and he left us. Do you know what job my father occupied when he moved to New York?"

"No. I didn't know he worked." Allard felt the shame in his voice when he said the word "worked."

"He was a taxi cab driver. With all of his gifts, he was a driver for others. He didn't use his gifts for wayward means even though he was cast aside."

"He was honorable."

Riesha was within a foot of Allard. Her pretty mouth smiled at him. Her eyes beamed.

"I'm sure you considered what my father meant by protecting me. Do you think he wanted you to...partake of me so I wasn't spoiled by man?"

Allard could sense the fullness and firmness of her bosom through her burka.

“No. I think he wanted me to save you from your uncle.”

“Save me. Me? My gifts way exceed his. I could charm him into walking off of a cliff right now.”

“He’s way more skilled than he likes to let on.”

“Let me bathe you, Allard. The water is getting cold.”

“Let it freeze.”

She turned from him and walked slowly toward the basin. He watched the fabric hug her curves. The burka slowly fell from her body revealing smooth skin and a healthy round rear end. She looked over her shoulder and he felt a warm sensation in his loins. He wasn’t sure if the sensation was her gifs or his hormones.

“I practiced that a lot too and slow is overwhelmingly better. Let me bathe you, Allard.” She turned exposing her full nude body to him. The firm suppleness of a much younger woman stared back at him tauntingly.

Allard drifted to her in a haze. He watched himself disrobe carefully. Her hands were gentle. The warm sponge scented with vanilla water massaged his muscles and relaxed his hesitations. There were no more inhibitions. He could feel the warmth of her body pressed against his when she reached around him and washed his back. She perched on her tippy toes to stare deep into his eyes. The sponge eased around his manhood softly.

"Shhh. Relax." She whispered though her lips didn't move. When he moved there was a change in her stroke on him. A smile lit her face. She blushed as they stared into each other's eyes. "Will you take me?" She asked innocently with a modicum of youthful uncertainty.

He felt his stomach drop. There was a thunderous rumble. A large gust of wind blew the curtains high and wide. Fabric floated in the air like jellyfish in saltwater.

"I will." He smirked and grabbed her hand.

There was a loud thunderclap in the room and they were gone.

Manesh's guards stormed into the room nearly tearing the door off of its hinges. Manesh hobbled into the room angrily. He knew without investing that Allard had indeed kept his word and took Manesh's most prized possession. Almost immediately there was a pounding at the front door of the brothel.

"Answer it!" Manesh bellowed to no one in particular.

By the time the guard had reached the door, one of the women had already raised the flap and asked for the password. There were two men talking, one in English the other translating for him in Tunisian.

"It took him a day's travel to get here. He does not speak Tunisian." The translator was an old Tunisian man pulled from his daily events and brought along for the adventure. "He was sent to you by Shalako to ask about a man named Allard. His name is Dustin."

"Allard left!" The guard growled and shut the peak slot.

The Guard returned to Manesh and told him of an American that wanted information on Allard. The devil was in the details and the guard, with hopes he'd return to Manesh's good graces, inadvertently left out the most important ones. Talk of Allard had already cost Manesh his most prized gift. There would be no more of it in his house. For all he cared, the American could continue roaming the countryside. Manesh sat back sipping a glass of the expensive whiskey he stashed for himself. He thought about the events and a way he could angle himself at the head of it all again. He did not know he had just let his brother's killer walk away.

CHAPTER TI O

Iara could have rubbed Michelle's shoulders to the bone, but there was no amount of soothing that could take away the pain. Michelle sat on the dirt street and sobbed with tears streaming down her cheeks. Marjorie was on all fours as she vomited in nearby bushes. Lisa was dead. The small tourist area in Ilha Grande, Brazil had become over-run with men in black fatigues. A small drone plane circled above again and again. The center of the activity was in a small bed and breakfast. It was in there, the soldiers told Michelle, Jury and Iara, that a person they believed to be Dr. Lisa Lucas lay dead.

Natives of the small island community buzzed nearby in groups. This wasn't the first time they'd seen the men in black fatigues. The soldiers often came into town to eat and flirt with the local women. This same bed and breakfast had served as a pit stop for the men who were lucky enough to get more than flirting. The natives recognized Iara as well. She was a local of sorts. They kept their distance from her. An older woman knelt by Jury with bottled water and slowly fed her sips while massaging her hair backward. The old woman understood the kind of pain Jury was experiencing.

Lieutenant Wellspring walked out of the bed and breakfast with a concerned look. A soldier walked two steps behind him and pointed amongst his comrades that stood nearby. Iara didn't believe her eyes at first. A woman stood amongst the solders. She had silken dark hair, her high heels were expensive, her dress more so. She wore sunglasses over her eyes, but still Iara knew. Alala lowered her sunglasses and approached The Lieutenant with a cocked eyebrow. Almost immediately, he began to nod his head. She was now in charge.

Alala and Wellspring approached Iara and Michelle. They whispered to each other the entire way without removing their gaze from the two women.

"I'm sorry for your loss." Wellspring said in a genuinely somber tone. "This is Alala. She was sent from Scilymax to consult on the situation."

“Hello.” Alala stared Iara dead in the eyes. “We’ve met before.” Iara’s eyes cast downward toward Michelle. “Hmm...” Alala looked at the other two sensing something in them. “Allard’s been busy.” She smirked.

“Did he do this? Was it him?” Jury’s anger bubbled just beneath the surface.

“We don’t know that. We received a call from Dr. Lucas telling us he was here. She agreed we’d rendezvous at the pier and the team, minus her ,would recapture him. She was very adamant that we take him peacefully. I’m not positive of anything outside of that.”

“I need someone to come inside with me to identify her.” Alala looked over them.

“I can go.” Iara volunteered.

“No. I want her.” Alala pointed to Jury. “You’re closer, you’ve worked with her, right?”

“I should go. I’ve known her almost all of her life.” Michelle choked back tears. Deep in her aching heart she knew she couldn’t handle it, but this was the right thing to do.

“You don’t look up to it. You stay here.” Alala shook her hair off of her shoulder. “Let’s go before it gets too crazy with the locals.”

Jury didn't appreciate the attitude of the rookie to the situation. However, considering Michelle's fragile mental state, she knew Alala had made the correct choice.

Inside, the bed and breakfast owner was exhausted from retelling the story over and over. This time he spoke into a recording device held by a security team member. Little did he know, that device fed directly into a small handset that measured fluctuations in tone and vocal stress. It was a handheld lie detector, a Scilymax product yet to be released, but being tested for police forces. The rollout was planned for Russia in consideration of their more lax laws as compared to the U.S.A.

"How much contact have you had with Allard?" Alala asked as she and Jury ascended the staircase.

"What do you mean?" Jury was distracted by this complete stranger saying the name of the man that killed her fiance' and her good friend.

"You weren't as close to him as the other two?"

"The other two? Iara hasn't had much contact with him. Just since we've been on the island."

"Yeah. She's had contact alright."

"What does this have to do with my friend possibly being dead in this shit bag hotel?"

"Don't mean to offend. I'm just trying to figure out how everyone gets along."

"Well considering y'all are saying he killed Lisa, I guess that means we don't." Jury said.

The soldier standing watch at the door nodded as they approached. He solemnly opened the door for them. Jury took a deep breath and slowly entered. Her head hung low with her eyes closed as she prayed. She prayed that it was a mistake. Her eyelids fluttered open and immediately filled with tears. A guttural sob erupted from her throat. The soldier held her up by her elbows when her legs involuntarily buckled.

"Why?" Jury screamed.

Lisa lay on the bed fully dressed. She was as still as she'd ever been. Somehow she already did not look like herself anymore. Her hands were placed across each other on her chest. Jury slipped to her knees and kissed her friend on the cheek. Lisa's skin was cold, but not yet stiff like other bodies she'd touched. There was a rumble in Jury's stomach and saliva began to well in her mouth. She held back the vomit this time. She didn't want to soil Lisa. She definitely didn't want Alala to see her too vulnerable. Jury began to say a silent prayer for Lisa's soul.

"Do you notice anything different about her?" The soldier interrupted.

Jury ignored him and begged God to keep Lisa close. She asked him to forgive all of her transgressions and to tell Lisa she loved her.

"Outside of her being dead?" Jury huffed to the soldier.

"I'm sorry. I meant..."

"Thank you. You can wait outside." Alala raised her hand banishing him from talking again. After the door clicked, she continued. "Is this what she was wearing when she left you?"

"She left early, before I got up, but this is her workout gear." Jury stood and walked slowly on uneasy legs to the window. She inhaled deeply then exhaled trying her best to get herself together as much as possible.

"Did Allard give her anything? A gift maybe?"

"Not that I know of." Jury had just lost her friend, but she was still a therapist and knew when she was being probed. "Would that be a motive for him to kill her?"

Alala stood silent for a moment then handed Jury a tissue for her tears. She'd forgotten how sensitive these souls were during war.

While on the boat to the Scilymax pier, Jury and Michelle made the decision that Lisa would be stored in the basement storage area. They preferred her close despite the fact she'd be sharing close quarters with the man that had attacked them just days before. They chose to ride on the back of the cargo truck with Lisa's body. The serene vistas of the island gave them both a moment to themselves.

"So you know this means we have to find him now..." Michelle broke her silence. Her voice was unsteady and raspy from her wailing.

Jury nodded her head. There was vengeance in Michelle's words, but her tone was more worrisome. She and Jury had quite a day and moving toward the evening all either of them wanted was to stop and wake up from their collective nightmare.

Iara and Alala drove in the Jeep behind the truck. Iara sat behind the wheel and stiffly stared ahead. She was scared. She tried to no avail to get either Jury or Michelle to ride back with her forcing Alala into one of the vehicles with the soldiers. She glanced in the rear view mirror at the soldiers' vehicles following several meters behind them. She pulled closer to the cargo truck with hopes Jury and Michelle would keep an eye on her, but mostly an eye on Alala.

"How is he doing?" Alala broke the silence.

"He's fine."

"Hmmm, I'm sure." Alala could feel Allard's power on her. "Where did he go?"

"I don't know."

"You can tell me the truth. I know you don't want to betray him." She looked Iara up and down. "Especially since he must've taken a liking to you."

Iara sat silently. A small bead of stress induced sweat surfaced on the tip of her nose.

"I understand. You wanna link yourself with a winner this time. No matter what your true allegiance is." Alala said.

Michelle and Jury wept as the soldiers lowered Lisa's body into the storage area. The soldiers who weren't acting as pallbearers saluted or held their hands over their hearts with their heads lowered. Iara stood stone stiff next to Alala who watched the procession closely. There was a glint from a metal box deep within the sub basement.

"What else is down there?" Alala whispered.

"The supplies." Iara hushed back to her.

"You should go inside and start preparing something tasty for us. They won't have appetites, but it'll be nice to have." Alala had a commanding tone. "And it'll give you something to do."

Iara slipped away back into the house pissed off. How dare that bitch show up and tell her what to do. Iara wanted to just leave, but she knew Jury and Michelle needed her more now with Alala around. It was already dark when Michelle and Jury watched the soldiers drive away. It was deathly quiet. There was a solemn hush over The Hut.

Michelle and Jury sat on the hammock together and swayed with the breeze. They stared out to the beautiful sunset that was lit with so many shades of orange and purple that it looked like a watercolor painting.

"That's her saying goodbye." Jury smiled.

Michelle nodded and wiped a tear from her friend's eye.

"Are you ladies going to get in?" Alala's voice was close behind them. She stopped just ahead of them wearing a deep red sarong. Her red two-piece bathing suit was visible underneath. "They say if you bathe in a large body of water when a loved one dies, your prayers for them spread further and faster."

"I never heard that before." Jury was more than a little annoyed by Alala ruining their moment.

"You should try it. It'll relax you."

"I've prepared some tapas and there's some chicken that I'll be putting on the grill." Iara joined them. "Shall I bring some out?"

"No thanks." Jury and Michelle answered in unison.

"I was just telling them they should join me for a dip." Alala looked to Iara. "The water should be safe to-night, right?"

Iara looked out toward the water without a word.

"There's nothing out there that should hurt me right?" Alala waited.

"Right." Iara answered so curtly that Michelle tossed a look to Jury.

"That's what I thought. I'll say a prayer for your friend while I'm out there."

"I appreciate it." Michelle sighed.

Alala dropped her cover up and walked towards the water. While it was partially blocked by the straps of her bikini, her tattoo was too large to be covered. It was etched across the entire length of her back from neck to waist and nearly shoulder-to-shoulder. It was the symbol of the war-horn...

Michelle tossed another look to Jury.

"Where is she sleeping?" Jury's question hung in the air like a noose on an old oak tree. Lisa wasn't gone six hours, yet they might already have someone sleeping in her bed.

"Put her on the couch." Iara said watching Alala wade into the ocean.

"That's not right. She'll stay in my room. I'll sleep in Lisa's bed. It's only one night. The plane will be here in the morning for us. I guess that means I'll pack her bag too." Michelle wiped tears from her eyes. It was only the beginning and her eyes were already nearly swollen shut.

"Ouch!" A squeal rang from the beach.

Alala was quickly moving back towards land. She smacked the water with her open palm. The water splashed high and created loud pops.

"Ow!" She turned her back and peered down at the water as she backed away quickly.

"I'll go inside and check the chicken." Iara smiled and made away quickly.

"Why?" Jury began to cry again. "Why would he kill her?" He had so many chances before. Why'd he take her from us?"

"He must've heard her call the soldiers and he...I don't want to think about it." Michelle's heart ached with real physical pain.

"Jellyfish!" Alala grunted as she reached them. "They swarmed me." She picked up her cover up, shook the sand into the wind and wrapped it around herself. "Where'd Iara go?"

Jury flashed Alala a look of scorn. Michelle shook her head. Alala's angry expression dropped.

"I'm sorry. I'll leave you two alone." Alala walked to the water's edge and stared at the setting sun.

Michelle and Jury watched Alala rub her jellyfish stings from their perch on the hammock. A smile cracked Michelle's dour expression.

"That big ol' tattoo and she can't take a jellyfish sting?" Michelle said.

Jury let out a whooping laugh. Slowly their laughs rose and they relaxed.

The tension between Alala and Iara was thick that night, but they did their best to ignore each other. Michelle and Jury packed Lisa's bag together then turned in for the night emotionally drained.

Iara woke up early the next morning inspired to cook a big breakfast as a bon voyage gift for Jury and Michelle. She absent-mindedly climbed out of bed and made it half way down the hall before she remembered she had slept nude again the night before. She backtracked to her room, pulled on a small tank top and some barely there shorts. She washed her face and while she brushed her teeth she heard a whirring sound and a door close. She imagined it was Jury, the early riser of the two. Then with so much going on, she knew neither of them had gotten much sleep at all.

Her bare feet pattered against the stone tile floor in the hallway to the kitchen. She dialed into the computerized cabinet retrieval system some of the ingredients she needed from the pantry. Onions, jack cheese, eggs, three cups of grits. She checked the refrigerator and pulled out more ingredients for omelets. She returned to the computer and dialed in orange juice, wheat bread and heavy cream. The error display buzzed. Heavy cream was not available. She dialed "buttermilk", pressed retrieve and heard the dumbwaiter descend into the basement. While gathering her ingredients she noticed a foul stench. She sniffed the lettuce and bell peppers, but they were fresh. There was a burning scent as well. She hopped over to the dumbwaiter and tiptoed to peek inside the glass window to see if it had malfunctioned. Just as she got a good view, the platform shot into place with a rumbling click, startled her and sent her back on her heels. She opened the cabinet door to see a horrible mess. Molded bread, over ripe onions, the smell from the rotten eggs made her wretch. With one hand covering her mouth, Iara reached in and poked the hard mass that was once jack cheese. The system was designed to monitor freshness so the malfunction had to have been overwhelming. Her body registered the panic before the rest of her. She stumbled backward with her eyes wide.

Her back bumped into something hard and she felt a wet smelly hand cover her mouth. The smell overtook her. Had the hand not been over her face, her vomit would've shot across the floor. Instead it stayed trapped in her mouth until she swallowed it again. Her stomach heaved to get rid of its contents again, to no avail.

"What are you cooking this morning?" The heavy voice whispered. With the words came the breath, with the breath came another heave from Iara's belly. "I haven't had a fresh meal in a long time." The voice grumbled. His mouth was right next to her ear. She felt his sticky tongue slide across it leaving a trail of halitosis wherever it landed.

Iara squealed, but his hand pressed against her face so hard the pain convinced her to shut up. His massive fingers wrapped around her nose and mouth stifling what little air she could breathe.

"Stop playing with the fishies. We need to go." Alala's voice whispered from behind them.

The hand released Iara's mouth and with it a torrent of vomit from her lips. She stumbled forward slipping on her waste. The remnants of the tapas from the night before collected between her toes. She turned over her shoulder.

"Sundiata." She panted and wiped her mouth with the back of her hand. "Where did you..."

"Nice try. You sayin' you didn't know I was locked in the basement like a bad doggy?" He growled too loud for Alala's wishes.

"Shhh. Let's go." Alala huffed.

"You scared, sis? You're acting scared." Sundiata said to Alala all the while he stared at Iara like a well-cooked meal. Alala's hand wrapped around the back of his neck and pulled him back without effort.

"Who are you talking to?" Alala recoiled. "Ughhh, you stink. Let's go before I throw up."

Iara looked Sundiata up and down studying his disheveled homeless clothing and matted hair. She remembered him being well kept, even handsome long ago. He was a living breathing testament to bad choices and joining the wrong crowd. Although his crowd had gotten him further than hers had.

"I can't believe this..." Sundiata stared at Iara in awe. "Wait...you have a covenant. Who was crazy and desperate enough to give you a covenant?"

"Take a guess." Alala began walking to the front door.

"You've gotta be kidding me. A little trampy guppy like you? They must be handing those things out with happy meals."

"Let's go." Alala whispered a little too loudly across the room.

Sundiata blew a kiss and backed away watching Iara's curves the entire time.

When Michelle awoke she wasn't surprised that she had been crying in her sleep. She wiped her tears and lay there. Lisa's scent was still in the pillowcase. She was still present in the room. There was no sun that morning and it was dreary out, a sign of a brewing storm. Perhaps the angels in heaven were crying tears of joy for Lisa's homecoming. When she listened closely she could hear their whimpers. There was an occasional sob. Michelle lifted her head from the pillow and heard more sounds of sorrow.

She popped up from bed and followed the sounds out to the kitchen where she found Iara mopping up vomit. There was a pile of spoiled food in a kitchen garbage bag.

"Are you OK? What happened?" Michelle spoke softly, but her voice startled Iara.

Iara turned quickly. She was ready for trouble this time. She held the mop aloft like a weapon. Her eyes shifted wildly in her head.

"Hey!" Michelle screamed.

"Sorry. I didn't know...I... I didn't hear him. They're gone."

Iara had barely begun the story before Michelle screamed for Jury. Jury came barreling down the stairs ready for business. The phone rang almost as soon as she reached the kitchen. Everyone stood still, paralyzed by shock.

"Hello?" Jury finally answered as she watched the strange expressions of her housemates. "What? Sir, I don't speak Portuguese. Hold on..." She turned to Iara. "I think it's for you. Some guy speaking Portuguese."

Iara took the phone. She could hear Michelle whisper the news to Jury.

"What do you mean GONE?" Jury screamed. "The two of them together?"

The man on the phone was older. He was the owner of the bed and breakfast where Lisa had died. In the fracas and excitement he had forgotten that the man who rented the room where Lisa died had left a message for whomever asked for it. No one had. The small envelope sat unread until his wife asked about it that night. He tried calling the number the Team Captain gave, but there was no answer. His wife, a very curious woman bordering on very nosey, opened and read the letter. It didn't make sense, so they tried the number again. No answer. His wife suggested they try one digit lower and higher in case there was an extension system and besides, the Team Captain really did have bad penmanship.

Iara shook her head.

"Get to the point." She told the man.

"Is it written in English?" She asked. "Can you not understand?"

"It is written in Portuguese and it is addressed to my wife. As if he knew she would read it. How does this man know my wife!" He screamed.

Jury immediately picked up on Iara's change in demeanor.

"What's wrong now?" Jury asked.

"Read the note." Iara said calmly.

"Dear Dolores, thank you for being a curious soul. Please try a different number. Tell Michelle to remove the dragon. Thank you. Signed A." The old man huffed as if he'd read it a million times.

"Read it again." Iara commanded. This time she repeated it aloud for the other two.

"Remove the dragon?" Michelle's eyes squinted. "What does that mean?"

Iara hung the phone up on the man as he steadily rambled about his wife and her infidelities.

"It means we have to go downstairs." Iara explained.

When the elevator door opened the three of them were hit with a foul stench. It wasn't quite death, but was rank just the same. The refrigerators were open. Much of the food in them was spoiled. The storage chamber for the dried goods looked to have been scorched by a flamethrower. Lying in the middle of the room was the open container that once held Sundiata. The refrigerator that held Lisa's body was only slightly ajar. Jury opened the large metal door. The body bag lay on a stretcher. Their friend lay amongst the other carcasses in a meat locker. It was an ominous sight. Iara rushed over and unzipped the body bag.

"What are you doing?" Jury grabbed Iara's hand halfway through the motion.

Lisa's grayish face protruded through the opened slit.

"Oh my God!" Michelle covered her mouth.

"Let go of me!" Iara screamed and with one flourish knocked Jury aside. "Where's the dragon?" She asked to no one in particular as she fully unzipped the bag. Her eyes roamed Lisa's body.

"What are you doing? What are WE doing?" Michelle's voice trailed off. She couldn't take her eyes off of her friend's lifeless body even though she tried. She tried with all of her might, but she couldn't stop staring.

"Does she have a tattoo?"

"She has a couple." Jury stood close by to make sure Iara wasn't going to desecrate Lisa's body.

"Is one of them a dragon?" Iara scanned Lisa, starting from her head and worked her glare down her body.

"No. One is like a tribal thing and the other..."

"There! What is that?" Iara pointed at a cord bracelet on Lisa's wrist.

Jury gave it a sideways glance. She'd never seen it before. It didn't even look like something Lisa would wear. Jury shifted it around Lisa's cold arm. The emblem stared back at them.

"That has to come off." Iara stood back. Her face registered a tinge of fear.

"Why?" Michelle's eyes had begun to tear again.

"TAKE IT OFF NOW!" Iara screamed.

"Fine!" Jury screamed back and grabbed the clasp. She winced in pain when Iara grabbed her hand tightly.

"Not you. Michelle. He said Michelle." Iara warned.

Jury yanked her hand from Iara's and put her index finger an inch from Iara's face.

"You're gonna stop putting your hands on me or every bit of Brooklyn is gonna come up outta me and whup your ass!" Jury warned.

"Stop it!" Michelle pleaded. "I'll do it."

Michelle pushed between them and looked down at Lisa's cold dead body. It was the first time she'd noticed a small round hole in the chest of Lisa's shirt right over her heart. She tried to touch only the bracelet, but her finger brushed the cold skin and it sent a shiver up her spine. She tugged at the rope, but it wouldn't budge. With a little more force Lisa's arm rose stiffly from the stretcher and thudded as it landed.

"Unhook it." Iara instructed softly.

Michelle looked back at Iara angrily. Didn't this bitch realize she was touching the dead flesh of a loved one? Hadn't she any feelings buried in that perfect body of hers.

"I'll do it." Jury huffed.

"I have it." Michelle sighed.

She slowly took Lisa's hand in hers with one hand and unfastened the bracelet hook. She pulled it off slowly and held it aloft offering it to Iara. Iara shook her head wildly like a three-year-old refusing her dinner vegetables. A slight whimper gurgled in her throat.

"Now what?" Jury asked as she finally took a breath.

"I don't know." Iara shook her head.

"What do I do with it?" Michelle asked.

Suddenly, the lights in the refrigerator began to flicker slowly. Before they could react, the power in the meat locker shut off and on wildly. The fan ground to a stop then began again. One of the bulbs above shattered and sent glass over their heads and across the floor. Iara reached forward and grabbed Lisa's body as it shook violently. Lisa's arms shook wildly. Her head bounced up and down off of the stretcher as Iara tried to keep her down.

"Some help! Some help!" Iara pleaded.

Michelle grabbed Lisa's left leg, Jury grabbed her right as Lisa's body bound sickly. Green foam bubbled from Lisa's lips and a guttural groan thundered from within her. Her body emitted a foul smelling gas from her rectum that filled the meat locker with the smell of sulfur. As quickly as the spectacle had begun, it stopped. The three of them stood quietly. Only then realizing they had been screaming throughout the ordeal. Then Lisa's eyes opened.

"Lisa!" Iara spoke as if trying to wake her up.

Michelle squealed at the sight of Lisa's jaundice eyes open and looking at the ceiling of the refrigerator. Her eyes closed again.

"Lisa!" Iara shouted louder.

Lisa's eyes fluttered open. Her head creaked slowly toward Iara.

"I...I want food." Her hoarse voice whispered. "I want BIG food." Lisa breathed a heavy inhale.

The gust of wind sent the curtains in Shalako's "work room" billowing wildly. When the fog cleared, Allard stood naked with Riesha in the middle of the room.

"Catch you at a bad time?" Shalako adjusted his glasses on his face.

Riesha hid her naked body behind Allard's. If she could've, she would've disappeared into Allard's back. Her plentiful hips were too wide to hide so parts of her were still visible. She covered her breasts with one arm and cupped her innocent vagina with her other hand. Allard stood bare and perturbed.

"You did, but only because traveling naked isn't fun. Hand me that, please." Allard pointed to an ornate tapestry on the wall.

"That's The Cloth of The Transition!" Shalako fumed.

Allard grimaced. Shalako unhooked the multi-colored, heavily woven piece from the wall and tossed it to him. Allard spun around and covered Riesha's body with it.

""Riesha, this is Shalako The Courier. Shalako meet Riesha. She's Mohana's daughter."

"By the looks of it, you're lucky he's no longer with us. Knowing Mohana, I don't think he'd approve."

"It's not like that." Allard assured him.

"Mmmhm, sure it isn't." Shalako said. "How was Brazil?"

"Productive." Allard nodded.

"Did you get what you went for?""

Allard led Riesha to a chair. When she sat, part of her nether regions was exposed. She quickly covered herself.

"You didn't see anything." Riesha's voice echoed in Shalako's ears though her mouth did not move.

"You're right, I didn't." Shalako spoke aloud. "But that stuff doesn't work on me, young lady. Teach her something will you, Allard."

"Nothing works on him. Not even common sense." Allard whispered to Riesha with a wink.

She smiled.

"Wait. You don't have your clothes or the bag. Do you need to go back and get it?" Shalako worried.

Allard's tongue contorted in his closed mouth. He opened his lips exposing the golden glint of the needle hidden under his tongue.

"Of course." Shalako nodded and tossed Allard a towel to cover himself. "Did you speak with Dragon?"

"I sent him a gift."

"A gift? You've sent a gift to him?" Shalako poured a cup of hot tea and handed it to Allard.

"I'm kind hearted. Haven't you heard?" Allard handed the cup to Riesha who sipped it slowly.

"How was Tunisia?" Shalako glanced at Riesha. "Besides the obvious."

"Productive."

"You saw Carver then?" Shalako poured another cup of tea.

"Carver? Dustin Carver?"

"Yes."

"Dustin Carver was in Tunisia?" Allard was gob smacked.

"Yes. Why do you think I sent you to Tunisia?"

"For her!" Allard shouted. "For Manesh!"

"You never saw him? I sent him there. I told him to ask Manesh for information about you." Shalako was confused.

"He never came. I never saw him." Allard was furious. Riesha got more nervous as the two yelled to each other.

"He must've gotten lost. Americans have got to be the most directionally challenged souls of them all."

"I thought you were trying to *help* me!"

"Help you? I'm a neutral observer. It isn't like that."

"Mmmhmm sure it isn't." Allard said.

"Is it safe to assume, with you sending gifts to Dragon, that you are..." Shalako looked up from his cup of tea.

"I am pissed I missed Carver. I learned some things in Tunisia. I'll need to get some clothes, but right after I need to go to Italy."

"I hear the airfares are cheap." Shalako shrugged.

"I can't fly. You know that." Allard said.

"Yeah, it's been a long time since you've done that." Shalako laughed.

"I'm serious, Shalako. Italy, as soon as I get some clothes."

"I'm not a travel agent. I've done enough."

"Even after I brought you a gift?" Allard paced the floor.

"What gift is this?"

Allard opened his hand and gestured to Riesha.

"Absolutely not! I am not a babysitter!"

"I am not baby!" Riesha interrupted in accented English.

Allard nodded with a smile.

"She is not baby." Allard mocked her accent. "She's a charmer. She's gorgeous. She can be a clerk and get the people to buy more of your stuff."

Shalako smirked. A beautiful hostess with Riesha's gifts would work well for his business.

"Fine, but I'm charging you full price AND you have to pass through the seal." Shalako pressed.

"You know I can't do that." Allard stared at Shalako.

"Sorry old friend. If you're sending Dragon gifts and Alala is popping in here. I'm playing it straight." Shalako bowed his head and shrugged. He was ashamed he had to treat his friend like a stranger.

"It's been fun while it lasted." Allard reached his hand out and shook Shalako's.

"Take care of him, OK." Allard bent to kiss Riesha on the cheek. At the last moment she turned and kissed his lips softly.

"I'll be waiting." Riesha batted her sad puppy dog eyes.

"Mmmhmm." Shalako smiled.

Allard reached to a coat rack, retrieved a long all-weather coat and covered himself. He walked out onto the cold cobblestones of the Soho street to find some clothes.

Iara served as many dishes as she could make from what little food that wasn't spoiled. It hadn't seemed like a lot, but when Michelle pushed back from the table after her second helping of French toast, she couldn't help but groan. Lisa was quiet. The only sound she made was the sucking sound of her licking her fingers. The table was filled with platters scraped clean of their contents. Every time someone tried to ask her a question she'd make a guttural "uh uh" moan and kept eating.

Iara had nearly used up all of the remaining ingredients in the kitchen. Everyone began to worry that Lisa wouldn't be satisfied when all was done and she would go out to the ocean, catch fish by hand and bite the heads off. She *was* a zombie, wasn't she?

"Let me tell you something." Lisa mumbled between double-fisted handfuls of turkey bacon. Everyone else stopped. "This fucking turkey bacon is incredible. We have any more?"

"Ummm..no. I'm sorry." Iara tossed a look to Michelle who sent another to Jury.

"Babyyyy." Jury touched Lisa's hand and stopped its mouthward progress. Lisa's response was a deathly glance. Jury retracted her hand quickly. "Who killed you Lisa?"

They all watched Lisa carefully.

"Oh!" Lisa abruptly stopped her hand shoveling.

She covered her mouth with the backs of her hands and belched. She slowly dropped the food, wiped her hands and covered her mouth in traumatized shock. It was as if she hadn't remembered until Jury reminded her.

"Maybe we shouldn't talk about that just yet." Michelle rubbed Lisa's shoulder.

"No, It's ok. We have to. I have to tell you a story." Lisa took several large gulps of her cranberry juice. "Oh that's so good." She panted.

"A story?" Jury was more worried about Lisa's state of mind.

"Well..not a story...umm..I guess it's history." Lisa thought about it some more. "Did I tell you guys that I love you?"

They nodded.

"Good." Lisa sighed.

Iara sat down. She was more worried than the others. Worried what happened when Lisa died, worried about what she saw and what she learned. She was mostly worried about what she remembered.

"I remember the whole story. It's like I was sitting watching a movie. I'm going to tell you the whole thing just like it was told to me. I think that's important." Lisa had suddenly become so fragile and solemn.

"Take your time." Jury patted her hand. "Maybe you should start with why you left with Allard..."

"We went for a run. We ran through the forest."

"Did anything try to kill you?" Michelle interrupted.

"No." Lisa was confused as to why the others were giving each other looks. "The run was fun. Then we went and had breakfast at a little restaurant. That was OK. Not as good as this Iara. Then we stopped at a market. I bought you guys souvenirs. Did you get them?"

They shook their heads impatiently.

"Then Allard bought me a bracelet. That was nice." She rubbed her wrist where it once laid. "We had to call for security to come get me so we went to the bed and breakfast. That wasn't so nice. He took a shower then I joined him. That was very nice. Then we had sex. That was very very nice."

Jury looked at Michelle with a look of shock, but was confused when Michelle looked away uncomfortably.

"I came out the bathroom and then it got cold. He had stabbed me in the chest with something."

"Sonuvabitch!" Jury went from calm to irate in a blink of an eye.

"That wasn't so nice." Lisa continued her pre-school manner of telling the story.

"You're back here with us now." Iara interrupted.

"I'm not done. That wasn't the story I wanted to tell. That's not the story I was told." Lisa continued. She took another gulp of the cranberry juice. "After the cold, I woke up at the end of a long hallway. The place was filthy; it smelled like cigarettes, vomit and cheap liquor. Instead of turning towards the noise, I felt something calling me from behind a curtain so I walked through. He was sitting behind a little table with a white tablecloth. He was a big fat guy, biker type with a bunch of tattoos. You know how Allard's are all one color and look like charred flesh almost? This guy had all types of colors and it was all over his body, like a child went berserk with a crayon and made all of these little pictures.

He didn't seem mean though. His voice was kind of soft. He stood and offered me a seat and after he made sure I was comfortable he poured us some wine, a Shiraz, it was REALLY good. Like amazingly good. Almost as good as sex with Allard good." She smiled.

"I'm gonna need you to stop talking about how good the sex was with the man that stabbed you in the chest." Jury shook her head.

"I asked him where I was and he said with him at his table and I didn't need to be with anyone else."

Iara dropped a glass. The shatter was deafening to the rapt attention they paid to Lisa. She shook her head to bring herself back to reality and apologized for the disturbance. Jury desperately wanted to know what was up with Iara and Michelle. They weren't taking Lisa's resurrection too well.

"In the beginning." Lisa began to stare in Michelle's eyes. "The Creator made a peaceful realm. He wanted company and loved to give life to new things. Creating new planets and sparkly stars bored him. Dimensions didn't talk back, though he considered making them talk so he could have company. Instead, he created beings that he thought were very exceptional. They were different than him, but it was fun just creating them. They lived with him in his kingdom. They came and went as they pleased and some of them were allowed to create other beings in their likeness. They weren't able to procreate with each other. So The Creator gave them that ability because he knew how boring it could be without someone near you that you cherish. As time continued, The Creator continued to create beings and as he continued they began to look more and more like him. Some of the original beings didn't like that he was making more beings. They took offense. They began to feel insecure. They felt that The Creator wasn't happy with them, but none of them ever said anything about it. The Creator knew the feelings were there, but he believed that over time they'd love and cherish the new beings like he did.

One day he created another new being and was so happy with them, he showed them off to everyone within The Kingdom. They looked even more like him and to top it off, he decided that all of them would have a small wisp of him inside of them that made them who they were. He called them Souls."

Iara sat at the counter in the kitchen and stared at Lisa intently.

"So..." Lisa continued. "He built a place for the Souls, but decided he'd inhabit it little by little. He saw what happened when his Kingdom was populated too quickly. The Beings got in each other's way, animosity and arguments began and he needed to keep expanding his kingdom to give them more space. Still, he bred them all. He loved them all. Like a new parent, he doted over the Souls. One of the original beings, Dragon, didn't like it at all. He thought it was unfair for The Creator to like the

Souls better because they weren't nearly as powerful or as loyal to Him as the original beings or even the Beings that followed the originals.

To prove his point, he went down to their home, found two very new, very gullible Souls and put them in a situation where they could either follow The Creator's rule or disobey him. They disobeyed him immediately. Dragon went back to The Creator and said '*see they aren't as loyal as us. They do whatever they want.*' The Creator responded in defense of the Souls. He told Dragon that the Souls had disobeyed him, but it wasn't as bad as Dragon seemed to think. To make matters worse, he threatened Dragon with expulsion if he ever challenged The Creator's rules and his Souls again.

Of course, Dragon was pissed. Expulsion!? Over some little play things? It was bad enough The Creator gave them parts of him. Parts that he hadn't given to the Beings. Dragon asked a few other Beings if they thought it was fair. The more he spoke to the other Beings of his class, the more he found that he wasn't alone. In fact, there were angrier Beings than even he. They asked Dragon to plead with The Creator to just get rid of these Souls. Just the presence of the Souls was causing discord. Dragon knew it was impossible, he knew The Creator wouldn't choose a side or destroy any of his creations."

"Ummm..." Michelle interrupted. "We've heard this before, Lisa. It's the story of..."

"Not like this. Trust me." Lisa shook her head. "Dragon went to The Creator and told him of the issues and the animosity. The Creator admonished him and accused him of causing trouble. After that conversation, Dragon noticed that he was pushed to the side. The Creator didn't answer his requests for conference." Lisa paused and looked at Jury for effect. "Dragon slowly grew chilly towards The Creator, but he still loved him. He actually adored him, looked up to him and idolized him. His anger built too high. He started acting out more and more. He was the rebel of The Kingdom and with that position came followers and friends. Other Beings agreed with him and they started to torment and torture Souls. They'd go down to their residence and cause trouble in the name of Dragon. They wanted Dragon to lead them. Dragon wasn't a leader, Beings liked to follow him. They believed in him and he believed in the cause.

The Creator had his loyalists as well, Beings who called Dragon a traitor and a separatist. They asked The Creator to toss Dragon out of The Kingdom, but he didn't. It was going too far. Soon, Dragon had an army of followers and they demanded Dragon take the helm. He wasn't sure he should, but the civil war was coming. Finally, Dragon gathered his strongest allies and discussed a takeover. They knew that with the force they had amassed, they could take at least a portion of The Kingdom to themselves, but they all agreed that they would fair better with one specific Being on their side as opposed to against them." She paused to sip her cranberry juice.

"Allard." Jury finished her sentence for her.

"He was the fiercest and best warrior in The Creator's army. While the archangel Michael is the leader, Allard was the best soldier, the best fighter. He was created with that in mind. He was The Creator's definition of vengeful, skilled destruction. He was the mold for everything a warrior was going to be. A mold The Creator never used again for reasons I'll tell you. Although The Creator did use attributes in others like Achilles, Genghis Khan, Hannibal..."

"Bruce Lee?" Jury cracked lightening the mood.

"Allard refused the requests. He told them he wanted no part of it. When the word got out that Allard wasn't with the opposition, the furor quieted some. Dragon was upset. He didn't like that one being choosing sides could disrupt the revolution he had begun. He set out to show Allard how deceitful the Souls had become. Dragon and Allard visited the land of the Souls and Dragon showed him how the Souls lied, cheated, were deceitful and enslaved each other. Allard was moved, but not wavered. Then in a sudden stroke of kismet, Allard was attacked by a band of ruthless Souls. They beat him unmercifully, but he refused to fight back because he knew he would decimate them. Allard returned to The Kingdom and showed The Creator the bloody body he wore. The Creator accused him of being manipulated by Dragon and chastised him for being entertained by the lies.

Upset that The Creator had become a deadbeat father to his kind, Allard joined Dragon. The plan was to move swiftly. They started by taking over small sections of The Kingdom. The battles were easily won. With Allard on his side, Dragon's strategies were flawless. Allard killed tens of his own kind by the time The Creator got involved. It was too much. It went on too long. Michael, the leader of His army begged for help. Peter warned of breaches in the perimeter of The Pearly Gates. Beings were coming and going as they pleased. Offspring of Beings were sneaking into The Kingdom and tilted the balance in Dragon's favor. The Creator was incensed. In a historical show of magnificent force, he destroyed much of their army. He flooded the world of the Souls destroying many of his precious children along with the second and third generation Beings that resided there. He wanted to start over fresh without the presence of the hatred and malice induced by Dragon's cause. He had his soldiers bring the leaders of the resistance to trial. Dragon was banished from The Kingdom forever. He was sent to live in one of the worst dimensions. A dimension The Creator made when He himself was lonely and had little room for love within Him. In that place, the same rules applied. Loneliness thrived and love was absent forever.

Others in the opposition were sentenced based on their crimes. Many were allowed to stay in The Kingdom under probation. Some were banished to the land of the Souls to help rebuild it. They were told that they could not return until they learned how to love and care for their little brothers and sisters. Knowing that animosity persisted, The Creator sent his own personal platoon of soldiers to look after the Souls. They became known as The Guardians.

The Creator didn't want Allard and Dragon associating so he sent Allard to the land of the Souls. His sentence was similar to the rest of the banished Beings, except he had a monitor placed on him. If ever he killed any of The Creator's Beings, he'd receive a mark. Those marks would be counted when he was finally judged and he would be dealt with accordingly. Those are the tattoos we saw. That's who Allard is. He's a traitor. He is treachery. He's a traitor to God and he's here on the Earth and he's hell bent on reclaiming his old position and restarting the war."

"That was a dream. The facts of the stories are wrong in places. That's not how it is told in the scriptures." Michelle shook her head.

"I know. I didn't believe it either until the fat man told me, you three would bring me back to life...and it happened. He told me I was dead and he had my soul now. He was the one they called Dragon and Allard had taken my soul with Dragon's needle. The cold needle he killed me with. It was built as a tool for the Beings. They could remove the soul from the body in cases of emergency, but then someone realized it could be used to just take souls and use the power. So no more were made. I'm here with you now, but when I die...my place in hell is set."

"Calm down." Michelle was physically agitated.

Lisa sat calmly so Michelle's direction to calm down was really for herself.

"People that have near death experiences always report visions. Walking into the light, long dead relatives telling them it isn't their time, none of it is real. Tell her Marjorie."

"She has a point. The shit with the bracelet was pretty freaky, but I'm sure there's a medical reason for it. You said you ate. Maybe Allard slipped something in your food that reacts with the metal in the bracelet. You told me yourself about those natural herbs that slow your heart rate down to near nothing and people think you're dead!" Marjorie backed up her friend. "Iara, you..." She stopped short remembering the flowers in the jungle. "You have things like that on the island right?"

Iara sat silently and stared down at the kitchen counter top.

"She believes it." Lisa nodded. "I told you when I was told the story it was like I could see it, like a movie. I could see it like I was there. I saw Michael and Peter and..."

"Did you see God?" Michelle blurted.

"No." Lisa shook her head. "I didn't see The Creator. It was like He was always just out of the shot or I'd see Beings looking at him, but never saw...I saw Allard. He looked different. He looked more regal, but still strong. He looked more naïve and younger, if you can imagine. I saw you." Lisa looked over to Iara. "You were there. You were with the rebellion. A face in the crowd of Beings helping Dragon."

Iara wiped tears from her eyes and nodded her head.

"They called you a traitor in the jungle, they said you were gonna die for being a traitor." Jury breathed.

"I'm not who I used to be. Neither is Allard, but we're doomed to finish what we all started. I never met him there. He was a different class. It's like meeting a celebrity. I was honored when he approached me here and asked for my help. He likes all of you. His interests are mine and I'm going to make sure nothing happens to you as he and I agreed." Iara's voice wavered only slightly.

"Until..." Lisa felt a dangling addition.

"Until..." Iara continued. "It's all said and done. I can tell you this. Alala and Sundiata together is a very clear sign."

"Clear sign of what?" Michelle couldn't fathom how she had now become a believer.

"Allard's war is beginning, but his time is coming to an end."

CHAPTER THREE

BO[F2ELL THE CHa[

The Archangel Michael found it troubling that The Creator had given all of the Souls little pieces of himself. The problem wasn't that The Creator gave the little pieces. Those pieces were what drove the Souls. Michael didn't like that some of those pieces gave the humans gifts. In some, the gifts were small. There were trace amounts of psychic ability here and there. On occasion there were humans that could run extraordinarily fast or jump abnormally high. Others were gifted with the ability to recreate natural life in a drawn form. These were simple gifts. Others, however, were gifted with abilities Michael found to be a little too dangerous for the child-like Souls. It was tantamount to handing a six year old a loaded automatic weapon.

Michael requested and received approval from The Creator to form a small commission of Beings that would travel to Earth and disengage the gifts. In order to achieve the best results, disengagement was found best done during the child years. As the Souls got older, those gifts became too intertwined in their bodies and could result in death during disengagement. The last thing Michael wanted was to kill The Creator's precious children. He was, indeed, a vengeful God. It would take quite some time before He softened.

Michael's commission worked tirelessly over time monitoring the Souls and appointing some of the most skilled, trusted and at times, highly respected, Beings to handle the disengagements. For once those gifts were removed, they had to be returned to The Kingdom wherein Michael would personally return them to The Creator Himself. The risk of the gifts falling into the wrong possession, or even worse a confederate of Dragon, could result in disastrous results. His commission and their agents were used less and less over time, but on occasion Michael would have to call up a round of disengagements.

The process of disengaging a part of the soul is just as delicate as it sounds. The agents were picked according to their unique abilities to recognize the portions of the soul to be retrieved. Some Beings were just better than others. One Being's ability to locate a gift of dimensional sight (the ability to see what we know as ghosts, Guardian Angels, etc.) may not be so great at sighting the portion of the soul that allows for hyper-movement (the ability to move quickly through air and space similar to transporting without the sci-fi colors and beaming sounds.) The delicate process was micro-managed by Michael. His stance was fairly simple in argument. He believed Souls were just too immature to handle the more advanced abilities. They also created a strategic and logistical issue for his troops guarding other Souls and the Pearly Gates of The Kingdom.

At five years old, Michelle Bonds loved playing on her Queens, New York street with friends. It wasn't often that her strict mother allowed her out, so when she did, Michelle took advantage. Usually, most of her time was spent in church. She'd sit bored and beleaguered by the constant talk. While it helped to instill a relationship with God and religion, her time in church also created a rebellious side. She was often the loudest in the group of kids.

While not the leader, she knew how to manipulate them into doing as she wished. If they didn't, she was prone to tantrum.

Michelle was in the middle of one of those tantrums when she heard her mother's voice. The sing-song texture of her mother's Trinidadian accent was unmistakable and by the tone, Michelle knew she was in trouble. She grabbed her Barbie doll, the center of the tantrum and stormed away stomping in her jellie sandals. Her mother stood in the doorway with one hand on her hip, the other held the screen door open. Her eyes were squeezed into tight angry almonds.

"Is that how you speak to your friends?" Her mother asked angrily.

Michelle was shocked at the range her mother could hear. She dropped her head and dragged into the house knowing that the belt waited for her. She knew that the next Sunday she would be held back by the Sunday school teacher to discuss her anger. The last thing she wanted was to talk about it with Pastor or Mrs. Drugans, but they always persisted. Church people bothered her. Even as an adult they weren't her favorite folks to deal with at close range.

"Go get the belt." Her mother announced as soon as the door latch clicked.

The belt was kept on a hook her mother installed in the headboard of her bed. Michelle's mother kept it close by so if Michelle and her siblings decided to talk instead of sleep at night, the belt would be handy for quick capital punishment. Michelle glared at the belt then took the double-sided leather hide into her hand. The belt had weight to it and was rather long. It was a man's belt. A leftover article her father forgot when he packed his stuff and moved out. Michelle wished he'd forgotten one of his hats instead.

As she descended the stairs slowly one by one, she heard a rapping on the screen door. It was a hard enough knock that it made the door open and close with a steady bang. That door latch never worked right since her father let it slam behind himself when he left.

"Hello?" A man's voice echoed through the doorway.

"Hi. May I help you?" Her mother's tone broadcasted a sunny disposition.

Michelle knew immediately that the man must've been to her mother's liking.

"Good afternoon, Madam. I saw your children outside and thought you'd be interested in the research assistant I'm offering."

Michelle had stopped halfway down the steps, enough to see him standing as a hazy vision behind the screen door. He had a stout body and cherubic face. His fat fingers where wrapped around large cases of tightly weaved burlap. The handles were made of thick twine. The corners of the large rectangular cases had small pearl ends.

"Research assistant?" Her mother's head tilted. "You mean encyclopedias?"

"It's so much more than that, m'am."

"Mother. I have the belt." Michelle broadcasted as she stepped to the main floor.

Her mother turned with an embarrassed eye.

"Thank you, Michelle." She said through smiling teeth.

"Ah, another beautiful child. Such an angelic soul that one." He smiled through the screen. "I'm sure she would enjoy hours of quiet time reading through the research assistant. May I come in for five minutes? Just five minutes, to show you and your daughter. If I don't impress..."

"Five minutes, sir." Michelle's mother loved to entertain men, even for just five minutes.

"Don't call me, sir. My name is Herman." He nodded to Michelle's mother as she held the door for him.

Herman sat the heavy cases on the floor near the living room coffee table and unclasped the brass fastenings.

He lifted out a large leather bound tome with gold leaf edges. The book made a heavy thud as he sat it on the table. He flipped open the book to a page of finely printed words and elegantly drawn pictures.

"There's quality in this. Look at...wow and look what page I turned to... angels." His eyes batted in shock. Even he was surprised by the coincidence.

Michelle looked closely at the beautifully composed pages. She hoped this distraction would make her mother forget about the belt.

"This book is expensive." Her mother shook her head.

"I won't sugar coat it. They are pricey, but they will provide you with decades of information right at your fingertips." He turned to Michelle. "Come closer. You can take a look."

Michelle eased in beside the two and began to turn the pages.

"Doesn't look like something we can afford. I'm a single parent. A woman reserves her money for simple things." She not so subtly hinted at her single status. "It's hot out. I won't just shoo you out into the street without something to drink. Would you like some cold water?"

He nodded and as Michelle expected, *SHE* was sent to fetch Herman a cold glass of water. Michelle dropped two ice cubes from the tray into the glass and poured the water. Pouring glasses of water for guests was her only chore and she had become a proud expert at water fetching. She heard her mother giggle and coo at the things Herman told her. When she returned she was disappointed to see the book had been put back into the case. Herman thanked her for the glass and drained the icy water in one gulp. Michelle noticed a gleam in her mother's eyes as she watched him drain the water across his lips. The look in her mother's face made Michelle uncomfortable, but she didn't understand why.

Herman picked up the cases, one in each hand and bowed to Michelle.

"Wonderful to meet you." A sparkle gleamed in his eye.

He sized her up, nodded then turned quickly. His bags flailed and swung with a woosh. Michelle never saw it coming...

The case connected with the Michelle's head right at the base of her left ear. She felt a piercing, cold sensation. It wasn't pain, but a hollow silence as if too much water had filled her ear at the public pool. The sharpest point of the pearl corner dislodged as quickly as it had entered her skull. Michelle fell to the floor shaken.

"Oh my word! I'm sorry!" Herman yelped, dropped his bags and bent to attend to her.

Michelle's mother leaped over him and pushed him away.

"What are you doing with those bags, Mr. Herman?"

"Hermes...I mean Herman. Just Herman. I'm so sorry. These heavy bags get away from me some times."

Michelle was shaken up, but laughed aloud at being pushed to the floor so swiftly. She rubbed her ear and found a tiny dot of blood there. Herman helped her to her feet.

"I really am so sorry little Soul. Are you feeling OK?" He asked.

She nodded her head. Her mother pulled Michelle back towards her.

"She'll be OK. Thank you, Herman."

Herman nodded, grabbed his bags and made his way to the door. Before he left, he turned to Michelle and smiled.

"You're welcome." He whispered to himself.

Herman didn't visit any other homes that day. He walked down the suburban street carrying his two cases and seemed to disappear in a whirlwind. Michelle's mother took the drinking glass back to the kitchen and began to cook dinner. Michelle hung the belt up on the hook and went back outside to play. By the next morning, neither of them would remember Herman's visit.

When Dr. Lisa Lucas was twelve years old, she was jumping rope in the schoolyard of St. Mary's Catholic School. She swayed back and forth ready to jump between the double dutch ropes set to begin her elaborate display. Tameka and Jessica kept the double ropes turning with a steady rhythm. Lisa's hands bounced forward and backward. Her body moved in the opposite direction. Just as soon as she caught the rhythm and was ready to jump in, she felt a slap on her rear. She turned in anger to see little Justin Robinson running away laughing like a devilish monster. He held his hands high in victory as he had touched, what already in her tween years, had become an embarrassingly big rear. Justin Robinson didn't realize how fast a runner Lisa was until she was tight on his heels chasing him around the schoolyard. Her fingers narrowly missed grabbing his shirttails.

"You're gonna get it Justin!" She wailed.

Justin had just cause to be petrified. Everyone in school knew Lisa meant business...all the time. He ran passed the boys playing "flys up" barely evading the speeding handball. His feet scattered the soda tops of the boys playing "skelly" and he stumbled over the stone markers of the girls who played hopscotch. Lisa didn't falter. She was dead set on payback.

"Stop! Stop! I'm sorry!" Justin screamed.

"You'll BE sorry, Justin." Lisa screamed back.

Suddenly and with alarm Lisa felt the air leave her lungs at a terrifying rate. Her speed slowed to a crawl as she coughed and fell to her knees. She shredded her knee-high socks and scratched her knees as she gasped for air. Her friends screamed for help. Teachers ran to assist. Almost immediately, a young woman pushed through the crowd, announced herself as a doctor and demanded everyone back up. Her burlap satchel was unlike any the teachers had seen, as was the gleaming apparatus she pulled from the bag. The apparatus looked like a fancy asthma inhaler. The handle was pearl and she placed a small spoon like lip into Lisa's mouth.

The woman held Lisa's head back while her eyes rolled sickeningly back in her head. The woman depressed a tab, which didn't act like a normal asthma pump. It slid something deep into Lisa's throat. Although a huff of air did expel like a normal pump. The woman retrieved her fancy item quickly from Lisa's mouth and dumped it in her bag. Lisa recovered quickly. The device left a numb sensation in her chest like she'd rubbed too much vapor rub on it. Lisa breathed well again.

The woman accepted a few thank yous from teachers, but was quick to make her way to her car. No one knew who she had come to the school to visit and overall she had been a mystery. Lisa was a little weak the next day and happily stayed home from school. She didn't have an asthma attack before then and none after. She never knew the full effect of that apparatus on her body and her abilities.

Marjorie was done with her PSAT course and waited for all of her friends to gather and walk home together. She sat in front of her Brooklyn high school laughing at the boys dancing to the latest hip hop songs. The sun had already set on that late fall evening and they knew that there was safety in numbers. No one wanted to get caught alone by "The Decepticons", one of the gangs that had been terrorizing students on the subway and in the streets. Their claim to fame was robbing and beating kids with hammers. Once Barbara Dewitt finally joined the group of students, their safe patrol was complete and it was time to go.

"Let's stop at the pizza place." Barbara commanded more than requested.

Marjorie never did like Barbara Dewitt. Barbara thought she owned the world because she had long straight hair, light skin and green eyes. Of course, because she wanted to go get pizza, all of the guys wanted to go too. The other three girls wanted to be where the boys were going.

"I have to get home. If I'm not home by six fifteen my father is gonna come looking for me." Marjorie shook her head.

"Well...see you tomorrow, Marge." Barbara shrugged dismissively.

Marjorie hated being called Marge. She hated it even more when Barbara Dewitt said it with her stank-ass tone of voice. Marjorie turned to Wesley. It was a known fact Wesley had a crush on her. He wilted under the peer pressure with a shrug and a half mumbled excuse about being "kinda hungry". Marjorie was hurt and disappointed in him. She thought he was different. Two years later, Wesley asked her to the senior prom. She shook her head and told him his only chance was left on the corner when he left her for pizza with Barbara Dewitt.

Marjorie headed home in the opposite direction as the others. Halfway down the block, she turned around with hope someone had decided to walk home with her. All she saw were the backs of her now former friends laughing and dancing away. She walked a little faster than normal avoiding eye contact as she passed the crack house next to the empty lot two blocks away. There was a permanently funky smell that arose from that house. She covered her nose and mouth so as not to inhale any smoke by accident. She'd heard you could become hooked on crack just that easily. There was no way she'd become a crack head for anyone. The last thing she wanted was to be sucking on a glass tube full of something that dealers often hid between their ass cheeks. She surmised that was the true reason they called it crack.

She turned and watched as two fiends bobbled out of the house huddled around their prize. They rushed to a quiet corner. There were few faster than a crack head with a new rock. Michelle was sure they could break Olympic records.

"Excuse me." The Man stood just inches from her.

Marjorie screamed in fear then realized the simple looking White man wasn't any harm to her. Although, being in her neighborhood after dark was a sure sign he was probably looking for drugs.

"Do you know which way is Nostrand Avenue?" He asked bright-eyed.

Nostrand? That was her street. There were no crack dens on her side of Nostrand. Well...not on the two closest streets anyway. He must've been someone's parole officer.

"Yes. It's three blocks straight ahead."

"Thank you." He nodded with wide eyes.

She continued to walk and felt his presence behind her about three steps, so she sped up. His hard bottom shoes clopped against the sidewalk faster. When she turned over her shoulder, she saw him looking at her with a broad smile. He nodded. She sped up. He was a little too creepy. She passed a group of young guys on the street, mustered her biggest "hey fellas" and kept her pace. Maybe the white guy would lay off if he thought she knew the thugs on the block.. The thugs ignored her.

"Jumbos. I got jumbos." She heard one whisper loudly when the White Guy was within earshot. They tried to make the sale to the obvious sore thumb on the street.

Marjorie sped up and crossed the street just as the light changed. There was no way the White Guy was...

Clop! Clop! Clop!

He was right on her heels getting across the street just before the gypsy cabs and cars with thumping stereos could drive through the light. She pivoted her feet and slid into a corner store bodega. Merengue played on the radio. The lone clerk was ringing up a lotto ticket. Another rather wide guy sat up high on a ladder keeping an eye on the merchandise. He was the bodega equivalent of a security camera.

“Hey Mami! Quieres hamon con queso on a roll tonight?” The clerk said as he retrieved the lotto ticket, handed it over to the patron and collected the money without needing to count it.

“No. I ummm...there’s this guy following me...and” Marjorie started, but before she could finish the guy on the ladder had already jumped down and headed out the door with a New York Yankees commemorative bat in hand.

“Don’t worry, Mami. He gots it.” The clerk nodded.

The bodega family was used to protecting their customers from crackheads, perverts and on occasion, providing alibis to la policia. It was just something they offered as a free service to protect their buying public. Marjorie stood against the quarter water refrigerator breathing heavily and trying to get her nerves together. The first thing she would do when she got to school the next morning was curse out every last one of those so-called friends of hers.

The security guy walked back into the store shook his head and dropped his bat back into the corner with a clang.

“He must run. Didn’t see anyone. Want me to walk you home?” He asked.

“No thanks. I’ll be ok.” Marjorie sighed. To show her gratitude, she bought a bag of chips and a quarter water for her walk home.

Marjorie walked so quickly her school bag nearly rubbed a hole in her jeans where it collided with the fabric. She was never so in tune with her surroundings before in her life. She could see the lights and cars of her street about a half block away. Her house was just on the opposite end of the intersection. The brisk air chilled her lungs, she clenched the school bag tighter in an effort to keep it from annoyingly rubbing her legs again. Suddenly, the bag lifted high up over her head, she reached to pull it back down when her whole body whipped against the brick wall of a nearby building. Her face pushed against the hard brick with a smack. She could feel hands pushing against her back. The air escaped from her lungs as her chest pressed against the wall. She couldn’t find the air to scream.

“Be still. This won’t hurt. Just remain still, young lady.” His voice whispered behind her. She could feel one hand pulling her shirt up and his cold fingers on her back.

"MIRA!" The voice of the bodega security guy bellowed nearby.

She heard a whoosh and the sickening thud of wood connecting with bone. The pressure of the hands on her back released immediately. The man tumbled to the ground gasping for breath. Loud Spanglish yelling filled her ears. There were foot stomps and more whooshes and wood against bone, wood against concrete and screams of anguish. Marjorie rolled to her side and saw the anguished face of the white man that followed her, his arms covered his head as feet stomped against him. Hands grabbed her ankles and pulled her away, more hands grabbed her wrists and pulled her to her feet. She was face to face with the bodega clerk.

"Go home! Don't turn around. You aint seen nuttin, ok? We got this piece of shit." The clerk yelled pushing her back away from the scene.

Marjorie ran as fast as she could. As she reached the intersection she couldn't help but to turn around. Five Puerto Rican men were stomping on the man. Bats swung high in the air then collided with portions of his body. He was overwhelmed and overcome by street justice. Marjorie turned and ran as fast as she could. She made it to her house panting and huffing. She shouted a quick "Hi" to her father as she ran to her bedroom and sat quietly praying her saviors didn't kill her assailant.

The next morning, Marjorie went by the bodega to thank the men for their help. None of them acknowledged her presence outside of attending to her like a normal customer. On her way out with her jamon con queso, she noticed the security guy had a new bat sitting behind his ladder. Her case was one of a few where the gift was not retrieved.

The Jeep approached the pier at a high rate of speed kicking up lots of dust behind it. The soldiers watched at alert. If they hadn't known better, they would've thought someone was chasing the women. Lieutenant Wellspring peered through his small field binoculars to check the occupants. His gaze dropped to the ground, he squeezed his bright blue eyes closed tightly,and then refocused the binoculars as the Jeep got closer. He turned to his men looking for his retrieval squad. They weren't back yet. Looking back to the road, he saw the small flatbed truck finally come into view pursuing the Jeep.

"Weapons!" Wellspring shouted.

In a flash, several of the team snipers aimed their weapons at the approaching Jeep. Lieutenant Wellspring pulled his service handgun, cocked it and walked slowly toward the forward position. He held his hand up to halt the Jeep. It sped without acknowledgment.

"DO NOT FIRE WITHOUT MY CALL!" Lieutenant Wellspring yelled. He felt his vocal box tighten.

The Jeep skidded to a stop just at the end of the platform. The soldiers lowered their weapons. Lieutenant Wellspring held his at his side.

"Is that the kind of welcome I get?" Lisa smirked from the passenger seat as Marjorie and Michelle hopped from the vehicle.

Wellspring stood stiff, numb to what he witnessed. He watched Lisa stand, walk past him and head toward the pier. He'd seen many odd things during his time at Scilymax. This was just another in a litany of unexplainable occurrences.

"Where's Alala?" He glared as the flat bed truck arrived shortly after them.

"She jumped ship with the guy in the basement." Marjorie huffed walking quickly down the pier.

"What are you saying?" Wellspring waved off the quizzical looks from the retrieval squad in the flatbed trucks.

“We need to go right now. We have to catch up to them.” Lisa slapped the back of her hand with her palm.

“You were dead yesterday. All of a sudden there’s a rush?” Lieutenant Wellspring followed them down the pier.

“When you’ve seen just how short life is everything seems to move in slow-motion.” Said Lisa.

“Right.” He shrugged. “Well I can’t just put you on that plane and have you show up in New York. There will be questions”

“Don’t be such a dick! We told you WE have to go. So WE have to go. We don’t have time for an interrogation. Let’s go!” Marjorie shouted.

“I can’t do it, ladies. Bad enough YOU’RE supposed to be in a crate in the cargo hold.” He pointed at Lisa. “We’re missing Alala and we have a missing prisoner? I’m not getting shipped off to some shit detail for you guys. You’re lovely ladies, but I’m not going to The Country Cage for you.”

“The Country Cage isn’t there anymore.” Lisa said matter-of-factly.

“What?” Lieutenant Wellspring was confused. “That’s classified”

“She means, it’s time for you to start this boat, take us to the plane and for us to fly our asses back to New York.” Marjorie yelled.

Michelle sat on the yacht quietly watching Marjorie and Lisa argue with Lieutenant Wellspring. Her hands twitched uncomfortably in her lap. She wasn't nervous. She was afraid Iara would hear them.

"Everybody please step off the vessel. I'll have someone escort you back to The Hut." Lieutenant Wellspring stared off to the plane that floated in the middle of the ocean. As usual, he played it by the book.

"Do we really have to?" Michelle asked as she watched the ocean swell.

"Yes you do." Lieutenant Wellspring put one foot on the gangplank and extended his hand to the first person that would take it.

There was a small thump on the hull of the boat.

"No!" Michelle shouted but it was too late.

The yacht jerked from the pier ripping the tie rope from the metal tether. Wellspring lost his balance and dove, rather than fall, into the water. The ship moved from the pier quickly. Two soldiers dove to catch it, but the boat evaded them leaving them splashing in the water. The soldiers on the pier aimed their weapons at the boat.

"Stop the ship!!" One of them shouted.

"We're not doing anything!" Michelle raised her hands. "It's not even on!"

The yacht moved swiftly across the water. Beneath the surface, Lieutenant Wellspring saw the waves above him as it sped away. Underneath the boat was a figure holding the hull. The feet whipped together, quickly up then down, pushing a torrent of water away. Was the person holding on or pushing the boat itself? He pushed his body upward breaking the surface and gasped for air.

"Sir?? Sir?? Do we fire?" One of the men on the pier aimed his weapon. Marjorie's head was dead in his scope.

"No." Lieutenant Wellspring peered at the boat.

The engine wasn't on. The yacht sat bobbing with the current forty yards away. Lisa, Marjorie and Michelle looked confused. Lieutenant Wellspring took a deep breath and submerged his head in the water. His eyes adjusted to the change in salinity. He focused on something a foot in front of him, Iara's big toothy grin. Had he screamed in terror like he wanted, he would've swallowed a mouthful of salty water. Instead he reflexively threw a slow blow at Iara's head, which she caught with her own hand and pulled him quickly toward the ship. He had never moved that quickly underwater without the assistance of a mini-sub. Looking back, he saw the pier get further and further away. Her grip on his hand was tight and uncomfortable but the last thing he wanted was for her to let him go.

When she swam, her arms didn't move, but her torso, legs and feet undulated quickly.

He felt his oxygen level decreasing and quietly prayed she wouldn't lead him out into the middle of the ocean and leave him for the sharks to feed on his body. Suddenly, she stopped, spun to him and lifted his body above the surface by his armpits like one would a baby. The air stormed through his nostrils as he inhaled with shock and relief while Marjorie helped pull him into the boat. Looking back, he could see Iara's beautiful form just under the surface of the water. Her barely there bathing suit seemed to shimmer. She winked at him and dropped deep into the water. The yacht pushed off again moving towards the plane. The sudden movement of the ship nearly sent him over the side.

"Get a grip, darling." Marjorie said with the utmost bitch in her voice.

"You ok, sir?" A voice crackled in his ear. Wellspring jumped when he heard it, he'd forgotten his earpiece was still in his ear.

"Yes. I'm fine."

"Shall we fire?"

"Huh?" Lieutenant Wellspring had momentarily forgotten his position. He looked out to the pier at his entire squadron aiming their weapons at the boat. Some of them didn't have the firepower to reach them, but the snipers could've shot the head off of a nail on the stern. "Do not fire!" He said emphatically.

As he watched the team lower their weapons, he felt the boat slow and ease against the loading platform on the plane.

"I hope you're ok to drive the boat back." Lisa checked his eyes for signs of shock. There were some, but no more than would've been expected.

"I guess there's no way you're gonna stay, huh." Lieutenant Wellspring shrugged.

"Awwww I think he likes you." Marjorie nudged him as she stepped on to the platform and handed the co-pilot her bag.

"I've got a life to live." Lisa smiled climbing on to the platform behind Michelle. It immediately began to rise to a doorway on the tail of the plane.

"If you write a report, you may wanna leave out the part about the chick in the water." Marjorie shouted down to him.

"And the woman that came back to life?" Lieutenant Wellspring shielded his eyes from the rain drizzle bouncing off the magnificent fuselage of the mechanical bird.

"Act of God." Michelle shouted back.

Lieutenant Wellspring waited until the door closed and locked before he started the yacht and headed back to land. He watched from the pier as the plane sprayed a large plume of water behind it creating splashing waves against the pier. Soon it was climbing up into the dreary sky. The large booming jets echoed as the plane ascended swiftly and soon became a shrinking black insect in the sky.

The flight back to New York was excellent with one exception, the food. They had all become so spoiled by Iara's cooking of fresh ingredients and exotic cuisine that their Scilymax in-flight lunch required imagination in order to complete. The Scilymax airline meals were much better than the average airline food, but still several levels below the cooking of their private chef...and helper. Lisa found herself running back and forth to the bathroom, while Marjorie nearly tore the cabin apart looking for a gas reliever. Michelle chose to sleep it off with hopes she'd wake up in New York sans bubble guts.

"You're going to the bathroom again?" Marjorie laughed.

"Remind me to never eat so much again. This airplane food on top of Iara's food has me about ready to just relocate my seat to the toilet." Lisa feigned sitting on the toilet while wiping real sweat from her forehead.

"You may need this." Marjorie tossed Lisa the Stephen King book that stuck out of her bag. Lisa flipped it back to her, along with the bird for good measure.

Lisa was careful to watch her step on the way to the bathroom. The passenger quarters were very elegant for what was really a jumbo cargo carrier. She braced her hand against the mahogany overhead baggage compartment when she lost her balance. Finally in the bathroom, she looked at her sweaty face in the mirror then without notice or build up, she threw up the remnants of the airplane food in the sink. After she rinsed the food down the drain, she soaked a plush white washcloth in some cool water and placed it on her neck. Her eyes burned red and she felt a burning sensation in her chest. This was way beyond indigestion.

She took a seat on the toilet and tried her best to get it together. When the long inhales and soft exhales didn't work, she counted backward from twenty and then again from fifty. Lisa didn't want to scare her friends, but coming back from the dead wasn't nearly as uncomplicated as she had made it seem. Her spirit felt overwhelmingly reinvigorated as if she rebooted her entire spiritual system. However, her body felt like it had gone through the ringer. As a doctor, she could tell she was having some type of arrhythmia. Every attempt she'd made at checking her pulse had been foiled by an erratic and irregular heartbeat.

This was her turn to fight and press on. As she sat on the toilet bowl, she whispered to herself that this time would be different. Death's kiss, as welcome as it would've been the first time, was not granted a return audience. She sat on the bowl replaying her after death experience.

Lisa sat across from that large sloppy slouch of a Being named Dragon, listened to his story and drank his wine. She watched him suck from his wine goblet with his red drool pattering against the crisp white tablecloth. She nervously laughed when he wiped his mouth with the back of his hand. She didn't know how she'd mustered a smirk when Dragon told her he would sodomize her for all eternity. He actually squealed with delight when she stood at his request and turned to show him her backside. She sat as quietly as possible while mentally tabulating just how fast she could make it to the exit before he could catch her with one of his fat fingers.

It wasn't long after he'd told her more disgusting details of her eternity with him, that he'd said something that sparked a memory.

"Keep that bracelet on until I say you can take it off." He said.

But he didn't just say it so much as warn her. He warned her with a tinge of fear. Allard had said something about the bracelet too. What was it? She thought so hard she bit her bottom lip trying to remember. A chill up her spine interrupted her thought. The thin wisp of hairs stood on the back of her neck. Dragon's eyes peered over her shoulder and she saw that he was displeased with the interruption. What she could never forget were the words she heard from behind her.

"You know she's mine first." The sweet bass heavy voice said.

"Fucking semantics." Dragon growled back.

The chill traveled from her neck to the hairs on her arm as he moved across the room. He floated passed her on her left side. She saw the long robes first. They were like something from a graphic novel. The endless reams of tattered dirty black fabric billowed and waved when he walked as if a fan blew them. The hood was large and a chasm of darkness enveloped the unseen face. His hands were gangly thin. The thin, yellowed skin was pulled taut against the boney appendages. His boney fingers tapped against the table as he floated by.

“Still mine first.” His sweet bass voice said.

Lisa looked up to him following Dragon’s own gaze. He took a slouched seat far behind Dragon. It was Kronus, known to most as The Grim Reaper himself. He looked as he was depicted in so many books, films and TV shows she’d seen. He sat with his hood draped over his head and his body slumped in a ratty old recliner chair in the back of the room. His sickle was made of a hard oak staff with a rather large jagged old metal blade. The staff sat flat across his knees like an old man might sit his cane.

“Don’t look at him, look at me.” Dragon fumed.

Lisa hadn’t realized she was staring at the billowing robes and the lone scrawny index finger tapping against the hard wood staff. She felt the chill to her bones. Her teeth had begun to chatter intermittently. Her hands shook against the crisp white tablecloth with the stains of wine. Her nipples were so hard they hurt.

“You’re mine remember that. I like that. I like you. Just remember that story I told you. You’re mine.” Dragon’s jowls shifted like a chubby bulldog. His gaze caressed the bracelet on her wrist.

She covered it with her hand. It was the only thing she had left from a world where she felt comfortable.

"Don't worry. I'll make sure you keep it. I won't take your jewelry, but I will take your ass." Dragon said.

Allard had said something to her about that bracelet.

"You're so charming, Dragon" Kronus said sweetly.

Dragon huffed exasperated with the constant interruption.

"How could a woman resist your charms? You really light them afire, ol dog." Kronus continued.

Lisa imagined a smirk on the skull beneath the hood.

She thought about the exit again. Kronus had come in quite fast. She figured if she ran she could maybe get back to the hallway in about six large steps. She picked up her wine glass and drank from it trying not to reveal her thoughts. As she drank, she looked at the maroon color of the Shiraz, the curve of the glass and the fun house image of that reaper's billowing robes. The boney hand rose and pushed the cavernous hood back. The fun house image through the glass didn't make sense anymore. She pulled the glass from her lips quickly and focused.

"Kronus!" Dragon shouted startling Lisa.

The Grim Reaper was gorgeous. He had well shorn blonde hair and a pair of the most beautiful blue eyes. While he wasn't young, his face was youthful and not without a wrinkle or three. He did indeed have a smirk on his face, which stretched his movie star good looks one way while his eyebrow cocked his forehead, the other. Dragon mustered the weight of his torso and turned to face him.

"You had to take off that fucking hood. Your semantics are not appreciated." Dragon roared.

"What's semantics to you is a tradition to me. A ritual. You know about rituals don't you? All kinds of goats and wild shit gets slaughtered for you." Kronus shook his head while mussing his blonde locks with his boney fingers.

Lisa rubbed the bracelet under her fingers. The smooth metal was warm to her touch.

"Whaddya say we blow this dive joint sweetheart?" Kronus floated to his feet. "It smells absolutely fucked up in here. You need a cleaning lady, Dragon."

"Kronus!" Dragon stood to face him.

It was the first time Lisa had noticed how tall the grim reaper was. Tall and sexy.

Sex...

It was after sex, after Allard had stabbed her in the chest, he whispered to her.

"This is how it works, sweetheart..." Kronus began. "You can give me a kiss. A nice warm passionate kiss or I can..." He held up his staff and looked it over. His bony finger slid across the blade, stopped at the very jagged tip and plucked it. A low metallic thump resonated. "I can bring this over to you and..." He frowned his face. "I'm sure you've been penetrated by a few large dicks in your time, but mine, honey..." He held the staff out in front of him showing its length. "Mine will take your breath away."

It was the first time she'd noticed a slight effeminate touch to Kronus' voice.

Allard's voice, on the other hand, was very masculine. He'd whispered to her.

"Just take off the bracelet." She heard Allard say again in a rush of recollection.

"Kiss her and go away. She's mine. That ass is mine." Dragon looked up at Kronus.

"Classless." Kronus shook his head.

Lisa touched the bracelet pulling at the corded string. She saw Dragon's eyes drop to her wrist. He lunged across the table and wrapped one massive hand around her entire neck.

"What are you doing you cunt?" He roared with spit escaping his lips.

She tugged hard pulling the bracelet from her wrist. It dropped to the vomit, sweat and semen stained floor. The air left her lungs as Dragon's hand clamped tighter around her neck. An electric shock went through her body. Her stomach turned. She vomited the wine in torrents as Dragon tossed her body to the ground. The chair broke under the velocity of her body as she crashed to the floor. She didn't feel the pain of the chair just the white-hot electricity of something trying to occupy the same space in her head as her brain. Something tried to get into her arms, legs and stomach. She looked up to the beautiful face of Kronus. Kronus looked down at her shaking his head.

"You could be here forever, young lady. If no one opens the door you're just gonna keep banging against it with your body like some kind of retard. Look... you're already drooling like one."

Lisa felt that exact sensation. Like her body was banging against a door...more like a brick wall. Every portion of her body including the insides were wrecked with the pain of being pushed around internally. Her saliva foamed in her throat.

"Don't let her go! Do something!" Dragon shouted from elsewhere in the room.

"I don't work for you. I'm an independent vendor."

Kronus miraculously sat his large frame on the edge of the table. He rested his legs on pieces of the broken chair without it all collapsing under his size. Lisa wanted to scream but she couldn't. It was like her vocal box was fighting a civil war. Finally she mustered all of the energy she could with a projectile vomit...

...and watched it land on the bathroom floor in the airplane.

She looked around and found herself back in the living world, back on the plane with bloodshot eyes and sitting on the toilet. Her vomit slid across the floor sluggishly with the swaying of the plane. The strong smell of the vomit and the diarrhea she deposited in the toilet made her dry heave. Life was not one to fool with. Death was apparently gorgeous. Evil liked a nice ass. The last two she hoped to never see again.

All three left the plane feeling a lot better than they had mid-flight. Lisa was especially better. She sighed as she smelled the near winter air in New York City. A fifteen-passenger van with the Scilymax logo picked them up on the tarmac. The driver was a teenager who still hadn't gotten use to his first corporate job. He forgot to take his hat off when his passengers approached him. It was a shame for him. He had just had his ex-girlfriend re-braid his cornrow hairstyle to be more presentable. He also forgot to turn the music off in the van so when he opened the door, the latest hip-hop hit blared from the speakers.

"Aww man, yo, I'm sorry 'bout dat." He covered his mouth, certain his pink slip would arrive as soon as he got back to the office.

"Yeah, you need to turn that up." Lisa nodded as she climbed in the passenger seat.

"Umm ok." He grinned, happy that these middle-aged chicks were cool. They were also kind of fine for women that could be his momma.

He packed their bags in the back then closed the side door. Sliding into the driver's seat, he remembered his first order of business...engage the passengers.

"Good Afternoon m'ams. My name is Darshawn Wilkins. I'll be your driver. How are you today?" He said robotically. "Are you going to the office or your home addresses?" He pressed the buttons on the Scilymax Travel System display. It gave information on his passengers and the quickest routes to and from their homes and offices.

"Darshawn, we may have to stop off at the hospital. Dr. Lucas may need a quick check up." Michelle sat on the first bench seat with Marjorie behind her on the second.

"I'm fine, Shell." Lisa cracked the window to let in some fresh air.

Darshawn had the van nice and warm to combat the outside frigid air, but Lisa appreciated nature more today.

"Ok..uhhh..." Darshawn pressed the touch screen buttons over and over. He was pretty good with the STS, but he still couldn't find what he was looking for. "I don't see Dr. Lucas in the passenger list."

"Oh yeah, about that..." Marjorie sat up.

"All I have is Dr. Marjorie Houston, Pastor Michelle Bonds...."

"Just Michelle Bonds, please." Michelle corrected him.

"Sorry m'am." Damn another mess up. "And a Miss Alala" He pronounced it Al-allah.

"She didn't make it." Lisa pursed her lips.

"The system records where I go. So if I drive anywhere not on the approved lists I have to pay for the trip out of my pocket. It won't even let me add you in the system. Automated, you know how it is." He grimaced punching button after button.

"Is there an address for Miss Al-Allah?" Lisa tried to peer into the STS screen.

"No address, but I have the previous destinations she took with Scilymax drivers. You can go to any of those places." Darshawn shrugged.

Michelle leaned forward peering into the screen alongside them. She looked for anything that stuck out. They mostly saw restaurants and places to shop.

"Bergdorf, Saks, La Perla, Asia De Cuba, Rolls Royce of Manhattan, Le Bernadin, Heavenly Little Things, Wolford, Scilymax Main Branch." Lisa read aloud.

"What was that last one?" Marjorie shouted from the back as she pulled a piece of paper from her pocket.

"Wolford." Lisa shrugged

"Before that."

"Heavenly Little Things, m'am?" Darshawn didn't think telling a passenger's previous destinations were in the rules, but he didn't want to get in trouble for not being helpful.

Marjorie read the name on the piece of paper Iara had given her. She'd written down the name of the person that she was sure had helped Alala get off the island. Iara's penmanship was nowhere near as pretty as she was.

"Does that system have business info?" Marjorie asked as she bent over the seat trying to get a better look.

Darshawn was on it. He punched a few buttons and got a display of the business, it's operating hours and a picture of the storefront.

"Anything else? Like an owner's name?" Lisa looked around the screen.

"Wilson Management Incorporated is listed as operator." Darshawn read. "The only thing else is the manager's name Shal-akalo?"

"Shalako??" Marjorie pushed forward squeezing her hips over the first bench. Her hand squeezed against Michelle's shoulder for balance.

"Owww!" Michelle moaned. "That's it isn't it?"

"Yep!" Marjorie matched the name on the screen with the name on the paper.

"That's where we'll go Darshawn." Lisa tapped the screen.

Darshawn didn't like people tapping his screen, but she was the nice one with the big booty that told her to turn the music up. He pressed his route chooser and checked it off as the destination for Dr. Houston and (Don't call me Pastor) Bonds. He checked Miss Alala for Dr. Lucas.

"Ok. Our destination is Greene Street, Manhattan" Darshawn breathed remembering his guidelines. "Please, everyone fasten your safety belts."

Darshawn was kind enough to carry their bags into the entranceway at Heavenly Little Things. Michelle handed him a twenty-dollar tip and he disappeared before the door chimes rang a second time.

“Good afternoon ladies, Welcome to Heavenly Little Things. May I help you find anything?” Jessup smiled.

“I think we’re in the wrong place.” Lisa looked around.

Jessup returned a frown. It was a slow day and he was sure these three were a guaranteed sale.

“Well, we have lots to look at. If there’s a specific piece you’ve heard about I may be able to have it shipped in.”

“Is there a Shalako that works here?” Marjorie stepped up to the large wooden main desk and looked around for signs of anyone else working. She noticed Jessup make a face.

“He’s in the back with another customer. Maybe I can help you with something.” He tried to persuade her by raising his voice.

“I still think this is wrong.” Lisa held up a small metal sculpture of a flower.

Before anyone could react, a door opened and Shalako walked out quickly followed by Riesha. He stopped in his tracks when he realized there were customers.

“Shalako these ladies are here to see you.” Jessup waved, sat behind the counter and sipped his cappuccino.

"I'm sorry. Would you please let him take care of your concerns? I'm pretty busy right at this moment." Shalako tied his waist belt over his overcoat preparing to leave.

"It's ok, thank you. I think this is a misunderstanding." Lisa apologized.

"No it's not." Michelle stared at the large sculpture near the desk.

She'd seen the symbol before. It was the war horn that was tattooed on Alala's back. It looked more dynamic in it's full three-dimensional form.

"Iara sent us. She said you may be able to tell us where Alala ran off to with a big smelly homeless guy who has some kind of powers." Marjorie blurted.

"And can jump down the side of a building like a monkey." Lisa added.

"Gorilla?" Marjorie shot back.

"Gorilla." Lisa agreed.

"The names don't ring a bell." Shalako watched Michelle as she looked over the items in the store very closely.

"What about Allard?" Lisa pressed.

"No, I'm sorry. I think your friend is mistaken..." Shalako shrugged.

"Where is he?" Riesha blurted out of turn. By the looks she received, she automatically knew this was something she shouldn't have asked.

"You know Allard?" Lisa focused in on Riesha. "How do you know him?"

"You don't want to travel down this path. I suggest you turn and walk out of here. Go live your life and ignore this." Shalako warned.

Jessup excused himself and went on lunch, as was often the case when people from Shalako's side business came into the shop. He had heard enough in his time there to know that he did not want to be too involved in it. He glanced through the large glass window as he walked away. He could tell Shalako was three steps beyond angry with the new girl for telling his business. Oh well, he didn't think the business needed her help anyway.

Michelle could hear the conversation going on, but didn't want to add another voice to the mayhem and accusations that started to fly. She was more interested in the antiques in the shop. Some of them bore religious symbols, others were very odd and out of place for a SOHO antique shop.

"I understand you think you're helping but you're not, Riesha." Shalako brandished a growing annoyance. "These women are not qualified to discuss any of this."

"Here's a qualification, Allard stabbed her in the chest with a dagger. We'd like to talk to him about that." Marjorie's voice wavered on the cusp of breaking into a full yell.

"He wouldn't do such a thing." Riesha retorted.

"Quiet." Shalako commanded.

Riesha backed down. She was still a very traditional Tunisian woman at heart and while she believed in gender equality, she was still a new comer. Her uncle's brothel wasn't a shining example of the equality of men and women. Her heart ached to know when Allard would return to her and if he would take her with him. Her crush had grown exponentially and her needs as a growing woman needed to be attended to soon. She had fully decided that Allard would be the one to attend to them and there was no doubt in her mind.

Michelle was drawn to an area containing luggage, large steamer cases and small satchels. All of them were made with a very sturdy burlap material. It was all very similar to the bag she received from Herman. Amongst the luggage were two sample cases each bearing pearl edges. They were familiar. Way too familiar. She unlatched one and found it filled with three large leather bound books engraved with the words Encyclopedia Astrales. She lifted volume one and flipped it open. The term "angel" stared back at her with beautiful pictures and adorned gold lettering. She dropped the book to the side and looked down at the other case. Her fingers thumbed the pearl ends. She found one end sharper than the others. When she opened it, there was nothing but a pretty gold silk lining. The case was empty. It had always been empty. This case wasn't to carry large books. It was to carry something more precious. She recognized those cases. She was hit with one as a kid. They were in her house. She had seen those pictures before. Those cases belonged to a salesman. A salesman named Herman. The same man she had seen later. He had said she hadn't changed when he saw her in the Homeland Security building. Shockingly enough, he hadn't changed at all in the thirty years since she had seen him.

"Mr. Shalako..." Michelle bellowed over the negotiations. Her stern command quieted everyone. "How much are you selling Herman's cases for?" She glared at Shalako with a knowing look.

"You know those cases?" Shalako asked.

He walked to the door and locked it. He pulled the large shade down over the large front window removing much of the natural light from the space. He pensively considered the cases.

"I do. Herman brought them to my house when I was a kid. I got hit with one of them by mistake."

Shalako laughed.

"If you got hit with one of *those* cases it wasn't by mistake." He said with his mouth twisting left and right.

"People know we're here. Don't try anything slick." Lisa warned.

"If I wanted to try something slick, there's nothing those people could do about it, young lady." Shalako walked toward the cases. His hand rubbed the burlap material. "And you were stabbed in the chest by Allard?" He said aloud as he brushed his hands in the gold lining of the bag.

"Yes." Lisa responded. "And I died."

Shalako nodded.

"You were the gift to Dragon." He looked from Lisa to Michelle. "You brought him Dragon's Needle." He looked back to Marjorie. "So, what's your purpose here?"

Marjorie stood stone stiff. She wasn't sure if it was a question, a threat or a prophecy of some kind.

"Are you going to help us find Alala?" Lisa interrupted the uncomfortable silence.

"You don't want to find Alala. You're looking for Allard. You want to undo everything he's done. You can't. That is done. Your fate has been sealed, miss..."

"Doctor...Doctor Lisa Lucas." Lisa corrected him with a sigh.

"Doctor Lucas, I'm sure you know that you belong to Dragon when you leave this world. You do know this?" Shalako put the encyclopedia back in the case and closed them both.

"Yes."

"So what is left to do? Live your life. All of you live your lives." Shalako aimed his words at all four women standing in his shop. "Allard will be Allard. He will do what he plans to do. You want to help. You think you can help, but he is responsible for his decisions. I'm sorry all of you have learned way more than any one Soul can manage to comprehend, but this is a war you cannot fight."

"What about me? I might be like Allard. I might be one of those things. I heard the trees and flowers talking in the jungle." Marjorie wanted some kind of closure.

"The flowers were trying to kill us?" Michelle shouted.

"You heard the flowers speak? You've heard the trees talking? You're a gifted Soul as was this young lady at one point before she was relieved of that via Herman and these cases." He gestured to Michelle. "It's really a burden. Something you shouldn't have to deal with at all. I'm certain someone tried to relieve you of that burden once. It's very disappointing that they failed. If I were granted the ability to extract it, I would, but unfortunately I have the tools..." He patted the cases. "But not the skills, you see. Even I can accept the things I cannot change. You are all very blessed and gifted people. You should accept that."

There was a dense silence in the room. The triumvirate had come for answers and received way more than they had expected. Shalako straightened a few things on shelves allowing all of them to come to grips with their newfound truths. It was a nice day, a beautiful day to relax and think about truth. He felt a warm sensitive kiss on his mind. His tension relaxed. Yes it really was a nice day out wasn't it? These were beautiful young women that needed help and deserved it so why couldn't he give it? He thought. Perhaps it was worth a try to help them. Technically it wasn't infiltrating or picking sides. The warm kisses on his neck increased. He shook off the fuzzy drunken sensation in his mind. Suddenly, he had difficulty making decisions. He felt high on life, on movement, on the world and helping these three women.

"Ok. I'll help you ladies find Allard, but I can only grant you safe passage through the seal as I did him." Shalako nodded dreamily.

His demeanor had changed noticeably. Lisa and Marjorie recognized the haze immediately and tossed each other looks.

"What's the seal?" Lisa asked.

Shalako walked them to the large circular sculpture that hung above the main desk. The small fingerprint indents on it looked as if it were molded by lots of different skilled hands

"It's a dimensional passkey." Riesha explained. "You walk through and it will lead through to where he wants to send you, but there is some issue with the passage."

Shalako stood still staring at the seal motionless.

"As I've heard it explained, you have to pass through a section of Purgatory to reach the other side. You never know who or what you can come in contact with. As Souls, if something captures you there, you can't come back ever. Dr. Lucas, if your soul belongs to Dragon, you would go to him immediately." Riesha explained.

"How far do we have to walk through purgatory?" Michelle fretted.

"I'm not sure. Shalako, how far through purgatory is it?" Riesha asked.

"Maybe only about a hundred yards." He glared dreamily at the seal. His eyes began to water.

"You ladies need to go now. I can't hold him like this much longer." Riesha grimaced.

"Hold him?" Marjorie waved her hand in front of Shalako's face. He didn't move.

"Go! Now!" Riesha yelled.

"I'll open the seal. It will take you." Shalako's pupils disappeared. His eyes shone translucent and with it a small swirling wind began to move in the seal. It was like looking down into a tornado funnel cloud.

Riesha grabbed a library ladder and pushed it into place. The three stepped up to the ladder and climbed up slowly.

"Don't touch anything and don't let anything touch you. Nothing!" Riesha warned.

Lisa, her normal protective self, was first. She stepped to the top rung and placed a foot on the edge of the seal. It vibrated under her foot. She took a deep breath and just as she was about to step in, a small hand reached out and grabbed the top of the seal. She lurched back nearly tumbling down the ladder.

"Go! They know it's open! They're gonna try to come out!" Riesha screamed.

Shalako's pupils began to flicker slightly and with it the tornado wins diminished and raged alternately. He was regaining consciousness. The hand at the top of the seal pulled to get out leaving more little fingerprints in its surface. Lisa nodded and stepped through the seal. One moment she was there, the next she was gone. Michelle stepped up. More hands began to pull at the sides. She squealed when she saw a pair of eyes coming into view just through the winds. Jury pushed Michelle on her backside plummeting her into the winds. Jury barreled up the ladder. When she reached the top, the winds began to flicker more. Shalako grabbed his temple and dropped his head. He was almost back.

"Will it work? It looks like it's dying out?" Marjorie braced herself on the edge.

"I think so." Riesha tried to focus on Shalako's mind. She forced him to feel a kiss on his lips. He relaxed some.

"You think so? What if it doesn't?" Marjorie felt a slight pull from the winds.

Riesha just shook her head. Suddenly, a figure burst through the seal. He tumbled downward knocking over a bookcase. It was a large blue Being with green eyes and small tusks on his face. All he wore was a small loincloth. His muscles flexed in his back as he stood.

"Shit!" Riesha screamed.

Marjorie jumped through the winds, felt a push downward and she was gone. Shalako's pupils ffaded back to full color. He turned to Riesha.

"What did you do to me?" Shalako squinted. His head slowly lifted from the haze. "Where are they?" He looked to the seal.

There was a grunt behind him. He turned to see the tall blue Being stand to his feet. It flexed its neck and looked down at Shalako in fear.

"Riesha, get our guest some clothes. You'll need to figure out how to get him back in Purgatory before they find out we let him go." Shalako leaned against the edge of the desk. "I may send you with him." He fumed.

Riesha nodded leading the Being slowly to the back room. Shalako cracked a smile. The youngins were so easily duped. He just hoped the three Souls could make good on their wishes.

CHAPTER GODR

Jury was enveloped in darkness. There was a strong rush of wind in her face. She felt like she was sky-diving in pitch-blackness. The horrible feeling in her stomach wasn't from the drop but from her realization that they didn't know exactly what the hell they had gotten themselves into. Or what in the purgatory, for that matter. She opened her mouth and screamed as loud as she could. The sound left her mouth, but disappeared into the abyss. She quickly closed her mouth because the air rushing into it caused a horrible sensation in her throat. She extended her hands and felt herself slow slightly and then without notice she landed in a soft cushy substance. It was like resting in cotton. The impact should've knocked the wind out of her, but the spring of the cushion absorbed her fall. She sat quietly listening to heavy breaths and the thump of her own heart.

"Hello?" She whispered.

"Jury!" Michelle's voice shouted from nearby on her left.

"Over here!" Lisa shouted from far to her right. "Climb out and walk on top of it. Walk this way."

"I can't see shit!" Jury pushed until her legs were free. She crawled across what felt like sponge under her hands and feet.

"Don't leave me Jury. I'm coming." Michelle was scared. She never did well with mystery and the dark was her secret fear.

Michelle crawled as fast she could. Her heart thumped in her chest worrying that she would be left alone. The silence alone was deafening. The cushiony surface was unnerving.

"Where are you?" Michelle shouted.

"Here!" Jury shouted from nearby.

Michelle crawled some more, reached out and clamped onto Jury's arm.

"There you are. Lisa where are you?" She shouted.

"Here!" Lisa seemed to be moving further and further to the right.

"Why are you moving away from us? Stay put until we get there." Jury shouted from about ten feet away.

"Jury?" Michelle turned her head.

"What? Come on, Michelle. I'm over here."

Michelle retracted her hand. She sat quietly listening to the other person breathing softly. Slowly, she pulled away easing on her knees trying not to alert whoever she touched.

"Michelle, Where you at?" Jury shouted.

Michelle sat back on her behind and scooted backward. She peered as hard as she could into the darkness trying to glimpse a look at what it was she touched.

"Michelle?" Lisa's voice wavered slightly.

Michelle used her arms to pull away inch by inch. She listened to the breathing. It was getting further away. She needed to move around it. She needed to get the hell out of there.

"Michelle??" Jury shouted. She hadn't moved.

Michelle stood slowly. The spongy surface made it hard to stand so she crouched and slowly crept to the right.

"Girl, there you are. Let's go!" Jury said. "Hold on to my arm."

Michelle began to run toward Jury's voice as fast as she could.

"No! I'm over here!" Michelle shouted.

"What?" Jury's distress was audible. Her screams were bone chilling.

Michelle ran at full speed and suddenly collided with something hard. It shifted with her touch and grabbed her around the waist. She screamed at her loudest.

"Where are y'all? What's going on?" Lisa screamed from further on the right.

"Michelle what is it?" Jury was not too far away. She swung her fists as hard as she could hit it, but it barely moved. It barely registered the blows. It grabbed her by the leg, pulled her down to the ground and began dragging her along the surface. There was a thump nearby and with it came the sound of heavy breathing.

"Jury it has me!" Michelle's voice screamed from just to her left.

Jury reached out and touched what she was sure was Michelle's arm and Michelle screamed again. Michelle punched back at her.

"It's me! It's me!" Jury yelled.

They were both being dragged along the ground faster and faster.

"Lisa help!" Jury screamed.

Moving as quickly as they were, the surface didn't feel as soft anymore. They were getting rub burn on their exposed skin. Kicking and screaming didn't work and they had the horrible feeling whatever it was, was hunting after Lisa next.

"Where are you?" Lisa screamed. She was closer. They were headed right for her.

"Run! It's coming for you! Run Lisa!" Michelle shouted nearly blowing her vocal chords.

"What is?" Lisa was even closer.

"Run!" Jury's voice wavered as she bounced against the ground.

"I am!" Lisa didn't seem to be moving any further away; a clear sign whatever was pulling them was running faster than she was.

Suddenly there was a wide shining spotlight from ten yards away. Long shadows cast across the ground. The entire ground was covered in a red pulpy mass. Jury looked up to their captor, but could only see darkness. It held a dark hand over its face blocking the light aimed at it. Lisa turned behind her and screamed. Jury could see the terror in Lisa's face as she covered her mouth and began to back away quickly.

It was faceless. A black form shaped like a human, but there was nothing there, like a shadow in three dimensions. When it blocked the light, the light bent around its hand and showed nothing but deeper darker blacks.

"Drop them and back away!" A male voice called out to the captor.

The captor made a motion to run out of the light and the light became brighter and wider. It was so bright Michelle was forced to avert her eyes. She stared at the red pulp ground. It looked like the translucent flesh of a blood orange. She could see vessels within it and some kind of liquid pustules giving it shape. Where the light shone she could see that the mass was also very deep and dense. When their captor released their legs, Jury realized that it had more than two arms. There were four arms in total, two now blocking where its face would be and two dangling at its sides. Jury and Michelle jumped to their feet. The Captor raised two of its arms to shield them from walking away.

"Walk towards me, Souls...Quickly." The voice within the light said.

They walked around their captor and began walking towards the light. Michelle peeked over her shoulder and saw the faceless form. If it had eyes it would've been staring directly at her. She turned quickly and picked up her pace. Her heart thumped in her throat. They heard footsteps, turned and saw the figure running deep into the darkness. They quickly rejoined Lisa. All three tried to look beyond the light to see their savior.

"Keep walking towards me. Let's go! You don't want him going to get any of his friends, trust me." The voice commanded.

They reached the light and it disappeared just as their savior was about to come into view.

"I'm going to open this door, when I do, do not look back at me. Just walk through it and keep going about your business. Do you understand?" He said.

"Yes." They said in unison.

They heard a lock unlatch. A long metal bolt slid open and then the door opened. As the light pierced the darkness they could see that the door was at least twenty feet high and twelve feet wide. He opened it just wide enough for them to walk through. Lisa walked through first. Jury was second. Michelle picked up the rear. As Michelle made it through the threshold she couldn't suspend her curiosity any further. She glanced down then slightly behind her as the door swung to close. As the door moved to shut, the side of his face was illuminated. His face was long, not vertically, but horizontally. There was hair; almost like a dog, but wilder, like a jackal's. His large round dark pupils peeked back through the doorway as it closed. His sharp dog teeth snarled at her as he closed the door.

They found themselves standing outside a large red barn. Fields of tall wheat blew undulating in a warm breeze. In the distance, one hundred yards at the end of the dirt path, was a windmill.

"That must be the other side." Lisa pointed down the path. "Let's go. Remember they said not to touch anything and don't let anything touch you."

"We're beyond that I think, Lisa. Remember the big black shadow thing just dragged us across the ground." Jury said.

"Well don't touch anything ELSE!" Lisa began sprinting down the path.

It descended into a small valley half way through and rose again to the windmill on the other side. The air was fresh. The breeze was comforting. There was a clear blue sky. The sun shone brightly but they didn't see it. They trotted side by side. Jury glanced out over the fields to see just the tops of people's heads. Up, down, up, down. Large scythes moved with them. Up, down, up, down. They were tending to the fields.

"There are people out there." Jury slowed watching as the workers went about their business.

"Let's keep moving." Lisa huffed. The three slowed to a walk.

"There has to be thousands of people out there." Jury stared out amazed at the fields on either side of the path. It was big and rolling and extended for as far as she could see. "It's a plantation. Purgatory is a plantation." Jury froze. She felt the urge to walk through the fields and see the people up close. Lisa grabbed her arm and tugged.

"Jury, Let's keep moving." She said.

They reached the bottom of the valley and started walking up the hill to the windmill. Every now and then, Jury looked out to the fields to watch the work. Lisa did too, but she wanted to make sure everyone stayed exactly where they were supposed to be.

"What are they doing here?" A voice whispered.

"They are Souls. Why are they walking the path?" Another voice mumbled.

"The natives are getting restless." Jury huffed.

"What do you mean?" Lisa wiped a handful of sweat from her forehead.

"You didn't hear that?" Jury stopped.

"Hear what?" Michelle turned to Jury.

“They’re listening. They can hear. They don’t belong on the path. Get them off of the path” A voice whispered.

“That!” Jury pointed out to the fields.

“I didn’t hear anything.” Lisa looked out to fields. The heads and scythes were still moving. Up. Down. Up. Down.

“Is it the flowers again?” Michelle looked behind her.

The large red barn still looked enormous. The tall, darkened silo on the back end had wheat dust littering its old metal ceiling.

“They want us off the path?” Jury shrugged.

“Let’s go before they get mad again.” Michelle picked up her pace.

“Off the path?” Lisa jogged alongside Jury.

“Yes.”

“Get off the path. You don’t belong there” A voice erupted.

“Who belongs here?” Jury shouted back.

“NOT YOU!” A voice rumbled.

“So get us off then!” Jury shot back.

“Stop talking to them!” Michelle fast walked up the hill a few more feet.

"Shhhh." Lisa was starting to panic. "Do not make this tougher than it already is."

"Too late!" Michelle screamed and started running even faster.

Lisa and Jury couldn't believe their eyes. All of the workers were swinging their scythes and running towards them. They seemed to grow exponentially. The fields were waving to and fro with a growing surge of people. The trio made a frantic run for the windmill. The words in the fields grew in Jury's ears.

"Get off the path!"

"Souls are not allowed on the path!"

"Get them! Don't let them endanger us!"

"We need to get off the path!" Jury shouted. She moved toward the fields.

"No detours." Lisa warned pulling Jury up the hill by her hand.

As they got closer they could see a man sitting on a bucket outside the windmill door. His head was held low as if he'd fallen asleep while sitting there. He didn't make a move; not when the fields moved, not when the women shouted. The natives were getting closer, but they stayed in the fields chasing the women without stepping on the path. It was only a matter of twenty feet to the windmill when the man raised his head. The three stopped in their tracks. Dust kicked up from their planted feet. Their fear was unmatched and their confusion was daunting. Boyce stood before them and folded his arms.

"What kind of test are you this time? Boyce grumbled.

"Test?" Michelle tried her best to reconcile the fact she had just responded to Jury's dead boyfriend.

Jury's face quivered. Her tears silently flowed from her eyes in torrents. She stepped toward him. Lisa blocked her way. Boyce held up his hand to halt her. The murmur of the natives grew louder. They lingered just inside the path line in the fields. Michelle glanced over and saw a little girl no older than seven. Her face was smudged with dirt and she had little flakes from the wheat in her hair. She shied behind a wheat stalk when Michelle made eye contact.

"Now you want to test me with Marjorie and her friends?" Boyce's eyes welled up. "Let's go. What do you have for me?"

"Boyce we're not a test...I don't think. We have to get into that place and cross over the next seal." Lisa pulled Marjorie closer.

"Get them off the path Soul. Get them off the path!" A native shouted to Boyce.

"You can't do this to me. This isn't fair." Boyce shouted to the fields. His lips quivered.

"Is it really you?" Jury finally spoke.

Boyce shook his head, turned and walked back to his bucket. He lifted it and pulled something from beneath it. When he faced them again, he held a small dagger with a pearl handle. He brandished it in a closed grip, holding the blade downward close to his wrist.

"Get them off the path!"

"Shut the fuck up!" Jury shouted.

The fields didn't like that. They mumbled and grimaced. The scythes began to swing wildly, some waved high in the air. Boyce sighed. He mustered as much energy as possible and began the speech he had repeated at least a dozen times.

"I am Boyce Lindens. I am a Soul. I am here to prove my worth to the one and only true Creator. I was sent to this place unfairly, but without malice by Allard. I will continue to defend this position until the time comes that I am no longer needed. Please get off the path." His eyes were bloodshot by the time he finished his words.

"Unfairly but without malice..." Michelle repeated quietly.

"Boyce it's me. It's really me. Is it really you?" Jury stood stone stiff.

"How do I know it's really you?" Boyce grimaced. "Where are we?"

"Purgatory." Lisa responded quickly.

"Not you." Boyce pointed the knife in Lisa's direction. "What is this place? If you're Marjorie, you would know."

The noise in the fields got louder in Jury's ears. More and more people began to charge toward the path. They began to resemble a lynch mob. Screams of "kill them" and "off the path" grew. Jury looked around herself. Her teary eyes batted as she watched the rolling fields become more murderous. The red barn behind them looked vaguely familiar. She glanced up at the windmill and she was suddenly and without pretense in a world she had once visited.

"Oh my God!" Jury twirled on her heels looking at all of the details. "How did? This isn't possible..." She said.

"Time's running out, Soul. You will join us soon. Get them off the path." Said an old man. He resembled Andy Griffith right down to the red hair and freckles except he had murderous eyes.

"We're in your grandmother's yard - on her land. We visited here when we first started dating. She's buried right over there." Marjorie pointed deep out into the fields by a large weeping willow tree. The tree stuck out like a roach in flour.

Boyce dropped his head.

"I thought I'd never see you again. This place is so hard. Too hard." Boyce looked up with an easing smile.

Jury pushed by Lisa and ran to hug him. Her heart ached to feel him, to touch his face and kiss his lips. She wanted to be in his arms again. Just one hug would remove the ache. If not one then she would take as many as she could get. If it meant she violated some rule or doomed herself to this place then at least she would be with him forever. He recoiled quickly holding up the knife to ward her back. She was hurt and perplexed.

"Don't touch him!" Michelle shouted.

"She's right." Boyce nodded. "We can't. It'll mean I stay here forever. I can't touch another Soul until mine has a home. This place is a waiting room. It changes often. Now it's my grandmother's land before this was the military academy, before that it was my elementary school. Imagine having to deal with hundreds of kids all day for what seems like forever until it changes again. Each time there's another test. I guess you guys are another."

Jury walked as close to him as possible. She wanted to smell his scent, but it wasn't there. In the excitement she had forgotten that he had no body. His Soul was here, but that was all. Suddenly, he jumped in the air and blocked a thrown scythe from hitting her. He waved his dagger at the fields.

"If any of you dares, I'll cross over there and cut you down." Boyce warned.

"Boyce we have to cross over. We don't know how much time we have." Lisa spoke slowly. The experiences had become odder by the moment.

"I'll lead you in." Boyce assured her.

"I don't want to go anymore." Jury shook her head. "I'm staying here."

"You can't! Do you understand where we are? This is where you go to wait for your soul to be judged. You're not dead yet!" Michelle pleaded.

"I won't let you stay. You can't stay. Come on." Boyce opened the door to the windmill and led them in to a rugged old wooden building.

Large metal gears filled the building. A large pole extended from the ceiling all the way through the floor. The windmill was powering something that lay beneath the ground. The gears spun rapidly and made a clicking sound as each gear slipped into its slot. Boyce led them to a winding spiral staircase in the middle of it all. He climbed it without hesitation. Dust kicked down from the stairs as he walked. He'd made it nearly an entire flight before Jury followed behind him.

"When I first got here Anubis told me that no one was allowed through this seal without his approval. He's not the final word though. I think he's a bit corrupt, but he doesn't bother me and he saved me from The Shadows." Boyce looked back to make sure they were all behind him.

"Those are those faceless things..." Lisa assumed.

"Yes. They're smugglers. They steal Souls and trade them or sell them to the highest bidder. Next thing you know you're a slave to some Lost Soul in Hell. They linger around the seals waiting for Souls to come through."

"Those Souls in the fields, are they slaves?" Jury asked. She tried to walk as closely behind Boyce as she could, but he moved too quickly and the air here was the thinnest she'd ever experienced.

"Those aren't Souls. They're Beings. They're like a level up from us in creation." Boyce began.

"Lisa told us about them." Jury didn't want to waste any conversation rehashing the things she knew.

"How do you know about Beings?" Boyce turned to Lisa.

Lisa immediately felt uncomfortable. While he looked and sounded like Boyce, there was something lost in his eyes. Overall, he seemed gaunt and without most of his golden brown skin. She always imagined that the soul of a person would be more vibrant.

"Long story." Lisa mumbled.

"They're like drones. Always worried about someone passing through the seals. Every now and again one of them tries to go through and I have to...make them not." Even after death Boyce spared Jury's feelings. "The path is only for Soldiers and Guardians. They can move quickly between wherever you guys came from and wherever this takes them. Where did you guys come from?" Boyce stopped. He seemed to be testing them again.

"Ummm...Shalako's. He told us we could pass through and find Allard." Lisa said quickly.

"Speaking of Allard." Michelle found her chance and jumped at it. "You said that you were sent here by Allard without malice...does that mean you came at your own volition or..."

"He killed me." Boyce said matter-of-factly as he reached the top level. He extended a hand to Jury to help her up, but then quickly retracted it before she took it. "Sorry. I forgot."

"He killed you..." Jury's anger grew.

"Calm down Marjorie." Boyce made a brief moment of eye contact with her then walked to a round wooden circle hanging on the wall of the building. The wood looked older than the rest of the building, parts of it were scorched by fire and others were damaged by water. The rotating windmill blades vibrated the floor. It was like being trapped inside a large fan.

"You just told me someone killed you, how am I supposed to be calm?" Jury shouted.

"You have to be peaceful." Boyce admonished.

BANG! BANG! BANG!

The door below rocked with the pounding of wood against wood. It wasn't as loud as the whirring moan of the windmill blades swooshing through the air.

"Who's that?" Michelle screamed.

"The Beings. I need you guys to cross over. If they get upset I could have an issue on my hands." Boyce spread his arms touching the top portions of the wooden circle. "They all seem to think this seal will lead them to The Kingdom. It's jealousy. I've only seen it once before and that one didn't turn out so good."

"They think this goes to Heaven?" Michelle asked as she approached the seal.

"Yes." Boyce inserted his dagger into a jagged hole in the circle like a key. Immediately the winds began to swirl. "I know it doesn't."

"How do you know?" Michelle stared in amazement.

BANG! BANG! BANG!

"Let me in Soul! You must let me pass through the seal!" A voice shouted from below.

"Get off the path or I'm calling Anubis!" Boyce shouted.

The four of them looked down the spiral staircase at the old wooden door. It wasn't the sturdiest of doors. If it burst open with a swell of angry Beings running through it, there was little doubt they would make it up the stairs in a hurry. Lisa grabbed Jury's reluctant arm and pulled her toward the seal.

"It's definitely not to The Kingdom. Allard just walked through. If what they tell me is true, there's no way he's walking or even sneaking into The Kingdom. He was nice to me though. Who's first?" Boyce shrugged.

"Marjorie should go." Lisa didn't want to risk Jury being last. There was no way she would leave if she were last, even with Boyce in disagreement with her.

"I'll go second." Jury nodded.

BANG! BANG! BANG!

“LET US IN SOUL! THIS IS UNFAIR!” Another voice boomed from below.

“The thing you said about Allard... without malice.” Michelle stared back to Boyce.

“I don’t think he wanted to, it was a mistake. He even held my hand when I died. I remember that. He held my hand. He told me to remember his name. I didn’t know why until I found myself being pulled away by The Shadows. I said his name and Anubis popped up out of nowhere. He scared off the shadows then said since Allard sent me I could stay. It was like a get out of Hell free card.” Boyce looked down at the door to make sure the Beings weren’t listening or coming through it.

He preferred not to retell this story, but he was happy to have company, human company - Marjorie’s beautiful company. He wanted to cry, but he couldn’t. This Soul business was odd. It was odd enough that it took less effort to move without his body, but there were so many other adjustments, like the lack of physical reaction to emotions. If he’d had tear ducts, he’d cry a river for his love that stood in front of him and was about to leave him again, possibly forever.

"Get out of Hell Free, huh. I guess I got the deluxe package." Lisa pushed Jury toward the seal.

"So he was nice to you?" Michelle pressed.

"Yes. I returned the favor when he came here." Boyce smirked. "I guess we're even. Had I not intervened those Beings would've torn him apart. That's why I have to get you guys out of here. I know what they can do, especially if they drag you out into those fields. It's not pretty. I was surprised Allard could take so much punishment, but he refused to fight them back…well except that one."

BANG! BANG! BANG!

"You guys have to go…" Boyce's head bowed. If he still could have the physical reactions to stress the way humans did, his stomach would have been full of butterflies.

"I'll go first." Michelle nodded.

She didn't hesitate. She blew a kiss to Boyce with teary eyes and jumped through the seal. A low whistle and a howling wind whisked her away.

"Jury you're next." Boyce and Lisa said in unison.

The hurt in Jury's eyes was overwhelming. Her eyes flooded with tears. Her stomach tightened and twisted. There was no way she could leave. She couldn't leave her man to sit on a bucket in purgatory guarding a windmill for the rest of eternity. Her heart couldn't take the pain. There was too much of a flood. She clutched her chest. The pain was overbearing, she was having a heart attack. The air got thinner as she wheezed and bent over in severe pain.

"I can't leave. I can't go." She sobbed.

Boyce leaned as close to her as he could without touching her. His proximity sent chills up her spine.

"I love you, baby. I'll love you forever. You have to go. You have to live your life. If you step through there and you are in Heaven, just hold on to faith that I will join you soon." He whispered in her ear.

Jury used every bit of will in her to stand straight. Her hands were wrapped tightly around her midsection. When she looked in his face again, the sobs returned. Before she recognized what caused it, she felt more pressure against her chest. She looked down to see Lisa's hands releasing from her chest. As if in a dream state, she saw the two of them watch as she fell through the seal. Boyce smiled at her as the winds engulfed everything she saw and he was gone.

"Don't worry. I'll take care of her." Lisa smiled at him.

"She's a big girl. She'll do just fine." Boyce stared out into the seal.

"That she is. You would've been proud how she handled this shotgun in Antarctica." Lisa smiled with a tear in her eye. "Take it easy, Boyce. We all love you."

Boyce grabbed her hand so hard it sent a screeching pain up her shoulder. An electric shock left her entire arm numb. He raised her arm in the air and peered at a small burn on her wrist. It was in the shape of The Dragon.

"What are you doing?" Lisa screamed.

"No, the question is what are you doing with this?" Boyce glared at the brand. "I can't let you go through the seal with this. You belong to Dragon."

Lisa tried forcing her wrist away from Boyce's grip to no avail. His touch was like a prolonged static shock.

"I don't belong to Dragon. Allard did this. You let him go and he's the one that started this mess. He killed YOU! He killed ME!" Lisa struggled to get to the seal.

"Yes, but you were pretty enough to make a deal, huh. I didn't get a pretty girl deal. I got an assignment guarding a broken seal on The Kingdom. A seal he probably broke in the war he fought. You've picked sides. I've already let one through that I wasn't supposed to. If I let you through, those Beings out there will want to do to me what they did to Allard. I may not understand everything, but I do understand that you, Allard and that Carver guy are on an expressway to Hell. I refuse to drive."

Boyce yanked her away from the seal. He faced her with evil intentions placing is back to the seal blocking her only way out.

BANG! BANG! BANG!

"You have her! Bring her to us, wandering soul!" The voices screamed.

"I don't have anything to do with Dustin." Lisa screamed. Her arm felt like a wet noodle hanging from her shoulder.

"You work for him and he left me for dead. He watched me die while he hunted after Allard. You're on the wrong side. I can't let you go, L." Boyce shook his head.

"Boyce, have I ever betrayed Marjorie? Have I ever betrayed you?"

BANG! BANG! BOOM!

The door burst open. There was a roaring cheer as the building began to fill with the sounds of feet. The steps thudded with a bursting wave of Beings storming upward.

"You're going to let me be judged by a wild lynch mob of drones?" Lisa pushed trying to get to the seal.

"They're prisoners of war, Lisa. The angels that refused to pick sides. I've chosen my side." Boyce dropped her hand. "And so have you."

The wave of feet and screams for the Soul got closer and closer. They were but a mere flight away from the top. Lisa pushed Boyce with all of her might, but like in the living world, he was just too strong.

"Whose side are you on?" Boyce's voice wavered. He had come even closer to crying.

"How dare you ask me that? You killed people for a living! I should ask you!" Lisa pushed Boyce hard. He stumbled backward effected by the energy from her hands.

"Whose side are you on?" Boyce asked again. He looked over her shoulder. There were Beings rising to the top level.

"I'm on The Creator's side." Lisa stared back. She felt the static shock of his hands on her shoulders as he flung her behind him.

"Stop there. You have broken the threshold of the seal bearer!" Boyce held his hand up as a few Beings charged up the staircase. "Go, Lisa." He whispered.

"What about you?" Lisa stood outside the circle. She could feel the pull of the forces within it.

"Tell Marjorie I love her." He said and pushed her through the seal.

Lisa reached out to stop her fall. She didn't want to leave him in peril. Her fingers slipped across the wood. She fell through the winds. The last thing she saw was Boyce reach for the dagger.

As soon as he retrieved the dagger, the winds immediately stopped. Boyce turned to the Beings. They looked like a rag tag lynch mob. He wondered if this is what many of his ancestors had seen post slavery and in the segregated American south before they were hanged from tress. Billie Holiday had called it "Strange Fruit". Here he stood in a windmill of a wheat field somewhere between The Kingdom and The Damned faced with the question: "which fruit would he be today?"

"They're all gone. Unlike you, they made their choice when they should have. You can make your choice now. Will you walk away or will you end on the tip of this dagger?" The dagger shook in Boyce's hand.

Before The Beings could respond. Before they could lunge forward, grab him and drag him down the steps. Before they could drag him through the fields with his body burning from the touch of each individual stalk of wheat. Before The Beings could punish him for being a decided Soul. Boyce ascended into The Kingdom through a shaft of light that whisked him upward as fast as the light had shone. He was now a freed and redeemed Soul. In his position now stood Anubis, the jackal-headed judge of Purgatory.

Anubis smiled a wild grin with his sharp jackal teeth. His onyx colored skin accentuated the muscles on his monstrously large human shaped body. He gained power from the terror in the faces of those he judged. He knew the ones that deserved the worst punishment; they were the ones standing at the top of the steps.

"Servicio in Camera." Said the woman on the other side of the door. Her accent was Southern Italian. She was most likely an art student working her way through school. "Vuoi asciugamani fresci?"

"No, thank you." Allard moaned as loudly as he could from his bed.

The towels she had given him the night before lay in a bloody crumpled heap on the bathroom floor. He tried his hardest to get used to the slow healing process of the human body. He had one for centuries and even though he never had injuries this severe, it was still painfully slow... with no puns intended. If he were a normal every day human, he would have needed extensive surgeries, physical therapy and rehabilitation. Since he was one of the most advanced Beings created, residing in a human body, all he had to do was wait for his multitude of gifts to take care of the issues.

Both Allard and Shalako knew the dangers that awaited him when he crossed through the seal. There was a longstanding bounty on him from the war. A bounty no single individual had dared try to collect. The danger came when there were groups of Beings with a rabid pack mentality. They wanted to collect the bounty or deliver him to justice. Only the most trusted knew that his justice had already been levied. The Beings on the other side of Shalako's seal were obviously not in the know. He easily could have decimated the majority of them and made it to the exit point, but then he knew that the only way to begin some sort of healing would be to allow them to have their way with him. That assault went too far and ended with him escaping. After, of course, he ripped the head off of a Being in the crowd. That Being had ducked his duties during the war and slid away like a snail denying his allegiance to Dragon; justice had to be served. Allard would have to answer for that slaughter one day. He held no guilt for it, but he also held no new tattoo brand on his arm for the slaughter.

Allard could feel his body repairing rapidly, but it wasn't fast enough for him. There was no amount of comfort the pillow top mattress could give his racing mind. The five star hotel services were exquisite, but he had business to finish. There were questions he needed answered. He laid resisting the body aches and quelling his rising body temperature with ice baths in hopes the damage wasn't too extreme. He fumed when he thought about the implications of the burgeoning war. There was no war without him. He was and would always be an egotist when it came to combat.

Late at night, at the end of his second day, he rose from his bed feeling eighty percent strong. His eighty percent was better than one hundred fifty of a normal Being. He showered his body, which now only showed the scars of the injuries he received long ago. He dressed in his new dark denim pants, black turtleneck, heavy black boots and long Italian all-weather coat. He checked out of the hotel and headed across the Via Novara to a beautiful five-star restaurant in the shadows of the brand new one hundred thousand seat Scilymax Stadium. The stadium, a widely controversial undertaking, was still under construction but would be the new home of Italy's famed A.C. Milan football team.

Allard sauntered through the front doors of the restaurant just in time for his eleven o'clock reservation. He was sat at a table by the large windows at the front. From his vantage point he could see the main stadium entrance and the small cafe where Jacob Mora sat drinking coffee and waiting impatiently. Allard enjoyed his meal ignoring the glances and whispers of the patrons of the restaurant. They were sure he was a celebrity or artist of some sort. What other man that looked like him could walk in and be placed in such a prime position? Moments after his entrée arrived, he saw movement in the façade of the café. The tide had rose quicker than he had expected.

The Shadows were quick and efficient. Jacob was seized and pulled from his seat in a gust of wind. Two Shadows held him, one by each arm and rushed him into the stadium before he could scream, before he could fight, before he realized that he wasn't sitting at the café anymore. He tumbled through the entrance finally able to release an echoed scream through the cavernous hallways. The Shadows whisked Jacob left and right, to and fro aggravating his motion sickness. They led him to the main field entrance and turned the corner.

"You can give him to me." Dezi said stopping them in their tracks.

Jacob vomited his exotic coffee at Dezi's feet

"He belongs to me." Dezi grimaced and stepped back away from the vomit.

The Shadows looked at each other, considered their opposition and dropped Jacob face first into his own vomit.

"That wasn't nice." Dezi dropped a crumpled napkin to the floor to Jacob to clean himself off. "Tell your master, I have him." He wheezed to The Shadows. "If he wants him, he can come get him."

Dezi lifted Jacob up by the nape of his neck like a puppy and carried him off into a dark corridor.

The dark hallways of the stadium were not kind to Allard's intuition. He trotted through peering in dark sections trying to get his bearings. He could feel Jacob's presence. He was nearby. Instead of taking a right, he made the left into a cavernous darkness. There was a presence there. It wasn't Jacob. He could hear light thumps. Some of them were erratic. It was an odd sound, but vaguely familiar. He moved swiftly across the surface, which soon changed to a spongy turf. He was on the soccer field now. He followed the thumping patter of Jacob Mora's heart ignoring the other vibrations. Suddenly a large spotlight exploded brightly in the middle of the field. Dezi stood over the kneeling Jacob Mora.

"Brother." Dezi coughed. His eyebrow cocked high.

Allard stared at the panicked Mora on his knees beneath the sickly looking Dezi. He was a long way from being a master of the financial universe. Dezi stepped in front of him guarding his prize. Allard raised his hands to his mouth as if pondering what else need to be said.

"Don't!" Dezi shouted making a quick defensive move.

The singing metallic swish of the Dragon's Needle echoed in the large stadium ten times over. Allard brandished it quickly striking at Dezi who ducked and dodged quicker than expected. His plagued body averted just a milli-second ahead of the golden lancet. Arching back, he projectile vomited the viscous black liquid in a stream. Allard ducked and sidestepped it as it flew. The stench-ridden sick landed on the turf in a bubbly black mass. It allowed Dezi a precious moment to unsheathe a black sword from a hidden harness. He raised his sword and introduced the duel. Allard crossed the sword with a hard, spark inducing clatter and their duel began.

Mora stumbled to his feet and watched from just out of the spotlight as the two clashed. A smile began to brighten across his face as he witnessed two abnormally gifted warriors battle. Allard was as beautiful and powerful as he was told. He was indeed the ultimate warrior. Even with Dezi using his viscous sickness causing spit, Allard seemed nearly unbeatable. Dezi pressed harder. Bright blue sparks erupted from the clatter of the weapons. Dezi grunted as he swung. His movements were labored but precise. Allard was fluid and deadly.

The black blade hummed swishing high then low. Its tip sliced through Allard's coat at his shoulder. Allard felt the hot burn and pain. An irritating numb enveloped the entire area. Dezi had coated his weapon with the black sickness. Allard could feel it eating away at the flesh on his arm like hundreds of tiny little bugs nibbling away at his flesh. Dezi smiled, proud of his exceptional element of surprise. Allard didn't let the burn and bite stop him, his lancet swung harder. Whenever one of the combatants was pushed out into the darkness, they fought to return to the light. Like Sumo wrestlers in the dohyo, they protected the boundaries the makeshift ring of light had created.

Allard's fierce swing split Dezi's sword in two. The severed tip shot across the spotlight into the darkness mere feet from Jacob. Jacob jumped back further in the darkness, but not too far for fear The Shadows would return for him. He didn't want to risk anything. He was too close to his goal. He watched as Dezi tried evading Allard's lancet, but with a splintered sword he struggled at every move. Allard shattered Dezi's sword with a swift spin, collapsed his own lancet to pin size and slipped it back into his mouth. He raised his hands and Dezi jumped as quickly as he could to take advantage of the hand-to-hand battle. Allard was too fast. With a spin, he had Dezi in a tight headlock spewing black sickness across his arm. Dezi coughed and sputtered trying his best to infect Allard. The harder Dezi struggled, the harder Allard squeezed. Finally, Allard introduced his other hand and pressed Dezi's jaw in the opposite direction. A sickening pop echoed through the stadium. He dropped Dezi at his feet with his head wobbling on a broken neck. Allard pulled the pin from his mouth, spread it longer and stabbed Dezi through the chest. He glared at Jacob with a sneer then dislodged The Dragon's Needle with a sickening pucker of organs while black sickness oozed from the body.

"Jacob Mora, come here." Allard growled.

Jacob stepped forward slowly. He had a snide pretentious smirk on his face. Allard knew why when he heard the erratic vibrations again. Six men followed Mora into the light. They were soldiers, different soldiers. The same type of soldiers Allard had fought in Manhattan the day he was captured. They too brandished matte black swords with brightly gleaming pearl tips, the kinds of tips that could mortally wound Allard.

"We need to talk." Mora nodded. He was a negotiator.

"I don't think we do. You'll be lifeless before long." Allard spun the Dragon's Needle playfully between his fingers.

"That's why they're here. They are my protection." Mora crossed his arms smugly.

Allard looked over the powerful looking soldiers with their black fatigues and sharp pearl tipped swords.

"You'll need more protection."

Mora reached in his pocket and produced a small remote control. He held it up high and pressed the power button. The large stadium lights exploded on. The enormous stadium filled with the loud hum of game time light. It was a magnificent stadium featuring typical Scilymax grandeur. Standing at each and every one of the one hundred thousand seats was a black clad solider holding a pearl tipped sword. Their eyes were focused on Allard. Their medically cloned and manufactured hearts thumped erratically in their chests. Allard looked at the vastness of Mora's army. Their sheer power was awe-inspiring, their silence and discipline impressive. Allard smiled.

"That's all?" He asked.

The battle was an incredible event to witness. At final count, Allard had slain ten thousand soldiers. Fixtures, seats and signs were torn from their couplings. Bodies lay strewn about like tossed newspapers on a train platform. It was a battlefield fit for spectacle with only one spectator, Jacob Mora. Finally, the soldiers rushed Allard, four thousand at once, smothering him under their sheer size. He was a captive again.

Michelle exploded through the edge of the seal into another cold darkness. After her second mouthful of salty water, she realized she had emerged into a flowing body of water. She fought the smooth tide by doggy paddling what she hoped was upward. Her lungs screamed for air as the pressure became too much to bear. She tried her hardest not to panic, but her body wanted to inhale. She prayed to God she could reach the surface before her body gave up. Her hands pierced the surface and her head shot up soon after. The chill of the air was an abrasive attack on her lungs, but she sucked in more of it. Her legs worked to keep her afloat as she caught her breath. It was nighttime wherever she was. There were old world buildings. The water way was in the middle of a small town. She saw brick walls and small signs. A small foreign car drove by. Its owner clutched a cigarette and seemed to mutter to himself.

Michelle focused on one of the signs as she swam to the closest wall. She recognized it from her theology studies. They were in Italy. They? No...she was... Michelle quickly took three deep icy breaths of cold air and dove back under the water. There was nothing but darkness. She looked for a sign of either one of her friends, but there was none. Michelle's lungs began to beg for air again. The chill of the water had evaporated her stamina. She turned to head to the surface after one brief paddle then turned back worried. Immediately, she saw Jury spinning upward from the bottom. Her body erupted from the darkness like a driedel. Michelle could see Jury's panicked arms flailing. Without a care, she dove back down, grabbed Jury by the collar and began to pull her upward.

Jury fought at first. She'd caught Michelle with a pretty good slow motion slap to the face before recognizing her friend. The two struggled to the surface together. An ice-cold blast of wind welcomed them to the world again.

"Good lawd!! It's freezing!" Jury squealed.

"We're in Italy somewhere." Michelle huffed. "We gotta go back down for Lisa."

"I don't think you can make it. Your lips are blue already." Jury shook her head. "I'm going back. You get out."

Before Michelle could argue, Jury was under the water again. Michelle waded to the wall. Her arms were stiff and her legs fatigued as she pulled herself up on to a cold stone walkway. She shimmied her hips between the metal and wood beams of the fence and looked around for signs of life. All she saw were the bright lights of a bar at least fifty yards away on the other side of the canal. She tucked herself into a tight ball in a small stone stairwell hoping it would shelter her from the wind. With her hands together, she prayed her friends would surface soon.

Jury swam toward the small current below. She could see the swirling waters erupting from the seal. Soon her friend would erupt from it and she would help get her to the surface. Jury waited hoping beyond hope that Lisa would come soon. She hoped even further that Boyce would be with her. The water felt tight against her skin. Her lungs began to tremble within her. Her body shivered. She would not leave her friend again. She would wait and if it took too long she would go back into the seal and get her. Lisa wasn't arriving. There must have been something holding her back. Jury quickly swam to the surface. Her head shot out of the water, she sucked in five quick breaths of air and ducked back beneath. She heard Michelle yell something, but none of it registered.

The water swirled. Lisa wasn't there. Had someone touched her? Had The Beings in the fields burst into the windmill and taken her? She prayed for forgiveness for leaving her friend the last time they were in such a predicament. She prayed Lisa would come from the seal and they could find Allard. She prayed they could make him pay for all that he had done. She prayed that if Lisa lived, this time, that she wouldn't take her love for granted. Her eyes focused on the seal. Her body shook. She needed to hold on a little longer. Jury began to move closer to the seal. She would have to go back and get her. There was air there. She would live if she entered the exit...wouldn't she?

Suddenly, Jury felt a tight tug on her arms. Her eyes opened in shock. Lisa was inches from her face shaking her awake. When had she lost consciousness? Lisa pushed her lips to Jury's and forced air into her lungs. The mental haze left her slowly. Lisa's hand pulled Jury's limp body upward. Jury couldn't hold it anymore. Her body gave up and with it; she felt her nose inhale water. She tried to move, but her body wouldn't respond. Her nose tried again and in came more water. Her legs kicked beneath her. She needed to get out, but she was panicking. You weren't supposed to panic, were you? Her nose tried to breathe again and there was a clash. Air mixed with water. She spat water from her mouth out into the icy air. Lisa pulled her to the side as Michelle helped pull her through the fence.

Lisa's lips covered hers again. She felt the softness of her mouth then a rush of warm air fill her lungs again. The water didn't like the air; it erupted from her mouth across her cheeks. Lisa looked down at her smiling.

"What were you doing!?" Lisa shouted.

"I was saving you." Jury coughed.

"Thank you." Lisa smiled. "How ya feel?"

"Better. What took you so long?"

"I got held up. Boyce told me to tell you he loves you." Lisa sat back shivering.

"I know he does." Jury smiled.

"Let's get out of the cold." Michelle helped Jury to her feet.

The three huddled as they walked up the stone staircase to street level. Small Italian cars were parked bumper to bumper all along the street bordering the Naviglio Grande, the first artificial canal in Europe. They walked passed the closed Italian boutiques towards a small bridge three hundred yards away. That bridge would take them to the other side of the canal where they would then have to walk back two hundred and fifty yards to the bar. It was either the walk or they could swim fifteen yards across the canal. All three preferred to stay out of the freezing water.

"Holy shit." Lisa whispered stopping in her tracks.

Jury and Michelle followed her gaze to a scruffy man in a worn wool coat on the other side of the water. He closed the door of his small car. He had parked horribly, leaving dents in the bumpers of the vehicles in front and behind his own small Fiat. He pulled his collar up shielding his neck from the wind and attempted to shield his identity from no one in particular. His head swiveled to and fro looking for an address. He was focused. He was on a mission. He walked up to the doorway of a blue four-story building. A beam of light shone across his scruffy face before he broke the lone light bulb with the crowbar he concealed in his right coat sleeve. It was Dustin Carver. The ladies pushed themselves into the dark corner of a boutique and watched him as he used the crowbar to break the old doorknob off of the door. After checking the street for witnesses and not seeing any, he dipped inside the building.

They ran at high speed to the bridge, crossed it and high-tailed it back up the opposite side of the street. Their clothes stuck to their skin. The wind and cold battered their faces, but they pushed faster toward that blue building. They galloped passed a group of men standing outside one of the open bars.

"Can I join you for your next swim meet?" A young man slurred in English, an American student "studying" abroad.

"Fuck off." Jury shouted back.

"Shhhh" Lisa hushed as they slowed to their destination.

Lisa looked behind them to see if the drunken men were watching them. When she was sure they had moved on to other business, she waved Michelle into the door, Jury followed, with her again taking up the rear. They walked slowly along the old hardwood floors trying not to make a sound. The room was filled with long drafting tables. Many of them still held their blueprints. A sign above a small archway read

Giorgio Architettura

Una divisione di Scilymax

There were creaks in the wood floorboards above them. Jury pointed up. Michelle raised her palms out signaling "obviously!" Lisa placed a finger to her lips as they shuffled beyond computer workstations to the small concrete staircase. They slid up the side of the staircase keeping their backs to the wall. Lisa peeked around the corner.

The open room was much like the one below it, more drafting tables and some computers on long tables in an open-air work environment. At the end of the room was a metal door. Dustin stood at the doorway picking at the wires of the keypad lock.

The lights turned on with a loud click. Dustin turned in shock to see his three employees standing with their arms folded at the end of the room. His eyes went wide.

"Turn the lights off!" He said between clenched teeth. His voice strained trying to whisper, but brimmed with anger.

Jury flipped the switch back off as Lisa charged towards him. She was fuming with all manner of feelings. He tried his hardest to brace himself for what was arriving. A tongue-lashing? A poke to the chest? A slap across the face? His teeth rattled in his mouth when her fist connected to his jaw and sent him backward against the metal door. He felt the pain of the metal crowbar as it connected to his sternum. Suddenly, he was looking up at Lisa; Michelle held her arms from connecting the crow bar with the center of his skull.

"What the hell are you doing?" Dustin gasped.

"I'm going to bust your head if Michelle lets me go!" Lisa whispered just below a scream.

A huffed sound of air left Dustin's lungs as Jury's foot connected with his gut. He buried his face in the hardwood meditating the pain away.

"Stop it!" Michelle said at full volume lurching the crow bar from Lisa's hands.

"What'd you tell me, Dustin? What'd you tell me?" Lisa panted as she paced back and forth.

"I don't know. What did I tell you?" Dustin made it back to his feet holding his stomach.

"You said 'Mora is on some kind of holy war. Trying to get us to drum up the recruits.' You said 'the thing in midtown was experimental'. That's what you said! I thought you were being metaphorical. I thought you meant he was trying to get us to produce better products and get better employees. I thought you meant when they captured Allard it was to see if the Scilymax soldiers could operate as a police force within the U.S. I didn't think about that until I was in The Cage. I didn't think it was serious until all types of shit hit the fan." Lisa said. "You meant this is REALLY a holy war. What was experimental in midtown, Dustin? Is Allard the experiment?"

Dustin's eyes said it all. He had vented too much at the end of a tough day of work and now she had put the pieces together. It made sense. She had come in contact with so many of the pieces herself, how could she not. How could all three of them not see what they had become complicit in?

"I need...we...we need to get into that room soon." Dustin said pointing to the metal door. He grabbed the wires and pulled and prodded at them trying to find the correct combination to hot wire the system.

"What's behind the door?" Michelle asked tapping it with the hard metal of the crowbar.

"I think this is where they've been storing the Seraphim Serum. They produce it in the Rome factory, but the manifests say they've been shipping it here to Milan." Dustin tried to decide between connecting the yellow and green wire or the red and black wire.

"The extracts for the disease prevention program. The cheaply made vaccines for third world countries." Lisa said realizing one of the projects she had worked on was part of the plan.

"Yeah, well that was the public relations spin on the program. We did create some great vaccines."

Green connected to red? He thought.

"The military uses helped soldiers recover from injuries faster. Some of them seemed to give them extraordinary strength. The teams found specimens with the proper D.N.A. to be cloned, which in turn created augmented soldiers. The Scilymax Amnio helped move the serum through the body faster. You know that." He nodded toward Lisa without looking away from the keypad.

Or was it black wire to yellow wire?

"That wasn't what it was supposed to be used for." Lisa said.

Suddenly a blaring horn sounded. Red flashing lights illuminated the room. It was a burglar alarm. It quickly shut off.

"Ok, not black to yellow." Dustin wiped sweat from his head.

"The alarm sounded. You know how Scilymax security is; they're on their way once that thing is tripped, regardless of false alarms." Jury shouted.

"I know." Dustin tied the green and red together and a loud metallic thump echoed through the room. "Lock is off." Dustin pulled open the door.

It was more than a room. It was a warehouse that ran the entire length of the remainder of the street. Inside were large metal shipping cases each branded with the Scilymax logo. Dustin ran to one and opened it. Matte black swords stared back at him, each case held twenty. He'd seen the swords before. He saw them in the streets of Manhattan when they captured Allard. Dustin needed both hands to lift the sword from the case. The density of it alone caused a strain in his back. The tip was different than the swords he'd seen. It had a glistening sharp pearl tip.

"Swords for an army? This isn't the middle ages." Jury shook her head.

"Maybe that's what Allard's army prefers." Lisa stared down into the box. She gave Dustin an angered look.

"This one's empty." Michelle said from the other side of the room.

Jury opened another case. It too was empty. Dustin opened another. It was empty as well.

"With no weapons here, that means someone has them. Lots of them." Jury banged on the case.

"Holy war..." Lisa whispered to herself.

"I met Mora at my church." Dustin started. "We happened to start talking about work and he told me that he was the chairman of Scilymax. He offered me a job running the medical research division. He said he needed people that had faith like I had. He'd ask me questions about religious figures or the apocalypse every once in awhile. That sort of thing. I thought he was just as devout as I was. He'd invite me out to lunch and we'd have these long conversations about religion. His belief was so much different from others I'd met. He wasn't just a believer. He didn't just have faith. He seemed to have touched it. He talked like he had personal experience with it all. He asked me if I believed like he believed. I told him I did. Then he asked me if I wanted to see it with my own eyes. I didn't know what to think. I thought he was kidding. I never thought about it again. It never came up again. Until one day, we were visiting the headquarters in Virginia. Part of the facility is space he bought from the government. It has all of these deep bunkers and weird security features. He asked me if I wanted to see it. If I wanted to see the proof of what I had been taught all of my life since Catholic grade school. I said yes. I still thought he was going to show me some new electronic gadget, some kind of invention or something."

"He took me down into one of those bunkers. Behind those thick concrete and metal walls, locked in a case like a zoo animal, was a demon, a true to life demon. It stared at me with its horrid teeth and it's blackened charred flesh. It glared at me. Mora was amused by it. He knocked against the case and it spread its wings and let out this howl that scared me half to death. The wings were like bat wings covered with melted plastic. It had hooves like a goat, but the feet had talons, sharp talons. I knew they were sharp because the window had these large scratches on the windows like it had tried to escape. 'There it is' he said. 'There's proof that your Creator exists and has a very real enemy.' He told me one by one he was planning to capture them and destroy them or use them to help us."

"Use a demon to help us?" Michelle asked with anger brewing.

"He did. He did it. I saw them do it. WE did it! We took blood from them, we used their bodies and their gifts and made cures and all kinds of things. We were able to replicate some of their abilities and put them into normal men and help them. He'd tell me about different demons they were tracking, ones that looked human. The next thing I know, they caught them and were using them to find others. Then one day he called me and he was astounded. They had found what all of the previous demons had called the ultimate catch. Allard, they said Allard was the one that no one could find. And we were just two degrees away from him. The idea was that if these lowly demons had given us the basis for so many wonderful medicines, what could Allard do?" Dustin sighed.

"He could kill you is what he could do." Jury said.

"When Allard broke out of that tube and Mora told us to destroy him, I knew something was wrong. How could you have the ultimate of all things to help mankind and just destroy it so easily without trying? We were doing well with what had been bad all along. Then I realized, he wasn't trying to kill the demons, he was trying to recruit them. The ideas had changed. It wasn't 'take them and create something from it.' They wanted to take them and bring them on board. The last thing he wanted was for Allard to go against him. He would've built an army of demons and genetically enhanced soldiers just to have it taken away from him by Allard. But then I thought again, what if Allard isn't a demon. What if he's something else...?"

Lisa glanced at Michelle.

"What do you think he'll do with this army?" Michelle asked.

"Only God knows." Dustin responded.

There was a ratchet of a shotgun. They turned to the doorway to see the adjoining room filled with soldiers aiming their weapons at them.

CHAPTER G5E

TAME G5E

The Scilymax soldiers handcuffed Lisa, Jury, Michelle and Dustin with tight shackles binding their arms to their feet. Their heads were covered with black cloth bags that served as masks. They barely let in air, much less light. Jury felt an overwhelming dread wash over. She knew that they'd be killed and dumped in the canal. The headlines would read the sorrowful tale of four tourists that had an unfortunate dealing with La Cosa Nostra or perhaps a drug deal gone wrong. She fought harder than the others and was greeted with severe manhandling. Jury wasn't a newcomer to a little manhandling so she fought back even harder, until a soldier raised her mask and quickly sprayed her in the face with pepper spray. She calmed after that. Not because of the pepper spray, but because Dustin had warned her that the soldiers often carried tasers. Pepper spray was one thing, but electric shocking a person was a whole different pain she didn't want to endure.

They were loaded into a vehicle of some kind. By the sounds of it, it was a paddy wagon. They could hear the rattle of each other's shackles against the cold metal bench seat. The sound was enough to assuage their concerns about the well being of the others. Only Jury made any noise. Her coughs and spits continued the entire ride. She sputtered and hacked in her best effort to clear her sinuses of the pepper spray to no avail. Her coughs slowly dissolved into a light whimper.

"Can one of you please help her?" Lisa spat over the roar of the motor and the rattle of the chains.

There was no response.

"I know you can hear me and I know you're sitting here with us. Help her! You shot her in the face with pepper spray. Her sinuses will swell and she could suffocate if she's having an allergic reaction." Lisa continued.

"I don't think they care if she lives or dies." Dustin whispered.

"They better care! They better care! If she dies back here because of their negligence it will be known. You can't hide inflamed glands and swollen eyes in an autopsy." Lisa warned.

She started to continue her tongue lashing when she heard the thump of military boots. A soldier removed Jury's mask. Before Jury could adjust her swollen eyes, a cold white liquid was poured over her head. She sputtered trying to catch her breath as it flooded her face. Between the cool sensation and the sudden calming of the burning, she recognized the taste of the fluid as milk. It ran down her body and further soaked her clothes. The others could hear the splash of the milk against the floor.

"You ok, Jury?" Lisa huffed.

"I guess..." Jury breathed as her mask was pulled roughly back over her head.

"What's wrong?" Dustin bellowed with authority.

"I'm lactose intolerant." Jury sighed.

The wagon turned this way and that. Suddenly they felt their stomachs drop and they were headed into what could only be a very large tunnel. The sound of the engine echoed off of the walls. The sounds of the other vehicles joined in, creating a loud mash up of revving engines and squealing rubber tires. The trucks stopped abruptly, the doors unlocked and they were tugged from the passenger hold with as much force and rough handling, as they were when they were loaded into the van.

"Those two then these two." A soldier's voice echoed.

Lisa felt her arm tugged by two men. Loud gates closed and she felt the rise of an elevator. She could smell Dustin standing nearby. The heavy breathing of several soldiers clogged the air around her. The elevator stopped with a jarring bump and she was pulled off the elevator. They stood silently while the elevator gates closed. Soon she heard the whistle of the elevator cables, the knock of the gates and more footsteps clattering against the concrete floor next to her. The bag was tugged off of her head. Dustin stood to her left looking worn and sleepy. On her right was Michelle and a swollen red-eyed Jury. Behind them were ten soldiers watching them very closely. They were in a conference hall that was still under construction. Work lights hung from the sheet rock. Nail guns and tools were scattered in a corner. There was a makeshift table built from two barrels and a piece of sheet rock. Sundiata sat at the table force-feeding himself from a small metal tin stuffed with pasta.

"I'm going to ask this question one more time..." He sucked a spaghetti noodle end-to-end with marinara scattering across his lips. "Where is Allard?"

"Why do you think we know where he is?" Dustin shot back. In his mind, he was still very much the big man on campus.

"You didn't travel to Milan for a fashion show." Sundiata said lifting his mouth up from his tin. "Especially not with the way you traveled here." He shoveled more pasta in his mouth, stopped, tasted what was in his cheeks then with an angry grunt, knocked the tin from the table.

As the contents hit the floor, they saw that his platter was now filled with blackened rotted noodles, fungus-laden marinara and maggots. Michelle averted her eyes and clenched her lips so as not to vomit.

"Just like mama used to make." Dustin grimaced at the floor.

The elevator whirred back into place. The loud door unlocked and whirred open behind them.

"I'll make you eat that up off the ground." Sundiata growled. His raspy voice trembled with every word.

The clack of expensive heels exiting the elevator echoed through the room. Alala sauntered by the soldiers and four others. Her hips switched back and forth as she approached Sundiata. The slit in her coat exposed the thigh high length of her boots, short skirt and bare caramel colored legs. She wore one bright red hibiscus in her dark wavy hair.

"How was dinner?" Alala asked as she stepped over the mess on the floor. "Can you please leave us alone?" Alala shooed away the soldiers.

Once they heard the elevator filled with soldiers begin its descent, everyone relaxed some.

"What's going on here Alala?" Dustin asked eyeing her legs through the slit in her coat.

"I need to find Allard and I need to retrieve Dragon's Needle. You four have been the most helpful in getting me close to him. You because of your overwhelming faith and these three because...hmmm....Allard has a healthy appetite." She smiled.

"What does that mean?" Jury growled.

"Oh well...maybe not for you." Alala smirked. "But these two have covenants." Alala approached Jury with a sparkle in her eye. "Maybe he decided your gifts were enough to get you by or maybe, you just aren't his type. Either way, while we get this cleared up..." She handed Jury the flower from her hair. "Talk amongst yourselves."

"Covenants?" Michelle asked as she watched Jury angrily toss the flower into the mess on the floor.

"Sex. The two of you had sex with Allard." Alala explained.

"I did, but not her..." Lisa shot back defensively.

Alala stared at Michelle carefully eyeing over her aura and energy.

"Yes, she definitely did. Didn't you Pastor Bonds?"

Michelle huffed embarrassingly. She wanted to tear Alala's pretty little head off of her shoulders.

"So, what are you his jealous girlfriend?" Jury snorted.

Hysterical laughter echoed throughout the space. Sundiata laughed so hard he beat his hands on the make-shift table. It was the first time any of them had seen him not serious.

"She got you there, Sis." Sundiata gasped trying to hold back his laughter.

"Shut up!" Alala ordered. "No, I'm not his girl-friend. It seems he took a liking to you...the two of you." She cut her eyes away from Jury. "For a Being to have sex with anyone is a lot of responsibility, especially for a Being of Allard's caliber and complex history. It's a covenant, an agreement he's made to watch over you for all eternity. If another Being was to kill you or take you off this Earth, he could immediately..."

"Track them down..." Sundiata's head rose. "That's quite a little trick big brother pulled."

"It is. He's taken the responsibility from your Guardian's and now is responsible for keeping you two pro-tected." Alala explained staring off into dead space. She was thinking it over again.

"He killed me and gave my Soul to Dragon. Is that the plan? To fuck and kill Souls giving them to Dragon as he goes?" Lisa barked.

"We would have to ask Allard..." Alala stopped in her tracks and stared into Lisa's eyes. "How'd you get that back?" She was perplexed. She tilted her head this way and that as if staring right through Lisa. "That's not supposed to be there. Sundiata, come here. Do you see that?"

Sundiata walked over slowly and stared at Lisa. He didn't see it. He stared harder, looked her up and down, but all he saw was a Soul with a covenant aura.

"I don't see anything." He responded.

"There." Alala pointed between Lisa's eyes. "You won't be able to see the whole thing. You're not as advanced as me."

Sundiata scowled at Alala's notion of being more advanced. He stared at Lisa and then saw a flicker, a flicker on her Soul. There was a ghostly image wavering on it. There were two Souls within her instead of one. One carbon copied just off of center of the first one. The second one had a strange hue to it. Sundiata watched the second as it glimmered and flared with a pulse. It's odd translucent milky color was almost imperceptible under the bright blue of the other.

"There are two of them. The other is odd. I haven't seen one like that before."

"Why are you staring at me?" Lisa felt a warm tension in her neck.

"The other is the gift. That was removed a long time ago. I *KNOW* it was." Alala turned away angrily. She walked to her large red purse and retrieved an item that tucked neatly in her palm.

"What gift?" Dustin said and took a position in front of Lisa blocking Sundiata's gaze.

"Is that what they look like on Souls?" Sundiata smirked.

"Yes and that one was retrieved. I know because I took it." Alala held up the small asthma pump looking apparatus with the pearl handle and strange lip. "How'd you get that back?"

Lisa backed away from Alala when she saw the unit. Her eyes squinted vaguely remembering what she'd heard the teachers tell her mother when she was picked up from school the day of her nearly fatal asthma attack. Her savior, most likely a doctor, had used an intricate asthma pump.

"Now that is very sly of him." Sundiata smiled looking around Dustin to Lisa.

"What is sly? How is that possible? How are there two? I don't get it." Alala was scared more than angry. Even in the world she knew so much about, she had come across something that left her stupefied.

"You see that on her wrist?" Sundiata pointed to the symbol of the dragon that only he and Alala could see. Boyce also saw it in Purgatory where only such things matter. "He gave her a covenant then promised her Soul to Dragon, but he made sure that she could come back by using something from this Earth as the bond maker. She died, but when she was resurrected, it was like a reboot on her entire Soul. The gift came back."

"They can't just come back!" Alala shouted refusing to be outdone.

"It did. You see it yourself. The original Soul that you tampered with is there and so is a new one." Sundiata pointed.

"You're saying I have two Souls?" Lisa stepped from behind Dustin to face Sundiata.

"Yes. Now that is a masterstroke. It's like multiple personality disorder. One has the gift the other is..."

"Promised to Dragon." Michelle finished his thought.

"That's the one with the covenant. So if Dragon takes it..." Sundiata smiled.

"He can always know where Dragon is." Alala's eyes widened. "And she'll still be able to rise to The Kingdom."

"Someone was studying loopholes while he was gone." Sundiata nodded walking back to his table. "But what about the gift?"

"I have to take that back." Alala raised the pump.

"You're not touching me with that thing!" Lisa shot back.

"It's my duty. It's my assignment." Alala stalked towards Lisa.

"WAS your assignment, Sis. Michael decides that." Sundiata kicked his feet up on the table.

"He already did. He told me to get it. I got it. It's back and I'll get it again." Alala said grabbing Lisa's wrist.

The two tussled, each trying to grab the other's hands. Lisa pushed but Alala was just too strong. Jury tried to push her way between them with Michelle following. Dustin tried his best to break it up. He reached for the apparatus but Alala quickly flung him backward. Sundiata's loud whistle stopped the growing scuffle.

"Alala that's not your job anymore. Let Michael send someone else for it if he wants it. We have bigger things to worry about." Sundiata's raspy voice shattered the commotion.

Alala backed away slowly. She tossed the apparatus in her purse and tried to calm herself. How dare a Soul try to tell her what she could and could not do? Didn't she know how hard Alala had worked to get to the level she attained? Retrieving that gift was a big part of her promotion to the next level. It was what brought her to the attention of Michael and Dragon.

"Where is Allard? Where is Dragon's Needle?" Alala said slowly brimming with fury.

"You think if we knew that we'd be standing here? Are you out of your fucking mind? We're looking for him too. I don't even know why the hell we're looking for him anymore." Michelle roared.

"I do." Jury gritted.

"If you know all of this about Allard and Souls and Beings and you can see Lisa's soul...or souls for that matter, then what are you? Angels?" Dustin pointed his finger at Alala and Sundiata angrily.

"I can't even tell you the last time I was an Angel." Sundiata shrugged. "What about you Alala?"

Alala ignored him. Her ascent wasn't as long ago as his and he liked to point out his seniority as much as possible.

"I don't even think you'd believe me if I told you." Sundiata stared at Lisa's Soul admiring the beauty an intricacy of its form.

"I've believed a hell of a lot more in the last five years than I'd care to admit. At this point, you could tell me that you're Santa Claus and I'd have to believe you." Dustin returned.

Alala turned to Sundiata. She wasn't about to say anything, but she knew that there could be no harm in speaking it aloud. Sundiata wasn't the bragging sort. If he spoke it, then it would be a tactic that would only help them. She flung her hair over her shoulder and shrugged. All the responsibility of that truth was left to him.

"I am Sundiata, the one time rider of the black. She is Alala, the one time rider of the red. We and our other two comrades were sent to find Allard. Before this assignment we were joined for a special mission. In fact, Dragon found us and used our distinct abilities to bring us together on behalf of The Creator. Of course, this was before Dragon was expelled from The Kingdom. The assignment was the destruction of this Earth." Sundiata watched the Souls of the four others stir and become uneasy. "Our comrade Dezi, was honored to bring sickness. Alala would bring war. Myself..." He glanced to the food rotting on the ground. "Famine. Kronus, the reaper, would bring Death.

We are two of the Four Horsemen of the Apocalypse. The fact that we were called down to find Allard means this is very serious business." Sundiata said.

"The Four Horsemen of the Apocalypse? She doesn'-t look like a man." Michelle pointed to Alala.

"Unless she's tucking some extra meat." Jury said.

Alala lunged in Jury's direction, but was held back by Sundiata's long arms.

"You'll have to excuse my sister. Sometimes she takes her order a little too seriously. You shouldn't take her kindness or her beauty as a weakness." Sundiata explained.

"The same goes for me." Jury replied.

"You two are sister and brother..." Dustin began.

"At arms. Brother and sister at arms and under the laws of The Creator. Alala wasn't always a Horseman. She took over the position not too long after our other left us and refused his charge. He took up with Dragon and became a henchman." Sundiata continued.

"Allard. Allard was the Horseman of War. That's why he was created as the ultimate warrior." Lisa said.

"Allard was indeed a horseman. I think he was more interested in fighting than doing his duty as the referee. Earth wars are not in our interest to fight." Said Sundiata.

“They lack beauty and true honor.” Alala added. “His successor couldn’t cut it either. His reign was short lived.”

“However, when it was time for your friend and keeper Allard to be brought in, The Arch Angel sent us, The Four Horsemen and Alala. You’ve seen him naked. You’ve seen the scars that were left when we fought him and brought him to justice. After all of his fighting and his wars, those are the wounds that will never go away. Here we are again, looking for Allard. And now he has Dragon’s Needle which makes him even more powerful and with his new slick way of operating.” Sundiata pointed to Lisa’s Souls. “It seems we have our hands full with Allard’s antics.”

“The Four Horsemen and Alala?” Dustin’s question was pregnant with accusation.

“I took over the war position after that. My predecessor didn’t make it.” Alala smiled.

“The last time, it took five of us to bring him in; five very talented and gifted Beings. I think you can pretty much see that you are well over your heads. Tell us where Allard was headed. What he was looking for and let us handle it.” Sundiata’s raspy voice quaked under the pressure of his using it so much.

As if on cue, Alala's cell phone began to ring loudly in her bag. She reached in, looked at the caller ID and smiled.

"Jacob Mora. How are you this late evening?" Alala purred. "Mmmhmm...oh is that right? So, what are you going to do?...I see...Well, I'll come down. I have some people you may want to see." Alala hung up the phone. "Sundiata, pack the kids in the car. Mora has Allard and we're going to pick him up." She smiled.

Allard awoke slowly. He kept is eyes closed while he listened closely to his environment. There was a steady hum of an air intake unit. His breathing sounded hollow in the room. He was lying against something hard and slippery, most likely Plexiglass. He was seated on something similar. It reminded him of the tube, but it felt bigger and there was no fluid to swim in. He listened intently waiting for someone nearby to talk. He didn't want to lose the element of surprise. He raised one eyelid peeking to see his surroundings. He was indeed in a thick plexiglass chamber. He saw consoles on the other side of the glass. There was monitoring equipment, but an otherwise empty room.

He opened his eyes fully to see his body slumped in the corner of the holding cell. His clothes were tattered and singed from the battle, but in overall good condition. His muscles were sore, also from the battle, but he wasn't any worse off than he was when he went head to head with the army. That alone was a welcome feeling. Allard knew he had been on a long road to recovery after his first capture. He stretched his hands out in front of his body and slowly rose to a standing position. Why had they left him alone? Didn't they respect his power?

"Hello darling. How's the sleepy head feeling?" Her voice was unmistakable, playful yet mature.

Allard stood stone still as the clack of expensive high heels echoed in the room. She walked from behind his cage looking straight ahead. She turned at the corner, walked to dead center in front of it, turned and faced him. She was still a beautiful Being. As was customary, she was wearing all red and she was unmistakably sarcastic when she smiled and cocked her eyebrow.

"You know to be the best warrior ever created, you sure do get captured a helluva lot." Alala shook her head shamefully.

Allard's face was stiff as stone. His eyes traveled down her body, taking note of all of its wonder. He gazed over her red trench coat. It was fashionable but made of a very sturdy material. It was also waterproof. She hadn't buttoned it, but instead had only tied it high above the waist leaving a long slit down the front. That slit made it possible for her to access her weapon, which bulged just slightly from the left side of her hip. By the size of the bulge, he could tell it had a slim handle with a bulbous end. The cross guard of it was curved and had extra protection for the hand of the bearer. The length was twenty-six inches, which was the proper length for Alala's height.

By the way she stood, he could tell it was a saber with a descent blade width. Most likely, it was the same saber that she copied and gave to Atilla the Hun many centuries before. The Sword of Atilla was a weapon of legend. His was a cheap knock off of what she hid beneath her coat. She rocked her legs side to side at the ankle, which let him know that the indent on the right side of her waist was the leather handle of her slingshot. A small bag of course diamonds hung behind her, dangling just below her round bottom. It was surely tied to a belt around her waist. Her legs were still thick and sturdy. She could use the solid shape of her thighs as a shield to kick and defend. Her boots were high and made of tough leather just for that purpose.

Beneath her coat he could see the impressions of the buckles and straps of her armor. The material was a form fitting leather, one of Alala's preferences. A corset (another preference) and considering how her breasts sat higher, her waist was also cinched with a chainmail huberk girdle that would stave off sword slices. The huberk was a chainmail armor shirt created by Alala and given to The Celts some time in the fourth century. Hers was a variant that fit neatly under her corset and extended the length of her skirt. Her arms were bare except some small bracelets on her wrists. They were certainly jagged to the touch when she swung her arms. Possibly a barbed wire made of platinum. With no arm protection, her trench coat must have had chainmail lining in the arms. To the layman, she looked like a sexy woman ready for a night on the town. To Allard, she was a soldier ready to fight a war.

"You're not talking to me?" Alala pursed her lips. "Are you embarrassed to see me like this? I'd think you are. This isn't the first time they've had you like this, is it? I heard they had you locked up in a tube. A tube! Wow. Are you that far out of practice that you let the same people capture you not once, but twice?" She shook her head and walked towards the back of the room.

Allard watched the sway of her hips. He knew her well. He could see her passion in the steps she took. He could see her anger in the way her fingers rubbed together. She was frustrated. She wanted more than to antagonize him.

"Funny thing about Dragon's Needle..." He said stopping her in her tracks. "...With all of the celebration and then all of the fear, it's really not that stupendous."

"But it is stupendous." She stood with her back to him.

"I'd call my spear stupendous. Dragon's Needle is more...cute." He chided.

"Cute? Don't try to play me for a fool. I saw your little spear Allard. Mora has it in his office upstairs. It's all shined up nicely and he has a little placard next to it engraved with the date he got it. The date they captured you, Tube Dweller. Allard's Spear sitting in an office like a trophy instead of being used, it's really a shame. You outta go see it while you're here."

"I intend to." Allard bristled. "Since you've seen my spear Alala, you know there's nothing little about it."

She smirked. Alala walked to his cage. She got so close to it when she breathed condensation rose on the glass. She touched the glass at his chest.

"You can use your spear all you want, but your heart belongs to me." She purred tapping the place on his chest where the scar resided.

"I could say that about certain parts of you as well..."

"Where's Dragon's Needle, Tube Dweller?" Alala whispered.

Allard moved directly in front of her face. He leaned in so his nose was nearly touching it.

"Why do you want to know?" His breath fogged the glass.

"Where's The Needle, Tubey?"

"Ask the question you really want to ask, Understudy."

Alala roared in anger and punched the glass so hard the vibration echoed loudly throughout the chamber. Allard didn't move. A smile spread widely across his face. He pushed the button on her self-esteem. Alala had never taken it lightly that she was the back up to the replacement in her position as the bringer of War. She was easily the best suited and the most efficient war bringer since Allard's short tenure. She was better than even he at designing weapons and although she could fight well, she didn't get the visceral response from it that Allard would.

Her predecessor, Mars, was a great strategist and an even better politician. He often took credit for many of her advancements in war and strategy. At heart, he really was a farm boy and in her opinion, undeserving of his job. Alala took his position in a hand-to-hand duel after he attempted to force his covenant upon her. Her only punishment was the branded tattoo emblazoned across her back as a resounding symbol of not only her deed, but of her power. His name, however, was often referenced in many of the things she created and he took credit for such as martial arts and martyrdom.

"Did I strike a nerve?" Allard sneered. "Here, let me kiss it for you." Allard extended his tongue and licked the glass where her face stood.

She glowered squinting her eyes at him wishing she could reach through the glass and tear his tongue from his face. As his tongue retreated back into his mouth, she saw the smallest gold sparkle of Dragon's Needle on the very tip of his tongue where it was hidden. Her eyes broadened.

"Alala! I asked you to tell me when he got up! What did he say?" Mora screeched as he entered the room flanked by two burly soldiers.

Allard could tell by their essence that they were fallen angels, the real ones, not the scientifically enhanced version. Allard straightened his posture and stared down his nose as Mora looked up at him in awe.

"I have to admit, I expected something a little more stupendous in size." Mora bellowed.

Alala stepped back amused.

"Last time, you were all catatonic, my friend. We didn't get a chance to speak. You were all docile in the tube. Tonight...tonight you were a warrior. That's what I expected to see out there on that field. And now once again, you're kind of biddable. Saving your energy for a scrap, chap?"

Mora's voice annoyed Allard immediately. He folded his arms and sized up his captor.

"No need for that. We've gotten off to a rocky start, but I'm hoping we can eventually put every bit of that behind us. Shall we start with a nice meal or some coffee? I have a wonderful exotic blend you will flip over. How's that?"

Allard's gaze turned to Alala. She feigned excitement over the coffee with a sarcastic smile.

"Jesus is he always this serious?" Mora looked around the room to the others.

Allard felt a tinge of anger when he heard Mora say the name.

"What can I get you? What will start us talking? I have a proposition, but it's impossible to make a deal if one party isn't talking." Mora whined.

Allard knew what he wanted and it was already within the building. He could feel the aura and the beat of the heart pounding.

Elsewhere in the stadium, Lisa, Jury, Michelle, Dustin and Sundiata waited in a theater sized meeting room. The purpose for the room was for team meetings and watching films of the week's opponent. There were large comfortable leather recliner chairs which all faced the large screen at the front of the room. A large table sat in front of the screen. It was a place for the coaches to hold materials to be handed out and studied.

That night, Dezi's body lay on the long table adorned with a crisp white tablecloth. He was still and no longer sick. His eternity had begun and ended with pain and he had endured a life of sickness. Sundiata stood over Dezi brushing his hair backward with his hand. Dezi had been his comrade for so long and even when they disagreed, they disagreed agreeably. Now without life, Dezi seemed at peace. Sundiata's anger with Allard for killing his friend was only simmered by Dezi's healthy appearance. He had achieved a glow and peace on the business end of Dragon's Needle. Sundiata would have to remember to thank Allard for bringing that to his friend Dezi, before he killed Allard himself.

Lisa stood just behind Sundiata watching how he carefully wrapped Dezi's body in the cloth. He was precise and steadied with each piece of fabric, wrapping them end over end tightly binding his body together in a mummified wrap. The doctor in her wanted that specimen to study. She wanted to learn more about the difference in Beings and Souls. She wanted to see if there was any way she could use his body to help mankind.

"Can you even do anything with only three horsemen?" Said Jury as she sat watching from the opposite end of the room.

Sundiata ignored her. He didn't want to, but he was steadying the last wrap of the fabric. Once he began, it was considered a disgrace to stop.

"There will be another. There is always another." Sundiata looked up as he wrapped, feeling a hatred for Jury. "What you are witnessing is the end of an era. This Being lying before you was the first of the horsemen. He has touched the hand of The Creator Himself. He was sickened his entire existence as a favor to you Souls. Without his sickness you would not be healthy. Every sickness known to Souls was first coursing through his body to see if it could inhabit this Earth without irreparably destroying it. That is enough to drive anyone mad, Being or Soul. He was a loyal servant."

"Would you like me to say a prayer?" Michelle offered approaching the table as Sundiata finished the wrap.

"There is no need. He is no more. He has no more. There is no more for him. Unlike you spoiled children; there is no Soul to move on to The Kingdom. His service ended on the tip of Allard's wrath." Sundiata said.

"Even though he tried to kill me, I'm sorry for the loss of your friend." Michelle sighed.

"I'm not." Dustin shot back quickly.

Everyone turned to him. Dustin sat with one leg crossed over the other in the last row of the room. He stared down at Sundiata and Dezi with a sickened expression.

"Watch your mouth Soul. You are not fast enough to outrun my fury." Sundiata rasped.

"There is only one fury that I fear and it is not yours." Dustin replied.

"That's poetic." Sundiata turned to Lisa. "Be sure to put that on his tombstone."

Sundiata leapt from a standing position. By the end of his second incredible jump, he had already reached the back of the theater and grabbed Dustin by the throat. The women screamed and rushed to Dustin's aid.

"Carver, the faithful warrior. You are the cause of this. You are who the Beings spoke of when they said they were being hunted. They were scared of you. Beings everywhere will rest easy tonight as I will rid them of their nightmares." Sundiata pressed harder on Dustin's throat slowly. He enjoyed watching Dustin flail as his color slowly left him.

Jury grabbed Sundiata's right arm and pulled as hard as she could. Sundiata's muscles flexed. Underneath his smell and his ratted old clothes, he was incredibly strong.

"Please let him go. He isn't the cause. It's Allard." Michelle screamed pulling Sundiata's left arm.

Lisa grabbed at his legs trying to tug him off balance. She could hear the air leaving Dustin's esophagus in spitters and sputters. She punched upward landing a shot dead square where Sundiata's testicles should have been, but there was no reaction. She punched again then again. Her anger rose within her. She felt the fiery burn in her throat again. Her head felt dizzy, but she kept punching and pulling. Sundiata kicked backward hitting her square in the chest and sending her tumbling down three rows of theater seats. She lay nearly upside down in an aisle, her head nearly wedged beneath a chair. Her fire grew, her anger exploded. A fervent roar exploded from deep within her. Her legs pushed beneath her. Her body catapulted towards Sundiata. Lisa's legs wrapped tightly around his waist and her arms slipped underneath his arms. She tore at the flesh on his face.

Sundiata squealed. His grasp broke as he tried to pull Lisa from his back. She tumbled off falling in the aisle. Sundiata turned to her with a shock she had never seen. His face had been clawed across each of his cheeks. Bright red marks were torn into his face. He panted as he watched her. Her Souls were erratic. They were flickering and flaring wildly.

"Hell Cat." He grinned.

Lisa was scared for her life. Sundiata's eyes were wild and crazy. She looked down to her hands where his gaze rested. Her hands were normal, but her nails looked to be on fire. She screamed and beat her hands against the carpet. Was this the punishment for attacking one of The Creator's Beings? Her hands scorched. She couldn't calm the fire nor put it out. Jury rushed over to help, but backed away when Lisa raised her hands.

"What the hell?" Jury screamed.

Sundiata laughed. The claw marks in his face throbbed with the stretching of his cheeks.

“It saved your friend this time, but next time, let Alala take it from you.” Sundiata warned. He stormed from the room quickly in a rush to find Alala.

Lisa looked down to her hands. Deep red flames flickered within her nails. It was her gift; the gift of an angry rage. Her passion personified in the blazing flames of Hades trapped within her claws. Lisa waved her hands around trying to cool them. She was overcome with hot flashes as she tried to calm herself. Sweat poured down her face as she fanned her hands to and fro. Finally, Dustin covered her hands with his coat. With her eyes no longer concentrating on what she was seeing, she slowly felt the heat diminishing.

“That’s a very unusual gift.” Dustin patted Lisa on her back in attempt to calm her. He hugged her as she shook with tears of extreme anger rolling down her cheeks.

“Hold up…I hear talking flowers and this bitch gets fiery claws? How is that fair?” Jury said.

“You’re the top draft pick, Allard. What I have built is the best franchise team in the league. I know about building franchise teams. I own a baseball team and two football teams, one American and one real football. I know how to put the pieces together. Look at my company, nothing goes overlooked." Mora spoke passionately through the glass. "With your leadership, there's no stopping this army."

Allard watched Mora with the sound off. He saw the fidgety hands and the wild eyes. This was a Soul that could not be trusted.

"Do we need to talk alone? Is that it?" Mora rationalized. "Fine. Let's do that. You three step outside." Mora commanded.

Alala stood still. There was no Soul that would order her out of a room, definitely not a male Soul. Mora's guards turned towards the door, but realizing Alala was being stubborn, they turned to face her.

"Alala, leave so I can have a moment alone with Allard." Mora pleaded.

"No." She said matter-of-factly.

"Well...why the hell not?" Mora was angrily perplexed. He nodded to the soldiers.

Allard saw it coming and knowingly shook his head. The easiest thing was to mistake Alala's pretty face for the inability to destroy everything in her path. The soldiers flanked her. She was quicker than they expected. Her sword sung with a whistle as she pulled it from its sheathe and stabbed the first guard three quick times in his chest, he stumbled backward clutching his wounds. The other raised his hands to subdue her. Alala dipped low and slit his Achilles Tendons with one slice. He fell to his knees screaming, but the noise stopped when she stood and removed his head with a sickening chop. She turned again and decapitated the first soldier. The high-pitched hum of her blade resonated and shook as she held it in place just over his fallen body. She peered over the blade at Mora. His back was pushed against the glass. His eyes bulged with fear.

"You didn't say please." Allard whispered just near Mora's ear.

Mora jumped away from the cage when he realized he had turned his back to Allard.

"I'm sorry. I must've forgotten who I was speaking with..."

"You need to mind your manners Mora." Alala lowered her sword.

"May I please have a moment alone?" Mora's chest rose and fell heavily as he spoke. Allard could hear the thump of Mora's heart in his chest.

Just as Alala re-sheathed her sword, the door exploded open. Sundiata charged in with his hands smoking. His gift was lit. His hands smoldered ready to deliver the rotting curse of famine and an unending hunger into whoever opposed him. He saw Mora standing wide-eyed trapped between Alala and the cage. Allard stared down at him.

"What are you doing?" Mora panicked.

"This doesn't concern you, but it could..." Sundiata turned his hands toward Mora.

Immediately Mora felt his stomach empty. The acids fought against the lining and burned. They refluxed burning his esophagus and higher.

Alala grabbed Sundiata's hands and pushed them downward unaffected by his gifts. She pushed him backward. She reached inside her coat to the right side with one hand and behind her with the other. Her hands squeezed tightly on her slingshot and the bag of course diamonds that she propelled into the brains of her enemies.

"Sundi, wait! Don't do this." Alala pleaded.

Jacob slipped away through the exit running down an adjacent hallway. He was headed to the field where his soldiers waited patiently. If he couldn't bring order to the situation, they surely would.

"Are you threatening me? Are you choosing the Soul's side over mine?" Sundiata bristled.

"I don't choose sides. I'm the referee. If there is going to be a war, I prepare the battlefield. If you want to get in the way of that then I'll have to deal with you as well." Alala shot back.

Allard watched the stand off from the cage. They had given him the distraction he wanted. He quickly slipped Dragon's Needle from his tongue. Pulling and waving it, he shaped it into a long thick piercing blade then fashioned a hook around his wrist. The Khopesh, the Egyptian sickle-sword, was a perfect weapon for his needs. It could make hard slashes using the lion's share of his strong arms. He swung it hard at the enclosure. The front wall exploded and fell away. A storm of thick glass fell across the floor. Allard stepped from the cage swinging his weapon testing its weight and fit in his hand. He waved it quickly giving the blade more length then twirled The Needle in his hand like a drum major would a baton. Allard tapped his thigh where his scar resided. The scar Sundiata gave him when he stabbed him unexpectedly so long ago.

"I've forgiven you for your previous act of betrayal. There will be no mercy for another." Allard glared at Sundiata.

"This doesn't have to happen." Alala said. "Hand me Dragon's Needle."

"You didn't say please." He replied.

CHAPTER LXI

RACHEL FREI

When Jacob Mora II was a teenager, he had to deal with his mother's constant nagging. She was always asking for help with cleaning the house or mowing the lawn. He always considered those to be jobs for the help. As a child, he had become used to various black and brown faces handling those jobs as well as the cooking, laundry and occasionally taking him to the park to play. His father, the elder Jacob Mora, had done well by himself after serving in World War II.

Shortly after returning home a medaled war hero, his father opened his own fish market in Flushing, Queens. Life was well and the money flowed. His father had made a great living from selling reasonably priced new and rare fish. People would come from all around to buy fish from Mora's Fish Market. There was even a special wall with a picture hanging from it: Jacob Mora hand in hand with Frank Sinatra both holding a gigantic Rainbow Trout. Jacob Mora II smiled sheepishly in front of the two. Well...most of the boy's face was cut off in the shot, but you could see part of his smile, his bright eyes and his messy hair. Those were the good days.

The elder Jacob Mora died suddenly and tragically in a boating accident off the coast of Brazil. He had been visiting the South American country looking for new species to import for his fish market. Jacob Mora's wife, Harriett, did her best to continue living the high spending life she had with her husband, but soon the money dried up much like the fish tanks at his shuttered business. Harriett took a job in a steno pool and her son was expected to lend a hand wherever he could. Jacob tired of his mother's incessant complaining. He'd often hide away in the attic of the house reading comic books and listening to the radio broadcasts of the New York Yankees games. When he didn'-t steal enough nickels from his mother's purse for comics, he'd look through boxes of his father's belongings. He appreciated the pin up magazines and the black and white postcards featuring nude women, often very chunky women, photographed doing very sexually explicit things... quite often with other women. Most of all, he enjoyed reading his father's journals.

It was the sweltering summer of 1962, when his mother had been on quite a tirade. She followed him from room to room telling him to clean this and that. She told him he was lazy and always wanted to find a shortcut "just like his father". As far as the younger Mora had seen, his father was a hardworking man, unlike that bitch. Young Jacob told her he didn't think his father was really dead, he just ran away from her constant spending and bitching. Harriett Mora slapped her son that day. She slapped him hard with an open palm when her son lashed out angrily. With the red palm print on his face still burning, Jacob ran to his hiding place in the attic. He turned the radio on loudly to cover up his mother's yells. When she banged on the door, he turned the station and settled on "Night Train" a "race song" by the "Negro" singer James Brown. He turned the music up loudly hoping the squeals and soul of the man's voice would drive her away...and it did.

Jacob shuffled through the box of his father's journals and began reading where he had left off. His father described a beautiful whorehouse where he relished in not one, but two beautiful Tunisian women. His father's lush description made the younger Mora feel as if he were sitting there in the room. His father continued to describe another man he met that day, a man by the name of Welk. Mora was gripped by the descriptions and the quotes.

More than once he re-read paragraphs wondering if his father had branched off and started writing his own novel in the midst of his memoirs. But it was his words and what he had witnessed and learned.

There were paragraphs about the power of a mighty army and their leader. His father described the man Welk and others that had helped the Allied forces overcome The Nazi. His father detailed his own efforts to help them find a man they considered to be the strongest of warriors and a demon in true form. A demon Welk called Allard. With Allard's help, he'd said, one could harness as many riches as man wanted. With Allard's help, everything man desired would be at his fingertips. Mora pledged his help in finding the man and ridding the Earth of such a dangerous temptation. However, Mora wrote, it tempted him to see what the demon Allard could do for him and his family. Mora vowed to keep his pledge to help Welk, if not only for himself then for his legacy.

It was there on that attic floor, with tears streaming down his face, a red handprint across his cheek and his mother's loud bitching erupting from the floor below, that the seeds were planted for Jacob Mora's plan. A plan brewed in desperation, childishness and anger.

Lisa led the group through the hallways of the stadium. She shook her hands trying to get rid of the numbness. She was happy that the flames had disappeared when she calmed down. Once this mess was over, she had to make an appointment at her nail salon...then again, she wasn't sure if that'd be a wise choice. None of the others discussed her sudden gift "flame up"; they were too appreciative it had shown up when it did. Jury walked closely behind Lisa knowing the inner turmoil that the abilities could stir.

"Look." Dustin whispered.

Jacob Mora was at the end of an adjacent hallway walking towards them. He looked panicked, but very much focused. In fact, he'd walked nearly half the hallway before he realized they were waiting for him at the other end. He stopped in his tracks trying to figure out how to handle them.

"Mora!" Dustin yelled.

Mora took a deep breath and ran as fast as he could up another hallway with the four quickly gaining on him. Dustin screamed his name over and again as if he hadn't been heard and obviously Jacob Mora couldn't have been ignoring him. He was headed for the stadium. He was headed for protection. Dustin quickly gained on him and tackled him against the cold stone floor. Mora struggled to run until he realized he was quickly outnumbered.

"We have to go. There are some very unsavory things that way and we can't risk being caught by ourselves." Mora panted.

"You weren't concerned about us when your ass was high-tailing it up the hall!" Lisa poked Mora in the face.

"Watch yourself Lucas!" Mora said sternly.

Lisa was impressed that the chairman of the multi-billion dollar conglomerate knew her name, but not impressed enough to back down.

"You haven't been honest with me." Dustin glared at him with fierce eyes.

He wished the pearl dagger were at his side again. If Mora said the wrong thing, it would pierce his chest just as it had the man in St. Patrick's Cathedral. He considered using the other weapon he had strapped to his calf.

"Honesty is an evolving construct. What may have been true yesterday, may not be today and then again it can change tomorrow. You know the business we're in, some information can't be shared all the time." Mora responded checking behind him for signs of Alala or Sundiata.

"Let me share something with YOU..." Jury charged Mora but was quickly held back by Michelle.

“Can you help me understand something?” Michelle spoke softly.

“Certainly. Make an appointment to see me reverend and I’ll have a nice chat with you.” Mora moved to escape, but was blocked by Lisa.

“You have a pretty powerful Army already. Why increase the strength? Are you crazy enough to believe you can just overpower the world with demons and super soldiers?” Michelle asked.

“I’m not trying to overpower the world. I own too much of it. I’m a businessman. I know when I have a good thing. My holdings on this Earth are a great thing. I plan on offering the world the best of the best in hired military professionals. When the opportunity arose to take it to the next level with Allard, I bit at the chance. I’m afraid I’ve always had an opportunist’s ego. Please excuse me. I need to go. You’re welcome to come with.” Mora slid passed Lisa and rushed hurriedly up the hallway.

Alala felt a chill up her spine when Allard handed her Dragon’s Needle. Sundiata stood perplexed unsure of whether he should attack Allard or be fearful of what other weapons he bore. Allard stepped back crossing his arms and shrugged. He knew giving his weapon away was a gamble, but his faith in Alala's integrity when it came to battle was unwavering. If she were to attack, she would hand him her own sword to defend himself before doing so. Sundiata on the other hand couldn't be trusted. The element of surprise was his specialty. The moral fiber in his body had long been frayed and brittle. Allard's strategy was to play Sundiata's own mistrust against him. When Sundiata took a nervous step backward, he knew it had worked perfectly.

"Why did you do that?" Alala huffed. She had become sweaty with the idea of battling Allard.

"I don't want it." He answered.

"Why did you request it?" She pressed.

"To get your attention." He nodded to Sundiata. "And his and Dezi's and Kronus. I couldn't just ask you to meet me for brunch, now could I? But if I decided to use such a powerful...yet cute, weapon, then of course there would be interest in what I was doing. I was attacked at a church by Beings dressed as Souls using sulphur swords from Hell. I figured Dragon was preparing a new war and was testing my readiness."

"He was telling the truth. You are on his side." Alala felt her breath quicken.

"Dezi was." Allard said. He watched Sundiata's jaw muscles clench. If his hands flinched it would signal an imminent assault. He glanced to his hands and they were still.

"Watch your mouth, brother." Sundiata growled.

"It's a hard truth, but a truth just the same. We all know Dezi liked Dragon. Dragon was the only one that kept in touch with him after the war. After you all took me in for war crimes... Dragon was a mentor to Dezi. He taught him so much. Even when Dezi turned his back on Dragon and you four escorted him to Hell, Dragon still didn't stop sending kind word to him. Dezi was jealous of my relationship with Dragon as well. I wasn't surprised when he went straight for Dragon's Needle and killed Souls just to retrieve it. He didn't want me to have it and he made that painfully clear. He didn't want me joining up with Dragon again without getting his own top spot in the army...until he found out there was no army." Allard looked down at Alala's boots. He noticed the bright tip on the toe. Pearl tipped retractable blades. She would've surprised him with that little tidbit.

"What do you mean there's no army? There's thousands of them standing upstairs in the stadium." Sundiata said.

"That's not Dragon's army." Alala responded with a nod.

Michelle watched Jacob Mora trot up the hallway towards the stadium. As usual, there was something he said that nagged at her.

"His holdings on this Earth are a great thing." Michelle said.

"Yeah and he just built himself a devilish army to profit from it." Jury groaned.

"I can't believe I fell for that. He told me I would help him destroy the greatest evil. Meanwhile, he's suiting them up and going to make millions." Dustin huffed.

"His holdings on this Earth...why would he say that?" Michelle asked no one in particular.

"Because he has holdings on the moon too..." Jury responded angrily.

"Or he has interests not of this Earth..." Lisa mumbled then began a sprint chasing behind Mora.

The others followed behind her. Jury, her running partner, caught up to Lisa quickly and sprinted step by step alongside her. Their breathing synced and soon it was just like another run at The Country Cage.

"He can't be serious!" Jury huffed. "He can't be serious! Is he serious??"

They saw Mora run out into the lit stadium. An overwhelming thunderclap erupted above them, ahead of them, all around them. It sounded like the building was crumbling. They stopped and looked, but soon realized the sound came from the army. They had welcomed their commander in chief with a rousing salutation. Jury and Lisa froze. There was no way they would run into the lion's den. Dustin pushed by them and charged Mora at full speed.

Mora basked in the overwhelming power of his army at the entrance to the field. He raised his arms high above his head and waved as the army quickly and thunderously snapped to attention. He felt a crushing blow in his back, went toppling onto the pavement and slid across the concrete, stopping at the turf's edge. Dustin rolled him over on his back and grabbed him by his collar.

"You told me that we were going to fight evil! You made me kill people!" Dustin shouted.

"We are going to fight evil Carver! If they don't join us then we'll destroy them. If they join us then we'll create a new power. Either way, you get what you want and I get what I want." Mora wiped blood from his scraped mouth. "Every man has a beginning, every god a creation, every ruler has an ascension and a demise. Tell The Devil he's been usurped. Jacob Mora has taken his crown."

"Run Dustin!" Jury's shouts echoed from the hallway.

Dustin turned in time to see several soldiers jumping down from the stadium seats and running to help their leader. He sprinted onto the field trying his best to escape. Soldiers jumped from the stands end to end chasing towards him. Dustin zigged and zagged but they were too quick. The soldiers closed in on him in a large circle formation and charged at him with all of their speed.

"STOPPPPPPPPPPP! Don't hurt him!" Jury screamed.

Her commands were heard. Her words were immediately obeyed. Every blade of grass stiffened razor sharp. The soldiers' boots ripped and shredded. Some of them tripped falling face first into thousands of sharp slashes. Others tried stopping, slipped and blades of grass sliced through their knees. Others slid on their hands leaving fingers in the wake of the blades. Dustin stood still in a small circle of unaltered grass watching as the men tumbled and screamed around him.

"How in the hell did you do that?" Lisa wondered aloud.

"I-I-I don't know..." Jury stood wide-eyed. "I guess talking to flowers isn't that bad a deal."

The soldiers regrouped. Those with their boots still intact stood carefully and unsheathed their weapons. Ten in all slowly approached Dustin walking carefully over the turf like glass walkers. Their matte black swords were trained towards Dustin, in case he decided to run he would impale himself on the approaching weaponry. Without warning, there was a loud screech and a hot scorching mist engulfed the soldiers one by one. Their faces turned gaunt, their bodies shriveled, their eyes bulged. The swords became too heavy to carry, their clothes too heavy to bear. They collapsed into the turf hard like diving onto a bed of nails. Their emaciated carcasses smoldered around him.

"Michelle?" Jury said turning to her friend.

"Wasn't me. I just made it up here. You guys run too fast." Michelle panted.

On the other side of the field, they saw Sundiata emerge from the darkened tunnel. He held his hands aloft smoldering with the mist of famine. He stopped before he reached the grass and scorched much of it, burning it to ash as he crossed it. Alala entered the field after him; she held her sword in one hand, in the other twirled Dragon's Needle.

"Shit...we've gotta go." Jury hushed.

"You'll be fine." He said as he approached them from behind.

Jury turned quickly and was face to face with Allard. Thousands of words went unsaid as they stared at each other. Allard nodded, Jury returned his gesture and let him pass. As he exited the tunnel, he removed a small metal placard from the brush metal of his spear. The placard bore the date he last held it and the date of his capture. It slid across the pavement echoing a hollow tink in the tunnel. There were audible gasps as he stepped onto the field and walked towards Alala and Sundiata.

"We've gotta get Dustin out of there." Lisa worried.

"Even after I killed thousands of your comrades, you still remain here." Allard began. "I applaud your sense of duty and I honor your will, but none of you will serve in a war. Your leader...no...your assembler, brought you together under false pretenses. There is no sanctioned agreement. He took advantage and lied to those who rightfully initiate these proceedings." He bowed to Alala who smiled back to him. "He said he was acting on behalf of Dragon. He even claimed to some of you that I would be your general. Those were all lies. Therefore, there is no war!"

The soldiers booed loudly. Hisses and grumbles filled the stadium.

"Now I understand some of you are bolstered and even energized by your capture of me earlier. That might make you feel that you can challenge me now. However, I'd like you to know, you didn't capture me so much as I grew bored with killing your comrades."

The soldiers booed loudly. Unrest began to grow.

"I don't care what Allard says we need to get the hell up outta here." Jury tugged on Lisa's arm. Lisa stared at Dustin who was frozen in his position looking nervously side-to-side.

"I understand that you feel that with such an awe-inspiring group, you could initiate your own guerilla style operation and make some big wins. We are telling you together that this is not allowed and you are hereby disbanded. We are giving you a one-time amnesty and suggest you accept it. To challenge us is to forfeit the life you have. This is the second chance some of you have been given, you will hand it all over to the blackness of death. While individually we are each masterful in a morose tone, together we are the dark ensemble. If you choose to fight, you will be initiating your finale. This will be your final note. There will be no bravo and there is no encore!" Allard stood in the middle of the field. His spear gleamed brightly in his hand.

A howling whish erupted from the sky. Alala looked upward watching a small sparkle descend. She took two steps to her left and watched as a black sulphur sword drove through the turf where she had stood. The stadium roared with approval. She quickly laid her sword and Dragon's Needle at her feet. Her hands slipped inside her coat and retrieved the slingshot and one marble sized course diamond. With sniper precision, she rapidly loaded the diamond aimed and shot. Her ammunition zipped through the sky with a buzzing whistle. Her target made a jump to move but it was too late. His body plummeted from the second tier crumpling to the ground with a thud.

"So be it." Alala shrugged.

The stadium exploded into a guided chaos. A tidal wave of soldiers rushed towards the field in formations. Allard, Sundiata and Alala stood at three points of a triangle waiting to sign the death certificates of each and every combatant that approached. Without a word spoken, Lisa, Jury and Michelle ran back through the tunnel hallway in search of an exit. Michelle turned behind her and saw Dustin running in Jacob Mora's direction.

"Dustin!" Michelle screamed. She considered running back to get him, but there was no way she'd part from her friends.

The three of them ran left and right following the exit signs through the labyrinth of hallways. They turned to a darkened tunnel and two soldiers guarded the exit.

"Freeze!" One of the soldiers shouted.

They turned on their heels and headed off in the other direction with the soldiers quickly behind them. Not even Lisa and Jury's speed was a match for the long strides exhibited by the soldiers. Jury kicked and punched as one lifted her by her waist and attempted to subdue her flailing limbs. Lisa was pinned against the wall while her captor reached for his handcuffs. Michelle tried her best to help Jury pull away, but was pushed to the ground. Her head ricocheted off the concrete casting a haze over everything around her.

Suddenly, Lisa's captor howled in pain. He stumbled back away from her with his eyes as big as saucers. Lisa turned to him clutching his severed hands in hers. Her claws lit a fiery red. She stared up at him with evil terror in her eyes. She tossed his hands at his feet.

"I think you dropped those." Lisa growled.

The other soldier unsheathed his sword and pointed it at Lisa. He swung at her wildly backing her down the hallway. This was a combat Lisa wasn't ready for. Self-preservation was one thing, but hand-to-hand combat with a soldier was not her forte.

"Aren't you a pretty Soul. I'll have you sodomized before day break." He slurred.

The next thing to leave his mouth was a pained gurgle. The next thing to leave his body was the pearl tip of a sword erupting from his chest. Michelle stood on the other end of his partner's sword holding the heavy weapon straight with both hands. She pushed harder plunging the sword fully through him. The soldier collapsed, shook and then his eyes blackened. The three bolted through the hallway towards yet another exit.

Dustin chased Mora laterally across the chaos of the field through a tunnel and into the darkness. He was focused not just on the man, but his mission. There had to be a reprisal. He hated the horrible feeling of vengeance in his heart, but he would ask for forgiveness later. Dustin didn't want to kill Mora, but he wanted to hurt him. He wanted to make Mora explain why he had brought him on the journey with him. If he were to be damned alongside Mora then he wanted it to be a good reason. Perhaps then he would kill Mora as a final act of destroying evil.

Mora slipped into an elevator. Dustin sprinted the long hallway towards it as he watched Mora feverishly pressing the control buttons. The door closed in Dustin's face just as he reached it. He waited, watching the display illuminate as the elevator rose. Dustin braced to run for the stairs, all he needed was a confirmation on which floor Mora was slinking off to like the coward he had shown himself to be. When the light progressed beyond the executive office floors, his heart sank. He immediately knew Mora's plan and he ran to the stairs as fast as he could.

Allard felt the energy surge within him when he swung the spear. He hadn't felt like himself in so long he nearly forgot the tingles he received when he fought with it. The spear made an unmistakably unique whistling sound when it swung. He stabbed, adjusted the size like he had done with Dragon's Needle and cut, he elongated and poked, spread it thin and sliced. Soldiers collapsed around him with blackened eyes and severed heads. To his left, Alala spun both her sword and Dragon's Needle in tandem destroying demons at every turn. She peeked over her shoulder at Allard and couldn't help, but to feel an attraction. His swagger on the battleground was gloriously beautiful. She smiled at him; he smiled back and tossed his spear directly at her. She kneeled quickly, it whistled over her head impaling three soldiers like a shish kabob. Before she could rise, she felt his foot use her knee as a step stool. He catapulted into the air spinning head over tail, clenched the spear and kicked the bodies from it like falling domino.

"Real cute, Tubey." She growled.

Loud pops echoed through the stadium followed by bullets whizzing by the two of them.

"So much for a fair fight." Allard said turning to Sundiata.

Sundiata held two soldiers by their limp broken necks and dropped them in a crumpled heap on the ground. He shook his hands at his sides then waved them upward blasting a hot mist across the stadium. It engulfed the sniper in a fog emaciating him within seconds. Sundiata turned his aim at a large swell of soldiers charging them from his right side. A sickened cough accompanied the fog as it bursts from his hands. The first line of soldiers was scorched so badly their skin evaporated. Those that followed crumpled to the ground shaking as the nutrients and vitamins in their bodies quickly depleted.

"You're much better at that than I remember." Allard said sarcastically as he struck down two opponents swinging swords. "Think you can hit that guy right there?" He pointed far off in the distance to a soldier standing in formation on the third tier of the stadium waiting for his line to engage.

Sundiata glared back at Allard. There was no way he'd turn down a challenge. He flexed his fingers, pivoted on his feet and shot a streamline blast of mist high up the stadium. Soldiers scattered running for cover. The mist followed one of them as he ducked and dodged with the rest, he tripped on the staircase tumbling backward into the scorching mist. Sundiata shot a smile back to Allard as he pulled a dagger from his coat and stabbed an oncoming soldier in the chest.

"Not bad." Allard nodded breaking the chest plate of a soldier with a fierce kick.

"Can we focus here?" Alala admonished as she kicked and eviscerated opponents one after the other with what she called "Alalatial" arts.

"We're going to be here for awhile. Might as well pass the time." Allard speared two soldiers. "Where's your other partner? The quieter he is, the more I think he's with the other side."

"You can never make Kronus join a fight. He's a little prissy for all of this." Sundiata's hands exploded a large plume that demolished a charging line of five soldiers.

"If he doesn't show, I'll go looking for him." Allard shouted over the screams of anguish.

"He'll show...or he'll have me to deal with." Alala assured him.

Allard felt a pull at his senses. His intuition bothered him. He closed his eyes and tried to locate Lisa, Jury, Michelle and Dustin. There was something ominous there. There was a darkness he didn't like.

"Allard!" Alala screamed as a soldier jumped high above him and descended with his sword.

With his eyes still closed, Allard raised the spear and blocked the pearl tip. He swung the spear knocking the soldier to the ground and speared him through the chest. The spear vibrated with the impact. Allard removed his weapon and opened his eyes.

"Keep busy until I come back." Allard said as he ran off towards the tunnels.

"Where are you going?" Alala shouted, but she knew. She knew how much Allard cared for those Souls.

Dustin wheezed as he ran up the steps. He started out running two steps at a time, but his aging muscles quickly got the better of him. He panted as he pushed his legs to climb the last step. His only hope was that Mora was still up there when he arrived. Sweat soaked his button down shirt as he pushed the crash bar and rushed out into a gust of wind.

The Scilymax Pinnacle luxury helicopter sat on the heliport with its blades causing a mini windstorm. Dustin pulled his desert eagle handgun from under his pants and aimed it at the pilot. He slowly raised his hands from the flight controls and shook his head. He mouthed something to Dustin with a shrug. Suddenly a metal bar hit Dustin's arm fracturing it and sending his weapon to the ground. Before he could reach down, Mora had picked it up and leveled it at Dustin's head.

"Geez this thing is heavy. What are you doing with such heavy firepower?" Mora complained over the sound of the copter.

Dustin stared at him with disgust.

"You've gotta be kidding me, Carver. I gave you what you wanted...a cushy job, a chance to help the handicapped and infirmed, that sexy secretary you were banging for so long. You couldn't honestly be upset with me." Mora walked around Dustin without dropping his aim.

"I never would've worked with you if I thought you were going to take advantage of so many people's faith."

"Take advantage of who? No one is faithful. No one is loyal in this world. Who's faithful? The board isn't. They know all about it. They know! They know the plans.

They love the plans. They're going to make billions off this plan. Who else your two little doctors and the Reverend that doesn't want to be called a Reverend? They don't care. They'd stab you in the heart if I paid them enough. No one is faithful. I'm the only one in this with a true goal. I'm the only one led by a vow. A vow my father made decades ago and while I was at it, I took a little bit for myself. I'm pretty sure he's looking down on me proud. I made it from the son of a fishmonger to a master of the universe in less than a generation. I own it all. Look at it. Look at this view, Carver."

Dustin stared out to the view of Milan just before dawn. It was breathtaking. He looked off into the stadium. The legions of soldiers were moving in a formation towards one center point like ants converging on a cookie crumb.

"You can come with me. We still have work to do, Carver. No hard feelings at all. I'll give you a bump up in pay and a new title...Senior Executive Vice President of Research. You can keep making sick people better, give a nice handsome donation to that church I recruited you from. The company will match whatever you give...Hell, I'll toss in an extra hundred k." He pointed out to the stadium. "Don't let THAT bother you. That's not your concern. Consider that insurance. How many employees care about their bosses insurance policies?"

"I'm supposed to fly away with you and forget this ever happened?" Dustin said.

"It's either that or walk out of here...and trust me, those guys aren't going to let you do that." Mora shook his head. "Geez, this gun is really heavy. How do you carry this thing?"

"You can just hand it back to me, if you'd like." Dustin shrugged.

Mora laughed a big hearty cackle. He dropped the gun by his side resting his arm.

"So, what is it ol boy? You fly with me or you walk outta here?" Mora asked.

"You're not flying anywhere and I damn sure am not walking back down those steps."

"Well, my flight is ready to go. Thank you for all of your hard work." Mora turned and walked toward the copter.

Dustin charged Mora reaching for the gun. Mora spun and fired one shot into his chest. The heat of the bullet was the most painful thing Dustin could ever feel. He collapsed to his knees then slid to his back. Mora leaned over him and looked him the eye.

"Sorry old friend, but I saved you a walk down those stairs. See you on the other side." Mora dropped the gun at Dustin's feet. He stepped onto the copter taking one last look back at Dustin gasping for air on the heliport then closed the door behind him.

Dustin tried to calm his breathing. The feeling left his extremities. All that was left was the white-hot sensation in his chest. Whenever he tried to take in more air, he felt it impossible and would cough. The last few coughs he tasted blood. He stared up at the copter as it rose above the stadium then he felt a warm hand take his.

“Hold my hand. Relax. Don’t fight, good soul. It will come swiftly. Just go with it.” He heard.

“Whoever designed this place oughta have their ass kicked.” Lisa shouted to no one in particular as they walked down yet another hallway.

They were lost in the various service tunnels built for moving concessions and engineering crew. The loud rumble of battle could be heard above them.

“See! We should’ve taken that left. I think we’re back under the field again. Why does every exit sign lead us into another tunnel?” Michelle harped.

“Wait. Let’s stop and think about this.” Jury began. “We don’t want to be on the other side of the stadium because that’s where we’re most likely to run into a guarded exit. We walked west then got turned around in that dead end. We passed the kitchens and then..."

"We followed the yellow brick road!" Lisa screamed.

"Let's just keep walking straight there has to be a way out up here." Michelle pressed. She pushed by them and walked laboriously down the dark gray corridor.

Knock Knock Knock

"What was that?" Jury asked.

"More shit hitting the fan in that stadium. We gotta get out of here." Lisa huffed.

Knock Knock Knock

"That wasn't in the stadium." Jury stopped. She tried to calm the thumping of her heartbeat so she could listen.

Knock Knock Knock

It sounded like old oak tapping against concrete.

"I heard it that time too." Michelle stopped dead in her tracks and tried to look ahead to the darkness that occupied the end of the corridor.

Lisa felt a chill down her neck that made the hairs there stand up. The tiniest little hairs on her arms rose. Her nipples stiffened so hard they hurt.

"Oh my God! Nooooo!" Lisa grabbed Jury and Michelle's hand and began to pull them as she ran.

The three of them sprinted back up the tunnel. The knocking grew louder then a whisking howl echoed through the corridor. Lisa turned and saw him floating towards them quickly. His robes billowed around him like smoke caught in an overturned glass. His sickle was extended in the bony fingers of his right hand. His gigantic hood covered what she knew were movie star good looks. Kronus was in pursuit. Death had come for them. Michelle screeched when she saw him barreling down behind them. Everything turned cold. Jury could see her breath leaving her nose and mouth in short puffs like smoke from a locomotive. They burst through a set of double doors and Kronus stood there waiting for them. When they turned back the doors were locked. Jury screamed at the top of her lungs.

"Oh! Do you have to do that? Why does everyone do that?" Kronus shook his head.

"You're not what I think you are...you're not what I think you are." Michelle chanted.

"I am." Kronus said.

“He is.” Lisa confirmed.

“You remember me, huh. Dr. Lisa Lucas, you got away from me last time and I’ve never heard from you again. You never call, you never write. I figured I’d have to make a house call.” Kronus cracked. His voice left his hood in a hollow echo. “Care to introduce the posse?”

“No.” Lisa shivered in the chill Kronus created.

“Selfish.” Kronus floated closer to them. The closer he got the colder it became. He pointed his left bony index finger in their faces. “Dr. Marjorie Houston. Pastor Michelle Bonds. My name is Kronus.” He slowly slipped his hood back revealing his sparkling smile and ice-cold blue eyes. His bony left hand mussed his blonde hair. “This is how it works...you either give me a kiss or...” He thumped the edge of his sickle. The thump echoed in the tunnel and reverberated eerily. “I make the final cut. Today is the last day of the rest of your lives.” He laughed at his own over-used joke.

“What if we don’t wanna go?” Lisa stepped forward. She felt a growing strength inside of her.

“I know why YOU don’t want to go. Dragon’s stubby little penis awaits your orifices and there are no little bracelets or doo-hickies that’ll save you from it this time, is there...?” He gave her the once over.

"Alala said we have covenants. You're going to go against that?" Lisa pawed for an escape plan.

"Covenants? What do I care for those made up rules by bored little angels and demons? I'm not scared of any of them." He replied.

"It's Allard." Michelle spoke softly.

"It's Allard." Kronus mocked her soft voice. "You might as well tell me it's Santa, The Easter Bunny and The Tooth Fairy, darling. Allard is about as dependable as a knife made out of cream. You're telling me none of you have noticed that when the going gets tough, Allard gets going?" Kronus smiled. "He's a deserter, babies. He's a traitor and a turncoat. The only thing he's brave towards is the sunset. He likes to turn and walk off into it."

Jury's heart raced. She didn't have a covenant. What would happen to her? Why hadn't anyone come to her rescue? Where were the bodega owners tonight?

"I hear you." Kronus whispered to Jury. "Wondering where your savior is? Wondering what happens to you with no covenant? None of that matters. I can tell you now what will happen to all of you. My shadows failed to bring you to me when you went on your little purgatory trip. This time they'll get you. You'll be sold off to some low level Lost Angel where you'll spend your eternity as a slave in the fire pits of Hell. Horrible work, but at least there's no need for health insurance. Oh, except for the pretty Dr. Lucas here. She has a date with Dragon. Well one of you does. The other Soul is coming with me. I could sell that little gift of yours or return it for a handsome reward." Kronus floated ominously up and down lengthening his already abnormal height.

"Stop talking and get it over with." Jury said.

"Shhhh" Lisa hushed as she tried to think of a way to get them out of there alive.

"What did you say?" Kronus grew angrier by the second.

"I said, stop talking and get it over with. I'm not going to stand here and live in fear of you. You said it's over then it's over. Stop running your cute little prissy mouth and make it happen." Jury shouted.

"You, my dear, won't get a choice." He floated over to Jury and glared down at her. "You will get the hard metal dick." He tapped his finger against the staff of his sickle.

"I'm not scared. You look flaccid anyway. You actually sound like you have sugar in your tank. Do you even like women?" Jury taunted as Kronus turned his back to her.

"I like them all." He said lifting his hood over his head. "And I'll show you how much."

Kronus spun around and swung his sickle down hard on Jury. At the last moment it collided with metal and large blue sparks erupted. The impact against the spear buckled Allard's knees. He held the spear blocking Jury from the sickle and slowly knelt under the pressure. Jury jumped back pushing Lisa and Michelle with her. Allard slowly rose to his feet again pushing Kronus' staff up and away. Kronus pushed down harder. Allard grimaced and with a grunt overcame his power and heaved Kronus backward.

"Fancy meeting you here." Kronus shrugged dropping his sickle to his side.

"Did you not see that they have covenants? Are you that willing to turn our relationship that ugly?" Allard pointed the tip of his spear inside Kronus' hood.

Kronus pushed it away slowly with the tip of one boney finger.

"These two maybe, but not her." Kronus pointed at Jury.

She got a chill up her spine when he referred to her.

"I'm here on behalf of her guardian as well. He asked me to keep an eye on her."

"You've always been a dashing gentlemen." Kronus lied. "How chivalrous and honorable."

Kronus lowered his hood.

"Speaking of honor, you have a vow to honor yourself. Yet you're not topside handling the wayward army." Allard tapped the tip of his spear against the concrete.

"I'm on my way." Kronus rolled his eyes.

"I also hear you showed up when Hermes was bringing me Dragon's Needle."

Kronus sneered at Allard.

"If I ever find out you're working with Dragon, it won't bode well for you, Kronus." Allard warned.

"I'll consider myself informed then." Kronus nodded. "Good day ladies. Hope your knight in dusty denim serves you well this day."

Kronus quickly shot upward dissipating through the ceiling.

"What does that mean?" Michelle asked.

"It means I gotta get you three the hell out of here fast." Allard said leading them back through the double doors.

The Scilymax Pinnacle hovered over the stadium. Mora watched as one of his greatest architectural achievements was broken here and shattered there. He saw his army being picked apart and decimated by only two figures standing in the middle of the field.

"No, no...not the display screens those are HD and were specially made. Arghhh!" He moaned as he watched a soldier get thrown through a display as it exploded in a shower of sparks. "I'll call the insurance adjuster in tomorrow; tell them we were filming a movie here and things went awry. Let's go." He told the pilot. "This is depressing me."

The pilot pressed the throttle and the engine stalled. The Pinnacle swayed in the air and the engine seemed to hiccup.

"What's going on?" Mora yelled from his plush leather bucket seat in the back.

"No idea." The Pilot squawked through his headset.

"I tend to have that effect on electronics." Kronus shrugged from his seat across from Mora.

Mora screamed in shock.

"Ughhh you too with that screaming, huh." Kronus deadpanned.

"What are you?" Mora pushed his back against the seat.

"I thought I was the bringer of death until you shot Carver down there. Are you trying to take my job like you tried to take Dragon's place?" Kronus asked as he pushed back his hood. He pulled a granny smith apple from the small fruit dish that sat between them and took a healthy bite.

“I'll give you anything you want. Whatever you need.” Mora stammered.

“You know what I've always wanted? Nicer hands. These frail things make it really hard on my social calendar, you know what I mean?”

“I have the best plastic surgeons in the world. Whatever you want.” Mora huffed.

“Sir, are you ok?” The Pilot squawked as he turned knobs and pressed buttons trying to stabilize the copter.

“Dragon put a nice bounty on your Soul. I think I want that.” Kronus took another huge bite from the apple.

In the stadium, Alala and Sundiata destroyed soldier after soldier. Alala pointed to the sky and the sputtering aircraft.

“Guess who finally arrived...” She said.

“Took him long enough. The nerve of that guy.” Sundiata shouted over the screams of soldiers shriveling beneath him.

"We'll need to keep an eye on him." Alala said. "He's taking this independent contractor thing too far."

There was a sudden wind gust beneath them. Small tornado shaped funnel clouds licked at their shoes. Errant turf and pieces of signage got caught in the whirlwind then kicked out. The two lifted off the ground individually in a lopsided current.

"Time to go home." Alala shrugged.

"What about Allard?" Sundiata shouted over the growing winds.

"You know my Tubey, he likes the Souls." She smirked.

A loud concussive explosion shot the two of them out of the stadium on their winds and off to another place.

The helicopter careened downward spinning out of control. The blades chopped up the top tier before landing in the field and creating an abnormally large explosion for an aircraft its size. The building rocked and exploded in small fires.

"The building is coming down!" Lisa shouted as she pushed open the exit door and was hit by the combination of the early dew of Milan and the fiery smell of ash being emitted from the stadium.

Michelle was right behind her with Jury and Allard following behind. Ash and debris began to fall from the stadium as they tried to rush further away.

"Over there. Go to that restaurant. The overnight staff will be there prepping. Tell them I sent you. They'll keep you safe." Allard said as he watched the winds launch the small specks that were Alala and Sundiata high into the sky and out of view.

"Where are you going?" Jury was more worried than the others.

"I have to go answer for all of this." Allard shook his head.

It was a bittersweet farewell for him. He'd grown to really care for them all. Even though it was written for him, he couldn't help but take note of the surprises it all held. He hugged Lisa.

"That doesn't define you." He pointed to the unseen Dragon stamp on her wrist. "There's a way around it. I won't you let you go to him."

"If I go, he better hope I don't take over." Tears leaked from Lisa's eyes.

"Thank you, Ms. Bonds. You're a beauty and a God send." He said hugging her tightly.

Suddenly a thorny bush wrapped itself around his arms and pulled him into it. The bush subdued his legs entangling him within it. The thorns tightened around his legs cutting him. A long vine swirled around his throat; the thorns sliced him as it tightened.

"Hold him! Hold him!" Jury shouted as more vines overtook Allard.

A large explosion within the stadium sent ash and into the air and part of the building façade crumbled into the street.

"Jury, what are you doing?" Lisa screamed.

"Let him go!" Michelle protested.

"It's ok." Allard moaned through a tightening voice box.

"I have one question." Jury glared at him. More vines shot from the ground as his muscles strained and popped others. "Why'd you take him? Why Boyce?" Tears welled in her eyes.

"It was his time. He had to go. It was the only way he could look after you." Allard struggled speaking through the constricting vines. He felt the winds pick up right around his heels. There was a sudden gust of wind bouncing him within the bush.

"We saw him in purgatory!" Jury grimaced.

“He was watching the entrance looking for you or I. It was a favor from Anubis to me. He kept him behind for me. That’s why you don’t have a covenant. I didn’t want to take him away from you. He’ll be a great guardian.” Allard broke the vines with the strength from his neck.

“He’s guarding me?” Jury’s eyes welled with tears.

“Forever.” Allard said. “You’ll need it. That gift is getting stronger.”

Lisa walked over and with one slash from her claws she pulled away the vines. They smoldered in her wake.

“And yours too...” Allard shook his head. He felt the winds pulling him. “I’ve gotta go.” He hugged Jury and kissed her cheek. “I’ll give him your love.”

“Please do.” Jury smiled.

The ground rumbled as the stadium rocked and exploded. Fire engines and police cars began to surround the building. Emergency workers shouted to each other in Italian as they weighed the situation.

Allard walked quickly down the street. His feet tripped beneath him, he couldn’t keep his balance. Suddenly he lifted off the ground. A loud explosion shot him quickly into the sky and out of view. They watched him become a small speck in the sky then a bright colorful light sparkled where he once flew.

“Oh no!” Lisa squealed. “I hope Dustin got out of there.” She sighed.

The three of them watched as the stadium shot large flames into the air. They all knew in their hearts, Dustin was no more, but they held out hope that somehow he made it out.

CHAPTER LE5EN

A2O5E LDPREKE

The memorial service for Jacob Mora was a grand affair held at St Patrick's Cathedral on a cold December morning. Two former U.S. Presidents and the sitting United States Vice-President attended, as did the Prime Ministers from Italy and The United Kingdom. The President of The United States and The President of Brazil sent their condolences to his family. He was offered a grave in Arlington Cemetery, but his widow decided he would rest in the family plot in Queens, New York. Every major news network broadcast at least portions of the funeral. Most chose to "break in" coverage as his eulogy was given by a world-renowned music star/humanitarian.

Traffic in Manhattan was snarled for a greater portion of that morning as the procession moved from the Cathedral, down Fifth Avenue, passed each of the Scilymax headquarters in Manhattan and crossed The Manhattan Bridge to his final resting place. The tragic story of his passing had sold tons of papers. The international business community was shocked when they learned his helicopter crashed into the stadium during the filming of a commercial for the new venue.

The experimental fuel used in the helicopter was blamed for the quick spreading inferno that destroyed portions of the stadium. Though none of the families of the thousands of "extras" used in the commercial sued, they were all sent handsome condolence checks.

Scilymax Corporation guaranteed the stadium would be rebuilt and fortified within two years. The newly renamed Mora Arena would be an addition to his legacy and bare a statue of Jacob Mora at the main gate. A dome was also worked into the plans so none who entered would fear a similar fate when they saw aircraft pass overhead.

The funeral for Dustin Carver was a much smaller affair. Attended by mostly family and close friends, there were still a few empty pews in the back of the small church, if anyone cared to drop in and pay their respects. Many of his research team attended wearing crisp white lab coats in homage to his preference for a clean staff. His widow was escorted to the front row by security staff provided by Scilymax. The corporation also paid for all of the services and provided the widow Carver with a healthy settlement payment. The Dustin Carver memorial scholarship was initiated and maintained by Scilymax granting full tuition and fees to ten deserving students in the medical profession with an emphasis on research.

Dustin's longtime assistant, Janice, mourned heavily in the third row finally confirming to his widow that they had more than just a working relationship. Upon his death, Janice left her employ at Scilymax and wrote a book on finding prize antiques amongst everyday yard sales. The book went on to be a New York Times Bestseller. The cover featured a small accent table, which turned out to be worth more than two hundred thousand dollars, even with the small nick on its surface.

Michelle stood in the back office fully dressed. Her pastoral collar looked up at her from the table expectantly. Accepting the request to officiate Dustin's funeral was easier than the simple act of...

"Just put it on, girl." Marjorie nudged her.

"It won't bite." Lisa assured her.

"I know, I know. I was just thinking about all of this and how we all really were delivered through evil. It's just amazing." Michelle sighed.

Lisa and Marjorie sat in hard wood chairs dressed in funeral black. Their mourning had a different layer of sadness that most did not understand. They knew of Dustin's transgressions...well some of them...and hoped he wasn't sitting on a bucket outside of a windmill waiting for his trials to be over.

"Can't help to wonder what's next..." Lisa's voice tapered off as she considered her own destiny.

There was a knock at the door.

"Come in." The three said in unison.

"Pastor we're about ready to begin." The Deacon said entering. "Having trouble with your collar?"

"I was wondering if you have one that comes in red." Marjorie joked. "Something that'll really make it pop."

"Or chartreuse?" Lisa egged her on.

"Chartreuse! You have a collar in chartreuse, Deacon?" Marjorie pressed.

"I'll be waiting for you out by the altar." He smiled and excused himself.

"You guys are crazy." Michelle shook her head laughing.

The door knocked again.

"If he comes in here with a chartreuse collar, you know that's a sign from God right?" Lisa cracked.

"Come in." Michelle said.

"The gang's all here." Allard said as he closed the door behind him.

The silence was deafening. They stared at him hoping beyond hope it was a collective dream.

"Don't everyone say hello at once." Allard crossed the room and poured himself a glass of water from the pitcher. "Traveling makes me thirsty." He gulped the water quickly.

Michelle looked to Marjorie, Marjorie looked to Lisa. Lisa shrugged her shoulders.

"Soooo, what brings you to the neighborhood?" Lisa asked.

"Dustin. I escorted Dustin."

"You were at the funeral home to pay your respects?" Marjorie asked not once looking him in his eyes.

"No, I escorted his Soul here. He wanted to be here to say goodbye. To be amongst you all."

"We really miss you, Dustin. We're so sorry you couldn't make it. We love you." Tears streamed down Lisa'-s face. "Did he hear that?"

"No." Allard shook his head.

"So he can't hear us?" Marjorie dropped her head further.

"No...he's out in the sanctuary saying goodbye to his wife. He said he'd see you guys when you come out. Oh, he also asked that you not let the altar boy sing Amazing Grace. He's not a fan." Allard shrugged.

"Making music demands from the grave. That is so like him." Lisa shook her head.

"Tell him we love him." Marjorie said raising her head to look Allard in the eye.

"I'll do that." Allard dropped his gaze to his shoes. "I also wanted to apologize to you...all of you. Sometimes it's hard for me to express myself. I spend most of my time alone. I don't have the pleasure to be close with anyone. I'm not really allowed to trust. When you've spent so long living like that, it affects you. These bodies you Souls have are so complex. My Being body didn't really have these types of...emotions. I guess that's why I was only meant to fight." He placed his hand on Lisa's shoulder. She stared up at him from her seat. "I know it doesn't seem fair now, but I sent you to Dragon because you could handle it. None of you were put in front of me by mistake. I won't let him take your Soul."

"Ehh don't worry, I have another." Lisa laughed.

The joke lifted the tension in the room.

"That's what I don't understand." Michelle turned to Allard holding her collar. Her fingers rubbed across the course fabric. "You told me you were a servant of the unholy. Dragon told Lisa you're a traitor to God. How can we trust anything you say?"

An uneasy smile spread across Allard's face.

"I told you trusting doesn't come easy to me, but I will trust you with this. You're on this journey with me whether you realize it now or not." He walked to Michelle and extended his hand. She laid her collar in it. He investigated it. "Holy is what is desirable; what is complete. I bet if I looked in that book..." He pointed at The Bible sitting on the table. "I will read lots of Holy Fathers. No matter how many times you Souls refer to it, you always forget the part about a vengeful God. You'll talk about the apocalypse and the Four Horsemen or the seven deadly sins. It's not just in *your* religion, but also in others. You all speak about the vengeance as if it isn't a tangible thing. Tangible Beings sent to carry out the meaning. We're all The Unholy Servants, the personification of what you consider His least Holy will. Parts of The Creator sent to serve what you young Souls don't see as being the love that created you. Holy is desirable and complete. We're the undesirable and incomplete. We serve Him as he instructed. However, what happens when He decides that he will no longer flood this Earth? What happens to that Being whose lone purpose was to carry out that will? Or the Four Horsemen that are no longer needed to bring about an apocalypse they were created to make? Servants of a once vengeful Creator, retired like battleships on the docks waiting to be called into action." He fitted Michelle's collar around her neck perfectly.

"Even Heaven has forced retirement, aint that a blip." Marjorie shook her head.

"I resigned my job." Allard shot back.

"Dragon said you were a traitor." Lisa said sternly.

"That was a long time before I was hired to do my job. When I was brought to be judged, He offered not to punish me, but to reward me for seeing what was righteous and coming back to fight on his behalf." Allard explained.

"You're God's double agent?" Michelle checked her collar in the mirror and decided she liked it.

Allard laughed a booming laugh.

"With the medals to prove it." He tapped his shoulder where his tattoo brands were hidden. "Beings, saints and holy men, granted mercy on the edge of my spear. Granted a painless death for those who chose his way even in the face of adversity. Even when they were misled about their missions or didn't have all of the facts... like young scouts named Welk that tried to bring me to justice. It's an honorable job and I'm sorry I resigned it. Thankfully, my Father isn't too prideful to let me back in his house...and smart enough to enlist a few new soldiers along for the war." He looked to them. "Well...I need to go. There's work to be done." Allard opened the door and began to head out.

"Hey wait!" Lisa stopped him before he could leave. "Dragon said..."

"The Devil is a liar." Allard smiled and closed the door behind him.

The sanctuary was adorned with pictures drawn by the patients of Scilymax Children's Hospital. Most didn't know that Dustin not only helped develop several of the treatments in the hospital, but on weekends he would volunteer as "DooCoo The Clown". This would be the first time in five years that he wouldn't roam the hospital's halls as Santa Claus, handing out presents he paid for himself.

As Michelle stepped to the pulpit, she spied three words painted on a picture near the front. It read "We Miss You! May you be blessed with Forgiveness, Grace and Mercy." Taking a deep breath, she looked out to the mourning group and thought about those three words. Forgiveness. She looked to Marjorie who had learned how to forgive the pain and animosity of losing Boyce. Grace. She looked to Lisa who had been given the ultimate in grace returning to life and finally allowing herself to not only be the protector, but the protected. Mercy... She'd met him herself and saw the beauty it could bring.

Later that evening, after a small repast and sharing of memories, Lisa, Marjorie and Michelle found themselves at Lisa's house. The wine flowed freely. Marjorie brought chicken and came without a security detail. Michelle kicked her feet up on the couch and sipped from her goblet. Lisa thumbed through vacation pamphlets for a much needed getaway without work.

"Wherever you pick, make sure there's no Scilymax branch within a hundred miles. You know they'll come looking for you to do work." Michelle said.

"You didn't tell her?" Marjorie turned to Lisa.

"Tell me?"

"We resigned. We're going the freelance route. Opening our own consulting business and practice." Lisa delivered the news with a smile.

"Those settlement checks won't hurt either." Marjorie added.

There was a knock at the door. The three of them turned to each other. It was too late for company and this was not an expected visitor.

"Don't answer it." Michelle warned.

"Why not?" Marjorie stood and walked toward the door.

Lisa skipped in front of her and blocked her off. She looked through the peephole.

She saw the unassuming face of Mark Silverman. He looked a lot better than he had on his flight to New York, perhaps because he stayed away from the last minute burritos.

"May I help you?" Lisa's voice had all the chill of a sub zero night in the Antarctic.

"Hi, I'm Mark, your neighbor from 12C. The doorman left this box..." He held up a rather large one. "...in my package area, but it has your apartment number on it. Didn't want to leave it out here even with the security and all. It looks kind of special."

"Thanks Mark. I'll come out and get it later." Lisa said with faux cheerfulness.

"A box delivered to the wrong address?" Jury folded her arms suspiciously.

"You think it's some Dragon shit?" Michelle whispered.

"Excuse you, pastor foul mouth." Lisa chided. "If it is I'm ready for him this time." She clicked her nails together.

Lisa unlatched the door and peered out. There was no sign of anyone. She unlocked the door and poked her head out. The hallway was empty. She looked at the ornate writing on the box and her eyebrow cocked. She pulled the box in, locked and latched the door behind her.

"What is it?" Jury stood over it.

"It's for you!" Lisa pointed to Michelle.

"Me?? I don't live here!" Michelle ran over and read the ornate gold lettering on the box. "No return address."

"If you don't wanna open it, I will." Jury pulled a letter opener from the foyer table, split the tape on the box and opened it.

The box was filled with soft gold crepe paper. Michelle dug her hand in and removed another small box made of burlap. Although it was small, it weighed quite a bit. There was a small twine crank lever on the back of the box. Jury fished around in the gold paper looking for a note or card. Michelle spotted a small symbol branded on the bottom of the box.

"It's cute..." Michelle shrugged. She cranked the lever seven turns and music began to play as the crank turned the opposite way. "I know that song. What is that?"

Suddenly, the top of the box popped open. A small figurine shot out of the box and stuck Michelle just on the side of the head behind the ear. She screamed clutching her head and dropped the box to the floor. Lisa picked it up and examined it. It was a small figurine shaped like a goat. The figurine bounced and bobbed held aloft by a gold spring.

"That thing stuck me in the head." Michelle examined the small drop of blood on her finger.

Jury pulled a small card from the bottom of the box. The words on the card were written in finely adorned gold ink.

"Dearest Michelle, I am returning this. Please take great care of this gift. Sincerely Yours, Herman. P.S. Send your mother my kind regards." Jury read. "Who the hell is Herman?"

Lisa held the box up to Michelle so she could see the pearl tips on the horns.

"...and what kind of gift did he just give you?" Lisa smirked knowingly.

The evening was the same as always at Tart's bar. The inhabitants sat huddled at the bar with their third too many drink. The booths were fairly empty except a straggler or two eating greasy half-cooked hamburgers. Dragon sat at his normal booth drinking a whisky talking to his thinner shorter companion.

"What happen there?" His companion said pointing to one of the tattoos on Dragon's arm.

The once perfectly drawn letter "L" had dark red welts scratched into it.

"It irritates me. I don't think I want that one anymore." Dragon replied.

"You? You're turning down a Soul?"

"Not every one is worth the pain. Did I tell you I hate pain? Hate it. These Souls and their bodies." He shrugged.

The door creaked open allowing some of the loud rock music to escape into the normally quiet streets of the neighborhood. The quiet non-assuming shlub of a man dragged in and addressed the bartender.

"Dragon, please?" Herman asked.

"We don't serve that." The Bartender shot back. "Maybe you should try SOHO."

Herman reached in the pocket of his tight tweed overcoat. His stubby fingers produced a rather large gold coin and placed it on the dirty bar top. The Bartender considered the coin, turned and pulled a bottle of whiskey from the uppermost shelf. He poured an overflowing shot of the liquor, slid it to Herman and pointed to Dragon's booth. Herman turned and began to walk.

"Hey!" The Bartender bellowed. "Don't forget to take that with you." He warned.

Herman reluctantly picked up the shot glass and walked with it extended out from his body so as not to spill it on himself. He felt the eyes in the bar following him as he approached Dragon's booth. He wasn't worried; he had delivered worse in harsher conditions. Dragon looked up at him as he approached. Herman felt himself stop on a dime. He stood on one tippy toe staring back into the eyes of The Prince of Darkness.

"Hermes...to what do I owe this dubious honor?" Dragon spoke in an exaggerated British accent.

Herman took smaller steps to the booth.

"Good evening, Dragon." He turned to Dragon's drinking companion. "Hello, Loki." He placed the shot on the tabletop and slid it across to Dragon leaving a slick trail of whisky behind it like a snail's mucous.

Loki motioned to leave.

"You don't have to leave." Dragon assured him.

"It's ok. Last time that bitch Alala tried to burn my bleeding eyebrows off." Loki slurred and stumbled to the bar.

Herman flopped into the worn leather seat of the booth across from Dragon, reached into his pocket and produced a small card with writing on it.

"A message for you..." Herman began.

"Oh wait..." Dragon interrupted. "Let me get myself together for the almighty message as delivered by Hermes." He straightened his dirty black t-shirt brushing off the shells of beer nuts and smearing the drops of Barbecue sauce and whiskey. "OK...you may proceed."

Herman sneered slightly then smiled as he read the card to himself first.

"Dear Losers..." Herman began. "You attacked me and I wiped your slate clean. I am a soldier and I will continue to fight."

Dragon bristled.

"Sincerely..." Herman concluded. Instead of reading the signature, he slammed the card down on the table. The reverse side of the card was emblazoned in gold letters...

Allard

"Is that all?" Dragon spat.

Herman nodded with a smile.

"Good. Get the fuck out of my establishment before I have your dumpy ass slaughtered."

Herman slid the card directly in front of Dragon, stood and walked out of the bar whistling the same tune that played in Michelle's gift box.

Dragon sat stewing in his own anger. He stared at the card with the name yelling back at him. It had been a very bad year. Mora's attempt to usurp him was only a fraction of the trouble he would have to deal with if Allard was blatantly on the offensive. Dragon drained the shot glass and stumbled from the table towards the bathroom.

The bathroom smelled worse than it looked. The red and black paint job had seen better days. Torn stickers and worn posters shouted names of unheard rock bands that pissed there after rocking shows in bigger venues. Graffiti smeared the walls, as did excrement in the stall closest to the door. Dragon relieved himself in the urinal as he plotted. He would need new recruits. It was time to drum up interest amongst his other former warriors. Proactivity was important. He also needed to capture some of the more gifted Souls. He shook the last drips of urine from his stubby penis and glared at the tattoo with the welts on his arm. She would have to do. He would have to bring her on board sooner than he thought. Dragon stared in the mirror above the sinks and splashed cold water on his face. That last shot was doing a job on him.

"That bastard doesn't know what's coming." He said to himself in the mirror.

Suddenly, the stall door behind him burst open. Dragon felt hard, work worn hands grab his face. Thick arms forced his own arms behind his back. He tried to fight but the strength was too much for him in his drunken state. He saw a mirage of glaring light as he tussled trying to fight off his attacker. His head smashed into the mirror. Blood dripped into his eyes. The cold sensation of metal punctured his throat then he felt searing hot pain. His throat was torn open with the jagged blade. Horrible pain, shot through his throat. Warm blood spurted across his chest and his hands as he tried to stop the spillage. Pain... Too much pain...human electric shocking pain through his body. He felt the hard, work worn hands digging at his throat. He choked and flailed trying to stop the assault but he became weaker with the loss of more blood.

There were fingers in his throat. He could feel the scratch of the fingernails digging in his face. He tried to speak, but could not. He tried to moan but the pain prevented it. He put his lips together, but could not make a word. His tongue was pulled through his throat. His body was thrown to the ground. He convulsed then looked up to the face of his assailant. An old Columbian face glared back at him. The man rinsed his hands leaving blood smeared all over the sinks. Dragon tried to muster a word. He tried to muster an offer to please save this body. There was too much tied to this body. He would endure the pain of a hospital and give this old killer a deal if his killer just helped him save this body. Before he exited the bathroom, the old Colombian man bent close to Dragon's ear.

"They call me El Cuello, I am with God. Allard says there is no mercy for you." Tomas Colon whispered and spat in Dragon's face.

The last thing Dragon saw through those eyes was the old man turn the light off and close the door behind him with a slam.

THE END

EPILOGUE

SANCTUARY

The beauty of the lush tropical flora was unmatched. The sound of a roaring waterfall mixed with the sounds of chirping birds and rustling animals. Allard walked down a small hill of plush green grass and took a deep breath. He'd only once seen such a beautiful place, but this place had easily taken the top spot. He crossed through thick brush and along a bubbling creek. The creek led to the waterfall, which poured gallon upon gallon of water into a fresh natural pool. He held his hand above his eyes to shield the sun so he could see the top of the falls. A rainbow stretched across the wide expanse in a perfect arc.

Allard looked left and right and automatically understood the dare. He shed his clothes and jumped in the pool of water. It was refreshingly warm. The temperature was perfect. He swam across the pool then dipped underneath the rushing waters of the falls. The current was strong and pushed him further than he expected. He quickly adjusted and dove under the rocky surface toward light just on the other side.

He made landfall on a mossy embankment and continued walking across the plush landscape looking for a sign. It came in a clearing. A very large apple tree sat in the midst of a bright sunlight. It was so tall it eclipsed all the other plants and trees around it, though they still grew colorful and beautiful in its shadow. Allard hiked to it. He took a deep breath and knelt.

"You could've kept your clothes on." The Voice echoed.

"Thanks for telling me that now." Allard said sarcastically looking up to the swaying limbs of the tree.

"You're welcome." The Voice returned.

"I assume you want to talk to me about Dragon."

"He's already looking for a new body. You don't serve yourself or your mission well playing tit for tat with him. I'd like you to be more focused on the assignments I give you." The Voice huffed.

"I apologize Father." Allard's shoulders slumped.

"Don't be. You were protecting the Soul, Lisa Lucas. She is worthy of your efforts." The Voice agreed.

"They all are." Allard said.

"How does it feel to be back?" The Voice asked.

"Good. Thank you for allowing me to return." Allard rose stretching his legs.

"I didn't like that you left, but I'm happy you're back. The only reason I granted you a leave was because I know how trying this can be. You'll understand how important it is to me soon." The Voice boomed. "Your replacement wasn't too happy that you returned though..." There was a sigh from the tree.

"As long as you're happy, I'm happy." Allard shrugged.

"Would you like your other body? I know the human form causes you some great pains." The Voice said.

"I'll stay the way I am. It makes me understand them."

"Not even your wings...? You may have those back, if you wish." The Voice offered.

"No, thank you." Allard bowed. His hands involuntarily rubbed his shoulders at the wingless area.

He looked around and took in the beautiful view of rolling green mountains and plush foliage.

"The Garden of Eden, huh."

"Care for an apple?" The Voice asked.

Allard jumped up and pulled a rich red apple from the lowest laying branch he could find. He brought the apple to his mouth and paused just before biting it. His eyes drifted to the tree with a cocked eyebrow.

"Yes! You can eat it!" The Voice said.

Allard took a bite and tasted the fresh juices and plush fruit. He sat leaning with his back against the tree and enjoyed the apple. The breeze calmed his tension. There would be many days to stress. This moment would be his only rest. At heart and in his being he was a servant and he would never stop.

Acknowledgments

No man is an island and even though I wrote portions of this book on a very beautiful island (those pages are probably the most relaxed of all) The Unholy Servants wouldn't have been complete, had I kept it to myself as I usually do.

First I must thank my parents for teaching me what hard work and love are supposed to be and that you can't have one without the other.

My three ladies, Keli, Imani and Jayden for giving me the most tangible motivation anyone can have and inspiring me to stay up long nights even when I wanted to go to bed early. I was actually doing work, Keli, See!

To all of my first readers, who kept me crossing "I"s and dotting "T"s..huh? Oh...damn! – Andii, Yan and Debbie for inspiring lots of dialogue, asking lots of questions and testing my mythologies. If you didn't push me to write something I'd let others read, this never would've happened. Nikki, thanks for reading it alongside your other eighteen books to compare if it had some staying power. Ed, your late night text messages were full of such excitement for the characters, it really gave me hope people would enjoy it. Kimya, do you still hate me for doing what I did to Dr. Lucas? I told you it all makes sense in the grand scheme of things. Thanks for your many corrections. Morten, no more dialogue is "spat", thanks to you. You upgraded my language with that observation. Monique T., your fine-tooth comb surely will be done soon right? I know I'm not as good at that grammar thing as you. Thanks for reading Tjamal, if you ever get time to finish you'll be able to read this line and ask why I waited until the very end for the best part. Thanks Kerri, Mike, Mark, Monique M. and Denise for being cheerleaders and motivators during the web preview. If you guys can do the human pyramid for the full release, I'll appreciate it.

To my siblings Prez, Eric, Stacy and Shannon because you've always been there...even when all I wanted was some quiet bathroom time.

Alton, Dave, Dean, Devin, Leandre, Redd and Ron because I can never do it without friends like you. Set Free never gave up on my writing, even though this isn't the one he wants everyone to see, he keeps me motivated to put the plan together. Had I listened to Daddy-O about not multi-tasking this book would've been finished a lot sooner. I'll remember that for the next one.

Last, but not least my Grandpa Artie, one of the strongest Souls I've had the pleasure to be around.

Andre Cole

April 2011

P.S. If you believe your name is missing, motivate me to write another book and I won't forget you, promise.

About the Author

Andre Cole is a freelance film and television researcher, writer and producer who has spent much of his life creating content for a broad spectrum of audiences. As a former consulting project manager for an international disaster recovery firm, Cole's client was based at the World Trade Center the day of the 9/11 attack. He helped them resume normal business just days later. Andre has written bios for people well known and unknown, but he hates writing bios for himself. The Queens, New York native and Syracuse University graduate resides in New Jersey with his wife and daughters.

www.ingramcontent.com/pod-product-compliance
Lightning Source LLC
Chambersburg PA
CBHW030823310726
48980CB00006B/613/J

* 9 7 8 0 9 8 3 6 8 4 2 0 6 *